THE VERY NAUGHTY LIST

CALLIE ROSE

Copyright © 2024 by Callie Rose

All rights reserved.

No part of this book may be reproduced in any form or by any electronic or mechanical means, including information storage and retrieval systems, without written permission from the author.

This is a work of fiction. Names, characters, organizations, and incidents are either products of the author's imagination or used fictitiously. Any resemblance to actual persons, living or dead, is purely coincidental.

For updates on my upcoming releases and promotions, sign up for my reader newsletter! I promise not to bite (or spam you).

CALLIE ROSE NEWSLETTER

MERRY CHRISTMAS...

For all the readers who put "being spit-roasted by three hot triplets" on their Christmas list.

The Cooper brothers will be happy to give you a spanking, you naughty girl.

1

HAILEY

N*EVER RETURN to the scene of a crime.*

Isn't that what they say on all those murder mystery shows? But I'm guessing the investigators on those shows wouldn't exactly consider running away from the altar a crime. And my reason for doing so is definitely *not* a mystery.

Still, it feels like I shouldn't be back here in Chestnut Hill, Montana. It feels a bit like defeat.

My old beater of a car sputters a bit as it hugs the familiar curves of the road. And as comfortably familiar as everything in my small, tight-knit hometown feels, it also feels downright weird to be back.

The whole town is covered in a blanket of snow that would make the perfect holiday card, especially since everything is already decorated for Christmas, with twinkling lights casting tiny pools of color against the pristine white backdrop.

I roll down my window to let the cold air kiss my cheek, and the breeze picks up a few tendrils of my honey-blonde hair to toss around my shoulders and spin around in the air. The cold is starkly different here than in LA, and I'm not sure if it's the temperature or the fact that I'm driving past the exact spot where Dylan proposed to me that sends a chill up my spine.

I try not to think about my ex, since being mopey isn't in my nature. But catching your fiancé cheating on you with none other than your best friend—on the actual day that you're supposed to get married—is enough to make even the most upbeat person a bit sour. And driving past all the places that dig those old memories out of their graves makes it pretty damn hard to forget why I ran away from Chestnut Hill to begin with. It's all so small here. Small enough for gossip to travel and form faster than the snowdrifts along the edges of the road.

I grimace as I drive by the bar where my friends and I went for my bachelorette party, and just past it, I can see the church where Dylan and I were supposed to get married. Right behind that church is where I found him screwing my now ex-best friend, Brielle, mere hours before we were supposed to walk down the aisle.

Well, fuck them both.

I sigh, trying not to let my emotions get the better of me.

My mom always says that whenever I tear up, it makes my green eyes look like sea glass. I know she just says that to make me feel better though, and crying is definitely not something that I want to start with right off the bat as soon as I pull back into town. Besides, it's Christmas time, and there's magic in the air.

When I pass by Gus's General Store, I pull into the parking lot.

It's been two years since I've been back here, two years since I ran the hell away from this place right after the wedding that didn't happen, and it doesn't look like much has changed. The outside of the building still needs a new paint job, and the owner still tosses birdseed on the ground just outside the front door for the cardinals to eat.

Maybe the only thing that's changed is *me*, although I'm not sure that losing my faith in true love and happy endings is an improvement over how I used to be. Still, deep down I would be lying to myself if I said I didn't hold on to some minuscule thread of hope that maybe one day I'll find love again. But for right now, I need to get my head out of the clouds and get some shampoo.

"Hailey! Well, I'll be. Is that really you?" A wrinkled smile greets me from behind the counter as soon as I step inside the shop.

"Hi, Gus." I smile politely. I really don't feel like talking to anyone right now. It's getting late, and it's been a long drive. So I head straight to the aisle to find a few basic essentials that I didn't bring with me when I left LA.

I probably could've packed a bit better before tossing everything in my car and heading home. But losing my job happened so abruptly, and my mom's voice on the phone was filled with such desperate urgency for me to come home for the holidays, that I didn't stop to overthink the decision to move back here for a little while.

Besides, it will be good to take some time to get my feet back under me. When I first headed to LA, I was determined to rebuild my life with confidence. But losing my shitty office job as an assistant in a music production studio was *not* the way I saw things going. I thought maybe the job would give me an opening to pursue the singing career I've dreamed about ever since I was a teenager. But instead, it turned out to be nothing more than a soul sucking grunt work job that I'm honestly not shedding any tears over losing.

I grab the shampoo, a new toothbrush, and a few other things that I didn't bring with me.

Before I even reach the counter, Gus is already talking to me again.

"I see you haven't lost a single freckle in all of that California sunshine," he teases. "You're still just as pretty as ever."

Since he's trying to give me a compliment, I don't point out that sunshine would actually cause *more* freckles, not erase them from my complexion.

"Oh my god, is that Hailey Bennett?" A new voice rings out from the open doorway. "It *is* you!"

I'd almost forgotten how, in a town this size, everyone literally knows everyone else.

I look over in the direction of the voice and see a woman I recognize as one of my mom's friends from the salon she goes to. I don't remember her name, but she's surrounded by a gaggle of other women who all greet me and act overwhelmingly happy to see me.

"How great that you came back home!" The woman's patronizing smile hints at being disingenuous.

The two ladies beside her break into whispers amongst themselves until one of them looks over at me with carefully curated empathy.

"After the wedding was called off, and then your mother said you had run off somewhere to pursue some wild singing dream of yours, we figured Chestnut Hill might not see you again anytime soon," she says.

It's not hard to see that she's fishing for details—any information about me that she can use as fodder for the town gossips, I'm sure. Before I can say anything in response to her, the woman beside her chimes in too.

"Oh my gosh, I almost forgot about that wedding!" Her overly saturated, gushing voice tells me that she definitely didn't. These women have probably concocted a dozen different versions of what happened that day. "I don't think we ever heard the full story about why you called off that wedding with the handsome Montgomery man. Was it cold feet? Cold feet can definitely destroy a good thing if you let it."

"No, it wasn't cold—"

"Jesus, Myrtle, leave the poor girl alone," my mom's salon

friend interrupts before I can even get a word out. "I'm sure that she's embarrassed enough as it is."

My jaw clenches. I would love to tell them all about how I caught Dylan with his dick out right behind their holy place of worship, but it's not worth it. Besides, I don't want to rehash all of this. I just want to buy my toiletries and leave.

"Well, it's nothing to be embarrassed about," Myrtle continues as she ignores her friend's remark. "We all make mistakes sometimes. Was it a mistake, Hailey? Do you regret not marrying Dylan Montgomery now?"

I wish I could evaporate into the Montana air that's wafting through the intermittently open door as more people from town that I used to know stream in and gather around to hear the conversation about my called-off wedding.

"I'm sorry, but I really do need to get going," I say evasively. "I've had a long drive, and I haven't even unpacked my car yet."

"Oh yes, of course! We aren't trying to pry at all or keep you from getting settled in. It's just that you left in such a hurry the last time that everyone here just wants to make sure you're okay."

Sure they do.

More like everyone here just wants to know my business. If I don't cut them off and divert the topic, then I'll literally be standing here all night watching Gus slowly put each of my items into a bag at a snail's pace.

"I'm fine." I smile again. "How are *you* three doing?"

Instantly, the three ladies start filling me in on every little thing that's happened in the past two years. It's enough of a distraction that I can get Gus to ring me up and hand me my bag without any further discussion of my "would-be wedding."

"Thanks, Gus. See you around."

I grab my stuff and leave, my exit barely even noticed by the trio of women who have now moved on to talking about how the Christmas tree tent has been set up too close to the road for comfortable parking. I make a beeline for my car, hoping to make it to my family's diner before I get stopped and interrogated by anyone else tonight.

But in my rush to get back to my car, I'm not watching where I'm going and wind up crashing right into a man who's coming around the corner of the building.

"Oh shit," a deep voice says as I reel backward a step. "Sorry!"

My heart drops, my body suddenly freezing as if the ice on the sidewalk has flowed up through the soles of my feet and rooted me in place.

I'd recognize that voice anywhere.

My stomach twists as I look up to see Dylan Montgomery, my cheating ex-fiancé, standing right there in front of me. His ears must be burning.

"Hailey? Wow, I didn't even know you were in town! What a surprise!" Dylan reaches out to hug me, and I can't help but recoil by taking another step backward. At least my feet are working enough to do that much.

This is the man that betrayed my trust and left my heart scarred and battered. It's because of him that my wedding turned into a disastrous spectacle and that I now find it tough to let anyone into my life at all.

I started dating Dylan right after high school, and I was absolutely convinced that he was "the one." Everyone thought we were the perfect couple—between his catalog model good looks and my reputation for being a "small-town sweetheart."

Little did they know that he's a cheater, and I'm not a pushover.

Dylan broke my heart, destroyed my relationship with my best friend, and crumbled my expectations for a fairytale future.

I was hoping I wouldn't run into him for a while, certainly not on the very first day that I pull into town. I'd been hoping to be prepared instead of getting caught off-guard.

"How are you?" he asks, giving up on trying to hug me after noting my instinctual reaction. "How have things been going in the city for you? Have you released an album or anything yet?"

He's smiling at me with that same pretentious smile that people often mistake as charming, and making small-talk conversation that serves as a polite, superficial gesture at best. But I don't want to answer him. I don't want to tell him that all my big plans for LA haven't worked out, and that I was working a shitty, menial job instead of becoming a singer the way I hoped to be by now.

Usually, I'm fast enough on my feet to come up with a clever response or comeback at the drop of a hat. But Dylan caught me by surprise, and my words stumble over themselves as I eye my car in the distance.

Fuck. Why did I have to park three spots over?

"I'm good, thanks," I mutter. "LA was great. No albums yet. I've been, um, too busy."

He lifts a hand to run his fingers through his blond hair, careful not to dishevel the perfectly styled pieces.

"Aw, come on Hailey. Too busy? Wasn't becoming a singer pretty much your whole dream? I mean, aside from getting married."

Ouch. Dick.

"I really am sorry about that, by the way," he apologizes, grimacing slightly. "I didn't mean to end things the way we did. I hope there are no hard feelings. I'm sure you'll find someone someday too."

The way Dylan can act both polite and condescending at the same time is a masterful art. He has a gift for making me feel small even when he's technically apologizing.

I force a smile at him and try not to let my sass take over and ask him if he didn't "mean" to plow my best friend on our wedding day. I heard the two of them wound up dating after that—him and Brielle—and I'm sure that they're just perfect for each other.

"No hard feelings," I grit out. "And getting married wasn't one of my life goals."

I incidentally glance down at his hand to make sure it doesn't have a ring on it yet, and his hazel eyes catch me looking.

"Well, maybe once you finish up chasing after your singing fantasy, you'll change your mind about settling down with someone," he says, giving me a look that I think is meant to be encouraging. "I remember how you used to sing in the shower. Are you still working on your pitch?"

The more he talks, the more this conversation makes me feel tenser and shittier. I preferred the mild interrogation of the town's busybodies inside the store to this. I feel like a deer in headlights, unable to toss back answers to Dylan without feeling like I'm shrinking right here on the cold sidewalk.

He used to always put down my singing. Toward the end of our relationship, I confined my singing to the shower under the cover of the background noise of running water because I doubted my talent so much. As much as I love to sing, it was hard not to internalize the constant criticisms about my pitch or whether or not I was in tune or enunciating my words enough.

He laughs abruptly as if he's just thought of a joke, and it startles me.

"If you ever do find someone that can put up with all that noise, send them my way, and I'll hook them up with some noise cancelling earbuds."

Anger twists my stomach, bubbling up inside me. I absorbed these shitty comments from him for too long when we were together, brushing them off or trying to excuse them. But I don't have to do that anymore. My tense jaw finally unlocks, and I open my mouth to say something, although I'm not sure what yet.

But before I can speak, a strong arm wraps around my shoulders.

I jerk a little at the unexpected contact and look up to see Reid Cooper, one of my older brother's best friends, standing beside me.

What the hell?

Not only am I surprised to see Reid, I'm even more surprised that he has his arm around my shoulder. I expected to cross paths with him and his two brothers at some point, especially since the Cooper triplets have been Lucas's best friends ever since we were kids. But his timing right now couldn't have been more unexpected.

"There you are!" Reid pulls me closely against the side of his body, gazing down at me with a grin, as if he's been looking for me.

I can feel the heat emanating from his rugged, muscular body, and suddenly the chill in the air seems like a distant memory. Dylan's face twists in confusion as he glances between the two of us.

"Hello, Reid." Dylan gives a little nod, subtly straightening his posture—probably trying to make himself look taller, since Reid is at least 6'3" and has several inches on him. "Here to pick up some more nails or something?"

His remark is clearly meant to be a bit of a dig, insulting Reid for his job as a carpenter who works with his hands instead of someone who's never needed to lift a finger like Dylan. Although maybe if Dylan wasn't so spoiled by his family's wealth and had ever done a day of manual labor in his life, he'd be less wiry and a bit more chiseled like Reid. Not that I'm thinking about how my brother's best friend's body feels pressed against me right now.

Fuck, who am I kidding? I'm totally thinking about it.

Reid laughs, a deep sound that I can literally feel vibrating in his chest. "Nah. I get my carpentry supplies wholesale. The only thing that I'm here to pick up is my girlfriend."

The look of shock on Dylan's face doesn't even come close to the shock that *I* feel at hearing Reid's words.

I turn my face toward him, instantly getting lost in his blue-gray eyes and suddenly hyper aware of the way his body is almost possessively leaning into mine. My grip on my bag of supplies slips a little as I reach beneath it to pinch my thigh and make sure I'm not dreaming.

Nope, not dreaming. Very much awake.

Which means this is real life.

And gorgeous, *off-limits* Reid Cooper just called me his girlfriend.

2

HAILEY

"I'm sorry, what?" Dylan asks as he stares at Reid in visible surprise. "You're dating Hailey?"

I'm grateful that he spoke before I could blurt out the same question, since it was on the tip of my tongue too. I'm also glad that he's looking at Reid for an answer, because I'm pretty sure my mouth couldn't form words right now even if I tried. I'm much too busy trying to think straight under the weight of Reid's muscular arm wrapped around me.

In all the years that Reid has been one of my brother's best friends, I don't recall ever having been in such a close proximity to him.

Sure, he and his brothers were always hanging around our house while I was secretly crushing on all three of them from afar, but he never touched me. None of them did—not like this.

"Yes, I am." Reid's answer is filled with unwavering confidence as he holds on to me protectively, dropping his arm down from my shoulder to hook it around my waist.

I blink up at him in shock.

"Isn't that right, babe?" he adds, looking down at me with a smile that makes heat rise in places I really hope no one can notice.

"Yeah. I mean, uh, yes." I stumble over my words. "We're dating."

I'm a completely shitty liar, but thankfully Reid has already taken the lead and all I need to do is go along with it.

"I'm so happy you're home." Reid sweeps a strand of my blonde hair away from my cheek. "God, I've missed your face."

I feel like my legs are going to give out from under me. It's a good thing he has an arm wrapped around my waist, or they just might.

"But I thought you just got back into town." Dylan eyes me skeptically, making my stomach tighten. I swear this man can *smell* weakness.

"She did, and not a moment too soon." Once again, Reid saves me from having to say anything. "Long distance is tough, especially when our chemistry is off the charts. I'm sure you can understand that, Dylan. Or maybe not."

The dig is an obvious one, meant to knock my ex into place.

I watch as Dylan seems to squirm in his own skin. He's not used to being shown up by another man. He still wants to think that I'm pining away for the relationship that he destroyed. And as much as I can tell he's trying to hide it, the tightened muscles in his jaw and the way he keeps glancing down at Reid's hand on my waist give away that his ego is bruised.

Good.

"Well, congratulations to the both of you, then," Dylan says through a thin-lipped smile. "Hope to see you around town some more, Hailey."

I don't say anything as I watch him walk away. Reid doesn't remove his hand right away either.

But when he finally does take a step back and releases his arm from my waist, the Montana winter air suddenly feels colder than it ever has before.

"Thanks." I feel the warmth in my cheeks against the kiss of chilly air. "You didn't have to do that. It wasn't your problem."

"You're always my problem." Reid shoots me a dimpled smile that could melt snow. "I've got your back. And you don't have to thank me. I'm more than happy to take that fucker down a peg or two. Dylan is an ass."

His smile melts into a scowl as he speaks, and he crosses his arms over his chest, making all the muscles in his shoulders and chest shift in defined lines under his long-sleeved shirt.

How is it that he's not freezing out here without a thicker jacket on?

For a moment, my mind plummets down a rabbit hole of all the ways we could stay warm together. But then I quickly shake the thoughts away and remind myself that he was obviously just doing this as some sort of obligatory favor to look out for his best friend's geeky little sister.

I like to think that I don't fit that description anymore, though. Despite the bumps in the road that I've faced, I've grown up a lot since I was the dorky little kid he and his brothers used to look out for.

"So, are you really back?" Reid continues, tilting his head as he gazes down at me. "Are you staying in Chestnut Hill?"

"No," I answer too quickly. "No, I'm only here temporarily. Just clearing my head for a bit before going back to LA."

"Clearing your head? Aren't things going well for you out there in the big city life?"

He runs one hand through his chocolate brown hair and takes my bag from me to carry to the car with the other. The light from the setting sun makes the lighter copper strands in his hair pop as his messy locks frame the sides of his face. Reid has a sort of rugged gorgeousness about him that I swear makes my heart actually beat faster against my ribs.

"No, they are," I lie as I walk alongside him back to my car. "It's just good to take some time for a fresh perspective sometimes. How about you? How have things been going with the carpentry business? How are your brothers and sister doing?"

He chuckles. "Business is good. Nick got a dog that doesn't like anyone but him, Sebastian is still at the garage, and the three of us are living together. Addison is great, and Iris is as adorable as ever. She's got all of us wrapped around her little finger, I swear. She's our only niece, so we've got to spoil her."

My attempt to divert attention off of myself and onto him seemed to work, but when we reach my car, I find myself wishing that I had parked much farther away.

"Thanks again." I smile, trying not to seem awkward as I force myself not to linger. "Maybe I'll see you around while I'm in town."

"Of course you will," Reid teases. He reaches out to pull the zipper on the front of my coat all the way up as if he's worried I'll catch a cold. "We are dating, after all, aren't we?"

He gives me a wink before turning to leave, and I fumble with my keys to unlock my car door. Just as I finally slip the key into the lock, Reid's voice sounds from a little way away.

"Oh, and, trouble?" The nickname he used to call me makes my stomach flutter, and I turn to look at him over my shoulder.

"Yeah?"

"I'm glad you're back."

I nod, clearing my throat, then quickly toss my bag into the car and slide into the driver's seat before he can see how flustered I am. He heads inside Gus's General Store, and for a moment, I sit in my car, gripping the steering wheel before even starting the engine. It might be cold outside, but I feel like I'm suddenly generating enough heat for a furnace as the wings of a thousand butterflies erupt in my stomach.

Finally, I shake myself out of my daze and crank the key in the ignition. The drive to The Griddle House feels unusually long, even though it's pretty much right around the corner.

That's because I'm impossibly lost in my thoughts about Reid Cooper the entire ride.

Reid and his brothers, Nick and Sebastian, have always been protective of me. I've always chalked it up to the fact that they're Lucas's best friends. The three guys were always spending time at our house hanging out with my brother, especially after their parents died in a car accident when they were eighteen.

And since I looked up to Lucas and always wanted to be around him, the triplets didn't have much choice but to put up with me—although they never made me feel like I was bothering them at all. In fact, they sometimes even carved out space for me, which I attributed to them just being nice guys and feeling an obligatory need to be kind to me, since they were sort of unofficially adopted into our family.

Truth be told, I've always had a crush on all three of them. How could I not? The Cooper brothers are all ruggedly handsome and built like Titans.

Obviously, I never let them know how I felt, since there was no way any of them would be interested in Lucas's little sister. But they did all still look out for me. Sometimes they even acted more insanely protective than *Lucas* did. I can even remember times when I let myself lie in bed and fantasize that their watchfulness over me might've meant something.

But I always circled back around to telling myself that it was just the way the triplets were—bonded closely together after the death of their parents and protective of the people they cared about.

So I'm not completely surprised that Reid stood up for me with Dylan, although *how* he did it sure knocked me on my ass.

By the time I get to the diner, park, and head inside, I've managed to talk myself down a bit from the encounter at the general store and I'm feeling truly excited to see my family. This place, my parents' restaurant, feels like home. And for the first time since I arrived back in town, I'm thrilled to be back in Chestnut Hill.

My sister Pippa squeals with glee as she runs toward me and squeezes the life out of me until I can't breathe. I hug her tight and bury my face against her artificially crimson-colored hair. It smells like a mix of strawberry shampoo and the coffee they serve at The Griddle House.

I've missed this, my sister's outgoing personality and the aroma of things that smell like home.

"Ahhh, Hailey! I'm *so* glad you're here!" Her face lights up when she lets me go so that my parents can get their hugs in too.

My mom looks me over and asks if I've been eating enough while my dad gives me a broad smile and echoes the sentiment that they're all glad I'm home. Then they both have to finish up some work in the back room of the diner before closing time.

Pippa and I slide into a booth together to catch up a bit.

"So where are you staying?" she demands. My old bedroom in my parents' house is being occupied by our grandmother now, which is just as well, because I don't know if I could've survived the indignity of being fired *and* being forced to move back in with my folks, no matter how much I love them.

"I'm renting a room from Ted Bigelow."

My sister grimaces and wrinkles her nose. "Ted Bigelow? Hailey, that guy is a weirdo. Everyone in town knows it. You shouldn't stay there with him. I told you that you could crash with me."

"It's fine," I reassure her. "Ted can be a little... different, but your place is so tiny, and I don't want to impose on you like that. And mom and dad have Grandma Dee living with them now, so there isn't much room. I'm perfectly fine renting a room from Ted for the time being."

I'm not sure if I'm reassuring her or myself, since I know that Ted Bigelow does have a reputation for being kind of creepy and odd. Not in a malicious or perverted sort of way—

he's just kind of socially awkward and strange. His place is on the outskirts of town, and when I was poking around for a last-minute place to stay in Chestnut Hill around the holidays, he offered to rent me a room.

"Okay, but if you go missing or some shit like that, I'm sending Lucas after his ass," Pippa warns, and her amused giggle makes me smile.

She and I both know that our brother would tear apart anyone who tried to touch either of us. Especially now that Lucas is working as a football coach for the local high school, as well as teaching some classes there—the pictures that he's sent me show that he's gotten even bulkier than before.

Without realizing it, the thought of muscular men has my mind flitting right back to Reid again, and I have to actually shake my head a little to get myself to focus back on my conversation with Pippa.

"How's work going at the diner?" I ask.

"Oh, you know, we're all hanging in there. Mom changed a few things on the menu to keep up with the food that they're serving at The Old Oak now."

"Really? That place serves food now?" The last time I was home, my favorite bar was drinks only.

"Yeah. You should go check it out, actually. Fair warning that you'll probably run into everyone from town there though."

I laugh, since I feel like I already accomplished that tonight in my first few hours of being back. It doesn't take much in a place like Chestnut Hill.

After catching up with my sister for a bit and promising to see the rest of my family soon, I head out to Ted's house so that I can get settled in and get some rest.

Thankfully, Ted isn't nearly as nosy as the rest of the town. He reminds me of an older, awkwardly lumbering bridge troll that doesn't mean to lurk about but can't really help it. At least he doesn't force me into awkward conversation.

"Need help with your bags?" he grunts as he leads me into the house.

"No, thanks. I don't have much." I follow him inside, trying to ignore the faint smell of tobacco that seems to have settled into the old wooden floor panels that creak beneath my feet.

Ted shows me to my room and then disappears into the rest of the house to carry on with his evening. I close the door of my room behind him, making a face when I notice that there's no lock.

Once I've dropped off my bag, I unload the small amount of other stuff I have in the car, then sit down on the edge of the bed to look around for a minute. The space is stark, not entirely clean, and definitely a far cry from the fancy big-city apartment that I envisioned myself living in back in LA by now.

Outside the window, it's starting to snow. The snowflakes are plump and feathery as they fall gently from the sky in a sort of suspended motion. But inside my head, there's a full-on blizzard of thoughts.

My first night back in Chestnut Hill, and I've already unintentionally stirred up gossip, taken more than one walk down memory lane, and practically had to clamp my thighs together to soothe the ache between my legs when Reid had his arm around me.

And now I'm sitting in a grungy room staring at my bag from the store, which is pretty much the only decoration in this place aside from the cobwebs in the corners of the ceiling.

"Perfect," I murmur to myself, attempting to make my voice sound sincere to my own ears. "This is all just *perfect*."

3

NICK

"Good boy, Bruno."

I crouch down to scratch my massive dog under his chin as he wags his tail so hard it thumps against the cabinet. He twists his head a little, trying to lick my hand, then changes his mind and goes for my face instead, making me chuckle. My rescued hound is always faithfully ready to shower me with slobbery kisses as soon as I get home from a shift at the fire station.

"Too bad he only likes you. If he gave me the same kind of warm welcome, maybe he'd lick some of this grease out from beneath my fingernails," Sebastian jokes, glancing down at where I'm crouched in front of Bruno as he strides into the kitchen.

"Dogs shouldn't lick grease," I grunt. "Especially not automotive grease."

Sebastian is the youngest of the three of us, if you're measuring our ages by the minute, since he was the last triplet to emerge during birth. Our mother used to always say that was the reason why he's the wildest out of her sons. I'm not sure if that's actually the reason, but she wasn't wrong in pointing out that he was the one who was usually getting Reid and me into trouble. Sebastian can't seem to help himself when it comes to seizing the opportunity for a laugh or a thrill.

At least now that he's taken over our father's garage, he has something to keep his hands busy and to keep him out of trouble. If Seb didn't have something to occupy his time, he'd be off the rails playing into the "bad boy" aesthetic that he showcases so well. Our dad was smart to get him working on cars at an early age. And honestly, he's good at it.

"Oh, come on. You'll never know until he tries it." Sebastian grins, holding out a hand toward Bruno. "Here, boy. Come here! Lick this."

Bruno ignores him. Not even his ears twitch as he gives me another lick, stoically pretending my brother isn't even in the room. It's been like this pretty much since I brought Bruno home. He doesn't give two shits about either of my brothers, although at least he doesn't actively growl at them anymore.

"See?" I arch a brow at Sebastian. "He knows who actually loves him around here." I give Bruno one more scratch before standing up. "That's right, boy. I'll take good care of you. You can just ignore that greasy fucker."

Seb rolls his eyes, making the scar across the corner of his left eyebrow arch. "He only likes you best because you're both so fucking grumpy. He probably recognized a kindred spirit the second he saw you."

"At least I'm responsible enough to take care of a pet."

He shrugs. "I had a lizard once."

"Which ran away."

"I like to think that's because I raised him so well that he knew when it was time to leave the nest and strike out on his own."

"Sure. Or he got eaten by a cat."

He scowls. "It's a good thing we're brothers, or I'd deck you for even suggesting that."

"You could try." I roll my neck out as the two of us banter back and forth.

"I'd sell tickets to that fight." We both turn around at the sound of Reid's voice entering the kitchen. "We're all pretty evenly matched, I'd say. We could probably raise a small fortune taking bets."

"Don't give him any ideas," I warn. "Next thing you know, Seb will have a whole underground fight ring set up in Chestnut Hill."

Reid isn't wrong though. The three of us are all built similarly—muscular and broad-shouldered, with the kind of physique that comes from working with your hands all day. All three of us have physically demanding jobs, even though we joke around about whose is better from time to time.

We're more alike than we're different, although we each seem to lean into the qualities that make us uniquely ourselves. But the bond between us is a strong one. We relied on each other after our parents died in order to get through the loss, and we all submerged ourselves into trades that allowed us to distract our minds with physical exertion.

Now we live in our parents' old house, which the three of us decided to keep after our older sister, Addison, moved out and got married. We owe her a lot for helping to raise the three of us after our parents died, and keeping the house seemed like the right thing to do. Plus, it's big enough that I have room for a home gym, Sebastian has a whole garage to store his collection of motorcycles, and Reid has a workshop out back where he builds furniture for his carpentry business. And even with all of that, there's still space leftover.

"You'll never guess who I ran into in town today." Reid grabs a beer from the fridge and gives Bruno a wide berth before sitting down at the table. It takes Sebastian less than a second to open the fridge and grab bottles for the both of us too. "Hailey Bennett. Apparently, she's back in town."

Instantly, my body tenses.

Hailey Bennett.

Our best friend's little sister, and the woman I've had a secret crush on for as long as I can remember.

There's a whole lot of history between all of us, but I've never told anyone that. While we all grew up around each other, looking out for Hailey and keeping her under our protection, I also couldn't seem to shake the constant awareness of how beautiful she was.

Every time she came around, I felt a visceral reaction to her. I just never fucking acted on it because she was Lucas's little sister, thus making her off-limits. That didn't make it any easier to breathe whenever she was in the room though. For years, I could barely string two words together anytime I talked to her.

Hell, she probably wondered if I could talk at all, since most of the time all I would do is speak in monosyllabic answers anytime she was around.

I pick up my beer and take a long swallow, trying to shove down the old feelings for Hailey at the same time. At least I'm not the only one who seems caught off guard about Hailey's reappearance back in town.

"Holy shit. Is she here to stay?" Sebastian leans forward, resting his elbows on the table. "I wonder what brought her back to Montana."

"No idea, but I'm guessing that it must have been a last-minute decision, since Lucas didn't say anything about it to any of us."

Reid's got a good point. Lucas and Hailey are still close, even though she hasn't been back here in two years. If he'd known she was coming home for the holidays, we would've heard about it.

"How did she seem?" Bruno barrels over and slams into the side of my chair to play, nearly knocking the beer out of my hand and making me spill some on my scruffy beard as I pull the glass away from my mouth to ask the question.

Reid shrugs. "She seemed fine, I guess. I only talked to her for a minute or two."

I want to ask more, but before I can, Sebastian's stomach growls. He declares that he needs food, and he and Reid launch into a debate about where we should go. It takes me a second to wrench my thoughts away from Hailey and focus on the argument playing out at the kitchen table, and I only fully snap out of it when Seb nudges my foot with his.

"I say we go to The Old Oak. Back me up on this, Nick. You know you want a nice cold beer on tap."

I frown, glancing down at the nice cold beer I already have in my hand, and he shakes his head.

"That's different," Sebastian insists. "Fridge beer isn't as good as draft beer."

He's got a point—and besides, they serve food, and I don't have the energy to cook at home tonight. So after a bit more debate, the three of us settle on The Old Oak. We disperse from the kitchen, going to our respective bedrooms to change out of our work clothes, then reconvene and head out to the bar.

When we arrive, the place is already packed. Sebastian flags down one of the servers, Chloe, who grins at the sight of the three of us and waves for us to follow her over to our usual table.

"Crowded in here tonight," I mutter as I let my brothers take their seats first.

"Sure is." She smiles back at me and touches the side of my arm as if she's testing to see if I've been working out harder than usual. "But you know I always save a table for you three. How can I resist those blue eyes of yours, Nick?"

I don't say anything in response, and Sebastian shakes his head at me as she gets pulled away to deal with another customer.

"When are you going to lighten up and hook up with her

already?" he asks. "She's been throwing herself at you for weeks. Seriously, Nick, you're all work and no play."

"He's not wrong," Reid points out. "You need to blow off a little steam one of these days, or you're going to fucking combust."

I brush off both of their remarks and head to the bar to get us all drinks. I'm not interested in flirting with the waitress. I'm interested in becoming the town's fire chief and making something of myself. When I decided to become a firefighter, I threw myself into it a hundred percent. I don't intend to get distracted and half ass anything. I intend to be the one in charge and take on the responsibility of this town's fire station.

Distractions only serve to—

Shit.

My thoughts about staying focused evaporate into thin air as I look over and see Hailey sitting at the bar.

The sight of how gorgeous she is stops me in my tracks. She's even more beautiful now than I remembered. Stunning, all grown up, and arguably the most attractive woman I've ever laid eyes on. Waves of her honey blonde hair fall against her back, and the outline of her curves sends a tremor through every tensed muscle in my body.

I can hear her voice as she talks to a few women sitting around her, and my brows draw together as I pick up on her tone. She sounds *stressed*.

I walk up to the other side of the bar and order me and my brothers a drink. While I wait, I listen.

The women around Hailey seem to be battering her with questions. Most of it sounds like they're being nosy, poking around in her personal life. Nothing overtly mean or malicious, just strings of questions that poke at an old wound—because apparently, the scandal of how Hailey left her fiancé on their wedding day makes for highly entertaining gossip. Even now, after all this time has passed, I guess.

One of the women asks her how it felt being left on her wedding day, and I can hear Hailey struggling as she tries to explain that *she* was the one who left Dylan, not the other way around. But the gaggle of women around her don't seem to care about details as mundane as the truth. They just want to breed drama as if it were profitable livestock.

"How on earth can you bounce back from something like that? I would just roll over and die."

"I would die too. I mean, to come back to Chestnut Hill and show your face here again? God, Hailey, you're braver than I would be."

Hailey looks between the women who are talking on both sides of her and sips her drink without saying a word.

"Inquiring minds want to know. Have you gotten back on the horse again?"

"Excuse me?" Hailey's eyes widen as she looks up from her drink at the woman sitting closest to her left side. I catch a glimpse of her expression and can read the shock and discomfort on her face.

"You need to get back out there, honey." The woman who asked the question leans in closer to Hailey as if she's providing some sort of sisterhood support, but Hailey just looks a bit claustrophobic. "Get back in the dating pool. There are plenty of fish in the sea, you know? I know it can be so scary after being dumped like that, but you just have to try."

She looks around at the other women, who all nod quickly. But Hailey's face drops, the light washing out of her eyes. It's clear to see that even if they're trying to be encouraging, it's just making her feel worse.

I fucking hate seeing her like this. I remember Hailey having an exuberant nature that was almost infectious, and a near-constant mischievous twinkle in her green eyes. But right now, she looks like she's trying to make herself smaller and smaller, as if she's hoping she can disappear entirely.

Fuck that. And fuck anyone who makes her feel that way.

The tension in her expression rouses something inside me, and before I can even think twice about it, I shove away from the bar and walk over toward where she's sitting.

I push myself right in between the girls sitting around her until I'm standing at Hailey's side with my chest pressed up against her shoulder.

"Ladies, you're not trying to steal her from me, are you?" The question comes out sounding smooth even though my posture beside her feels awkward and stiff.

Hailey's head whips up, and she does a little double take as she registers my face.

"Steal her from you?" one of the women asks, looking confused.

"Yeah." I nod. "She's with me."

I can't help but notice the way Hailey's lips part in response to those words, as if she is letting out a silent little gasp. I try not to get distracted by the sight of it—or thoughts of what it would be like to press my tongue between those plush lips and kiss her senseless—clearing my throat to regain my composure.

"We're dating," I elaborate. "And if you don't mind, I'd like to claim my girlfriend back for the night."

The space between barstools that I've wedged my broad body into in order to stand beside her is a tight one. So tight that our bodies can't help but touch in several places at once—my chest against her shoulder, my leg against the side of her thigh. I'm not normally great in crowds. I prefer to be the one *not* dancing at weddings and *not* standing in the center of the mosh pit at concerts.

I'm more comfortable running into a burning building to save someone than engaging in any sort of social event or conversation with strangers. But Hailey clearly needs some help here, and just like when we were younger, I will always show up if she needs something.

I reach down and rest a hand on her thigh, forcing myself not to give in to the thoughts racing through my head as soon as I touch her.

"Well, I guess that answers that," one of the women says with a raised brow. "I guess you've definitely gotten back on the horse, Hailey."

4

HAILEY

Everyone sitting around us at the bar seems a bit stunned by Nick's declaration. Even some people who weren't paying much attention to the women interrogating me before glance our way now, curiosity and surprise in their expressions.

Hell, *I'm* surprised too.

Not only did I not expect to see him here, but I sure as hell didn't expect him to jump to my rescue and claim to be dating me. What are the chances of this happening twice within the same twenty-four-hour time period? Not one but *two* Cooper brothers swooping in to save me from the perils of the small town rumor mill?

And just like with Reid, I don't know how to react.

"I thought you didn't really date anyone anymore." The woman beside me, Casey Powell, frowns slightly. She had a crush on Nick all through high school and was determined to have his baby one day, although that clearly hasn't happened yet.

I can't say I blame her for being a bit obsessed with him though. Despite the fact that he doesn't talk much, there's something about Nick that draws people's eyes wherever he goes. He's enigmatic and classically gorgeous, with hair the color of dark chocolate and a beard that I have to curb myself from thinking about too much. I bet it tickles *wherever* he kisses you, in the most satisfying of ways.

For fuck's sake, why do I keep doing this?

I keep letting my thoughts slide right down into my panties every time I'm around one of these Cooper men.

There's something so serious and capable about his demeanor that I've always felt safe and secure in Nick's presence though. And that goes for right now too.

"I don't really date... much," Nick confirms, nodding a bit stiffly. "But I made an exception for Hailey."

"Wow." Casey shakes her head, shifting her focus from him to me. "You are one lucky girl."

I nod in response to her words, although I feel a bit like I'm having an out-of-body experience. And just like I did with Reid when he swooped in to save me from Dylan, I lean into this lie too.

"Yeah." I nod weakly. "I know."

As the ladies around me all start to chatter excitedly, I'm very keenly aware of Nick's presence beside me. He squeezed himself right up between all the women and barstools, and his body is practically glued to mine.

Nick is the tallest, burliest, and grumpiest of the three Cooper brothers. And since he's so quiet, especially around me, I always thought he kind of disliked me. But maybe I was wrong because here he is, standing stoically beside me like a wall of muscle and claiming to be dating me just so that the gossip vultures in high heels will back off.

It was shocking enough when Reid did it, but it's even more of a shock now that Nick has proclaimed that we're dating.

"So how long have you two been a thing?"

I don't know which of the women around us just asked that question, but honestly, it doesn't even matter. I'm swimming around in my head trying to make sense of how nonstop crazy things have been since I've gotten back home.

"A while."

Nick is clearly following the same instinct as his brother, to save me from interrogation. His answer is a lot less elaborated on than Reid's was though. He's definitely not quite as good at bullshitting as the charming middle Cooper triplet is.

Once, I accidentally ran into him coming out of my brother's room with his shirt off after the two of them challenged each other to some stupid pushup contest. I actually *literally* stumbled and tripped over a rippled piece of the old carpet on the hallway floor and put my hand out to brace for my fall. But I never hit the floor, because my palm wound up landing on Nick's chest instead.

I was mortified, but I also didn't want to pull my hand away, because even back then the definition of his muscular frame was impressive. I remember trying to apologize and then standing there blushing as heat swept over me. In my teenage brain, I had a mini fantasy about how maybe Nick would put his hand over mine and we'd have some sort of romantic interlude in the hallway.

Obviously, I was amped up on teen hormones. The thought of that actually happening was a ludicrous one. Nick just muttered, "no problem," and pushed past me down the hall as if he couldn't stand to be in the same space as me.

After a few more minutes of chatter, the ladies around me seem to realize that Nick has no plans to move from his spot, so they move on and go hit up some of the guys at the end of the bar. Once they leave, my brain finally fully catches up with what has just happened. My breath whooshes out of me in a rush, and suddenly, I can't hold in a laugh.

"What's so funny?"

I turn at the sound of Reid's voice and see him standing nearby with Sebastian right beside him. All three of the Cooper men apparently decided to come out tonight, and being surrounded by all of them somehow makes me feel even more giddy and off-balance.

Nick shrugs in response to his brother's question. He jerks his chin toward Casey and her posse of pink rosé drinking friends down at the end of the bar.

"I don't know. I just told those ladies that Hailey and I were dating to get them to leave her alone."

"Wait, you *what*?"

Reid looks shocked, and then he too bursts into laughter.

"Am I missing something here?" Sebastian exchanges a look of mutual confusion with Nick while Reid tries to get his laughter under control.

"I told the exact same lie to Dylan Montgomery earlier today," Reid informs them, still chuckling.

Nick blinks at him in silence for a second. "Wait, what?"

"Yeah, Dylan was harassing her outside the general store, so I told him that Hailey and I were dating so he'd back the hell off."

"You failed to mention that earlier." Nick looks slightly annoyed at Reid's omission.

The middle Cooper brother shrugs. "It didn't seem relevant until just now."

Sebastian takes advantage of the space that opened up when the other women left and sidles up on my other side. When I turn my face to look at him, he grins, and I can feel myself instantly flush in response as his blue-green eyes pierce through me. He still has that "always messy" hair that I want to tousle between my fingers so badly, and the crooked smile that curves his lips is downright mouthwatering.

"I guess this is the perfect way to get people to stop talking about how you got cheated on by Dylan," he says. "Calling off a wedding isn't nearly as dramatically juicy as showing your ex that you've got plenty of prospects still here in town."

Sebastian has a solid point. It's kind of the perfect way to get everyone in Chestnut Hill to stop gossiping about the failed wedding and my attempt to run away from it all.

"But you know..." He drags the words out, a thoughtful expression crossing his handsome features. "Why stop there? I think you could take it even further. Really give people something to talk about."

"What do you mean?" I ask, my stomach flipping over. The look in Sebastian's eye is a deviously mischievous one.

I haven't forgotten how much he always liked pushing the envelope with things. Sometimes he went too far and would get his brothers into trouble, and then he'd rely on Reid's smooth talking and charm to get them all out of it. But there's always been something so alluring and fun about him that it's hard not to want to be caught up in whatever scheme he's getting into.

"I mean, if you really want to make Dylan leave you alone and snuff out all the gossiping busybodies in this town, then what better way to do it than shutting down all their questions by taking this really over the top?"

Reid nods in agreement as if he's already following along with Sebastian's train of thought, but I shake my head, confused about where this is heading. "Over the top, how?"

Sebastian grins. "Instead of just one of us, you could have a trifecta of suitors."

"You mean all *three* of you would pretend to date me?" My eyebrows shoot up toward my hairline.

I can't even believe I'm asking that question. It sounds like something I might have fantasized about after the lights were out during my teen years when I knew the three guys were just down the hall sleeping over in my brother's room.

"Yeah." He gestures to his two brothers. "We can pretend to fight over you, act jealous when we see you with one another, and make sure that people around town see you out on one-on-one dates with each of us."

I chew my bottom lip, trying to process what he's saying. Sebastian's idea definitely has the potential to stir up a lot of drama and trouble. *But* it also has the potential to shut down all of the comments about my almost-wedding and the pitying looks I keep getting.

"It would definitely show everyone that you're totally over all that shit with Dylan," Reid adds, clearly already on board with this scheme.

I glance over at Nick, whose expression I can't read. It's hard to tell if he's for the idea or against it.

"What do you think?" I ask.

Nick takes a moment before answering, and I worry for a second that he's going to shut down this totally insane proposal of Sebastian's. Maybe that would be for the best, but for some reason, I really don't want him to say no.

I don't know if he can read any of my thoughts on my face, but after studying me for a moment, he gives a single, decisive nod.

"I'm in."

My pulse instantly starts to gallop. I can barely believe this is happening. I feel slightly embarrassed to be accepting this kind of help from them. It feels more intimate than it probably should, and definitely more scandalous. Still, I can't help but be a little excited too.

"Okay," I whisper, barely loud enough to be heard over the ambient noise of the bar, even though they're all standing close to me. "Let's do it."

This is crazy, right? Yeah, it's definitely crazy.

But right now, I don't care.

"All right then." Sebastian's smile widens, and he glances around at the still-crowded bar. "There are a lot of people in here, which means we have a captive audience."

"For what?"

A little burst of adrenaline shoots through me, because I

know he's getting ready to do something wild. Sebastian's always been just one step away from being a complete troublemaker, and I can tell that the years since I last saw him haven't done anything to tame his wild side at all.

I like it though. I like how Sebastian brings a sense of unpredictable fun, and Reid coats everything with a sort of casual charm, and Nick can always be counted on to act as the responsible one. It makes it feel like between the three of them, this charade could actually work. They're like the perfect balance for each other—a true trifecta of amazing men with bodies to match.

Fuck, there I go again. *Calm down, girl.*

"It's my turn this time, shortcake," Sebastian informs me. "I think we should take things up a notch right now. Get everyone's attention and let the gossip mill start turning."

'Taking things up a notch' by Sebastian's terms means taking it up ten notches by everyone else's standards. I sit straighter on my barstool, glued in place as I wait to see what he's going to do. Nick sits down on the barstool next to me as if he's waiting for the show to begin too, and Reid mutters something under his breath that sounds like, "This ought to be good."

"I know my brothers are interested in you too, Hailey." Sebastian raises his voice, speaking loudly enough for everyone in the entirety of The Old Oak to hear him. "But that doesn't change how I feel about you. I've never known another woman like you, and I'm not gonna stop trying to win you over."

The women at the end of the bar set down their drinks and turn to stare at us with their mouths agape. The rest of the patrons in the bar turn to look too, and even the bartender, Craig, stops drying a whiskey glass and watches Sebastian.

"I'm going to prove that I'm the best man for you," Sebastian continues. "This town lost the best thing it ever had when you moved away, and now that you're back, I'm not gonna hide my feelings any longer. So, sure, my brothers can try their best to earn your heart. But I know that in the end, you'll choose me."

Yup, that's done it. He has the attention of every single person in this bar.

Sebastian moves in a little closer, the messy locks of his dark brown hair falling over his forehead as he gazes at me with a look that makes my breath hitch.

Maybe he should be an actor instead of a mechanic, because he's convincing as hell.

He tips my chin up with two fingers, and my heart stutters in my chest. His eyes bounce between mine, his scent enveloping me. He smells like cognac and amber, and I can feel his breath ghost over my lips as he speaks in a low voice meant only for me.

"If you don't want me to kiss you, stop me right now."

He hesitates for a moment, giving me enough time to decide.

But I don't say no. I'm not sure my voice would even work right now, but it doesn't matter, because I have absolutely no desire to say anything. Instead, almost unconsciously, I tilt my chin up a little more.

A slow grin spreads across Sebastian's face.

"Good girl."

Then he drops his head and presses his mouth to mine.

5

HAILEY

The moment our lips meet, I'm aware of the hoots and hollers that erupt all across the bar. Every raised voice around us reminds me that this is only pretend—this kiss is all for show, meant only for the benefit of our audience, which means we have to sell it.

It's a bit awkward at first, our lips stiff and unmoving. I curl my fingers loosely, unsure what to do with my hands as I wonder what this looks like to everyone watching us.

But then Sebastian's tongue slides out, tracing the seam of my lips. I gasp softly as a spark of heat shoots through me, and he takes the opportunity to deepen the kiss, angling his head to take it a bit deeper.

He pulls me up against him, and my hands instinctively reach up to press my palms against his chest as I melt into him. I can feel every tensed muscle of his pecs beneath my fingers, and it takes actual restraint to keep my hands from wandering any more than they already have.

I don't know how long the kiss lasts—it can't be more than several seconds at most—but in that short time, the kiss grows rapidly hotter and increasingly more *real* feeling. His tongue slides against mine, one large hand palming the back of my head, and I feel like there's nothing else in the world besides Sebastian's strong arm wrapped around me and his fingers threading through my hair.

In all the times I ever allowed myself to imagine what it would be like to kiss him, it was never as intensely *primal* as this.

I'm not sure which one of us pulls away first, but I have to physically restrain myself from chasing Sebastian's lips to get one more taste of him.

As soon as we break apart, all the sounds of the bar come rushing back in. It's like I was underwater that whole time, hearing nothing at all while submerged in Sebastian's embrace. But now that it's over, the reality around us comes crashing over me like a tidal wave. It's almost too overwhelming to take in all at once, especially since most of my brain is still locked in that kiss, trying to recall the exact sensation of his mouth on mine.

But the heightened noise level, along with the slightly chilly air that seems amplified now that my body isn't pressed against his, force me out of my head. All of the people at the bar are watching us, including Reid and Nick, who both seem to be glowering a little.

It takes me a minute to remember that this is all part of the show the three of them are putting on. It's just an act, and they're doing a good job of pretending to be jealous for the benefit of the onlooking crowd.

I feel flushed and a little unsteady, and my stomach is revisiting that same fluttering sensation it had when I pulled out of the parking lot after first seeing Reid. It only accelerates the fluttery feeling when I look at Sebastian and he winks at me.

He has the uncanny ability to make me feel things on the spot, as if my body responds to his commands on cue.

I open my mouth to say something to him, but before any words can come out, a large hand wraps around my arm and gently pulls me away.

"Dance with me." Reid smiles as he threads his fingers

through mine and walks hand-in-hand with me to the center of the bar.

This isn't really a dancing kind of bar, but there's enough space without tables in the center of it that most of the regulars get up and dance from time to time whenever their favorite song plays over the bar's speakers. Reid makes a big show of pulling me toward that empty spot, practically lifting me up off my feet and twirling me around as he looks over my shoulder back at Sebastian.

Oh. I get it now.

This is the pretend fighting-over-me thing that they talked about, to convince everyone here that there's jealousy between them. It's almost convincing enough for *me* to fall for it.

Placing a hand at the small of my back, Reid pulls me close against him and starts to move. The beat of the music pounds in my chest as every inch of my skin reacts to his proximity. I try to act like I don't notice the lack of any space between our bodies, but it's impossible not to be overwhelmed by it.

"You don't have to do this, you know," I whisper, my heart still thudding so hard that I can hear blood rushing in my ears.

But Reid just shakes his head, brushing off my attempt to let him off the hook.

"I wouldn't be doing it if I didn't want to," he replies, leaning down to speak quietly in my ear. His lips don't quite touch my skin, but I still have to work hard to suppress a shiver as my knees wobble a little.

As if he can feel it, he tightens his hold on me, steadying me by holding me even tighter against his body—which doesn't do much to help with the shakiness of my legs, if I'm being honest.

"Besides," he adds. "I meant what I told you today. Your problems are my problems, trouble. They're *our* problems. So my brothers and I are doing this. Fuck everyone in this town who made you feel small just because your ex was a dick who didn't appreciate what he had. Dylan didn't deserve you. Fuck him."

Reid's words make my heart race, and it has nothing to do with the tempo of the music. There's a fierce protectiveness in his voice that hits me right in the chest, and I wrap my arms around his neck, drawing back a little so that I can meet his gaze. He looks right back at me, steady and unwavering, and we're still staring at each other in heavy silence as the song ends.

Even though the music has stopped, Reid makes no move to let go of me.

"My turn, shortcake."

The deep voice behind me is all the warning I get before I'm tugged out of Reid's hold. Sebastian somehow manages to twirl me in such a way that even my uncoordinated ass looks halfway graceful, and even though I wasn't quite ready to be done with Reid yet, it's hard to be disappointed as Sebastian grins down at me.

His outgoing and flirtatious personality is a nice balance after the intensity of that moment with Reid, but it's no less intoxicating.

I can feel every inch of his body as he moves against me too —*every inch*—and I'd be shocked if my face isn't bright red by this point, but he doesn't seem to mind at all.

"Reid and Nick are both glaring at us, you know," he points out, inclining his head in their direction without taking his gaze off me.

"People are probably wondering if the three of you are going to get into a bar fight," I joke breathlessly.

He grins. "Actually, Nick and I were just talking about opening up an underground fight ring in Chestnut Hill earlier tonight. I think it's a great idea."

I laugh, unable to help myself. "Of course you do. Remember during senior year when you got into that fight with Tommy Keller?"

I can remember at least a dozen instances in the past when Sebastian got busted for fighting—usually nothing too serious, but he was always the type to swing first and think later. But with Tommy, it turned into a legit fight. Sebastian was suspended for a week, and when Tommy showed up to school the next day, one side of his face was purple and bruised.

Sebastian snorts. "That douchebag had it coming."

He pulls me closer and swings me around so fast that it's dizzying, only to grab me by both sides of my waist and steady me on my feet again. Every time he spins me around, he smiles, as if he's pleased with how my body fits in his hands and how easy it is to maneuver me like this.

"Oh yeah?" I ask as he wraps his arms around me again, swaying to the music. "What did he do to deserve looking like he got run over by a truck?"

For a second, the teasing gleam I'm used to seeing in Sebastian's blue-green eyes slips away, replaced by a spark of something heavier.

"He said some shit about you in the locker room. Talking about how good you looked in the skirt you were wearing, and all the things he wanted to do to you." His jaw clenches. "Trust me, he got off light."

It was for me?

He punched Tommy Keller out in defense of me?

I'm so surprised by the realization that I trip over my own feet, and Sebastian's serious expression clears as he catches me, gripping my arms to keep me from falling.

"Careful there." He grins. "If you go down, I go down, and you can't let me look bad in front of my brothers."

That draws a laugh from me, and we keep dancing. His words stay with me though, and I'm too lost in my thoughts to keep bantering with him. When the song finally ends, Sebastian looks like he's ready to dance to another—but this time, Nick appears and pulls me away.

"Let me guess, it's your turn now?" I chuckle, brushing a few strands of hair away from my sweat-dampened forehead. "You guys are really going all out."

"No." He shakes his head, his expression unreadable. "It *is* my turn, but I don't dance. I'm just coming to get you."

With that enigmatic answer, he tugs me through the crowd away from the makeshift dance floor. I follow after him, my mind still reeling a little. Going from Sebastian's dangerously flirtatious dancing to Nick's grouchy and commanding presence is enough to make my head spin.

Nick leads me to a table, and I glance back toward the bar in time to see Sebastian and Reid settle onto two barstools. Reid gestures to Craig for a couple of beers, and as the bartender delivers them, the two Cooper brothers shoot a look our way.

Ignoring his brothers for the moment, Nick pulls out a chair and motions for me to sit, which I obediently do.

Part of me wishes I could dance with him too, but I know that would be pushing this little fantasy into "obvious lie" territory. I don't think I've *ever* seen the man dance—not at any of the school dances back in high school, and not even at his sister's own wedding. If Nick had stepped in to spin me around the dance floor, everyone in the bar would probably have figured out we were trying to trick them. So it's probably better this way, despite the twinge of disappointment I feel.

At least he sits in the chair beside me instead of across the table, sliding his chair close enough that our legs touch.

"I'm not gonna dance with you, but I can at least feed you," he declares.

He pushes the menu in front of me, and I remember what my sister said about The Old Oak having good food on their new menu now.

"Oh. Okay."

My gaze scans the menu, and I realize suddenly how hungry I am. I haven't had a lot to drink tonight, but it's been long enough since I last ate that I can feel the buzz of alcohol in my system. And Pippa was right, everything looks really good.

"What do you want?" Nick asks.

He's staring at me intently, and it makes nerves sweep through me. I'm not used to getting this much direct attention from Nick, who usually doesn't say much and almost seems to avoid eye contact with me. It's hard to make a decision when I can feel his gaze boring into me, and I ramble a little as I peruse the menu, a nervous habit I've always had.

"Oh shoot, I can never decide. It's always too much pressure. The loaded potato skins look good. Ooh, so does the burger. Or maybe I should get the flatbread? That looks pretty amazing too."

Nick flags the waitress down before I've finished deciding on what to order. She smiles brightly at him, although the smile dims a little as I look up from the menu and she looks at me. I get the feeling she's a bit jealous—although she has no real reason to be, even though I can't tell her that.

"We'll have one of everything," Nick says just as his brothers come to join us at the table.

"Everything on the entire menu?" The waitress blinks at him with her mouth shaped into a surprised little 'O.'

"Yeah, one of everything. Except for the drinks. We'll get those from the bar when we want."

"Um… okay. I'll be back in a bit with all of that."

She slips back into the crowd, still looking slightly incredulous.

"Damn, dude. You trying to show us up?" Sebastian whistles, sharing a look with Reid.

"What? She needs to eat." Nick frowns at them as if he's only just now realizing that he ordered way too much food. "And she hasn't tried anything on the menu yet."

"Thanks, Nick," I stammer, touched by the gesture even if

there's no way I'll be able to eat it all. "That was... really nice of you."

He gives me a look, his expression hard to decipher. Then he nods, glancing away and rubbing a hand over the back of his neck. Fortunately, the waitress brings the food as it's ready instead of waiting for everything to be done, so it's not long before she delivers the first few plates to our table.

The guys tuck in, the four of us sharing all of it—although Nick makes sure I get the first taste of everything. They banter easily among themselves and with me as we eat, sometimes raising their voices a little to play up the ruse that they're still fighting over my affections.

Their deep, familiar laughter, combined with another round of drinks, makes everything feel looser and *very* enjoyable. I'm having such a good time that I don't even notice my phone buzzing until Nick looks down at me.

"You're vibrating."

His words make my cheeks heat instantly, my mind going to a million dirty places. "Uh, what?"

"Your pants, probably your pocket—your phone is vibrating. I can feel it on the side of my leg."

I'd forgotten that our legs are still side-by-side, and I shift away a little, blushing even harder as I tug my phone out of my back pocket. When I swipe across the screen, I see a text from my best friend back in LA.

LORELAI: Hey girl! How are things going so far back there in Chestnut Hill? Have you turned back into a country bumpkin yet?

The guys are all eating and talking, so I take a minute to answer her.

ME: No, not yet, lol. Things aren't as bad as I had expected here, actually.

LORELAI: Oh yeah? Please tell me you haven't shacked up

with some rugged cowboy in the back of a barn or something. Although if you have, I want ALL the juicy details!

I let out a small laugh. Lorelai cracks me up, and I'm feeling so good right now that everything is making me smile. She's constantly telling me that I "wear my heart on my sleeve" and warned me not to bat eyes at any "handsome hunks with pickup trucks." She would just about die if she could see me sitting here with the Cooper brothers right now in all of their brawny glory.

My thumbs fly across the screen as I type out a message, promising her that I haven't fallen for any cowboys. We text back and forth a bit, and when something she says makes me chuckle again, Reid reaches over and plucks my cell phone from my hands.

My head shoots up. "Hey!"

He arches a brow, giving me a serious look as his full lips twitch with an almost-smile. "No texting at the dinner table, trouble. You know the rules."

I have to hide a smirk too. That's a rule my parents always enforced very strongly in my house, and even though Reid is being all bossy, there's a teasing glint in his eyes as he reminds me of it.

"Besides," he adds, standing up and holding out my cell phone as if he's tempting a cat with a piece of fish. "It's time for more dancing. Can't let Nick think he's really gotten ahead of me and Seb with this feast."

I roll my eyes but push to my feet, shoving my phone back into my pocket when he gives it back to me.

Reid takes my hand and leads me toward the dance floor again just as another song starts blaring from the speakers. Heads turn to watch us as we go, and I do my best to keep a straight face. Normally, I don't like people staring at me, but all of the curious and jealous looks from the other patrons at the bar are doing wonders for my ego.

When we reach the empty spot in the middle of the bar,

Reid pulls me in close, molding my body against his. But before we can start dancing again, a loud voice cuts through the bar.

"What the *fuck?*"

My head snaps up to see my brother standing near the door, his gaze locked on me and Reid.

Shock contorts his features, followed quickly by anger. Before I can process what's happening, he barrels across the bar and drags Reid away from me.

Then he winds up and punches his friend in the face.

6

REID

The punch catches me off guard, sending my head snapping to the side, and Hailey lets out a startled yelp.

I grunt, ducking Lucas's second punch and backing out of the way. I'm not gonna hit him back, especially since he's got every right to be mad. We all promised him years ago that we'd never fuck with Hailey, and he has no idea that this thing with us and his sister is pretend.

"Hey! Whoa, whoa." Nick and Sebastian appear between us, and Sebastian holds his hands out. "Hold up, dude. Stop!"

"The fuck I will." Lucas glares at me over my brother's shoulder.

"Oh, for fuck's sake." Hailey huffs out a breath, grabbing her brother by the arm and pulling him back. "Stop, Lucas. It's fine, really. It's—"

He doesn't stop glowering. "No, it's not. He—"

She yanks on his arm, bringing his head down low enough for her to whisper some quiet, urgent words into his ear. I can't make out what she's saying, but I can guess the gist of it, because Lucas's eyebrows draw together as he listens. Some of the tension drains from his shoulders, and Hailey pulls on his arm again, urging him toward the door.

"Come on," she says. "We'll talk about this outside."

He nods, still looking a bit wary, and the five of us step outside the bar so that no one will hear us talking. We've already stirred up quite a bit of attention, not only with our very public fight over Hailey, but now with this scuffle with her brother.

Once we get outside and are around the corner of the building so we won't be overheard by anyone coming or going, Lucas looks between the four of us.

"What do you mean, it's fake?" he asks, confirming my suspicion that Hailey told him what's really going on.

"Dylan Montgomery was being a dick to your sister," I explain. "I ran into the two of them earlier today, and he was being a complete fuckwad, as usual. Trying to make her feel like shit for still being single."

"So Reid stepped in to help me by pretending to be dating me," Hailey pitches in.

I nod and then let her carry on with the explanation as I rub away the soreness in my jaw, working it open and closed a few times. He did manage to get in a decent hit, especially since Lucas's right hook has always needed a bit of work.

"They're actually..." She clears her throat. "Uh, they're actually *all* pretending to be dating me."

"What?" Lucas narrows his eyes. "Why?"

"Well, Nick saw some women talking to me at the bar about Dylan leaving me and what a disaster our wedding was, and I guess he felt sorry for me too, because he stepped up and—" She glances over at Nick, and I swear I see a flush creep up her cheeks. "He told them we were dating too."

"We couldn't exactly admit that one of them had been lying," Sebastian points out, spreading his hands. "So we decided to go for the trifecta. We'll tell everyone in Chestnut Hill that all three of us are dating her separately, doing our best to win her over. With the three of us supposedly fighting over her, people won't keep hounding her about the wedding, and Dylan won't have shit to say either."

"Oh." Lucas stares at the exterior wall of the bar, his brows pinching together as he works through all of that. Then he shakes his head, glancing over at me. "Shit, I'm sorry, man. I shouldn't have hauled off and punched you without knowing the full story."

I lift one shoulder. "Don't worry about it."

"Fucking Dylan." Lucas's hands curl into fists as if he's itching to land a punch on Hailey's ex instead. "God, I hate that guy. I can't believe he's getting married to Brielle, although I guess they deserve each other."

Hailey grimaces at her brother's comment, and I wonder if she knew that already. If she didn't, I wish she hadn't found out like this. I'm sure it stings to hear that the 'friend' of hers whom Dylan cheated on her with is now the guy's fiancée. Maybe the slightly nauseated look on her face isn't because she didn't know but just because it's so shitty. I hope that's the case. I hope she doesn't have any leftover feelings for that fucker. He isn't worthy to breathe her air.

Now that Lucas is on board with the lie and not trying to take a swing at me, we all go back inside the bar and dig back into the massive amount of food Nick ordered. It's nice to have us all sitting around the table together, and we easily all fall back into talking again.

When Hailey gets up from the table, I watch as she walks first to the bathroom and then to the end of the bar. It looks like she's getting a glass of water or something.

Lucas is telling us about how football practices have been going, and about a kid who's been giving him a bit of trouble.

"I swear to god, coaching high school football is gonna make me go gray before my time," he grouses, and we all chuckle. He loves coaching too much to ever quit, and everyone at the table knows it.

He tells us a bit more about the player who's been struggling, and my brothers and I toss in bits of advice here and there. I have my head turned toward the conversation when Hailey returns to the table, and I stiffen as I feel something cold touch the side of my jaw.

I turn toward her and realize that she's holding a little pile of ice that she's wrapped up in a bar napkin.

"Hold still." She lifts it back up to my face and presses it against the spot where I got punched.

"You don't need to do that," I murmur, reaching up to tug her hand away. "I'm a lot tougher than I look."

She laughs lightly before putting the ice right back on my jaw.

"You already look tough as nails to me. And I know I don't have to do it, but just like you said earlier, your problems are my problems. So I'm going to anyway. And there's nothing you can do to stop me," she adds with a smirk.

I chuckle. "You're so sassy."

"You're so bossy," she shoots back.

Her smile sparks something inside me as she locks eyes with mine, stubbornly tending to the small injury on my face. Her wrist is so close to the bottom of my nose that I can smell the faint scent of her body wash clinging to her skin. It smells like wildflowers and honeysuckle, and it's delicious enough that I want to lick it off.

Fuck, what in the hell was that all about?

I snap myself out of my thoughts as soon as I realize that I was just allowing my mind to wander down a dangerous path about my best friend's little sister.

Shifting a little in my chair, I glance away. I have to let my gaze focus on something else for a second because I feel like I might combust if I keep staring into Hailey's eyes. Or worse yet, if I let my eyes wander down over the full, enticing curves that I've felt pressed against me too many times tonight to ignore.

As my gaze wanders over the crowded room, I catch a glimpse of Dylan and his new fiancée standing on the far side of the bar. Brielle is saying something, and Dylan nods along with whatever it is. But I see his gaze dart in our direction twice when he thinks she's not looking, and there's a sour expression on his face. He looks entirely pissed off at the sight of Hailey hanging out at a table with me and my brothers, and I have to assume that the rumor mill has already fed him the story we concocted.

As far as he knows, all three of us are actively fighting over her affections, making her officially the most sought-after woman in Chestnut Hill.

And she's the woman he let get away.

I hope he fucking regrets losing her. That he regrets giving up a woman as beautiful and intelligent as Hailey. I hope it haunts him until his last damn breath. Hailey has a genuine enthusiasm for life that's infectious whenever I'm around her, and she's one of the kindest people I know. Dylan really fucked up his chance with a woman he didn't deserve anyway. And now he's sitting over there at the bar with his 'prize,' a girl who isn't *half* the woman Hailey is, stewing over how his ex looks like she's enjoying herself with the attention of other men while he's left with the scraps that he left the table for.

Good. I hope it keeps him up at night.

In fact...

Without hesitation, I reach over and pull Hailey up onto my lap.

She makes a little yelping noise, the sound so sweet and breathless that I have to immediately block it out of my mind—because I can't afford to let myself think about what *other* noises I might be able to get her to make.

"Dylan is watching."

I make sure to say it just loud enough that Lucas and my brothers can hear too, explaining my impulsive action before

Lucas can deck me again. Hailey's body goes still, but motionless or not, I can still feel the soft roundness of her ass pressed against my crotch. I clench my jaw, willing my cock not to react as I glance across the bar again.

If Dylan wasn't staring over here before, he sure the hell is now. I can see his fuming face out of the corner of my eye, and a grin tugs at my lips. I'm going to make this good.

I slide my hand down Hailey's back, resting my palm just below the curve of her lower back, almost on her ass. I can feel the way her body responds, tensing and relaxing beneath my touch, and I know that I should probably stop right here. This is enough of a possessive display to get the point across.

But for some reason, I really don't want to.

So I let that hand slide down just an inch or two lower, catching her chin with the fingertips of my other hand. I turn her head toward mine, and when Hailey reaches up to rest her palm on my chest, right over the tattoo that covers my left pec—I can't help myself.

I kiss her softly, pressing my lips to hers until I feel her melt against me.

When we separate, I bring my mouth to her ear, keeping my voice low.

"That piece of shit ex of yours should never be able to make you feel inferior," I tell her. "And if I have anything to say about it, he never will. Never again."

Hailey's fingers flex lightly against my chest as she draws in a breath. Even without looking at her face, I can tell she's smiling, and my chest goes a little tight.

7

HAILEY

By the time we all leave the bar, it's late, and I'm feeling positively wonderful. I'm no longer even a bit tipsy, thanks to Nick's decision to order the entire menu. Instead, I'm pleasantly full, happy, and warm. I feel much better than I thought I would being back here in my hometown, which holds so many of my best and worst memories.

I give my brother a hug goodnight as he heads out, and then the triplets walk me to my car.

"Okay, so who's taking her out on a date first?" Reid looks at his brothers before quickly suggesting that he should be the one to make plans with me first.

"Like hell," Sebastian argues. "I've already got a great idea for a date, so I'm going first."

"You guys really don't need to take me out on dates," I say with a laugh. "I think that what you did here at the bar was enough to get the point across to everyone."

As soon as the words are out of my mouth though, I immediately regret them. Because after the fun we had tonight, I really *do* want to go out with each of them one-on-one.

"Nah." Nick makes a noise in his throat, shaking his head. "It's a good idea for us to be seen doing stuff with you. If this were real, we'd want to spend every waking minute with you. We need to make it believable."

Something flutters through me at the sincerity in his tone, and I look away from him as I nod. He's got a point.

"Okay," I say to Sebastian. "So what's your idea?"

He arches the brow that has a little scar through it, shaking his head at me without answering.

"Not so fast there, shortcake. You have to promise you'll go with me before I tell you what it is."

"What? That's not fair!" I laugh and look to Reid and Nick for backup, but they're both staying out of it. Finally, I relent. "Okay, fine. I'll go. Now tell me what it is, please."

He flashes me his widest smile. "I'm going to take you to do the Polar Bear Plunge at Lake Monroe tomorrow morning."

My jaw drops. "Are you serious? There's no way in hell that I'm doing that with you. The lake is fucking *freezing* this time of year! I've heard they literally have to cut away the ice by the shoreline to make it possible."

"But you already promised! Besides, I'll keep you warm." He gives me a look that probably *could* thaw ice, and I have to work to keep the flush from traveling up my face. Then he waggles his eyebrows, taking a step closer to me. "Come on, Bennett. I dare you. You aren't scared, are you?"

The other two men chuckle—probably because they know that Sebastian has shamelessly hit on my weak point. Maybe it's from growing up with an older brother, but I *hate* to back down from a challenge. Sebastian and I managed to get each other into trouble a couple of times when I was younger by throwing down dares or bets for each other, and he clearly knows that it's his best chance of getting me to go with him.

And... dammit. He's right.

"All right." I scrunch up my face, already regretting this. "*Fine*. I'll do it. I'll meet you by Lake Monroe in the morning."

Sebastian raises his arm in victory, his blue-green eyes

shining in the dim light outside the bar. "There she is! The girl we know and love."

His easy affection makes something warm and soft spread through my chest. I know he doesn't mean it in a romantic way, but it's still nice knowing how solidly these three men are on my side. If I was worried that being away for two years would change things between us, those fears were clearly unfounded. If anything, the Cooper brothers seem even more protective of me than they used to be, and they all seem happy to have me back.

I like that. A lot.

"I'm taking you out too," Reid puts in. "Sebastian doesn't get to have all the fun. Besides, I'm the first one you technically agreed to 'date,' so that means I should at least get to go second."

It's kind of endearing to watch as the three brothers create a running order for who will take me out when, even if they are only fake dates. There's something about having these three ruggedly handsome men all arguing over their chance to hang out with me that's simultaneously sweet and a little daunting.

Nick clears his throat, his expression stoic and serious as he tells me, "My date with you won't be anything as dumb as taking you to the Polar Bear Plunge."

Sebastian makes an indignant noise, and I bite back a grin.

Reid opens my car door for me, and I climb inside behind the wheel. He bends down a little, the light from the neon signs in the bar window reflecting off the copper strands in his brown hair.

"'Night, trouble," he tells me. "Go get some rest. You're going to need it if you're doing that stupid plunge in the morning."

I nod, and he closes the door for me.

For a second, I stare out my window, watching as the Cooper brothers turn to head back toward their car. Their broad shoulders seem even wider when lined up side by side like that, and it strikes me—not for the first time—that although separately, any one of them would be a force to be reckoned with, together, they're devastating.

Without the heat on in my car, I'm starting to feel the cold, so I finally turn the key in the ignition and pull out of the bar parking lot, heading back to my temporary lodgings.

I figure Ted is probably already asleep in his room since it's late, but I'm surprised to see that not only is he wide awake and sitting on the couch in the living room, he's also smoking a blunt cigar and listening to the kind of music that makes me think someone's dog got hit by a truck. The whole thing is rather stomach-turning.

"Welcome back." Ted pulls the cigar out of his mouth as he looks up at me and holds it out in his hand.

"No, thanks." I barely suppress the urge to retch. "I, uh, don't smoke."

"Neither do I." He shrugs, putting the cigar back in his mouth and speaking around it as he adds, "Only when I'm about to jam."

Oh, dear god, no.

I cringe as he pulls an acoustic guitar out from the side of the couch and starts to play along with the music coming through the speakers. Giving him a vague wave, I make a beeline toward my room, slipping inside and closing the door behind me. I was hoping it would block out the sound, but unfortunately, it doesn't seem to make much difference. I'll have to pray he gets tired and gives it up before too long.

After such a wonderful night, it's kind of a downer to have to come back to a shitty place like this, but I brush it off, refusing to let it put a damper on my mood. At least I have a safe, cheap place to stay, even if it's less than desirable.

I get changed quickly, sliding a soft, oversized T-shirt over my head before washing my face and brushing my teeth and hair. Then I climb into bed and try to settle my mind down enough to fall asleep.

I could blame Ted's atrocious music for the fact that I can't seem to drift off, but in all honesty, I'm still too keyed up from my eventful day to be able to sleep yet anyway.

So instead of staring blankly into the darkness, I pick up my phone and text Lorelai. It's not quite as late where she is, so I'm pretty sure she'll still be awake.

ME: Hey, are you still up?

LORELAI: Of course! I'm doing my nails in bed.

I laugh out loud, because I can totally picture Lorelai doing that right now. It's just like her to be up late with her dark hair tied up in a messy bun while she paints her toenails alternating shades of pink. I can see her heart-shaped face peering closely at each nail to paint it perfectly.

ME: So remember how you told me not to get distracted by any hot guys while I'm here?

LORELAI: I knew it. You went and fell for some mountain man, didn't you?

ME: Calm down, lol. It's actually not nearly as exciting as I made it sound. It's my brother's three triplet best friends, and it's only a sort of pretend situation to get my ex to leave me the hell alone.

LORELAI: Whoa whoa whoa. Back it up there, sweet cheeks. I'm gonna need a hell of a lot more details than that. You're talking about the Cooper brothers, right? THE Cooper brothers??

ME: Yup. I'm fake dating them. All of them.

LORELAI: Holy. Shit! Fake dating? I didn't even think that was a real thing! How the hell did that happen??

I fill her in on everything, texting her until my eyelids start to droop and I fall asleep with my phone still clutched in my hand.

When my alarm goes off in the morning, I wake up feeling a little less enthusiastic about this whole idea.

Not the fake dating plan—which I'm actually very much still on board with—but specifically, my date with Sebastian.

Damn my past self and her inability to back down from a dare.

I throw one arm over my face dramatically, groaning into the quiet morning air. Ted stopped his racket a short while before I fell asleep last night, so it's blissfully silent in the house now.

"Are you seriously going to do this, Hailey?" I mutter to myself.

I was raised in Montana, so I grew up with cold weather. But I've had two years for my blood to thin out while living in Los Angeles, and even before I left Chestnut Hill, I was never really the type to participate in things like the Polar Bear Plunge. I always figured that winter is cold enough. Why add to it by voluntarily jumping into a freezing lake?

But Sebastian was always the daredevil of Lucas's brotherhood of best friends, and I like to think that I was part of that group more often than not, even if they were just indulging me by letting me join. I can remember how Sebastian had a way of getting me to take the leap on things, even back then. Anytime I felt skittish about something, he always seemed to be there helping me rise to the challenge.

It's funny, in a sort of sad way almost, how everyone always saw him as such a rebellious kid. I guess that maybe I saw a different side of him sometimes, a side that wasn't always just about thrill-seeking but about something a lot deeper. He had a gift for making me feel braver and bolder than I actually probably was.

So I'll rise to the challenge this time too. I refuse to wimp out on him. And to prove it, I'm even going to take things up a notch.

Hauling my ass out of bed, I pad over to the dresser where I put a bunch of my clothes when I unpacked. Then I rifle around in the top drawer until I find the very skimpy bikini I brought. I had several just like it in LA, since it made perfect sense to own a bunch of bikinis there. Of course, here it pretty much makes no sense at all.

Unless you've been tricked into doing a plunge into a freezing lake, in which case it's the perfect outfit to prove that you're not even a tiny bit scared of the cold.

I strip off my sleep clothes and put on the bikini, tying the pink strap around my back and pulling at the Brazilian bottom just a bit so that it leaves at least a *little* to the imagination.

Then I cover up with a big warm coat, and give myself a determined nod as I stand in front of the mirror on the wall.

It's literally freezing outside. There's snow on the ground, and underneath this coat I'm practically bare-ass naked—with the exception of enough fabric to dress maybe half a dozen Barbie dolls. The coat reaches almost halfway down my calves, thank goodness for that, and my boots reach the rest of the way up. From the outside, I almost look like I'm actually dressed for the weather.

I head out to meet Sebastian, pulling up to see a bunch of townspeople gathered at the edge of Lake Monroe already. The Polar Bear Plunge is an annual tradition, and almost everyone who's milling around on the shore participates every year, which is probably why most of them are smart enough to have wetsuits or at least long-sleeved shirts and pants on, and a dry change of clothes nearby.

At least I have that. I'm already looking forward to putting on the sweater and pants I brought with me for afterward.

Sliding out of the car, I wrap my arms around myself and look around, scanning the crowd. Sebastian isn't here yet. I must have beat him. If memory serves, he was never much of an early riser.

For a second, I'm tempted to get back in the car, drive back to Ted's, and crawl back into the bed in his spare room. But I've already made it this far, so instead of letting myself chicken out, I quickly shuck my coat and stride toward the shoreline. I join the rest of the crowd as they wait for the event to begin, my bright pink bikini like a beacon against the stark white snow that covers the ground by the lake.

"That sure is a statement."

I turn around to see a guy I vaguely recognize from high school. He was a year behind me, I think.

"Oh." I chuckle, my teeth chattering a little as I blow out a breath. "Thanks."

"Is this your first time doing the plunge?"

"First and *last*," I say fervently, making him laugh.

"It's not so bad," he assures me. "The trick is not to hold your breath, and not to try to keep yourself from shivering. You *want* to shiver. It's what keeps you warm."

"Noted." I nod as a visible tremor passes through my body, and his smile widens.

"You should've kept your coat on until right before we went in." He takes a step toward me, reaching out as if he's going to rub my arms. "Here, let me—"

"Hey, asshole. Beat it."

A sharp voice cuts him off, and we both glance up to see Sebastian bearing down on us. The guy from my high school blanches a bit at Sebastian's massive size and the hard, protective look on his face. He holds up his hands and gives me an apologetic look, then turns and quickly walks away.

I'm about to tell Sebastian that he didn't need to worry about that guy, but before I can, the youngest Cooper brother rounds on me—and he *still* looks pissed.

"What the fuck are you wearing?" he grits out.

I blink, surprised. I didn't expect him to be angry about it. If anything, I thought he'd find it funny that I met his dare and one-upped it.

"A bikini. Don't tell me you've never seen one before."

"Yeah, I've seen one before, smartass," he says, narrowing his eyes like he wants to bend me over his knee and spank me. "But why the hell are you wearing that here? Every guy at the lake is staring at you."

"So what?" I glance around, sure he's exaggerating. "I mean, why does it bother you so much? I'm only your fake girlfriend, not your real one."

"Good fucking thing." His eyes are still locked on me, his jaw tight. "If you were my real girlfriend, I'd throw you over my shoulder and carry your ass out of here."

A shiver that has nothing to do with the cold races up my spine at the dark promise in his words, and for some reason that I can't quite understand, instead of backing down… I poke the bear.

"Like hell you would."

I lift my chin, uncrossing my arms so that more of my stomach is bared, just to make a point. It's even colder without that extra bit of protection from the chilly air, but I don't care.

A muscle in Sebastian's jaw jumps, his gaze dropping downward before shooting back up to my face. Then he moves, scooping me up and tossing me over his muscular shoulder with ease. I let out a surprised yelp that turns into an 'oof' as my body folds over his shoulder, my head and arms dangling and my ass in the air.

He turns and strides toward his car, and I can feel the palm of his large hand against my butt as he tries to cover my ass on the way.

"Sebastian!" I hiss. "What are you doing?"

"What you dared me to do."

"I didn't dare you to do anything," I insist, squirming a little in his grasp but trying to keep my voice down so that we won't draw more attention than we already have.

"Like hell you didn't."

When we get to his car, he sets me down and stands in front of me. My back is up against the cold metal side of the back passenger door as he reaches into the front seat to pull something out. His body is practically pinned against me, and I feel as if I'm shaking all over.

"Here. Put this on."

He hands me one of his shirts and starts to pull it over my head before I can protest. I'm tempted to put up a fight just for the principle of it, but as he slips the oversized shirt over my head and tugs it down, it's hard to regret the extra bit of warmth the additional layer offers. Plus, it's surprisingly soft and smells just like him. Although I'd never admit this to him, I find myself wanting to pull it even tighter around me and never take it off.

"There, that's better."

Sebastian nods. He seems a bit more satisfied now that I'm covered up. And even though I know that the whole jealous display he just made was a fake one, likely for the benefit of all the guys gathered at the lake who will run their mouths until word gets back to Dylan... I still liked it. My heart flutters a little at the idea of Sebastian Cooper being that jealous of other men for looking at me. Jealous enough and possessive enough that he literally covered up my ass with his hand as if claiming it as off limits for anyone else to see.

"You ready?"

His question jars me back to reality. *Fuck. We still have to do that part.*

"Right, the plunge."

It's time for everyone gathered here to race into the water, and I suck in a deep breath as we walk back over to join them, studiously avoiding people's curious glances.

I've got no coat, no boots, and just a T-shirt and scant bikini with bare feet in the snow. I'm fucking freezing.

I watch as Sebastian sheds his coat, his arm and chest muscles flexing with the movement. He tosses it aside, leaving him in just a pair of swim trunks and a shirt. Suddenly, I don't think I feel the cold anymore, even though my toes are numb.

He extends his hand out for me to take. "Come on, we'll wade in together."

"Wait, aren't we supposed to *plunge*? Isn't that kind of the whole point?"

"I admire your courage, but let's take this slow. My brothers would never forgive me if I gave you hypothermia before they had their chance to go on dates with you."

I give him a suspicious glance. I'm sure they don't care *that* much, but I guess I should just be glad he wants me to live through this.

We walk into Lake Monroe together. Like they do almost every year, the event organizers have opened up a large section in the ice that covers the lake, allowing us access to the freezing water. As soon as my foot sinks into it, a shock of cold streaks up the inside of my leg like a lightning bolt.

Sebastian wraps his arms around me as we slowly walk in deeper, the frigid water surrounding us.

"Just breathe," he reminds me, and I let out a gasping exhale.

By the time we're up to our chests, we stop walking and face each other. He holds on to me, and I press my whole body against his out of the sheer need to combat the freezing lake water. I can feel his warm breath at the side of my neck as I bury my face against him, and his strong arms wrap around my back in an unwavering grip.

"Breathe with me," he murmurs again. "You've got this."

I nod, my teeth chattering and my entire body screaming at me to race for the shore. But I don't, and as the two of us breathe together, our chests rising and falling in sync, pressing harder against each other with each inhale... I start to feel less cold.

Taking one last breath in, I lift my head to look up at him. He's gazing down at me, our faces only inches apart.

"Okay," I whisper. "I'm ready."

He nods. "One…"

"Two…"

"Three."

At the last word, he tightens his arms around me, holding me close as we both plunge the last bit into the water, dunking our heads beneath the surface. The shock of it hits me all over again, and we both resurface like monsters emerging from the deep, gasping for air as we make unintelligible noises. We race toward the shore, one of Sebastian's large hands wrapped around mine.

By the time we finally get out, we make a beeline toward his car, dripping with each step.

"Here."

He pulls a towel from his back seat and wraps it around me, covering up my wet bikini and soaked shirt. Then he rubs the sides of my arms as if he's trying to start a fire. I laugh, giddy from the experience and strangely energized by it too.

"See? It was fun, right? I told you it would be a good time." His smile broadens, and he finishes helping me dry off a bit before grabbing a second towel for himself and wrapping it around his shoulders. I put my boots back on, and we lean against his car and watch everyone else come in from the water in a staggered pattern as they compete to see who can withstand the cold the longest.

Some of them grab thermoses out of their cars, huddling and chatting as they enjoy a post-plunge beverage. Sebastian notices and lights up, grinning at me as he opens his door again.

"Hang on. I forgot I brought you something."

He grabs a small bag and two cups from the cupholder in his middle console, then straightens and shuts the door.

"Here." He hands me a cup of coffee and a donut. "I thought this might help make up for the fact that I basically entrapped you into doing the plunge."

I take it from him, smiling because coffee and a donut sounds perfect right now. I take a sip from the cup, and my brows furrow.

"What is this?"

"It's a half-caff latte with cinnamon and vanilla. That's still what you like, right?"

I'm totally stunned. It's not the gesture that leaves me speechless, it's the fact that Sebastian remembered *exactly* how I like my coffee and what my favorite donut is. I can smell the vanilla and cinnamon wafting from the steam out of the top of the cup, and the donut is a perfectly crispy old-fashioned.

"Yeah, that's still what I like," I murmur, working to make my voice sound normal. "I'm just surprised you remembered, that's all."

"Of course I remembered, shortcake. You haven't been gone *that* long." He chuckles. "And besides, we're 'dating' now, aren't we? I'm not gonna half ass it and get my girl some shit she doesn't like."

His smile is teasing, but I know he means it. Sebastian doesn't half ass anything. He's the guy that drives the motorcycle full throttle and kisses the girl as if her life depended on it. That last part I know for a fact now, after last night at the bar.

"You're a good fake boyfriend," I say, trying to banish the heat that floods my veins at the memory. "I had no idea that you could be such a gentleman."

Sebastian's brilliant blue-green eyes darken. He runs a hand through his wet hair, dispelling a few water droplets from the messy dark brown strands as a devilish smirk curls his lips.

"Of course I'm a good fake boyfriend. But I'm definitely not a gentleman. In fact, I'm a great fake boyfriend *because* I'm not a gentleman."

I swallow hard, my heart crashing against my ribs as if it's trying to burst right through. "What does that mean?"

Sebastian gives me a look, almost as if I've just laid down another dare. He steps closer, plucking the coffee and the bagged donut from my hand and setting them on the roof of his car.

Then he pulls me into his arms and kisses me.

Unlike our first kiss at The Old Oak, this one doesn't start off awkward or stiff. Instead, it's like pure fire right from the start. His lips are firm and warm against mine as he presses me up against the car, pinning me between the cold metal exterior and his firm, muscled body. Even though we were just in a freezing lake, I can feel the heat radiating from his body into mine, and both of his hands slide into my wet hair as his thigh slips between my legs.

I gasp at the slight pressure on my clit, and although I have no idea whether that was intentional on his part or not, that doesn't stop my body from responding. I arch against him, breathing in the fresh scent of the lake mixed with a spicy cognac and amber scent that I recognize as being uniquely Sebastian's.

My arms wrap around his neck, pinning our bodies even closer together as I go up onto my tiptoes, chasing the pressure of his lips as he groans softly into my mouth.

I don't know who's watching us, or what prompted such a strong response from him.

I have no idea who we're putting on a show for, but I tell myself that I'm just following Sebastian's lead as I throw myself into our kiss without restraint, letting instinct take over.

He shifts his weight, making his thigh brush against my clit again through the fabric that separates us, and I bite back a whimper.

Holy shit.

He wasn't kidding. Sebastian Cooper is definitely *not* a gentleman.

And in this moment, I'm really fucking glad about that.

8

SEBASTIAN

Hailey whimpers against my lips again, and the sound goes straight to my cock. If it weren't for the freezing water we were just submerged in, I'd definitely be sporting a raging hard-on right now—as it is, I'm sure she can feel that half staff that's pressing against her lower belly as I tighten my grip on her damp hair, tipping her head back as I devour her lips with mine.

There are a lot of people still hanging out around the lake after the plunge, so it's easy to use that as an excuse for why I'm kissing her.

We're putting on a show, just like we all agreed.

But it's not quite as easy to find an acceptable reason for why I don't want to *stop* kissing her.

I tilt her head to one side a little, dragging my lips away from hers only to find the soft curve of her jaw. I scrape my teeth over the delicate skin just below her ear, and she shivers against me, letting out a plaintive little squeak.

Fuck, those sounds she makes.

I'd be lying if I said it didn't drive me wild knowing that I can elicit such involuntary noises from her. I fucking love how easy it is for me to get a reaction out of her. She's so damn responsive, even if this is all supposed to be a lie.

Her fingernails scrape across the nape of my neck lightly, and I hiss out a breath as my cock jolts again, even more of my blood rushing south.

I'm not quite sure what came over me as we were bantering a moment ago, but something about hearing her call me a gentleman made me want to show her just how *ungentlemanly* I can be.

How easily I could ruin her if she let me.

How perfectly I could make her fall apart.

Shit. Get ahold of yourself, Sebastian.

Even though my body seems to physically resist my command, I reluctantly draw back, letting a small space open up between us. This is my best friend's little sister, and what I'm doing with her here would be totally off-limits if it weren't for this charade we're putting on.

I need to remind myself that that's what this is—just an act, and nothing more than that.

Her cheeks are flushed, more than they were even in the cold water of the lake. I like that too.

Fuck, I like everything about her.

It's as though the second I started pretend dating Hailey, I've suddenly become hyper aware of how fucking gorgeous she is. Not that I didn't notice it before, but at least I was able to shove it all down back then. Now it seems to be rising to the surface regardless of how hard I try not to think about it, or about *her*.

"Um, point taken," she says, clearing her throat as a pretty flush creeps up her cheeks. "I don't think gentlemen kiss like that."

As she picks up her coffee from the roof of the car and sips on it, looking perfectly mussed and flustered, I wonder how the hell I'm going to get all of these things I'm suddenly feeling back inside the bottle when it's time for this whole fake dating thing to be over.

But when she looks over and smiles at me, I push those thoughts away. I don't want to deal with that yet.

"You want to go someplace to warm up?" I suggest, deciding not to follow up on her comment about our kiss.

Hailey nods quickly as if she's been waiting for me to ask. The coffee isn't doing a good enough job of chasing away the chill.

I grab her donut so she won't forget it, and we both climb into my car.

"My garage is close by."

"Please tell me it's warm in there."

She shivers as she slides into the passenger seat, and I'm tempted to reach out and touch her again to help her warm up, but I keep my hands firmly on the steering wheel.

"It is," I promise.

But as we near the garage, a bit of doubt starts to creep into my mind. I was pretty sure Hailey would end up having fun at the Polar Bear Plunge, but the garage where I service a good portion of the vehicles in Chestnut Hill isn't exactly in "date worthy" condition. It works great for what it is, but there are spare parts scattered around, oil stains on the floor, and it smells more of engine fuel than champagne and chardonnay.

Maybe my brothers were right to have laughed at my great idea for a date.

"Shit, this probably isn't the best fake date." I reach up and sweep my damp hair out of my eyes. "I should have—"

"What are you talking about? It's great." She takes a bite of her donut, making an appreciative noise. "Besides, the fake part of the date is over. We're not in public now, so this is just the two of us hanging out."

The thought of that seems even more dangerous somehow than the Polar Bear Plunge was, and I find myself oddly disappointed that I won't be able to use public exhibition as a reason to pull her into my arms again.

When we get to the garage, I pull inside and turn the thermostat up as soon as we get out of the car. The place isn't huge, so it should heat up fairly quickly.

"I always liked hanging out in here."

Hailey runs her fingers over some tools that I left lying out on the workbench, expression nostalgic, as if she's lost in her memories.

I can't help the grin that spreads over my face at that. "Yeah, me too. It's like my home away from home."

My dad used to run this garage, and I can remember working with him on cars in here as a kid. Then, after my parents died, I took over running the garage as a way to cope with the loss. I always felt safe and completely at home here, and I like that we share that feeling about this place.

"Do you remember when I used to come in here and study?" she asks, glancing my way.

Of course I do.

Lucas and my brothers used to come hang out in here with me all the time while I was tinkering around with stuff.

Once I was working on a set of motorcycles—three of them, to be exact. I got them from a scrapyard and was fixing them up for my brothers and me to ride. Lucas joked around about how they were "death machines," but I was determined to get them up and running and get us out there riding. Plus, after my parents' car wreck, I didn't want my brothers being afraid of things. Their accident was a brutal one, and it hit us all hard. Nick and Reid thought that I was just being reckless again instead of dealing with the grief. But I had a purpose. I didn't want any of us to be so traumatized that we were afraid to get behind the wheel.

And it worked—for a while anyway, until we all got too busy to go riding together. Or maybe the bikes had just served their purpose by then, getting us through the worst of the aftermath of our loss.

Hailey came and hung out in the garage a lot back then, since her brother was here too. But the funny thing was that she didn't *just* come by when Lucas was here.

"Yeah, I remember," I tell her. "You'd come by, and we'd all hang out and eat pizza. Lucas used to tease you about always wanting to get pineapple and pepperoni."

She laughs, and I take her coat from her and turn my back as she changes out of her wet bikini and into the dry clothes she brought with her. I'm enough of a gentleman not to turn and look while she's changing, but it takes every last ounce of my self-restraint to keep my gaze fixed straight ahead.

"I used to come by after school sometimes."

Her voice is right behind my back, and I try to stay focused on what we're talking about so that I don't start picturing what she must look like right now, her nipples peaked from the cold and her lightly tanned skin flushed.

I nod. "I remember that too. Sometimes you even snuck out of school on your free periods and came here. That clique of mean girls—what were they called?"

"The Divas," she says with audible distaste. "God, they were horrible. You can turn around now."

When I turn and look at her, Hailey is back in blue jeans and a sweater that looks soft enough that I want to bury my face in it. But it's the way her jeans hug the curves of her hips and perfectly showcase her long legs that makes it a little hard to breathe.

I turn around for a second and pretend to look for something in the garage just so that I can get my shit back under control, clearing my throat as I glance at her over my shoulder. "They really used to give you a hard time, didn't they?"

She grimaces. "They did. Which is why I came to the garage to escape. It was nice to just get away from the cliques and drama for a bit, and to be here with you."

Hailey's eyes dart away from mine after she mentions the

last part, and I round the workshop bench to stand beside her. It feels good to talk like this—natural, normal, the two of us alone instead of putting on a show for everyone else. Not that I don't enjoy the spectacle. I definitely do. But I also like having her all to myself behind a closed door too, where we can just talk and be real with each other.

Something about Hailey makes it feel easy to be myself, as if she doesn't judge me the way almost everyone else here in Chestnut Hill does. I got a reputation for being the town bad boy a long time ago, and that's never really shifted over the years. Usually, it doesn't bother me, but I think it would if that's how Hailey saw me. Or if that's the *only* thing she saw in me.

"Well, those Divas are a bunch of shallow bitches," I tell her. "Brielle started hanging out with them too, you know."

Hailey rolls her eyes at that piece of information.

"I'm not surprised. I thought she was my best friend, but obviously that wasn't the case. Looking back on it, Brielle always wanted to level up socially. She was never content with where she was, and never content just being my friend. I wonder sometimes if that's part of the reason she fucked around with Dylan behind my back. I mean, his family is wealthy and connected, and he was always super popular."

My blood boils just thinking about how either of those two people could have hurt Hailey as much as they did.

A fiancé and a best friend? Those relationships are supposed to be worth something, not the kind of thing you betray just because you want to climb the social ladder or get your cock wet with your bride-to-be's bestie.

"Fuck both of them. Neither of them deserves to have a place in your life or even in your head. You deserve so much better, shortcake."

She smiles when I use the nickname I used to call her when she'd come to the garage and hang out with me alone. She's not even that short at five foot five, but compared to me and my brothers, who are all well over six feet, she's always felt petite to me.

"You know, I wish I could've come back to town in a blaze of glory." She lets out a sad little laugh, as if her entrance back home was a pitiful one. She looks vulnerable, standing in my garage in the dim light with her blonde hair drying slowly around her shoulders. "I haven't though. To be honest, I wasn't really doing that well with my dream of becoming a singer. I was gone for two years, and in that time, all that I managed to achieve was working a shitty job in LA that just happened to be related to the music industry. I never even went on one singing audition."

"What? Why not? You have a great voice."

I can still remember catching her singing to herself when she would come to study in the garage. I'd be working under a hood, and she'd have her headphones on while doing her schoolwork. She'd always start off kind of quiet, but then the music would take over and she'd belt out a tune. Her voice always sounded like silk to me, melodic enough to tame ocean waves or calm dragons. It added to the many reasons why I liked having her keep me company as I worked.

Hailey shrugs, pinching her lips together.

"I tried, but... every time I set up an audition, I would end up bailing on it and canceling at the last second. I've got terrible stage fright."

"Since when?

"Since I listened to months of Dylan subtly belittling me and my abilities." She wraps her arms around herself, looking over at my wall of tools. "He always made me feel crazy for wanting to pursue music as a career. He would tell me how competitive it was, and how the odds were so low that I would never get anywhere with it. Even though I tried to shed all that negativity when I moved to LA, I guess it left a mark. And now I just feel kind of like I've failed."

My jaw clenches as I listen to her talk about how that bastard hurt her.

"That's just one more reason why Dylan Montgomery is a goddamn idiot," I growl. "You haven't failed, Hailey. Everyone's path is different, and it doesn't have to be a straight line. You haven't made it in LA yet? Fine, you haven't made it—*yet*. That doesn't mean you can't or that you won't. Your voice is beautiful. Like, *otherworldly* level beautiful."

I can see the effect that my words have on her as she swallows hard and then parts her lips like she needs to get more air.

"Thank you, Sebastian."

She smiles, almost tentatively, and my fingers twitch with the impulse to reach out for her. I curl them into fists lightly, wishing I had something to do to occupy them.

We aren't in front of anyone else in here. There's no one to put on a show for, no one watching. And that means there's no good reason for me to want to kiss her right now. No real excuse.

But *god,* I want to.

I take a step toward her, and I think she does the same. Unbidden, my gaze drops to her full, pink lips, and my throat tightens as her tongue darts out to wet them. Her delicate throat moves as she swallows, and she tilts her head back almost imperceptibly, like she's just begging me to—

A car pulls into the garage, and the rumbling sound of the engine makes us both jerk slightly.

Fucking hell. I left one of the bay doors open, and some invasive ass has decided to barge right in.

As soon as I see Maeve Gaskin step out of the car, I'm not surprised by the audacity. She's part of that Divas group that was in Hailey's class at Chestnut Hill High, and she's almost as prissy and stuck up as Brielle and the rest of that entourage of vipers in heels.

"Hey, Sebastian." Maeve's voice is like nails on a

chalkboard, the annoying sound rivaled only by the incessant clicking of her heels against my concrete garage floor. For fuck's sake, how can one person take so many tiny steps? Does she have Dachshund sized legs under her skirt? "I need you to fix my car. It's broken."

"Sorry, the shop's closed at the moment. And it's obviously not *that* broken if you drove it here," I point out. "I'm sure it can wait until tomorrow."

I couldn't care less about being rude. I don't need anyone's business badly enough to be barked orders at.

Maeve makes her way toward me, her face morphing into a pout that shifts into a look of surprise when she notices Hailey standing there too.

"Oh, Hailey Bennett, I heard you were back in town!" She smiles. "All the girls have been talking about your recent homecoming."

I heard Hailey mumble something under her breath, but Maeve doesn't catch it. Especially not when Hailey's smile hides things so well.

"Your mom must be so thrilled to have you back home. I know she's missed you. And just in time for the holidays too, that's great! You'll have to come help us get the Santa's Workshop display ready for the holiday bazaar!"

"No thanks. I haven't really had time to settle back in yet, and I—"

Maeve holds up a hand. "Nope. I'm *not* taking no for an answer. You helped every single year when you lived here, and we have to revive the tradition. It won't be the same without you."

I can tell Hailey doesn't want to, and I have to stop myself from speaking for her and telling Maeve to go sit on a giant candy cane and get the fuck out of my garage with her not-so-broken car.

But when Hailey grudgingly agrees to help with the setup, I

think I catch a bit of rebellion in her voice as she smiles back at Maeve.

"Sure, you're right. It will be great."

I can't help the grin that tugs at my lips as she lifts her chin a little, squaring her shoulders. Despite the fact that Maeve has clearly been trying to bait her, there's a quiet fierceness in Hailey's expression that I fucking adore.

That's right, shortcake. Don't let the mean girls win.

9

HAILEY

WAKING up in my rented room at Ted's place is completely underwhelming. At least he wasn't up all night "jamming" on his guitar again. I managed to get some much-needed sleep after the plunge and my day with Sebastian.

On today's agenda is my next fake date with Reid. As I get ready to go out, I take a minute to text Lorelai, filling her in on the events of yesterday and telling her a bit about my plans for the day.

LORELAI: *It's too bad you don't have "dating three guys at once" on your naughty list.*

I'm glad she can't see my face when I read her text. She may be my best friend, and literally the only other person in the world who knows about my naughty bucket list, but it's still enough to make me blush.

ME: *It's all just fake anyway, remember? So even if it was on my list, I couldn't check it off. That's for real experiences only.*

LORELAI: *I dunno, girl. It seems close enough to me.*

I look at the screen on my phone for a long moment. *Is it close enough?* Nah, I can't start thinking about things that way. I'll only wind up getting hurt again.

I let Lorelai know that I need to get going and then set my

phone down while I finish dabbing a bit of mascara on my eyelashes. I've never been one for a lot of makeup. Besides, I doubt I could cover all my freckles anyway. They punctuate the bridge of my nose and the tops of my cheekbones like the stars scattered across the night sky.

When I was little, I once took a black marker and drew lines between them, thinking that maybe they would form one of those dot-to-dot pictures. I remember being so upset when I tried to wash it off and found out it was permanent marker. But the next day at school, Lucas and the Cooper triplets stuck close by my side all day so that I wouldn't get teased, and Lucas told me that it looked like I had constellations on my face—which he said meant that I was as beautiful as a galaxy.

I smile at myself in the mirror as the memory washes over me. My older brother has always been there to protect me and pick me up when I've needed him. Which is why I should really stop thinking about his three best friends in the way I have been.

I'm sure he would be scandalized if he could see inside my head right now.

Thank god no one but Lorelai knows about my naughty list.

My mind flits back to my text conversation with her. The list was something I wrote after leaving Dylan, right around when I got to LA. It's mainly a bucket list of all the things I want to try in bed someday that I was too embarrassed to ask him to do with me—although some of them don't even require a bed.

I sigh as I tuck in my shirt and get ready to leave my room. Unfortunately, I've been in a bit of a dry spell ever since leaving my shitty fiancé, so the list has been rendered pretty much irrelevant.

I was too busy trying to get by in LA to have time to date, much less worry about my poor neglected pussy. It goes without saying that none of the items on my naughty list have been checked off. Not even one.

"And we won't be checking anything off the list in Chestnut

Hill either," I mutter, glancing down at my crotch. "So don't get any big ideas."

I wonder if it's normal to talk to your own vagina. Probably not, but she needs a good talking to right now. The past couple of days have been wreaking havoc on my nervous system, and all the attention from the Cooper triplets is definitely confusing my body. I feel like every little touch from any of them is enough to have sparks flying through my veins, lighting me up inside like the Fourth of July. I'm in a constant state of semi-arousal, and clearly some parts of my body haven't gotten the message that there will be no follow through since it's all just an act.

I tell my naughty bits to calm the fuck down one more time, then head out and make my way toward Chestnut Hill's small downtown area. I'm not feeling very confident that my pussy pep talk is going to do much good though, especially when I arrive and see Reid standing outside the door of the town bistro to meet me for our "date."

It's his turn now, and I feel as if I've barely even recovered from my day with Sebastian.

Seeing him outside the restaurant makes my heart skip a beat, even from a distance. The way the sun hits the copper strands in his hair and the way his steely blue eyes cut across the street toward me are nothing short of breathtaking. Who knew that such a ruggedly masculine man could be so *beautiful*?

But the best part about Reid isn't his intense good looks, as hard as that is to believe. It's how warm and kind and charming he is. He's such a down-home sort of guy that everyone in the entire town wants to be friends with him. Out of all three of the Cooper brothers, Reid reminds me the most of his dad. He seems like such a family guy, with love overflowing from his heart toward anyone that he cares about.

When I reach the door, he smiles and holds it open for me. And when we get to our table, he pulls out my chair and holds it as he waits for me to sit down before pushing it back in again.

He makes this little local bistro feel like a five-star restaurant simply by the way he treats me, and I can't help but grin as he takes the seat opposite me.

"You're quite the gentleman."

He shrugs at my compliment as the waitress comes and drops off some menus, and I chuckle when I think about yesterday.

"Sebastian seems to take pride in *not* being a gentleman," I say jokingly.

Reid rolls his eyes, clearly unsurprised that his brother said that. "There's nothing wrong with treating a lady right."

I nod at that, remembering vividly how I used to sometimes notice Reid with his ex—Sutton, a girl he dated semi-seriously for a couple of years. She was gorgeous, of course, and it always made me a little jealous to see how Reid treated her like a queen.

"Are you always a gentleman?"

I blurt the question out with genuine curiosity, but I'm not prepared for the heated look he gives me in return.

"Well now, not so fast, trouble. I didn't say all that."

His eyes blaze with a cold blue-gray flame as he speaks, and my body reacts to the implication in his words.

Shit. Yeah, that heart to heart I had with my pussy earlier definitely didn't work. I need to remind myself all over again to calm down. None of this is real. This is all just a fake game that the four of us are playing in order to gain the upper hand on the town gossips. Once we get through the holidays, none of this will even matter or exist anymore.

My brain tries desperately to convince my body of that fact, but neither my body nor my heart are listening to it. It feels like there's a war raging inside of me, with conflicting emotions jostling for dominance. Currently, level-headed rationalization is on the losing end of things.

"Do you know what you want to order?" Reid sets his menu

down on the table as if he's ready, but I haven't even really looked at the choices yet. Sure, I've been holding the menu up to my face, but my eyes may as well have been staring right through it.

"I'm not really sure. I can't decide what I want."

The waitress walks back over at that exact moment. She plucks the pencil from behind her ear as she tells us about a few specials, then she pauses and looks at us expectantly. Reid glances my way, probably seeing the panicked look on my face as I try to make a last-minute decision, then turns back to the waitress.

"Can you bring us one of each of those specials that you described, please?"

The waitress gives him almost the exact same look that the server at The Old Oak gave Nick the other night—although thankfully, Reid restrained himself a bit and didn't order the entire menu like Nick did.

"That's like five different dishes," she points out. "Are you sure?"

Reid nods. "And two sets of plates and silverware. We'll share everything."

After she turns to leave, he smiles across the table at me. "There, that ought to take care of it."

I pretend to mull it over. "Yeah, probably. If we're still hungry afterward, we can always get more."

He bursts into laughter, the sound warm and low.

"Seriously," I add in a quiet voice, shaking my head. "You and your brothers have to stop spoiling me like this. It's going to make my expectations way too high when I actually get back into the dating pool."

The smile on Reid's face slips a little, but he doesn't respond to that and I can't quite tell what he's thinking.

The food arrives pretty quickly, and we dig in, sharing all the dishes between the two of us. It's so much food that I'm floored not only by the spread but also by the gesture. I meant what I told Reid. I haven't been treated like this on a date before, not even when I was with Dylan. He would never spring for more than a burger and fries, even though he has more money than most of the town put together.

"My brother would be in hog heaven right now with all this food," I say, covering my mouth as I take a bite.

Reid laughs and nods. "Yeah, Lucas could always pack it away, that's for sure. But now that he's coaching the Chestnut Hill High football team, I'll bet those kids have him running around burning calories left and right. Hell, he's probably in better shape than any of us, thanks to them."

"I don't know about that. You guys are in good shape too. You were always working out at our house, remember?"

A flush heats my cheeks as I realize what I just said. I have more vivid memories than I'd care to admit about all the times I ran into a half-naked Cooper brother in the hallway after they came out of Lucas's small home gym following a good workout. Sometimes they had a shirt on, sometimes not. And once, Sebastian even came out wearing nothing but a towel on his way to shower after a particularly intense leg day.

I have a vague memory of Reid having a tattoo on his chest, although I think my brother might have mentioned at one point that he had more ink done since high school.

"I mean, you were over at our house doing a lot of things," I correct quickly, hoping my face isn't as red as it feels. Thinking about whatever ink Nick might've gotten in the years since I left town isn't doing anything to lower my internal temperature. "I know my parents were always happy to have you over."

Reid grins, a warm look passing over his face. "Yeah, they've always been super welcoming. It means a lot." He nudges my foot with his. "I'm sure they're on cloud nine about having you back in town."

I nod, trying not to pay attention to the way his foot keeps touching mine even as he leans back in his seat a little. It's just a tiny bit of contact, probably accidental, but I'm so aware of it that my heart beats a little faster.

"I think they are. It's been nice being home and getting to see everyone."

"It's been good seeing you too." He flashes me a crooked smile that disrupts the quickening rhythm of my heart, making it trip over itself for a beat. "I have to admit, I was surprised as hell when I ran into you at Gus's. I didn't expect you back in town, at least not for a long while. I figured you'd be too enamored with LA to want to come back to a place like Chestnut Hill."

A little twinge of nostalgia rises up in my chest as I glance out the window at the town beyond. It's weird. I didn't think I would miss this place, especially not after everything that happened with Dylan and the ruined wedding. But being back has made me realize how much of my heart stayed here when I left. In some ways, this will always feel like my home.

"No, not too enamored with LA to come back, at least not for a short visit like this. Honestly, I thought about Chestnut Hill a lot when I was in California. Little things that I missed would pop into my head all the time."

"Oh? Did you think about me at all while you were gone?"

My heart stutters at his question, and I take another bite and carefully swallow to give myself a moment before answering.

"Sure, of course I did. I missed everyone here. Well, maybe not the Divas or my backstabbing bitch of an ex-best friend. But I did think about all of you guys. And Lucas, of course."

There. That sounded good, right?

I hope I played it off well enough not to give away how much I actually did think about the Cooper brothers while I was away. I did my best to keep my tone light, but Reid still has a somewhat serious expression on his face. Silence falls across the table for a few heartbeats as he gazes at me, and I clear my throat and ask, "What about you? Did you think about me at all while I was gone?"

"Yes, I did. Every day."

The simple truth in his voice hits me like a ton of bricks. He's not joking. He's serious.

I don't know what that means, but my stomach flutters wildly anyway. The table gets quiet again, and I don't know whether I should look at Reid or look away.

Never in a million years would I have ever guessed that Reid Cooper would be thinking about me. My high school self is doing cartwheels in my head while my common sense is running around inside my brain telling her to stop before this gets out of hand.

It can't get out of hand, can it? It's all only a game. None of this is real.

But the way Reid is looking at me right now, the way his voice dropped a little when he told me that he's thought of me—none of it seems like something he's doing for public display. Besides, the bistro is mostly empty, so no one can even hear us talking or hear the questions being asked.

His answer was the truth, and it was meant only for me.

Before I can figure out what to do with that or what the hell to say in response, the moment is broken by Reid's two brothers walking up to our table.

"Damn." Sebastian eyes the array of dishes, which almost completely cover the table top. "How many people are you trying to feed?"

"Nick started it," Reid replies with a shrug, as if the oldest Cooper triplet threw down some kind of gauntlet at The Old Oak. Then he glances at the two of them. "What are you guys doing here? This is my date with Hailey."

Sebastian sits down at the table and helps himself to some food off one of the plates. "Sure, but we're supposed to be fighting over her, remember? And if I were really trying to win

Hailey's affections, I wouldn't just be letting her date my brothers without showing up to stake my own claim too."

Nick nods in agreement and nabs some food for himself as well. "True. But you already had your own date with her. I'm the only one that hasn't yet."

"Okay, but you're *both* intruding on mine." Even though Reid's tone is joking, the look in his eyes has a bit of a jealous edge to it.

If I didn't know better, I'd think there are some actual competitive feelings between the Cooper brothers.

"It's okay with me if they stay," I offer, unsure if the moment needs smoothing over or not. But the last thing I want to do is cause any kind of real strife between the triplets, who've been inseparable for as long as I've known them. "We really can't finish all this food on our own."

Sebastian and Nick end up sticking around for a bit to help us finish off all the food Reid ordered as we all talk and laugh over some of the small-town drama that the guys fill me in on. Things go back to being lighthearted and fun, but there is still a small undercurrent hinting at a brotherly competition between the three of them, with me at the center of it.

When we all get up to leave together, Reid makes a point of wrapping his arm around my waist and pulling me in for a kiss just after we walk out the door of the bistro.

The first thought racing through my head is that he's making a show of it for the townspeople who are walking by. But when the kiss turns from a simple peck to something a little more breath-stealing, with his mouth firm against mine and his tongue moving demandingly against my own, I start to wonder if this isn't as much a show for his brothers as it is for everyone else.

Is he trying to lay some sort of claim on me in front of them?

But why would he need to do that when they're only pretending to fight over me? They don't actually have to vie for my affections, since this is all fake.

And in all honesty, if any of this were real, I wouldn't know how to choose between them. I've had crushes on all three of these men for as long as I can remember.

As if he can sense that my thoughts have wandered a little, Reid growls softly against my lips. One of his hands slides through my hair, but instead of just running his fingers through the strands, he grips my hair tightly, tugging just hard enough to send a little sting shooting through my scalp.

I suck in a breath as a jolt of sensation rushes through me, the zap of pain turning into pure heat as it races down to my clit. My knees wobble, and I lean into our kiss as if it's the only thing keeping me upright, my lips moving hungrily against his.

We just ate, but I suddenly feel fucking *ravenous*.

It's not food I'm craving right now though.

Reid gives one more tug on my hair, sharply enough to send another bolt of pleasure and pain right to my clit. I swear I can feel wetness soaking the crotch of my panties, and my stomach flutters. God, if he keeps touching me this roughly and possessively, like he fucking owns my body and wants the entire world to know it, I might just come right here on the sidewalk.

When he finally breaks the kiss and pulls away, his fingers sliding out of my hair, I find myself dazed and a little giddy.

"That was… a great date," I whisper, trying not to sound too breathless. "Thank you, Reid."

A sinful smirk curves his lips, as if he can read every thought I just had on my face. "I'm glad you enjoyed it, trouble. So did I."

He brushes his thumb over my bottom lip before dropping his hand, and I will my legs to support me as I give a little nod and turn to head toward my car.

I'm debating whether to call Pippa and see what she's up to or head back to my rented room at Ted's crappy house, trying to figure out what to do with myself for the rest of the night that doesn't involve spending every minute fantasizing about that kiss.

But before I make it more than two steps away, Nick reaches out to stop me, tugging me in close to his side. The motion is so swift that it startles me, and I look up at him in surprise.

"It's not even seven o'clock yet." His face is as stoic and set as ever, but I swear I almost see his lips twitch into a smile. "It's my turn now."

10

HAILEY

I blink up at Nick, my heart thumping.

Honestly, I wasn't expecting him to really want a "date" with me to begin with. In fact, I was pretty damn surprised when he stepped up at the bar and claimed that we were dating at all. He's so antisocial and grumpy most of the time that I figured even though he said it in the moment to help me, he wouldn't actually want to do any of the performative aspects of fake dating.

At most, I figured he would make an occasional appearance and let his brothers handle the rest of the showcasing.

Clearly, I was wrong.

"Um, okay," I say. "Sure. I wasn't really ready to go home anyway."

Reid and Sebastian head out, looking like they're begrudgingly conceding their time, and Nick is completely silent as he starts to walk down the street with me, his massive hand wrapped around mine. It's not unusual for Nick to be silent, but I feel a bit awkward because I have no idea what to say to him. It just seems like it is so out of character for him to be doing this.

Is he enjoying it? I mean, why would he even be doing this if he didn't want to? It's not like he *has* to do the fake date parts. So why go all in?

Once again, my mind starts to wander down a rabbit hole of hopeful thinking, but it's too much of a stretch to think that Nick would actually be into me. So I try to ease the awkwardness by filling in the silence between us.

The evening is cold, and there's a gentle snow falling. Most of the little independent storefronts are decorated for the holidays with twinkling Christmas lights or those fake plastic candles that light up in the windows.

"Oh, look!" I grin. "MooMoo's Ice Cream! I used to love their triple berry flavor. It was so good, I swear I could eat it every day and never get sick of it."

I point at the window, which has a plastic cow decoration with a Santa hat on for the season. Nick glances, his expression unchanged. "I've never tried it."

"You've never had MooMoo's?" I demand, aghast. "They've been a staple of Chestnut Hill our whole lives!"

He shrugs. "I don't really like ice cream."

That seems like sacrilege to me, but I don't say so, and we lapse into silence again as we keep walking.

I almost have to laugh as we meander down the sidewalk for several more minutes. Nearly every shop or restaurant we pass elicits an excited gasp from me as I bask in the happy nostalgia of being home—but Nick is almost the exact opposite, as unimpressed by all of it as I am thrilled.

"You don't seem to like much of anything," I tease after he grunts something about how the fancy lattes from Deja Brew are all too sweet.

Nick chuckles, the sound rumbling in his chest. "That's not true. I like my family. I like your brother. I like my dog." He stops walking, turning to face me as something shifts in his dark blue eyes. "And most of all, I like—"

His voice cuts off, but his gaze stays fixed on mine.

I swallow hard, suddenly desperate to know how he was going to finish that sentence.

For a long moment, we just stare at each other in the gently falling snow. Little flakes collect on his dark hair and the close-cut scruff of his beard, and I watch them gather and then start to melt, my breath fogging the air in little puffs.

Then, without saying another word, he reaches out to take my hand and then turns to start walking again.

He falls quiet again as we continue on, almost as if that small exchange didn't happen, and I feel even more off-balance than before. It's not just awkward now, but also filled with a confusing sort of angst that swirls around me faster than the falling snow.

I can't stand the hanging silence. My thoughts are so damn loud inside my head that I almost worry he'll hear them in the quiet, so I talk to fill the space, trying to find a safer subject than the one we were just discussing.

"Um, how's it going at the station?"

"It's good."

At first, I think that's all he's going to give me. It would be about par for the course for Nick, who often speaks in grunts rather than words and especially seems less inclined to talk to me than his brothers or Lucas. But then he surprises me by continuing on.

"Things are busy there," he adds. "Thankfully not with devastating fires but with a lot of community outreach that the fire station has been doing lately. We're in need of new equipment though. Most of the trucks are pretty old. Sebastian has actually helped out a lot by doing some work on them, but I feel like we need some new gear and maybe a new truck in order to be really prepared in the event of a large fire. Which obviously I hope will never happen. You can never be too sure or too careful though."

I blink, stunned into momentary silence. That might be the

most I've ever heard him say at once, and it's nice to see him talking so enthusiastically about something. I can tell he's passionate about what he does.

"One day, I want to be fire chief." Nick rubs his free hand over his beard, brushing away a few of the gathering snowflakes. "I know I could be great in that role, and I already have a bunch of ideas that I want to implement at the station."

"Wow. That's great! I bet you'll be an amazing fire chief."

When I glance up, I think I actually see him flush a little at the encouraging compliment. It's true though. I don't doubt that Nick will achieve his goal. He's one of the most focused, hardworking men I've ever met. In LA, there were a lot of guys that liked to talk big about their ambitions and achievements, but most of them wanted an easy path toward getting there, which would never actually amount to anything. Nick, on the other hand, is capable and driven. He'll work toward being fire chief, and he'll get it.

He glances down at his watch suddenly, his brow furrowing. "We'd better get going."

"Oh. Okay."

I thought we were actually heading toward a destination, a "date" somewhere, but I guess our short stroll was the date in its entirety.

When we get back to the bistro though, Nick walks me over to his car instead of mine.

"Hop in."

"Where are we going?"

"You'll see." A tiny smirk tilts the corners of his lips, and I can't help feeling a flutter of excitement and curiosity. Maybe I was wrong, and we really are going somewhere else for a date.

I get in, and Nick drives us through town. The whole time, I keep peering out the window to see if I can figure out where he's taking me. When we wind up in my neighborhood, I frown, and when he pulls into the driveway of my parents' house, I glance over at him in surprise.

"What are we doing here?"

I definitely wasn't expecting a trip to my parents' house to be a date-worthy destination. Especially not if the goal was to be seen by the general public of Chestnut Hill. It seems to defeat the point of a public exhibition of romance, and I doubt my parents would understand this whole scheme I have going on with the Cooper brothers. We had to fill Lucas in on everything so he wouldn't kill them, but I have no plans to tell my parents the truth.

Instead of answering, Nick comes around to open my door and then leads me up the walk. The sidewalk is iced over, so he keeps one arm wrapped carefully around my waist to catch me in case I slip.

For such a gruff and grumpy man, whose thick muscles I can feel even with just his arm around my waist, it's really sweet.

Nick knocks on the door, and my face lights up when I see my grandmother open it. I've only seen her once since I got back, when I went over to my parents' house before heading to The Old Oak, and it wasn't nearly enough to make up for all the time I've been away.

"Grandma Dee!" I exclaim as my spry, gray-haired grandmother reaches out to give me a big hug.

"Hailey, baby." She squeezes me in the way that only a grandma can, then welcomes Nick and me inside. "Your parents are at the diner working. Come on in, I've got a kettle on the stove."

Grandma Dee is always making tea. It's one of my fondest and most frequent memories of her. Have a cold? Echinacea tea it is. Feeling blue? A cup of mint to ease away stress. And then there's my favorite—Grandma Dee has a "secret stash" of amaretto tea that she puts a drop or two of liquor in. That's the tea that she always brews whenever I need just to sit in silence and think.

We walk inside and sit down at the table while Grandma Dee sets teacups down in front of us and then goes to get the kettle, which is already starting to whistle. I look over at Nick, suppressing a grin at the image of this burly, bearded firefighter sitting there with a dainty teacup set in front of him.

But I still don't know why we're here.

Sebastian's date was a plunge in icy cold water, Reid's date was a dinner out that wound up getting crashed by his brothers, and now Nick's date is inside my childhood home with my grandma? It's been a whirlwind of experiences so far, but honestly, I've enjoyed every one, so I don't really expect this to be any different. That doesn't stop me from being curious though.

"So catch me up, Dee. What did I miss?" Nick smiles up at her as she pours the tea, as if they have some sort of secret conversation going on.

And surprisingly, they *do*.

I sip my tea and listen as my grandmother catches Nick up on an episode of *Shadow's Edge*, a show that they've apparently been watching together. The season finale episode aired earlier tonight, and Nick missed it when he came to the restaurant to find me and take me on a walk.

The two of them talk avidly, and he laughs when Grandma Dee makes a joke about one of the characters in the show. She goes on to tell him how excited she is about the next season of the show, and Nick nods in agreement.

"This strapping young man has been keeping me company through two television seasons already. I have to admit that if I were a *whole* lot younger, I'd think we were dating."

She bursts into laughter, and Nick's cheeks flush.

I look over at him, awed and a little stunned. I'm immensely touched by this hidden sweet side I didn't know he had. All this time while I've been off in LA trying to run away from my past and piece together a future, he's been here spending time with my elderly grandmother.

She looks at him with her soft brown eyes and gives him a wrinkled grin. I can tell by the way her entire face is lit up that what he's doing means a lot to her. And funnily enough, it seems like Nick is enjoying the show they're watching together just as much as she is.

"Do you want to see the season finale?" Grandma Dee asks me, clearly brimming with excitement. "I wouldn't mind watching it again. Nick and I can fill you in on what's happened up to this point in the show."

"Sure!"

The three of us go to the living room, and I sit down on the couch beside Nick to watch the show with my grandmother. About halfway through, there's a surprise reveal where the main character discovers that her long-lost sibling, believed to be dead, has been living under a different identity and is secretly involved in a major criminal organization. Nick's jaw drops, and he nearly jumps off the couch, shock clear on his handsome face.

In the chair next to us, Grandma Dee is cracking up.

"Look at you!" she chortles. "You'd think you'd seen a ghost!"

"That's because I had no idea that Lorenzo would be coming back." Nick rubs at his chin, disheveling his beard as he looks at my grandmother with a teasingly accusatory glare. "You didn't want to warn me?"

Grandma Dee is still laughing so hard that her second cup of tea is shaking in her hands, the liquid threatening to slosh over the rim.

"No spoilers," she finally says, affixing a more serious look on her face, although her eyes still dance with amusement.

"That's our rule, remember? Besides, I had to keep *some* surprises for you to find out for yourself."

I chuckle at both of them, completely entranced by how easily they seem to get along. Nick, who usually speaks only when absolutely necessary, banters easily with her as the show continues. I can't resist joining in and teasing him a little.

"I've never seen you get so excited about anything before," I point out, nudging him lightly. "Who knew that you were secretly a soapy TV show junkie? I'll have to keep that in mind."

My grandmother howls with laughter, and a flush works its way up from beneath Nick's beard. He clears his throat, leaning back against the couch cushions and relaxing his expression. "It's the first time I've done that. I don't normally get so worked up over fictional characters."

I'm pretty sure that's a lie, given how obviously invested in the show he is. And even if it's not, I make a secret goal to get him to do this more. I love seeing him so genuinely excited and not as stiff and withdrawn as he usually is.

Beside us, my grandmother snorts. "Oh, bullshit!"

"Grandma!" I laugh at her foul mouth.

"What?" She shrugs, taking a prim sip of her tea. "I'm old enough to have earned the right to curse like a sailor if I want to. And don't let him fool you. Nick is always shouting at the television screen."

"Ah hah! I knew it." I shoot him a triumphant smirk, and his cheeks flush again.

I find myself loving this fake "date" so much more than I expected to. It's absolutely wonderful, and I still can't believe that Nick has been coming over to hang out with my grandma. Lucas has never mentioned it to me.

When the show ends, we get up off the couch and get ready to leave. Nick and I wait in the doorway while Grandma Dee puts the teacups in the kitchen sink before coming to see us off.

"Oh, look!" She points up at the ceiling over our heads.

I tilt my head up and realize that Nick and I are standing directly under the mistletoe.

"You know what that means." Her grin is positively mischievous.

"Grandma, did you put that up after we got here?"

"Of course not."

The innocent look on her face makes me suspicious. I can't tell by her face if she's telling me the truth or not, although she would've had to be pretty quick to do it in the time since we arrived. But it's something I wouldn't put past her.

I glance up at Nick, who's standing as still as a statue, his broad shoulders filling up nearly the entire doorframe.

"It's okay," I murmur quickly. "We don't have to."

He clears his throat. "We *are* on a date."

"Right."

"So we should probably kiss. Under the mistletoe."

"Okay."

Despite our words, neither one of us moves for a moment. He's the only one of the Cooper brothers I haven't kissed yet, and my heart kicks against my ribs at the thought of his full lips against mine and the scruff of his beard against my skin. What would it feel like against my cheek? What would it feel like... against other places?

Heat instantly rises in my face, and I glance sideways at my grandmother, who's still watching us expectantly.

Then Nick leans down and kisses me. The scent of sandalwood and clove fills my nostrils as his lips meet mine, the masculine scent wrapping around me like an embrace. But despite the fact that his smell alone is enough to have me practically panting, the kiss feels oddly formal. No hands around my waist or cradling my face, no sudden burst of heat, just a simple press of our lips.

"How romantic!" Grandma Dee claps her hands, sighing happily.

She doesn't seem to notice at all how *un*romantic the kiss was as we break apart. On the contrary, she seems exceedingly pleased with herself that she somehow either strategically hung the mistletoe there in the doorway or orchestrated the two of us standing under it—or both.

We both give her hugs before leaving and heading out to the car. We're silent as we approach Nick's vehicle, and I miss the easy banter and camaraderie that we had going on inside the house.

Not wanting things to settle back into awkward silence, I bump my shoulder against his arm and joke, "Okay, so you can redeem points for that lame kiss by how much fun tonight was."

I reach for the door handle on the car, but before I can open it, Nick grabs me by the waist and spins me around to face him.

He presses me up against the side of the car, his wide, sturdy body pinning me there. The suddenness of it shocks the air out of my lungs, and in the space between one breath and the next, Nick crushes his lips against mine to steal what little air is left.

His lips are hungry and fierce, like he's been waiting a lifetime to do this, and for all I know, maybe he has. This is nothing like the restrained, G-rated kiss he did for Grandma Dee's sake a few moments ago, and my body responds instinctively. I cling to his broad, powerful shoulders as his tongue sweeps inside my mouth like his life depends on it.

My entire body catches fire, starting with my cheeks and burning all the way down as he kisses me like he's trying to devour me, to consume me whole.

Holy shit. This is what a kiss from Nick Cooper can be like?

11

NICK

I press harder against Hailey, squeezing out the space between my overpowering frame and her soft, small body that I've pinned against the cold metal door of my car.

God, I want her.

It's been nearly impossible hanging out with her this whole time and keeping myself together. I feel so drawn to her that even sitting next to Hailey on the couch at her grandmother's house was like torture. Whenever I'm near her, I can't help but be aware of her every movement.

The way her exuberant smile lights up a room, the curve at the edges of her lips when she laughs. The delicate lacing of freckles over the bridge of her nose and top of her cheekbones. And that mischievous little twinkle in her eye—fuck, that one really gets me.

Everything about Hailey makes me want to touch her. Even the way she's so unafraid to wear her emotions on her sleeve. And when she moves—even if it's just a casual brush up against me, a breath that I can feel on my cheek if we're sitting too close, or a strand of her hair that happens to fall against my skin—it's all the most delicious kind of torture.

Now that my hands are on her body, feeling the fullness of

her breasts and the delicate curve of her waist beneath my palms, I feel like I'm feasting.

With every passing second of our kiss, my lips moving against hers and my tongue sweeping into her mouth, I want *more*. I'm quickly reaching the point where I won't be able to make myself stop. Everything feels *too* good.

With my lips on hers and my hands on her body, I'm like a starving man at a feast. I just can't get enough, can't help myself.

My blood thunders in my ears with every pounding heartbeat, and Hailey's initial shock must have passed because she's responding to me now. She pushes up on her tiptoes, squeezing her arms around my neck to get closer and kiss me back. She even starts to lift one leg and wrap it around mine like she's trying to convince me to take her right then and there, and if she's not careful, that's exactly what's going to happen.

The warmth of her body against mine, and the way she's winding herself around me like a vine, turns me into a wild man. My hands find hers and my fingers link with hers so I can push her hands backward, pinning them against the car along with the rest of her. Her body arches as she wilts and lets out a moan. With her exposed like this, I can't stop myself from grinding against her, dragging my almost painfully swollen cock against her thigh through my pants.

"Oh my god, Nick," she whimpers as my mouth kisses and nibbles down the side of her neck to her collar and back up to her lips. I crush my mouth against hers, then again, and on the third time, I trap her lower lip between my teeth, biting down. She gasps, and the sound of it cuts through the fog in my mind.

My chest heaves as my senses return and I remember what the hell I'm doing.

This is Hailey. Off limits Hailey.

I can't touch my best friend's little sister like this. Not in the way I want to.

Fuck.

I press my lips harder against hers for a split second, then wrench myself away from her, releasing her hands. She looks up at me, dazed and clearly reeling as she tries to catch her breath.

Goddammit. It would be so easy to pull her against me again. My cock is straining against my jeans as if it's desperate to get closer to her and is pissed as fuck at me for stopping. I drag in a breath and step backward so that she won't feel the bulge of my hard-on against her stomach.

Hailey's eyes have a hazy sheen to them, the deep green of her irises dark in the dim light. Her tongue slowly darts out to lick her lower lip, as if she's trying to remind herself of how I tasted, and it almost fucking undoes me.

If things were different, if this wasn't all still supposed to be pretend and if she wasn't my best friend's little sister, I wouldn't be ending things like this. It takes everything I have not to kiss her again.

"That kiss under the mistletoe was because your grandmother was watching, songbird. This one was because she's *not*," I say, working to keep the rasp out of my voice.

She blinks, her expression clearing a little. "Songbird?"

Shit.

I've called her that in my head for years, but I've never spoken the nickname aloud. It was easy enough for Sebastian and Reid to get away with calling her teasing, lighthearted nicknames, but considering that I could barely ever work up the courage to talk to her, it would've felt strange to call her anything but her given name. I don't know why I said it now, and I instantly regret it.

I don't know how to answer the question in her voice, so instead of giving any explanation, I just take another step backward, shoving my hands into my pants pockets.

"Come on. I'll take you home."

My voice sounds gruff as I try to shut things down and regain my usual stoic composure. It's the only way I know how to deal with all the shit knocking around in my chest and keep myself from giving in to the desire to kiss her again. Because giving in to it would mean crossing a whole lot of lines that I know I shouldn't cross.

"Oh. Uh, okay." Hailey looks a little taken aback, but she nods.

I open the door for her to get into my car, then walk around to the other side.

As I drive her back to the place where she's staying, I can tell she's nervous, or flustered, or maybe both. She breaks the silence in the car by talking, but our conversation is stilted. There's so much tension filling the car that it's as if there's an entire extra person sitting in the back seat, and Hailey keeps fidgeting with the sleeve of her shirt like she's trying to keep her hands occupied.

"So the next season of *Shadow's Edge* starts after Christmas, huh?" she asks. "Now I kind of want to go back and start from the first episode."

"Yeah." I nod, almost wishing that Reid and Sebastian had crashed our date like Seb and I did to Reid earlier. I feel like one of them would be able to say the right thing to ease the tension, but me? I have no idea what that might be. "Good idea. You'll probably like it."

When we get to the place where Hailey has been renting a short-term room, I insist on walking her inside. It's not a "date" gesture or part of the act of fake dating her. It's more due to the fact that no matter what, I can't stop myself from being protective of her.

"Oh, you really don't need to," she says, making a face. "Ted's probably sitting in his underwear with a fat cigar hanging out of his mouth, since it's almost his self-proclaimed 'jamming time.' Trust me, it's not a sight you'd want to see."

She chuckles wryly as if it's funny, but I'm not amused by it at all. In fact, it pisses me off to think that she'd be living in such a shitty situation.

If Ted is going to charge money for a room rental, then the very least he can do is provide decent accommodations free of cigar smoke, noise pollution, and the sight of her apparent 'landlord' in his briefs. Now I really want to go inside and check it out.

I don't take no for an answer, and I don't let Hailey brush it off. Instead, I get out of the car and walk her up to the front door. The second we step inside, I realize just how much she *underplayed* what a dump this place is.

"Fucking hell, Hailey." I glance around, my brows pinching together. "This place is a shit hole."

Ted Bigelow strides into the living room—not in his underwear, thank fuck—and his eyebrows rise as he sees me standing beside Hailey.

"You're not allowed to have guests," he says blandly.

The fact that he sounds like he's chastising her makes me bristle. "*She's* not allowed to have guests? She's not the one doing something wrong here, asshole. You are."

He frowns. "What? Is there a problem?"

His feigned ignorance pisses me off even more. I take a step toward him, towering over him with my hands curled into fists at my sides. "Yeah, the problem is that you're a piece of shit for taking advantage of a woman needing a place to stay."

"Whoa, whoa! I have no idea what you're talking about. I've never laid a hand on her." He raises both of his palms in the air, a flash of worry entering his eyes.

"I don't mean like that, you jackass. I mean she's paying you to rent this room and stay in this house. The very least you could do is keep it clean and wear your fucking clothes in common areas. You're ripping her off because you know Chestnut Hill gets packed around this time of year. You knew she didn't have a lot of options, so you decided you could get away with overcharging her for a piece of shit room rental, huh?"

Ted's face pales. His gaze slides sideways toward Hailey and then back to me, and he licks his lips nervously.

"Okay, okay." He keeps his hands held out. "You're right, man. I'm sorry. I'll get the place all fixed up tomorrow. And I'll even credit her a night or two of rent for the trouble."

"Fuck that. Not good enough." I shake my head and turn my attention to Hailey. "I'm moving you out of here right now."

"You're *what?*"

I don't let her visible shock deter me from the idea. There's no way I'm letting her stay in a place like this and pay money for it too. She mentioned that losing her job in LA was part of what brought her back to Chestnut Hill for the holidays, so I'm assuming funds are a little tight. She shouldn't be paying at all.

And luckily, I know a way to fix that.

"Come on." I glance around quickly, looking for the room she's staying in. "I'm going to help you pack up your stuff."

Hailey's gaze darts toward a door to my right, so I make a beeline in that direction. The second I open it and step inside, I know it's hers. Despite the musty scent that seems to permeate the entire house, I can smell a hint of honeysuckle in the air.

She follows me into the room, shooting me a quizzical look as I grab one of the suitcases on the floor and set it on the bed before opening it. "And go where, exactly?"

I open a dresser drawer, fully prepared to reach in and start grabbing things, but Hailey rushes over and loads her arms up with a bunch of clothes before I can. She drops them into the suitcase as I answer her.

"I'm moving you into the house with me and my brothers."

Ted, who trailed after us and is standing in the doorway watching, throws his arms in the air and makes some sort of remark under his breath about how he "didn't really need the rent anyway," then leaves us alone to pack up. He's lucky I don't go after him and beat his ass into giving her a refund for every single night she stayed here already—including a surcharge for having had to listen to him play music all night.

But at this point, my only focus is on getting her out of this shit hole and back to our house where she can have a decent and comfortable living arrangement.

She might be okay with staying in a dive like this, but I'm certainly not okay with anyone that I care about getting charged to live in a dump. A home should be a place that you want to get back to and spend time in, even if it's just a temporary room.

Hailey stops packing and stares at me. "What about Reid and Sebastian? You haven't even run this by them or asked if it will be an imposition to have me there. It's a sweet offer, Nick. Really. But maybe you should sleep on this for a night and then—"

"No, I've already made up my mind. They'll be fine with it."

I shut down her attempts to weakly protest and motion for her to grab whatever toiletries and stuff she has in the bathroom.

As soon as her modest amount of belongings are packed up and in my car, we head out. I drive a little more aggressively than I mean to on the way back to the house I share with my brothers, but I'm still stewing about Ted thinking he can get away with treating Hailey like that. The car is silent like it was before, but it's a different kind of tension now—a better kind than the awkward, post-kiss one, at least.

Sebastian is in the living room, sitting in one of the easy chairs that bracket the fireplace, so he's the first to see us when we enter. He looks up, his mouth opening to greet me, but then his eyebrows shoot up as he notices Hailey by my side.

"Hey, no fair," he grouses, rising from his chair. "Reid and I didn't get overnight dates. I call foul on you getting to have Hailey sleep over. It's against the rules."

Reid walks in just as Seb finishes speaking, his gaze scanning Hailey and me and the suitcases we're carrying.

"Everything okay?" he asks, eyeing the bags.

"It will be now."

I set both of the suitcases down, recruiting my brothers to help me grab the rest of Hailey's belongings from the car as I explain the situation and describe the shitty living conditions that I moved Hailey out of.

Once all her stuff is inside, Sebastian pours us all a drink as we gather around the kitchen table, and I surreptitiously check Hailey's face to make sure she's okay. I know I caught her off guard more than a few times tonight.

First with the surprise visit with her grandmother, then with the reckless kiss by the car, and now I've uprooted and abducted her here to our house. That's a lot for a first "fake date." But at least I know that she's here now and all right. She looks like she's still reeling a bit, but the whiskey seems to be helping her relax a little.

"Damn, that's fucking bullshit. I can't believe you were dealing with that on top of everything else." Reid gives her a sympathetic smile, and Sebastian sits down on the other side of her.

I take a seat across the table from her and top off my drink from the bottle in front of me. It doesn't surprise me at all that Hailey never complained to us about living in that shitty room in Ted's house. It's just the way she is—always looking for the silver lining no matter how tough things get. She's tenacious while also being soft and contagiously positive. I could probably stand to have some of that rub off on me.

"All right, it's settled then." Sebastian raises his glass in the air as if we're toasting to something. "Hailey's staying with us."

Reid clinks his glass against our brother's, and I make the obligatory gesture as well, even though I'd already decided that she would be staying no matter what my brothers thought about it.

It takes Hailey a second or two, and she still looks a bit

worried that she might be imposing, but she finally lifts her glass and touches it to ours.

"Thanks, you guys," she says with a soft smile that makes my chest tighten in an almost painful way. "I really appreciate this. And I'm happy to pay you rent, of course."

"Fuck, no." Reid shuts her offer down instantly. "We don't want your money."

"But—"

"Sorry, shortcake." Sebastian chuckles. "It's three against one here. You're better off letting us have this one, or we'll be here all night."

Hailey purses her lips as if weighing whether or not to argue more. Then she finally shakes her head, making her honey blonde hair shift over her shoulders. "Okay, fine. But no matter what you say, I still owe you guys."

"Nope." Reid arches a brow, leaning back. "You don't owe us anything."

"Yes, I do."

"No, you don't."

She narrow her eyes at him. "Have you always been this bossy?"

"Yes," he answers instantly. "Have you always been this bratty?"

A faint tinge of pink colors her cheeks, but she smirks as she holds his gaze, clearly not intimidated by him in the least. "Maybe I'm only a brat to you."

Reid blinks, clearly taken aback by her response, and I can't help but grin as I down the rest of my whiskey in one swallow, relishing the way it burns down my throat.

That's my songbird.

12

HAILEY

Reid holds my gaze for a moment, and my stomach flutters as an expression I can't quite name passes across his face. I can feel Sebastian and Nick watching the two of us, and the warmth in my cheeks deepens as I realize how easily my words about only being a brat to Reid could be taken as flirting.

But we're not in public right now, so there's no reason for us to pretend to flirt... or for him to be looking at me with heat in his eyes, the way I could swear he just was a second ago.

Then Reid clears his throat and shifts his gaze away from me, breaking whatever that moment between us was.

I'm still reeling a bit, to be honest—from the kiss, from the dates, and now from Nick hulking out on Ted and getting all protective of me before moving me in with the three of them.

But I have to admit, it feels nice to be in a familiar space with the three Cooper brothers right now, nursing a glass of whiskey instead of trying to drown out the sound of Ted's guitar while breathing through my mouth to avoid the worst of the musty smell in his house.

I take another small sip of the amber liquid and am about to ask the guys where I'll be staying, but before I can speak, a low growl cuts me off.

I jerk in surprise, looking over to see a big hound dog with slightly floppy ears and saggy jowls pad into the room. He's got his eyes fixed on me, and although he doesn't growl again, I swear his expression says something along the lines of, *who the hell are you?*

"Easy, Bruno. She's our guest. Come here."

Nick reaches out a hand to the dog, who perks up instantly and swings his head toward the burly firefighter. His nails tap against the floor as he trots quickly over to Nick and happily receives a pat on the head and some scratches behind the ears.

"Don't take it personally, trouble." Reid chuckles. "Bruno doesn't like anyone. He's only attached to Nick. He doesn't growl at Sebastian or me anymore, but he basically just ignores us."

"Yeah, so someday soon, you can look forward to him ignoring you too," Sebastian jokes, topping off his whiskey. "You don't need to worry about him biting or anything though. He's perfectly harmless. Bruno just likes to act like a giant grumpy asshole. You know what they say about pets starting to resemble their owners."

Nick rolls his eyes at his brother's remark, and I watch as he leans down to let Bruno give him a big, sloppy kiss on the cheek.

"Hi, Bruno."

I reach out a hand slowly, knuckles forward, hoping he'll maybe give me a sniff and decide I'm not too bad. But the big hound rebukes my attempt at being friendly, making a quiet huffing noise before walking away to lay down under the large window in the living room.

Okay. I get it. I guess I can respect the feeling of not wanting to be bothered by someone you're not sure about yet. And although I'm determined to one day make friends with Bruno, especially since I haven't yet met an animal who hasn't liked me, I let it go for now. I have my hands full sorting through everything else first, then I'll try to win over Nick's dog.

"Where will I stay?" I glance through the open doorway into the living room, and the stairs that lead to the second floor. The Cooper brothers' house, which they inherited from their parents, is substantially larger than my folks' house. As much as I don't want to intrude, I'm also secretly hoping that if I'm going to be staying here, maybe I'll have to bunk up in a room with one of them.

The thought of sharing a room, or even a bed, with one of the three brothers sends an instant thrill down my spine. It would be like playing with a live flame, considering how wildly attracted I am to all of them and how tangled up and confusing things between us have gotten ever since I returned to town and they agreed to fake date me.

It'd probably be a bad idea, but... aren't bad ideas the most fun sometimes?

"We have a spare room," Nick answers, immediately dashing my secret, salacious hopes. "Come on, I can show you."

He stands up, and he and his brothers help me carry my stuff upstairs. Honestly, it's not much, and I could carry it all myself, but there's something about having all three of them around me at once that makes me feel like I won some sort of lottery. It's like being wrapped in a warm blanket on a cold night and not wanting to get out of bed. That's how I feel when I'm with all three of the Cooper brothers together.

I follow Nick into the bedroom, already feeling more at home here than I did at Ted's. Their guest room is clean, neatly furnished, and has a pleasant piney smell.

"Thanks," I say as Sebastian and Reid set down my bags on the bed. That single word doesn't seem like enough, so I add, "You guys have gone above and beyond since I got back to town, and I owe you so much for everything you've done. Standing up for me, the fake dating, and now giving me a place to stay? I'm seriously never going to be able to repay you for all of this."

"You don't need to repay us, trouble." Reid takes a step

closer to me, his voice taking on that bossy tone I remember well from my youth. He's always been an interesting mix of charmingly laid back and demanding—and right now, his bossy side is out in full force. "That's what we keep telling you. Of course we'd do all of this. We've gotta look out for you."

I wince a little internally at the phrase "gotta look out for you." It makes me feel a lot like the hot mess of a teenage girl they all once knew, crushing on them from afar and never quite having her life together.

"Well, thanks," I say a bit lamely, feeling some of the wind come out of my sails. "It means a lot to me."

"We'll let you get settled in." Nick jerks his head at his brothers in a not-so-subtle hint that it's time to leave, and all three of them walk out together.

It's fairly late by now, and I can feel exhaustion stealing over me. I've only been back for a few days, but they've been jam-fucking-packed. With the bedroom door closed, I sit on the edge of the bed for a few minutes, trying to wrap my mind around this new change in my circumstances before getting up to unpack my things.

Through the door, their voices muffled and distant, I can hear Nick, Reid, and Sebastian talking.

Nick is going on about what a shit hole Ted's place was, and the other two are commenting in agreement with his quick decision to move me out of there and into their home.

I stop in the middle of pulling a few sweaters out of my suitcase, blinking back sudden tears as a rush of warmth fills me.

This is what it feels like to be taken care of.

Just being in this house gives me such a happy feeling. I can remember coming here sometimes when I was younger, tagging along with Lucas or coming for one of the parties their parents would sometimes throw.

The triplets and their older sister, Addison, were so close with their folks and I could always *feel* the love inside these walls, like it had somehow permeated the wood and plaster. I know how hard all four of the Cooper siblings took their parents' deaths. I can't even imagine going through such a sudden and unexpected trauma as that.

At least in my tattered past, no one *died*.

I finish unpacking quickly, and even though my eyelids are drooping and I'm starting to drag a little, I decide to hop in the shower quickly before bed. Standing under the hot water always helps relax me and usually makes me sleep better, so I grab my toiletry bag and slip out into the hall.

If I remember the layout of the house right, there are two bedrooms downstairs and three upstairs, along with two bathrooms on the second floor. One of the bathrooms is already occupied, and I can hear running water behind the closed door.

Clearly, I'm not the only one who likes a late night shower.

I pad farther down the hall, trying to keep my steps quiet without actually tiptoeing. Once I reach the second bathroom, I set my toiletries in the shower and get undressed, letting my mind wander as I step under the hot spray and breathe deeply.

It's impossible to hold on to any tension here in this quiet bathroom, with nothing to focus on but the cascading water from the rainfall shower head and the smell of my wildflower and honeysuckle body wash.

A few humming breaths fall from my lips, and I don't even notice the exact moment when I start singing. It just sort of happens, which isn't unusual. I always like to sing in the shower since it's the only place where I can sing easily without getting any stage fright.

I used to just sing unconsciously everywhere, without any fear at all. But after Dylan and all of his needling remarks about the sound of my voice, I started to freeze up under pressure anytime I had an audience listening to me. It doesn't even matter if it's one person or one hundred. I always choke.

That's why singing in the shower still feels like my safe

space, I guess. There's no one in here but me and the sound of rushing water as my accompaniment.

I start to truly lose myself in it, running my hands through my wet hair as my voice gains more and more strength—but just as I'm rinsing the last of the shampoo from my hair, the lights in the bathroom flicker. Once. Twice.

Then they blink out entirely.

Shit.

13

HAILEY

I stand under the spray for a minute in the dark, hoping the power will come back on, but it doesn't.

Dammit.

Had I thought through this better, I would have brought my pajamas into the bathroom with me. But I figured I would just wrap up in a towel and walk back to my room to change afterward. After all, the guys would likely all be in bed by the time I got out. I was planning on leaving the bathroom nice and tidy and bringing my toiletries back to my room with me too, but it's impossible to see in the dark.

One thing that's *very* different about Montana versus Los Angeles is that the nights here are as black as the bottom of the ocean. There aren't thousands of city lights to provide a near constant glow of illumination. In Chestnut Hill, there are only the moon and stars shining in the sky. Or when it's overcast, as is the case tonight, nothing but pitch black darkness.

I fumble around in the bathroom as I turn off the water and step out of the shower, reaching for a towel without being able to see my hand in front of my face.

My hair is dripping wet, and I shiver as I wrap the towel around my body and hold it securely against my chest.

When I open the door, I grimace. For some reason, I was hoping there would be more light out here, but there isn't. I'm not familiar enough with this house to be able to walk the hallway completely blind and feel confident I won't run into anything, but I'll have to try. I can hear muffled voices from downstairs, but I don't want to call out to any of the guys.

I'd really rather not have to be rescued yet *again* tonight. I can handle this on my own.

Hopefully I won't run into that giant dog in the dark. As much as the guys say he's harmless, I still don't want to tempt fate by scaring Bruno and making him think I'm an intruder who needs to be taken down.

I walk as quickly and quietly as I can, trying to navigate the hallway by memory and reaching out to trail my hand along the wall so I won't accidentally bump into it. I'm feeling pretty confident about my skills navigating a somewhat unfamiliar space in the dark—until I crash into a wall of solid muscle.

"Ahh!"

I yelp in surprise as my body collides with a taller, broader one. My balance is thrown off, and as I grab on to whoever it is, I lose my grip on my towel ... leaving me pressed up against a very wet, very *naked* body.

"Oh shit! I'm sorry!" I blurt, reaching down to try to catch my towel before it hits the floor.

I don't manage to grab it, but I *do* grab something.

Something thick and warm, with what feels like a line of metal piercings along the underside of it.

Something that pulses in my hand, hardening and becoming even thicker than before as I give it an unconscious little squeeze.

Holy shit.

"If you wanted to touch my dick, shortcake, you could've just asked." Sebastian's voice is dripping with a husky sarcasm that makes me blush even in the dark.

Oh my god, oh my god, oh my god.

"Sorry! Sorry!" I step back, quickly releasing my grip on his rapidly hardening cock.

Heat flames in my cheeks, and I crouch down, scrambling to find my towel and awkwardly wrapping it around my damp body again. Then I straighten up, keeping one hand on the wall to steady myself.

"It's okay." Sebastian chuckles. My eyes have adjusted to the darkness enough by now that I can vaguely make out his features—enough to see the smirk curving his lips, anyway. "Could've happened to anyone. I was in the other shower when the power went out, and I was heading back to my room to get some clothes. I didn't think to grab a towel. Didn't realize how handsy our new roommate was."

His smirk widens as he adds that last part, and I smack at his bare chest, ignoring the way my stomach does somersaults at the feel of his damp skin beneath my palm. "I'm not handsy, I just couldn't see what I was reaching for!"

He chuckles. "If you say so. But that doesn't explain the way you were groping me."

"I wasn't groping, I just... squeezed a little."

"Potato, potahto."

He cocks his head to one side, and I bite my lower lip. It's a miracle that the flush of embarrassment rippling through me hasn't dried my skin completely and burned the towel to a crisp in the process. I have no response to that, because I definitely did feel him up a bit.

"I was just surprised, that's all," I insist. "I didn't know you were... uh... pierced."

"Yup. Did it a couple years ago."

"How many are there?"

His eyes glint in the darkness. "Wanna count for yourself?"

Oh god. *Yes.*

I know he's probably just teasing though, and there's no way

I'm going to humiliate myself even more by grabbing his cock on purpose this time, so I don't say that out loud. Instead, I let my gaze flick downward briefly before rising back up to his face.

"Did it hurt?" I whisper.

His chuckle rumbles in his chest. "Yeah. It hurt like a son of a bitch. Which you still owe me for, by the way."

I blink. "Wait, what?"

"Well, I got them because of you." I can practically hear his smile through the darkness.

My eyes widen, my jaw dropping open a little. For a moment, I have no idea what he means—and then it hits me.

"The dare," I breathe.

Years ago, when we were still kids, I was hanging out with the Cooper triplets and my brother one night, and I dared Sebastian to get a piercing. He didn't have any back then, and I remember teasing him about how he'd probably be a baby about the pain.

Guess I was wrong about that.

We dared each other to do stupid stuff like that all the time. His brothers and my brother never got quite as competitive about it as Sebastian and I did, but I remember dozens of dares being thrown down over the course of our childhood and teenage years. I didn't think he'd ever actually follow through on that dare, though. In fact, I forgot all about it until now.

But clearly, he didn't. He really did it. And he got that pierced, of all things. More than once.

The thought makes my face flush. I can't get the image out of my head, no matter how much I try to think of anything else. The harder I try, the more vivid the image gets as my mind tries to piece together what I felt and figure out what it would look like.

"I—I can't believe you actually did that," I mutter, digging my fingers into the towel where I'm holding it clasped above my breasts.

He lifts one shoulder in a shrug. "You ought to know better than anyone that I never back down from a dare. Especially not from you, shortcake."

His voice drops lower on the last words, and he takes a half step closer to me, until our chests are nearly brushing. An unspoken implication hangs in the air between us as his words settle in my ears, and it makes goosebumps race across my skin. I almost feel like he's goading me, like he's daring me to throw down another challenge.

My breath catches in my throat as his scent surrounds me, his features shadowy in the near total darkness. I wish I could see him better. I wish I could read the look on his face.

What would he do if I dared him to kiss me right now?

The thought zaps through me like a bolt of lightning, making my lips tingle with the urge to speak. But I can't quite say it out loud, so the silence hangs between us, thick and loaded with tension.

Sebastian swallows, his Adam's apple rising and falling, then moves another inch closer to me. I can feel the heat radiating from his body, feel the brush of air across my lips every time he exhales, and I feel like I might pass out from how hard my heart is pounding. Without even thinking about it, I tilt my head up, my tongue darting out to wet my lips.

His gaze drops sharply, and he makes a noise low in his throat that goes straight to my clit.

"Fuck it," he mutters suddenly, and before I know what's happening, his mouth is on mine.

He cups my face in his hands as he kisses me, turning us so that my back hits the wall and boxing me in, pressing his body against mine as he devours my lips. His cock is fully hard now, pressing against my stomach through the towel, and the feeling of it sparks something inside me.

I kiss him back like I've been waiting for this moment my whole life, pushing away all the voices in my head screaming at me that this is a bad idea. I never thought I'd be making out like this with Sebastian Cooper in his childhood home during a power outage, but here we are.

And if I'm being honest, there's something incredibly hot about the risk of getting caught like this.

I know each of the triplets are trying to "win" me in public, but this moment between us can't be for show, because there's no one around—and it's dark, so they couldn't see anyway. So what is Sebastian trying to prove? I'm not sure what the answer to that question is, but right now, I decide I don't give a damn.

"Fuck, you smell good," he groans, dragging his lips away from mine to nip at my earlobe. "It's been driving me fucking crazy."

He teases my clit more deliberately, making me arch against him, and he lets out a harsh breath as my stomach grinds against his cock.

"I bet you taste good too," he mutters, finding my mouth again. *"Everywhere."*

He rolls his hips, grinding against me again, and my towel falls open as I let go of it to wrap my arms around his neck. Our bodies meet skin to skin, on purpose this time, and it's the most incredible feeling in the world.

I can feel the hardness of his cock, the firm planes of his chest brushing against my nipples as his tongue tangles with mine, and the pressure of his fingertips as he slides them between my legs, spreading my wetness over them. It's so much all at once, but at the same time, it's not enough. I need more.

"Sebastian," I whimper. "I..."

"I've got you."

His voice is a low rasp as one thick finger finds my entrance. I gasp, my inner walls clenching in anticipation as he starts to press slowly inside. I barely even notice when the lights flicker twice then flare back on. I'm too lost in him, in everything he's doing, and the spell between us doesn't break until a few seconds later when the sounds of his brothers' voices echo from the stairs.

"We must have blown a fuse or something. Piece of shit house," Nick grumbles, his voice moving closer, and I shove Sebastian away from me in a panic.

Before Nick and Reid can reach the top of the stairs, I snatch up my towel and throw it around me before darting past Sebastian toward my room. With my heart pounding and my mind racing, I close the door behind me as quietly as possible and hold my breath, praying silently that no one saw us.

14

HAILEY

Resting my back against the wall, I stare up at the ceiling for several long moments as I try to catch my breath. I can still feel Sebastian's hands all over me, his lips against mine, and the phantom memory of his touch isn't doing anything to slow my racing pulse.

I have to call Lorelai.

What just happened is way too much to be relayed over text, so even though it's late in LA by now, I pick up my phone and scroll to her number.

I throw on some sleep shorts and a t-shirt, then press the call button. I crawl under the covers as I wait for her to answer, pulling them all the way over my head as if to create an extra layer of insulation to make sure none of the guys hear me. I heard them talking in the hallway for a bit, but I'm pretty sure they're all back in their rooms by now. Still, I'm not willing to risk it.

"This had better be good. I need my beauty sleep, you know." Lorelai's voice is groggy, but it sharpens a little as she adds, "In all seriousness, though, is everything okay?"

Shit, that's a loaded question. Especially considering how

far out of hand I'm letting things get with my brother's best friends.

"Yeah, everything is fine." I keep my voice to a whisper, holding the phone close to my mouth. "But, Lorelai, you're not going to believe what's been happening here."

"Okay, if it was worth a middle of the night phone call, it's gotta be good. So spill it already. I'm awake now!"

She suddenly sounds much perkier than she did a moment ago. I can just imagine her sitting up in bed on the other end of this call, shoving her long bangs out of her face with one hand the way she always does.

I take a deep breath, keeping her in suspense for a moment longer while I gather my thoughts. Then I let the words spill out of me in a rush.

"I kissed each of the Cooper brothers. And not just for pretend. Some of the kisses have definitely been real."

"*What?*" Her voice is loud enough that I wince, suddenly more worried that the brothers will overhear *her* than me. I quickly turn down the volume on my phone as she says, "The last I heard, you were fake dating them and that's all it was. But now you're telling me shit is getting real? Tell me about these kisses! Every single detail."

I start by telling her about how Nick pressed me up against the car outside Grandma Dee's house, giving her a play-by-play of exactly what he did and how he did it.

"It was so hot that it took my breath away," I whisper. "Like, he *actually* took my breath away, Lor. I wasn't expecting it, and it was so much more intense than I could've imagined."

She gasps as if she's hanging on the edge of her seat. Something I love about Lorelai is that she's blunt with her emotions and honest in her reactions. I can always count on my best friend to tell it to me straight, and to have my back no matter what.

"Damn, girl. That's the firefighter one, right? The one who had the beard in that picture you showed me of them?"

"Yeah, that's Nick."

"Holy fuck." She whistles. "You've had a crush on these guys since you were, what, thirteen? I bet you nearly died."

"Oh, that's nothing." I actually manage a laugh, despite the heavy pounding of my heart. "What just happened a little while ago in the hallway tops *everything*."

"You got pressed up against another hard surface? Did Nick come back for seconds?"

I roll over onto my other side, pulling one of the pillows down into my little cocoon. "No, not Nick this time. Sebastian. The power went out when we were both in the shower, and—"

"Hang on a second, you were *both* in the shower?"

"Not together." I shake my head, chuckling quietly. "Separate showers. But we ran into each other in the hallway... naked. I was fumbling around trying to pick up my towel after it slipped, and accidentally I touched his dick."

"No way! That's like my nightmare! Or my dream. Depends on the guy."

She laughs, and I can't help but grin. Then I bite my lip, closing my eyes as the memory of that loaded moment in the hallways rushes over me.

"Yeah, well. It turns out that a dare I gave him back when I was a teenager about getting piercings—well, let's just say that it's something he actually took seriously."

"You're kidding!" Lorelai gasps. "He has his cock pierced?"

"More than one piercing. An entire Jacob's Ladder on the underside of his shaft."

"What happened after that?"

"He kissed me. And I felt like the world shifted on its axis."

"*Shiiit*." I can practically see Lorelai shaking her head in my mind's eye. "Why the fuck did I not come with you to Chestnut Hill?"

For a moment, we enjoy the giddiness of our girl talk as I try to keep my enthusiasm to a low whisper over the phone. I'm finding it more and more difficult to contain myself though. Especially now that I'm literally locked in close quarters with all three of them. It's not like I have anywhere to retreat from temptation anymore.

"I haven't been out of my room since it happened, and I think I'm just going to stay in here and hide forever," I admit. "I'm not sure I can look Sebastian in the eye again without wanting to literally throw myself in his bed. At least there won't be any confusing sexual tension if I stay locked in here all by myself."

"Yeah, that's quite a conundrum you've got there." She laughs. "Seriously though, you'd better not."

"Better not what?"

"You'd better not keep yourself sequestered in your room. Obviously there's some attraction there, and not just on your end of things. It sounds like the guys are into you too. This isn't just your high school crush anymore. It sounds pretty damn real to me."

"Yeah, but Lorelai—"

"Uh uh. No buts," she interrupts before I can finish. "I know how much you were dreading going back to your hometown. So why not make the most of it and take advantage of this amazing new development? I think you should make a move."

"Make a move? On which one?"

When I think about each of the triplets, my heart races and my clit starts throbbing like it's begging for attention. I honestly don't think I could make a choice between Nick, Reid, or Sebastian without still feeling like I want the other two as well.

"On all three of them, dummy!"

Lorelai says it like it's obvious, and I swallow hard, my stomach dropping out like I'm on a roller coaster.

"You can't be serious. All of them? Three men?"

"Why not? They all seem to be showing interest in you, and we both know that you've been into all three of those brothers for as long as I can remember. Give me one good reason why you shouldn't take advantage of this once in a lifetime opportunity."

"Well, for starters, these guys are Lucas's best friends."

"Yeah, yeah, we've already covered that. Come up with something else that you haven't already used as an excuse."

"Okay, well... it would be pretty scandalous if anyone in Chestnut Hill found out."

"Who says they have to know? And who says it's any of their damn business even if they do find out?"

She's got a point there, although knowing how fast gossip spreads in a small town like this, I'm not sure it'd be as simple and straightforward as she's making it sound.

"I get what you're saying." I chew my lip, nerves racing through me at the idea that I'm even semi-seriously contemplating this. "But the biggest thing is, what if the guys have no interest in sharing like that? I mean, *assuming* any of them were even interested in doing anything with me, I definitely don't want to come between them. I don't want to do anything to risk their bond as brothers, or to mess up anything between us."

"I know." Her voice softens a little with understanding. "It's scary. I was sort of just kidding when I told you to make a move with all of them, but the more I think about it, the more I think you really should. This could be something fucking amazing, but you'll never find out if you don't try."

"But what if—"

"Look, I know that asshole ex of yours did a number on your self-esteem." She sighs, and I can practically feel her anger at Dylan, even across all the miles that separate us. "And maybe you're right and this is all just supposed to be fake dating. But what do you have to lose? Your brother doesn't have to know about it. You're literally staying in a house with the three hottest men you've ever known, and I honestly don't think that they would be kissing you in the way that you're describing to me if there weren't some honest to god feelings evolving over there."

I chew on my lower lip as I listen to my best friend speak, practically wearing a hole through it as my mind spins over her words.

On the one hand, I can barely stand how badly I want the triplets. I've always had massive crushes on all of them, and living in such close proximity is making that simmering attraction boil over. On the other hand, I know there's a lot at stake. Besides, I'm not quite so sure that I'm ready to open up my heart to any guy again, not to mention *three* of them.

I've all but given up on the idea of true love and happy endings. So the thought of taking a chance again with not just one, but possibly even three men, is a lot.

"I don't know," I whisper after a long beat. "I guess... I'll sleep on it."

"Good. I'm sure that will give you sweet dreams." Lorelai laughs. "And speaking of sleep, we should both get some. I'm really glad you called though. Keep me in the loop, girl, and if anything else sizzling happens, you know where to find me!"

I laugh. Lorelai always has a way of making things feel less heavy and taking some of the weight off my brain. "Thanks."

We say goodnight, and I snuggle down into the bed, pulling the blankets around my chin.

I'm hoping that I'll fall asleep quickly now that I've decompressed a bit and talked things over with my bestie, but after twenty minutes of staring up at the ceiling with my thoughts still racing, I scrunch my face up in frustration.

"Dammit," I mutter. *So much for sleeping on it.*

My entire body feels like it's buzzing with adrenaline and

lingering arousal, and I realize there's a good chance I won't sleep at all tonight unless I take the edge off.

Biting my lip, I kick the covers off and slowly slip a hand into my sleep shorts. If these thoughts are going to keep me up all night, I might as well do something about them.

I never had "spectacular" orgasms with Dylan. It was all just average. And most of the time, he wasn't even able to get me to climax. I had to do that part myself, which at least means that I'm well versed in what it takes to get me over the edge.

Sebastian's handsome features float through my mind as I trace slow circles against my clit with my finger. What would've happened if Nick and Reid hadn't come upstairs while we were kissing in the dark?

I imagine Sebastian's finger pushing into me as I work one into myself and bite my lower lip to keep from groaning. The last thing I need is to wake up any of the guys and accidentally alert them to what I'm doing in here.

But I can't stop either. I close my eyes, drifting back to the dark of the hallway with Sebastian, his hands and mouth all over me.

"I dare you to fuck me," I whisper into his mouth between kisses. "I dare you to make me come."

He draws back a little, then swallows hard and exhales, long and slow. His hot breath teases my skin as he stares hungrily down at me, and I shiver under his intense focus.

"Like I said, I never back down from a dare," he finally says with a smirk, his eyes glinting in the darkness.

Before I can speak again, he grabs me by the hips. With one powerful movement, he hoists me upward and my back slides up the wall until I'm at eye level with him. He holds me there for a second, his gaze searing me, and I feel his thick, pierced cock at my entrance.

"Did you really get those because of me?" I whisper.

"Why don't I just show you how perfectly they fit you?"

In my imagination, he grips his cock with one hand and holds it steady as he starts pushing into me. I work a finger into myself while I visualize holding on to his neck and biting my lip to keep from crying out as he fills me up. In my fantasy, with every piercing of his that slides into me, it becomes increasingly difficult to stay quiet. I don't know quite what they'd feel like, but even my best guess is enough to have my pussy clenching around the intrusion of my fingers.

Fantasy Sebastian leans closer, his mouth hovering above my ear.

"Does that feel good?" he whispers, just like he did when we were kissing.

I slip a second finger into myself, twisting both around inside while my free hand palms my clit. I think of the way his sturdy, strong body would feel, his hips clapping against mine with every thrust.

I'm still so turned on from the thrill of our hallway encounter that it doesn't take long for my body to rev up. My fingers glide in and out of me, slick with my arousal, and my clit pulses against my palm.

I imagine the feeling of Sebastian's body pressing me into the wall, his cock opening me up, his piercings sliding over my sensitive skin, and a groan escapes me as I fall headfirst into an orgasm.

I bite hard on my lip to keep from making too much noise while my body spasms and I arch up off the bed for several seconds until I melt back into it as the rush ends. I pull my soaked fingers out and idly drag their wetness across my clit, making myself shudder as I catch my breath.

Just like I did under Nick when he pressed me up against his car and kissed me like a wild man. There was something so needy about the way he was kissing me, his hands pawing my body. Even when he bit my lip, I liked it. Would he have fucked me just as intensely?

My heart skips a beat at that thought, and I shake my head to try to clear it.

Come on, Hailey, knock it off. You're playing with fire even letting yourself fantasize about Sebastian, let alone Nick.

What happened with Sebastian was one thing. We were so close to making it real anyway, although it never should've happened in the first place. And I've been on edge sexually since I got here, so I needed to let off a bit of steam. That's all it was.

But I still can't stop thinking about Nick. About what would've happened if I hadn't yelped in surprise when he bit down on my lip.

Before I can stop myself, my fingers trail along the inside of my thigh to my pussy once more. I hesitate, holding them there while I try to talk myself out of this.

"Fuck it," I whisper and shove a finger into myself again. I'm still sensitive as hell from the first orgasm, so it takes even more effort not to cry out, but at this point, I almost hope the guys will hear me.

My mind flashes back to that moment at Nick's car. The unspoken attraction and tension crackling between us after the awkward kiss we shared in front of Grandma Dee—and the real one that followed.

"I've never been kissed like that before. I wouldn't have known you had that in you," I say, and Nick flashes me a little smile through the darkness of his scruffy beard. His intense blue eyes darken like storm clouds as they rake across me.

"Most people don't know a lot about me. I like it that way."

He's so tall he towers over me, like a mountain come to life. I feel powerless pinned between him and the car like this, like he could do anything he wanted to me and there wouldn't be anything I could do to stop him.

"What other secrets are you keeping?"

"You'll have to work to find out."

I reach up to run my hand through his beard, and the wild, hungry look flashes back on his face. With a growl, he scoops me up into his arms and flings open the door to the back seat, then tosses me into it like I weigh nothing. I bounce against the cushions as he falls onto me, tearing at my clothes, and in a matter of seconds, he has me down to nothing but my panties. He shoves them aside with one of his giant hands, then unbuttons his jeans with his other enough to tug his hard cock out of them.

He sits next to me, then gruffly pulls me up off the seat and into his lap. I straddle him, facing him, and try to control my breathing as his hands paw my hips and force me down onto him. He enters me roughly, but that's exactly how I'd want it with him.

My hands rest on his shoulders while he starts bouncing me up and down on him, slowly at first but building quickly. He never takes his penetrating gaze off me, his eyes boring into me like they're trying to see into my soul.

"Good girl. Take my cock," he mutters, picking up the pace even more. In my fantasy, he lifts me up then lets me go, dropping me and impaling me on his cock.

I shove two fingers into myself, hard, the same way he's fucking me in my imagination. That's all it takes for me to come again, biting my lip to keep from crying out his name.

My heart hammers in my ears when I come back into my body. I'm breathing erratically, but at this point there's no way I can stop my mind from going where it's going to go, so I decide to just give in and get this out of my system.

I flash back to sitting in Reid's lap on the barstool where we put on such a show to piss Dylan off. Our lips are locked together, and heat sparks between us, melding us until Reid breaks the kiss and pushes my sticky, sweaty hair out of my face.

"What do you say we get out of here for a second?" he asks quietly, and my heart skips a beat.

"Where are we going to go? It's a crowded bar."

Reid smirks as he helps me back to my feet. "Don't you worry about that. Follow me." He jumps off the bar stool and offers me a hand and a wink, so I take it and follow him through the bar toward the bathrooms at the back.

"Are you serious?" I whisper and dig my heels in to slow him down as we get closer.

"Very. Come on, no one's around." He squeezes my hand to encourage me, and I give in. Reid takes one more clearing glance to make sure no one is around, then pulls me inside and kicks the door closed behind us. He blocks the door with the trash can—like that's going to stop anyone determined enough to get in—and pulls me into him again.

As soon as we're alone, he kisses me with even more heat, pushing me up against the counter. His hands find the waist of my pants and he tugs them off in one go, then spins me around and puts one hand on my lower back to bend me over. My palms splay across the counter for balance, and I watch in the mirror as he unbuttons his jeans and pulls out his cock.

His eyes meet mine in the mirror as his cock head teases my hole, and his expression simmers. "Do it. Fuck me, Reid."

"Mm," he growls and thrusts into me up to the hilt. I gasp and grip the counter's edge to keep from crying out, but Reid doesn't give me any time to adjust. He just starts hammering away at me, reckless and wild—and so fucking hot.

My fingers work my hole, wet and squelching, and the sounds fill the bedroom, but I don't care. I'm so lost in the fantasy, in the pleasure I'm giving myself, that all three of the triplets could walk in on me right now and I wouldn't stop.

But as I finger fuck myself and return to the scene in my mind, it shifts. Reid's still behind me, plugging me desperately, but we're here in my room. He has me bent over the edge of the bed, his hands gripping my waist. But he falls forward onto me, his chest against my back, and his lips flutter against my ear, giving me chills.

"Looks like I'm not the only one who wants you," he mutters, *and my head turns on the mattress to follow his gaze. Nick and Sebastian are standing in the corner, naked and stroking their cocks eagerly as they watch their brother plow me like his life depends on it.*

"Fuck," I gasp in both the fantasy and in reality as I erupt for the third time.

I can't keep the noise to myself, and a series of whimpers leak out of me along with my orgasm. I clench my lower lip between my teeth as it goes on and on, coursing through me like a current, until I finally melt into the mattress, heaving.

"Jesus," I whisper, my eyes fluttering open and darting to the corner of the room just to make sure Sebastian and Nick aren't really there watching me. The room's empty, and I'm not sure if I'm disappointed or relieved to find it that way.

I don't know why my fantasy switched like that at the end, but I'm too tired to think about it. I lie there in a puddle of my own sweat and release until the exhaustion that's been burning at the corners of my eyes for hours finally overtakes me.

15

HAILEY

When I wake up the next morning, I'm feeling a bit less frazzled. I was able to get at least some of the sexual frustration out of my system, and my head is feeling a little clearer—although I'm not sure how long that will last once I'm around the guys again.

I get up and get dressed, then follow Lorelai's urging from last night and force myself to leave my room. I pad downstairs into the living room, realizing with a mix of relief and disappointment that all three of the guys are gone. I'm sure they've headed off to their respective jobs already. Even though Sebastian and Reid work for themselves and own their own businesses, I know they put in a ton of hours. And Nick sometimes has early shifts at the fire station.

The only ones left in the house are me and Bruno.

"Guess it's just you and me, huh, buddy?" I look over at the dog, hopeful that he'll have warmed up to me a bit since last night.

He's standing at the base of the stairs, his back paws still on the bottom step and his front paws on the floor. He doesn't wag his tail or anything, just regards me with a serious expression as he clutches something in his mouth.

I frown, leaning a bit closer as I peer at it. He's such a big dog, literally the perfect mutt for a frequently brooding and burly guy like Nick, and whatever is hanging out of the corner of his mouth definitely looks like something too delicate for him to be allowed to have.

I take a step closer, still trying to figure out what he's got clenched in his jaw.

Then I let out a little squeak of surprise.

It's a pair of my panties.

"Hey! Give those back! They don't belong to you!"

I reach for them, completely forgetting the fact that I'm supposed to be a little afraid of him. But before I even get close, he darts to one side and lopes into the living room. I lunge for him again, and he evades me, seeming to want to make a game of having me chase him around the house as my black lace panties dangle from his drool-laden jowls.

"Dammit all," I mutter, trying to cut him off by feinting right and then going left. But he's too smart for me and sees the trick coming a mile away.

I try for several more minutes, until we're both panting a bit from the exertion. But even though his tongue is lolling out of one side of his mouth, Bruno doesn't let go of my underwear. When I finally sink down into the couch and give up, he takes a few steps closer, looking almost disappointed that the game has ended. Then he shakes himself out, saunters over to the large window along one wall, and lies down with my panties still firmly clenched in his jaw.

"Fine, you win. Keep them. But now you owe me, buddy. I'll accept my payment in licks and wags."

I shake my head at the panty stealing dog, then stand back up again to head out.

I have a lot on my agenda today.

First, I stop by the diner to say hi to my parents. Pippa told me that she usually stops there for breakfast, and I'm happy when I run into her too.

We grab some food so our parents won't have to wait on us and settle into a booth in the back, and I watch as our folks hustle around the diner. Mom is taking food orders, and Dad is working on a few cosmetic repairs.

"Man, they don't stop moving, do they?" I ask, thinking about how many times I've seen them do this throughout my life. Pippa and I both worked here during high school, so we're well acquainted with the hustle of a busy diner.

My sister laughs and shakes her head.

"Nope, never. I help out as much as I can, and they just hired a new guy to work behind the counter, so that's good. But it feels like they've been under a bit of extra pressure recently. I don't know if it's just the holidays or what, but I hope it eases up soon. I know how much they both love this place."

They really do. We used to joke about it being their fourth child.

"Sooo..." My sister drags the word out, giving me a look. "How are things at Creepy Ted's place? Are you two besties by now? Did he turn you into a cigar aficionado?"

"Actually, I'm not staying at Ted's anymore. The Cooper brothers offered to let me stay at their house."

"Oh, *did* they?" Pippa raises her eyebrows, and her fiery red hair makes the smirk on her face look almost devilish.

I grab the biscuit off my plate and chuck it at her face, but she snatches it out of the air and bites into it.

Dammit. Now I'm down a biscuit.

I refrain from throwing any more food at her since I know she'll just eat that too, but at least all the commotion hopefully distracted her from the flush that rose into my cheeks at her little innuendo.

"They're just being nice," I say firmly. "And they have a

spare guest room. Plus, you know they're only helping me out because they're best friends with Lucas."

"Whatever you say." Pippa grins again but doesn't press the issue.

The diner picks up shortly after that, and we both end up quickly scarfing down the rest of our breakfasts and hopping behind the counter to help our parents out. It's nice, all of us working together like this, the way we used to back when things were a lot simpler.

Once the rush dies down, I give my parents and Pippa hugs goodbye and step out into the wintery air.

The next thing on my to-do list is going to be a lot less fun than working at the diner. Today is the day I'm supposed to meet up with Maeve and the other women who all volunteered to help with the Santa's Workshop display this year.

I'm sort of dreading it, since it's likely going to be mostly Divas volunteering.

Maeve and Brielle are friends, and I could do without seeing my ex-bestie for a while longer.

Regardless, I refuse to let them think that they have won by scaring me off. So I head over to the town square where the display will be set up, stepping into the Courtyard Shops, a large building that houses several shops and cafes, with an open space and atrium in the middle. Most of the volunteers are there already, and I greet them with a friendly smile, even though it does feel a bit forced.

"Oh my gosh, Hailey! Hi!"

Amanda Swann, whom I distinctly recall dumping paint all over my hair in our theatre tech class waves at me, brushing her hair back over her shoulder with perfectly manicured nails. I nod at her, pressing my lips together as a few other women greet me too—all of them acting as if we're best friends, when most of them made my life miserable in high school.

Whatever. That was a long time ago, I remind myself. *Just smile and get through this, and maybe you can talk the guys into going out for drinks or something tonight.*

A woman named Tina is in charge of organizing the volunteers, and she leads us all into the storage area where all of the supplies for the workshop are kept.

"You three." She points to me, Maeve, and Amanda. "You're on wreath duty. The wreath will go on Santa's door, so it needs to look good. There are supplies in a couple of tubs somewhere, marked 'wreath.' Get to it."

Maeve gives a perky smile, gesturing for me and Amanda to follow her. "I'm pretty sure I know where it's kept," she tells us. "Hailey, since you've been out of town, I know you're a bit behind on how we do it, but we've been building a new wreath every year to keep things fresh."

"Sounds great," I say unenthusiastically.

She leads us over to a corner of the storage space, frowning slightly as she takes in the somewhat haphazardly organized supplies. "They're around here somewhere. Oh, wait, I know. They're in the crawlspace. We thought it would be better because it's more dry."

Maeve gestures to a metal ladder bolted to a nearby wall. It leads to a tiny door about halfway up the wall.

Jesus. I grimace as I look at it. How is it worth it to store the wreath materials in there? Personally, I would've just let them get dank and musty if it came down to it.

"Hailey." Maeve raises a brow at me. "Do you mind getting them? I'm not wearing good shoes for a ladder, and yours seem so... practical."

She gestures from her high heels to my boots, and irritation prickles through me.

"Sure," I mutter. "I'd love to."

Without waiting for her to respond, I march over to the

ladder and start climbing, yanking the metal door open as soon as I reach it. The crawl space isn't wide at all, but it's deep enough that I have to crawl all the way into it to grab the materials. I clench my jaw, muttering curses under my breath as I clamber off the ladder and into the small, dark storage area. I don't like confined spaces, but I wasn't going to admit that to Maeve, especially not when she was clearly already trying to get under my skin.

I'll just grab the wreath materials quickly and then get down.

Crawling on my hands and knees, I make my way toward the back of the space, heading for the plastic tubs that should have what I need. A creaking sound catches my attention, and I glance over my shoulder as the door I just came through swings shut.

The light cuts off immediately, and my pulse spikes.

"Shit," I whisper.

My hand scrabbles in my back pocket for my phone, and when I finally manage to turn the flashlight on, my breathing evens out a little. Instead of continuing on toward the tubs, I turn back to the door, wanting to prop it open so I won't lose the light again.

But when I try to open it, it won't budge.

Oh fuck.

My heart rate leaps again, and even though I've still got the light of the flashlight, it's not enough. Because now I'm trapped in here, and the panic I was holding at bay a moment ago is rising hard and fast, like a tsunami wave racing toward shore.

"Fuck, fuck, fuck," I mutter, shoving hard at the door. "Hey! Can anyone hear me? Maeve! I'm stuck!"

No one answers me, and my stomach twists. How thick is this door? Can they really not hear me?

From down below, I swear I hear a small burst of laughter.

My skin chills, my voice going quiet. Was that Maeve? Maybe she *can* hear me, but instead of coming to help, she and the others are just laughing at me. It's childish and petty and just plain fucking mean, but that doesn't mean it's above them, if their past behavior is anything to go by.

Dammit. Why did I ever agree to do this?

Anger surges through me, and I work harder to get the door open, this time even kicking it with my heel, but it still doesn't budge. The exertion only makes my heart thud harder, and I can feel myself inching closer to a full panic attack. Every breath is short and choppy, but I can't seem to slow them down.

My phone is still clutched in my hand, the small beam of the flashlight jerking wildly around the space, and I pull up the first contact I can think of and press the call button.

"Hey, shortcake. Did you miss me already?" Sebastian's teasing voice through the phone's speaker makes me feel so relieved that I practically burst into tears.

"Sebastian! Please, you have to help me! I'm locked in a crawlspace in the Courtyard Shops, where I was volunteering for the Santa's Workshop." I can't hide the urgent, spiraling panic in my voice. "Please come get me and let me out. It's so fucking small. I can't breathe."

"Shit." Instantly, the tone in his voice changes from playful banter to concern. "I'm on my way, Hailey, just breathe. Stay on the phone with me and breathe, okay? You're going to be fine, and I'll be right—"

He cuts off mid-sentence, and the light winks out too. I let out a gasping, startled breath as I look down and realize that my phone battery has died. Dammit, I forgot to plug it in after my call with Lorelai last night.

"No," I whisper, clutching the dead phone like I can somehow bring it back to life. "No, no, no. Come on."

There's no light in here anymore, and even though the space

is big enough that I'm in no real danger of being suffocated or crushed to death, it doesn't matter. The fact that there's no way out makes it feel as if my skin is crawling and I can't suck enough oxygen into my lungs.

I'm spiraling, and I dig the nails of one hand into my palm, trying to ground myself, but it's not working.

I need to get out of here.

Please, Sebastian. Please come get me.

My chest feels like it's being squeezed in a vise, each inhale sending stabbing pains shooting through my ribs as my body fights to draw in air. I force myself to keep breathing, tiny, shallow breaths that fill my ears with a harsh, raspy sound.

I feel like I'm drowning in darkness. Like I'm about to be pulled under, and I'll never fight my way back to the surface.

"Hailey. Hailey!"

A muffled voice slowly registers in my ears, cutting through a bit of the panic. There's a loud banging sound, and a second later, the crawlspace door swings open. Light floods the small space, illuminating Sebastian's worried features.

"You're okay," he murmurs as he reaches for me, and I practically throw myself into his arms. "I'm here. I've got you."

He lets me cling to him for a moment as shudders wrack my body, and when I finally loosen my hold a bit, he helps me down the ladder. When we reach the floor, I still feel lightheaded, my legs so wobbly that I almost collapse into a heap. Sebastian notices immediately and pulls me close, tucking me against his chest and keeping his arm wrapped tightly around me. Nick and Reid are here too, flanking us on either side.

Reid steps forward, rounding on the Divas. They've all gathered around us, no doubt eager to witness the spectacle of me being rescued from the crawlspace like some kind of frightened child.

"What the actual *fuck*?" His voice is low, but the anger in his tone is unmistakable. "What the hell were you thinking, locking Hailey in that crawlspace?"

"It was just an accident." Maeve gives him her most falsely sincere smile. "We had no idea that she was stuck up there. I assumed she was just taking her time with the wreath materials. We hadn't heard anything from her until the three of you barged in here like the place was on fire." Her gaze flicks to me, and she gives me a condescending look before adding, "Honestly, she probably just called you because she wanted the attention."

My stomach clenches. It's bad enough that I had a panic attack in front of the women who used to bully me, but for her to imply that I was faking it just so that the Cooper brothers would rush to my aid makes me feel even worse.

Before I can respond to that, though, Nick steps forward to stand shoulder to shoulder with Reid.

"You're almost as terrible a liar as you are a person," he growls, and Maeve's eyes widen, her cheeks flushing with arrogant embarrassment.

"I don't—" she starts to say, but Nick cuts her off.

"Save it," he bites out. "We don't need to hear any more of your bullshit, and neither does Hailey. We're taking her home. But if you ever treat her badly again—hell, if you ever even fucking *talk* to her again—you'll be dealing with the three of us. You got that?" His voice hardens as he sweeps the rest of the Divas with an icy glare. "That goes for all of you. Understood? Hailey is off fucking limits."

There's a moment of stunned silence as all the Divas stare at him in shock. Then they slowly nod, looking more cowed than I've ever seen them. Even Maeve seems thrown off by the force of the Cooper brothers' defense of me, clearing her throat and looking at the floor as she nods along with the others.

"Don't worry about finishing up the wreath," she mutters. "We'll get the materials down and do it for you."

"Damn fucking right you will." Reid glares at Maeve. "She's done here."

My legs still feel like they might give out at any moment, but with all three Cooper brothers surrounding me, I manage to make it out of the Courtyard Shops without my knees buckling. I can feel the Divas watching us as we go, but the men don't even spare them another glance, and neither do I.

Nick was right. I'm well and truly done with them—and now, thanks to him and his brothers, maybe they're finally done with me.

All of the men drove to the Courtyard Shops separately, since they were all in different places when Sebastian texted to let Reid and Nick know what was going on with me. They leave my car where it is, and I ride home in Sebastian's car, with the other two trailing right behind us.

Back at their place, they get me into the living room and onto the couch, and I curl up next to Nick, leaning against him more unabashedly than I might in other circumstances. I'm still trying to come down from the panic, and his steady, solid presence is helping.

"Thank you all for coming to get me," I whisper, trying to keep the quaver out of my voice. "I know it was silly for me to get so freaked out over it, but I really don't do well in confined spaces."

"It's not silly at all," Nick grunts.

Sebastian nods. "Seriously, Hailey. I've got a confined spaces thing too, so I get it."

"Everyone has things that they're afraid of," Reid adds. His expression darkens as he adds, "And I'm glad you called Seb, since those fucking bitches thought it was more fun to laugh at you than to help you."

Sebastian and Reid settle onto the couch too, all four of us crowding onto the large sofa. Reid rubs my back, and the palm of his hand feels warm and smooth as he traces steady circles.

It's rhythmic and relaxing, and Sebastian reaches for my hand, talking to me quietly about nothing important.

His deep voice soothes me, and as the adrenaline rush starts to fade, pure exhaustion fills its place. Even though it's nowhere near the end of the day, I feel like I can't keep my eyelids open, and a short while later, I fall asleep surrounded by my three handsome rescuers.

16

HAILEY

When I wake up, there's something hard and warm beneath my cheek. I blink my eyes open slowly, realizing that the 'pillow' I'm using is Nick's thick thigh. I must've been sleeping on him this entire time, curled against him with my head nestled on his lap.

I yawn and turn my head, looking up at his chiseled, bearded jaw. He's definitely awake, his posture a bit stiff as if he's afraid of disturbing me if he moves too much.

"How long was I out?" I murmur, sitting up and rubbing my eyes as I look around the room. Neither of the other two men are still here.

"An hour or so."

My heart swells, a little lump of emotion welling in my throat. It means a lot to me that he sat here like this the whole time I was sleeping, like a silent, watchful protector—especially since he was also serving as a human pillow. I quickly glance down at his leg to make sure I didn't leave a drool spot or anything, then shift my gaze back up to his face.

"Didn't you have to finish up your shift at the station?"

"I called in and got someone to cover for me."

Sebastian and Reid walk back into the living room as he

speaks, and I glance over at them, startled. When I didn't see them when I woke up, I assumed it was because they had both headed back to the garage and the workshop respectively.

"None of you guys went back to work?"

"Nah, we all wanted to stick around and make sure you were okay." Reid brushes it off casually, as if it's nothing. But it's definitely *something* to me. They didn't need to do that, especially since I was physically unharmed and mostly just freaking out. It's not like they needed to sit with me to make sure I didn't die or anything.

But they stuck close by me anyway, without me even asking.

I'm trying to figure out a way to say 'thanks' that will sound different than the dozen other times I've thanked them since I came back to town, but my thoughts are interrupted by something wet touching my hand.

I jerk in surprise, almost flailing a little to fling whatever it is off—but I restrain myself when I realize it's Bruno. He must have been lying near the side of the couch, where I didn't see him when I first woke up. Now he's standing in front of me with his nose pressed to my hand. As I look down at him, he drags his tongue over my hand in a long lick.

It tickles slightly, and I can't help but grin.

"Hey, look! I think I'm making progress on becoming friends with him."

"He must have known you were scared. Dogs can sense when you need comforting." Nick leans down and gives him a pet and some praise for being a good boy.

"Maybe." I grin as Bruno flops back down on the floor. "Or maybe he's just happy that I let him win the panty raid."

"The panty raid?" Reid's curiosity is visibly piqued.

"Oh, do tell." Sebastian chuckles. "This sounds good."

I fill the guys in on how Bruno stole my panties before I left for the Santa's Workshop fiasco, and how I ran all around the living room chasing him before finally giving up and letting the dog keep them.

Nick flushes deeply, and I can't help but laugh at his embarrassment over Bruno's behavior. It's not like it's *his* fault his dog stole my panties.

Unless…

I turn to face the muscled firefighter, giving him my best 'come clean' look.

"Did you train him to do that?" I demand.

"What? No, of course not!" Nick straightens, his shoulders going stiff. He looks like he's about to panic almost as badly as I did until he catches the expression on my face and realizes I'm just teasing.

Sebastian and Reid break into laugher.

"Still, it's like I said." Sebastian shoots me a wink. "Dogs often start to take after their owners, don't they? So if you didn't train him to do it, maybe it's just a habit he picked up from you. Come on, Nick. You're in a safe space, you can admit it. Do you have a panty stealing problem?"

"Fuck off."

Nick flips him off, and that makes me laugh. I feel so much better than I did when Sebastian pulled me out of that confined space, almost back to my usual self.

"You guys really don't need to stay here with me," I reiterate, not wanting them to feel like they have to babysit me all day. "I'm fine now. You can go back to work or do whatever you need to do."

"Nope. Fuck that." Sebastian claps his hands together, grinning down at me. "We're all taking the day off, so I say we do something fun to make the most of it."

"Agreed." Reid nods, then gestures to an empty space on one side of the living room. "Want to help us decorate our Christmas tree? We were planning on getting one soon anyway, and there's nothing like a little holiday spirit to forget about the damn Divas."

I don't even bother trying to give them another out, because the truth is, I much prefer the idea of decorating a tree with them all to hanging out in this big house by myself. So I just nod enthusiastically. I feel like I haven't properly celebrated Christmas in two years, and it used to be my favorite season. I like the magical feeling of it, the coziness of the lights and decorations, and the fun of staying indoors on cold, blustery days, all warm and snug in thick socks.

I love Christmas, and I'm starting to really love spending time with these three too.

"All right. I'll go put on my boots and get my ax." Nick is the last of the brothers to get to his feet, and when he does, Bruno starts to bark in excitement, clearly reading the vibe in the room and realizing that a romp outdoors might be in his future.

"Your ax?" I ask, frowning. "What for?"

"How else am I going to chop down a tree?"

My eyes widen with excitement. "Oh! I didn't know we'd be getting a real, live tree. Although this *is* Montana and not LA. I guess it's easier to do here than it would be there."

Sebastian rolls his eyes, huffing a laugh. "I bet all the Christmas trees in LA are plastic or some shit like that."

"They're probably pink or silver too," Reid adds with a smirk.

The funny thing is, they're not exactly wrong. And as a born and bred Montana girl, I definitely never got over the incongruity of seeing Christmas trees right next to palm trees or hearing Christmas carols in seventy degree weather.

The winter seasons that I spent in LA were lonely and underwhelming. There's nothing like a Montana winter, especially during the holiday.

"Hell yes, let's cut down a tree." I push up from the couch, excitement bubbling through me.

Nick gets his boots and ax, and Sebastian pulls a winter hat over his messy dark hair, tugging it down on his forehead so far that it mostly obscures the scar through his eyebrow. Reid digs out the Christmas tree stand and decorations from the basement while I try to keep Bruno entertained. The big mutt is practically beside himself with anticipation, eager to be let out so he can play in the winter wonderland.

Since I don't have thick enough outer layers—I got rid of the really heavy stuff when I moved to LA, since I'd never need it out there—all three of the guys bundle me up, handing me scarves and gloves and a hat, and enough jackets for three people to wear.

"Wait, wait! It's not *that* cold out. Did you guys forget that I still have Montana blood in my veins?" I laugh at their overly generous efforts to keep me warm.

"I was just afraid that you were going to try marching out there in the snow in that hot pink bikini again," Sebastian teases.

He gives me a wink, and when his brothers glance between the two of us burning curiosity, he ends up telling them the whole story as we head out the door and drive about thirty minutes out of town. We tromp through the woods until we find what I declare to be the perfect tree, and then Bruno and I watch as the three of them work together to chop it down.

Nick and Reid strap it to the roof of the car, bitching at Sebastian the entire time as he flirts shamelessly with me instead of helping.

Honestly, I don't mind one bit.

Once we get back home and have peeled off all of our winter gear and gotten the tree into the stand, it's time to decorate.

"How about Christmas music?" Reid suggests. "Any favorites?"

I nod and walk over to help Nick pick out some remixes of Christmas carols to play, and in a matter of minutes, the whole house is practically bursting with holiday spirit. Even Bruno, who's now lying contentedly in front of the fireplace after all that gamboling through the snow, starts to howl along a little.

I look over to see Reid standing with an armful of string lights in his hands. He must've been testing to make sure they work—which they do—and now it looks like he's holding an entire galaxy of blinking stars in his arms as he starts to untangle them.

"Hey, come help me with this," he says when he notices me watching him, lifting his chin to summon me closer. I go, and the two of us manage to untangle all the lights, laying them out carefully so they'll be ready when we need them.

As Nick opens a box filled with ornaments, Sebastian emerges from the kitchen, where he disappeared a few minutes ago. He's got two glasses in each hand, a finger or so of whiskey in each.

"No tree decorating party would be complete without this."

He passes the glasses around, and we all clink them together in a little cheers before sipping the spicy, smoky drink. The whiskey burns down my throat in the best way, warming me from the inside out, and I let out a small, contented sigh.

"See?" Sebastian nods in approval. "Aren't you glad to be home?"

"Yeah," I say honestly. "I really am."

We work together to wind the lights around the tree, and when that's done, we start hanging ornaments. Before I know it, the whiskey in my glass is gone—but almost as soon as I realize that, it's full again, thanks to a top-off from Reid, who grabbed the bottle from the kitchen.

All of us are getting a little tipsy by the time we run out of ornaments to hang on the fir tree's branches. The whiskey seems to be helping Nick loosen up a bit, or maybe he's just finally starting to hold back less around me, because he's more talkative than I've ever seen him.

"I have to admit, the town's been pretty dull since you left," he says as he puts a few stray pieces of packing paper back into the box that once housed the ornaments. "Chestnut Hill wasn't the same without you here."

I grin, unable to help myself. Then my smiles fades a little as I remember all the reasons I left in the first place. "I'm sure not *everyone* missed me."

Reid snorts. "Eh, if you're talking about that little prick, Dylan, I wouldn't give him a moment of your thought."

"That asshat and his family have been expanding their influence here at a record fucking pace," Sebastian mutters as he sticks the star on top of the tree. "They've been buying up real estate and making deals with various businesses in town, trying to monopolize their hold on property in Chestnut Hill. I don't like it."

"I don't like it either, but it's not like we can do anything about it." Nick frowns. It's clear that he doesn't like feeling powerless about anything. "They're not doing anything illegal—that we know of, anyway. Dylan is just a rich, smarmy scumbag, and that's that."

It's very clear that none of them have any love for Dylan Montgomery, and the open disgust in their voices is like a balm to the old wound inside me. Honestly, I'm embarrassed that I ever loved Dylan. I'm not even sure I actually ever did.

Thank god I didn't marry him.

Even if he hadn't cheated on me, I can't see how we would've lasted. And if we did manage to stay together, I can't imagine how I could've been happy.

Maybe it's the whiskey cutting down on my brain-to-mouth filter, or maybe my boldness comes from feeling more comfortable around the Cooper brothers than I ever have before. But either way, I blurt my next words without thinking.

"Well, he might be well-endowed in terms of money, but let

me tell you, that's about all he's got going for him." I snort a laugh, shaking my head. "My sex life with Dylan sucked."

All three triplets instantly stop what they're doing and look over at me with intrigued expressions.

"Oh? What do you mean it sucked?" Reid asks.

I shrug, my face heating a little as I realize I'm actually talking about my sex life with the triplets.

"It was... boring," I admit. "There were things I wanted to try, but he was never into any of it. He would make me feel like a freak if I asked for anything even vaguely kinky."

"Oh really?" Sebastian polishes off the last sip of whiskey in his glass and sets it down.

All three men are still looking at me, and I can feel the atmosphere in the room shift a little. I should probably try to find a way to steer the conversation into safer territory, but...

Fuck it.

I'm feeling loose and reckless, and this is the most fun I can remember having in a very long time. So instead of zipping my lips or changing the subject, I admit to the one thing that almost no one else in the world knows.

"I made a bucket list after I left Dylan," I say, my voice dropping a little. "Of things I wanted to do... in bed. Every dirty, filthy thing I could think of."

My cheeks burn, and I wait for one of them to make some sort of teasing remark—but instead, the room goes quiet.

17

HAILEY

My pulse races as the silence stretches on for several long seconds.

All three men are still staring at me, and I'm pretty sure not one of them has blinked. The combined weight of their gazes is enough to make me feel like my skin is on fire, and I lick my lips, trying to remember how to breathe.

"Did I hear you right?" Sebastian finally asks, his voice a low rasp. "You have a list of things you want to do in bed?"

"Yes," I whisper. Then I correct myself and add, "Well, technically, not all of them would be done in a bed."

"Fuck," Reid breathes, running a hand through his chocolate brown hair. Nick groans quietly.

"Honestly, I haven't made that much progress on it," I admit. I don't know why I'm still talking, but the silence feels too intense, making me itch with the need to fill it. "The dating scene in LA is abysmal, so I haven't had a lot of opportunities."

The muscles in Reid's jaw work as he shakes his head. "Clearly, whatever *boys* you've been meeting out in LA aren't the kind of real men who could take care of your needs. That's their loss."

"What's on your list, songbird?" Nick asks, his voice strained.

I already feel like my heart is about to pound its way out of my chest, and his question—not to mention the way he's looking at me as he asks it—only makes it worse. My pulse is racing so fast, and there's so much sexual tension swirling in the room, that I start to feel a little lightheaded.

But what do I have to lose? I've already told them that the list exists, so I might as well give them the details. I haven't forgotten what my best friend said to me the other night when I called her after I'd kissed Sebastian, and as wild and reckless as Lorelai's advice seemed at the time... it's starting to feel a little less impossible.

"I can show it to you," I offer, my voice breathless.

Instantly, all three men nod in response.

Swallowing hard, I head up to my room to get it. I'm intensely conscious of all three pairs of eyes following me as I make my way up the stairs, making me feel like a piece of prey for three very hungry hunters.

None of them have moved an inch when I come back a few seconds later with the list clutched in one hand. I don't quite have the guts to read it to them myself, so instead, I hold it out to them like an offering.

Sebastian takes it, and Nick and Reid crowd over his shoulders to read it along with him. Their gazes scan the page, and I hold my breath as I wait to see their reactions.

"'Have my hair pulled during sex. Be spanked. Ride a pierced dick. Be part of an orgy, three way, or four way.'" Sebastian starts reading aloud, and with every word he speaks, I feel my face getting hotter. "'Go down on a guy while being fucked by another. Have sex in a public place. Be fucked wearing only a pair of high heels. Be fucked against a window.'"

Jesus, is he really going to stand here and read the whole

thing? My face flushes again at the thought. I can't believe I'm letting these three men, my brother's best friends, read my deepest sexual fantasies—the things that Dylan was way too vanilla to ever even want to try—like they're front-page news.

But it's even harder to believe how hot I think it is.

Sebastian pauses in his reading, his gaze finding mine as his eyes gleam with heat, and Reid takes the opportunity to pluck the piece of paper from his brother's hand. He reads the next few lines silently, a slow smirk spreading across his face before he speaks them aloud.

"'I think I might have a praise kink. Do I have a degradation kink too? I'd like to find out.'" He lifts a brow at me, almost as if he wants to be the one to help me find out, then continues reading. "'I want a guy to get me all worked up and then make me beg for him. Have a guy spit whiskey into my mouth, then chase it with a soul-stealing kiss.'"

Reid glances up from the paper at me again after the last one, his dimples appearing as his grin widens. "That's vivid."

"Keep going," Nick barks at him, and Sebastian chuckles roughly as Reid's eyes return to the page.

"'Have a guy tell me to get on my knees and crawl to him. Have a guy tug my panties off and then drop to his knees in front of me to eat me out. Sit on a guy's face—like, really sit. Sex while blindfolded. Sex while tied up. Wear a vibrator that someone else controls. Be forced to come over and over until I literally can't take it anymore.'"

Reid pauses once more, something passing across his expression before he reads the final item on my list. "'And last but not least, find a guy who'd actually be into doing all of this with me.'"

The room goes quiet again for a moment, all three of the Cooper brothers staring at me like they're seeing me—or at least seeing this side of me—for the first time. Then Sebastian lets out a low whistle and chuckles.

"You dirty, dirty girl," he drawls. "These are all the things you want to try? Who knew that sweet face hid such a filthy mind?"

My face burns with embarrassment, and I squirm a little under their gazes. I feel kind of like the awkward little sister of their best friend again. But I'm not that girl anymore. I'm a grown woman, and there isn't a damn thing on that list that I should be ashamed of.

I hold his gaze and lift my brow a little, challenging him to say otherwise. But he just shares a look with his brothers instead, and then all three of them turn back to me.

Tension crackles in the silence that sweeps between us, like lightning through a storm cloud. I chew the inside of my lip, waiting for someone to say something to break it. But they just keep staring at me, their gazes hot and probing.

"You know I got pierced because you dared me to, right?" Sebastian finally asks, and my eyes snap to him.

I nod. "Yes. You told me in the hallway last night."

"Well, I have a dare for you."

"What is it?" My throat is so tight and dry I can barely get the words out.

Sebastian raises his eyebrows at me. "I dare you to let us do all of this to you. To let us bring your list to life."

My pulse spikes and my vision swims. I'm so turned on just by the idea of what he's suggesting, but the side of me that's always gone tit for tat with Sebastian whenever he throws down a challenge rises up before I can think about it.

I smirk, cocking a brow at him as I shoot back, "I bet you won't even get halfway through my list."

He grins confidently, running his tongue over his lower lips. "Oh, we'll take that bet. The real question is, do you accept the dare?"

My heart hammers in my ears as the reality of what we're bantering about hits me like a ton of bricks. This is crazy. Like, truly wild. Am I really about to act out my deepest sexual fantasies with the three Cooper triplets? My brother's best friends?

But I know the answer before I've even finished asking myself the question. I want this—want them—so badly. And now that I have the chance to make it a reality, I'd be stupid to let it go. I swallow hard and nod at him.

"Thank fuck," Sebastian murmurs, immediately striding forward.

He stops less than a foot away from me and reaches up to cup my face, tilting it up to meet his eyes.

"I've been thinking about this ever since last night in the hall," he says in a low voice. "I've been wanting to finish what we started."

My eyes widen in shock at his admission, and in the honesty I can hear in his tone. Then he presses his lips into mine, gently but firmly, and it's so much hotter than any fantasy my brain ever could've cooked up. It's our hottest kiss yet, not least of all because I know that this time, we won't stop. And this time, instead of pulling apart to keep it a secret from his brothers, Sebastian and I are doing it right in front of them.

Even with my eyes closed while I kiss Sebastian back, I can feel Nick and Reid's eyes on us, watching intently. And that just turns me on even more.

Sebastian keeps kissing me, his soft, full lips all over mine, until I'm dizzy from the charge of it. As if he can sense the way my legs are wobbling, Sebastian breaks the kiss but keeps my face in his hand. He winks and smiles at me, and I feel like I might pass out from the arousal and adrenaline coursing through me.

"Come here," Reid orders, and my body automatically obeys, as if it's known from the beginning that he should be in charge like this. I turn and walk slowly over to him, stopping when I'm close enough that I have to tilt my head up to meet his eyes.

"I wonder if you're as bossy in bed as you are everywhere else?" I whisper, biting my lip.

He chuckles roughly, reaching up to grip a handful of my hair in one hand. "I'm bossier, trouble. A whole fucking lot bossier. And you'll love it. I promise."

He drags my face toward his and kisses me, and it's nothing like the first time when he kissed me in public because he was pretending to be dating me. It's deep, all-consuming, as if he's been sitting on this desire for years and is finally letting the beast out.

This is as far from a small-town gentleman as I've ever seen him act. Without saying a word, he's completely in charge, using his grip on my hair to angle exactly where he wants me. And he's right, I fucking love it.

But just as I start to lose myself in our kiss, he tugs sharply, breaking the connection between our lips and leaving me gasping as my eyelids flutter. Before I can get any words to form on my lips, he releases my hair and Nick seizes me from behind, spinning me around to kiss him.

Our mouths collide, and without breaking the kiss, he hauls me closer in one easy motion, holding me up against his massive body.

He reaches around me and pulls my shirt up over my head, flinging it to the floor behind us as I claw at his shirt. I want his clothes off just as badly. I'm desperate to feel his hot skin against mine, to put our bodies as close together as possible.

When he finally sets me down, I feel like I can barely stand. My knees are shaking like leaves, and every inch of me, inside and out, starts to buzz like a nest of hornets when I realize the triplets are surrounding me, each of them shirtless.

Three pairs of hands reach for me, touching every bit of exposed skin, and I feel like they're branding me with each touch. Their hands are hot and raw on my flesh, giving me chills, and I spin between the three of them until my gaze lands on Sebastian.

He smiles at me, sinful and so fucking tempting as he cups my jaw with his calloused hand.

"You're going to get fucked the way you deserve, shortcake. I promise."

18

HAILEY

Sebastian's words travel right to the spot between my legs. Whatever part of me still can't believe this is happening falls silent as the rest of me revels in the incredible feeling of having three warm, solid bodies surrounding me. All three of the Cooper brothers are built as fuck, and with so much muscle on display, I feel like a kid at a candy store, wanting all of it and unsure where to even start.

I rise up onto my tiptoes, kissing Sebastian as I rest my hands on his broad chest. But when I draw back and reach for Reid's belt, desperate to get more of their clothes off, he catches me by the wrist and smirks.

"Uh uh, trouble. What did Sebastian just say?" Reid asks, his voice low.

I blink, staring up at him breathlessly as my brain struggles to function for a second. "That... that I'm going to get fucked the way I deserve."

"Exactly." He lifts my wrist, pressing a kiss to the inside of it and making me shiver. "The way you deserve. Which is more than some quick race to the finish line. You've had that shit with other guys—and clearly with Dylan too. But not with us. Tonight isn't gonna be like that. What was it you wrote down?"

Still holding my wrist with one hand, he pulls my list from his back pocket with the other and snaps it open with one easy flick of his wrist. His gaze scans the page quickly, and then he nods, heat smoldering in his blue-gray eyes.

"There it is. 'I want a guy to get me all worked up and then make me beg for him,'" he reads, lingering on each word. His eyes travel slowly back to mine, and when they meet, his expression darkens. "That sounds like a good place to start."

Another jolt of heat courses through me as Reid sets the bucket list aside and crushes his lips to mine again, and his brothers chuckle on either side of me. With Reid holding me in place so that he can kiss me senseless, Sebastian attacks the tender skin on my neck while both their hands deftly remove the rest of my clothes. In a matter of seconds, I'm completely naked between them, at their mercy and loving every second of it.

I lose myself in the almost overwhelming feeling of Reid's and Sebastian's mouths on me until Nick appears in my peripheral carrying a bottle of whiskey. Reid stops kissing me long enough to notice and pulls me away from his mouth by the hair. With a dark smirk, Nick raises the bottle to my eye level and swishes the contents. A thrill instantly rushes through me because I know what it means and what's coming.

We're about to check another item off my list.

"Open," Nick orders in his rough, commanding voice as Reid holds me in place by the hair. I drop my jaw, never taking my eyes off Nick while he lifts the bottle to his mouth and takes a deep swig from it.

He steps closer, gripping my jaw and tilting my head back. My mouth remains open, my heart thudding with anticipation as he leans over me, his fingers running lightly along the curve of my jaw. Then he parts his lips and spits the whiskey directly into my open mouth. It hits my tongue, spicy and strong, and before I can close my lips to swallow, Nick's mouth is on mine.

Our kiss is tinged with the taste of whiskey as it coats our tongues, and when I finally do swallow it, Nick sweeps his tongue deeper into my mouth as if he's trying to chase the drink down my throat. It's so intense that it almost incinerates me, and I let out a plaintive noise against his lips.

"At this rate, we'll have her list finished in a few hours," Sebastian jokes to Reid, who chuckles as Nick continues kissing me like a starving man.

"And I bet our dirty girl loves it, doesn't she?" Reid whispers in my ear, making me whimper again. "Yeah, that's what I thought."

"This is only the start, though," Sebastian adds, his hand sliding over my hip in a leisurely movement. "Like Reid said, this isn't a quick race to the finish line. If we do this, we're going to take our time and make sure you have an experience you'll never forget. Are you sure you can handle it? Can you handle all of us?"

Nick drops his mouth to my neck, giving me a chance to breathe and speak. Despite the tingling in my scalp from Reid's grip, I turn to face Sebastian.

"Are you sure *you* can handle *me*?"

He chuckles, low and gravelly, and I feel like I'm going to dissolve. "Oh, shortcake. You don't have a clue what we're capable of. But you will soon enough." He glances at his brothers, the three of them sharing a look. "Come on. Let's show her."

Nick nods, and Reid lifts me effortlessly into his arms. I yelp in surprise, wrapping my legs around him as he carries me up the stairs. Followed closely by Nick and Sebastian, he takes me to my room and lays me gently down on my bed like I'm the most precious cargo he's ever handled. It's a marked difference from the way all three of them were manhandling me downstairs, but it makes me feel safe and lets me trust that, as intense as this night gets, they're going to take care of me.

As if to prove my point, they surround me on the bed, smiling and stripping off their pants. My eyes can't settle on just one of them, darting from one set of toned abs to another and back again. Now that it's happening, I can finally admit that I've wanted to see all of these men naked since we were teenagers. But I never pictured it happening like this.

One by one, they crawl onto the bed next to me, their hard, muscled bodies flexing with every movement. I'm sure they're finally going to fuck me now, but the three of them descend on me instead, their hands and mouths exploring my body.

Nick and Reid settle on either side of me, each of them sucking one of my nipples into their mouths while Sebastian climbs between my legs and shoves them apart by the knees. He lowers himself down, teasing my clit with little flicks of his tongue and warm gusts of his breath.

I moan, tossing my head from side to side, and Reid chuckles, scraping my nipple with his teeth. "Look how sensitive she is. How badly she wants it."

Nick nods. "Wait until we're finished with her. She won't know what hit her."

"Oh, she'll know," Sebastian murmurs against my pussy. "I'll make sure of that."

He sucks my clit into his mouth, and I whimper, making all three of them groan.

"You were always meant for better than whatever the fuck Dylan did for you," Reid says. "Or any other man, for that matter. You were made to be worshipped."

His words make my breath catch, and when Sebastian starts to fuck me with his tongue, I arch off the bed, feeding more of my breasts to Nick and Reid.

Reid sucks hard on my nipple, then lifts his head with a wet pop. He glances down at where Sebastian's face is buried between my legs, then grips my chin in one hand to force me to meet his gaze.

"You like that, don't you, trouble?" he asks. I nod, and he squeezes my jaw. "Say it."

"I love it."

"That's my girl." His dimples pop out as he smirks and lowers his mouth to mine, cutting off the moan rising at the back of my throat as Sebastian's tongue pushes apart my folds.

"Fuck, wait until you taste her. She's so sweet," Sebastian murmurs, circling my clit again and making me quiver. Honestly, I'm not sure if my reaction is from his words, what he's doing, or both. The thought of them all eating me out like this is almost too much to bear.

"Let me see," Nick says, giving my nipple one last lick before elbowing Sebastian out of the way and climbing between my legs. He dives right in, his scruffy beard dragging against my inner thighs. The harsh prickle of it against the sensitive skin gives me chills, but it's nothing compared to the way it feels when he drags his tongue up my slit.

"Oh my god," I groan, gripping the sheets as my eyes flutter shut. But they jolt back open when Reid takes my nipple between two fingers and gives it a twist.

"That's it, eyes on me," he encourages. "I want to see how good my brother is making you feel."

I nod, my chest heaving for breath as I hold his gaze, following his command automatically. Even as I stare into Reid's blue-gray eyes, I still can't believe this is happening. That I'm being touched like this by not just one of the Cooper triplets, but all three of them—at the same time. If my entire body wasn't flooded with so much sensation, I'd swear I was dreaming.

But when Sebastian's mouth finds my clit again, and his tongue starts twirling around it while Nick plunges his tongue into my pussy, I know without a doubt it's not a dream. I'm being eaten out by two men at the same time, and I'm not going to be able to hold back the orgasm building inside me for much longer.

Reid smiles, clearly reading the ecstasy playing out on my face.

"This is what you wanted, isn't it?" he asks. "To have a man —or more than one—get you all worked up and then make you beg for him?"

I nod eagerly, my bottom lip locked between my teeth to keep from crying out. My legs are starting to shake, my entire body flushed and my clit swollen with arousal. I've had guys go down on me before, but never, *ever* like this. I've never come so fast from being eaten out in my life, but I can already feel the tingling sensation growing in my lower belly.

Reid reaches down, tugging my lip free from my teeth before pressing his thumb into my mouth instead. I bite down on it, sucking hard, the same way Sebastian is sucking on my clit. Nick keeps plunging his tongue in and out of me, and I squirm between the three of them, making noises I've never made before, my hips shifting as I chase the pleasure of their touch.

"Maybe I'm imagining it," Reid murmurs, his eyes dark with desire, "but I'd say you're pretty worked up, aren't you?"

"Oh my god, yes..."

The word ends on a moan as Sebastian gently locks my clit between his teeth and flicks the tip of his tongue repeatedly against it. It makes my toes curl and little stars pop in my vision, and I'm sure he's going to keep going until the torrent welling inside me comes crashing out—but he and Nick both pull away at the last second, just before my orgasm breaks.

"Don't... don't stop," I pant when Reid withdraws his thumb from my mouth, writhing on the bed, desperate to get both of their mouths back on me.

"Listen to you, shortcake. You're so turned on you can barely speak," Sebastian notes, his arousal coated lips curving into a smile as he lifts his head slightly. He massages my clit with his finger, just barely touching it, and I feel like I'm going to lose my damn mind. My body arches up off the bed, hungry for more of his stimulation, but he pulls out of reach, and I groan in frustration as I sink back against the bed.

Because he's right. I'm more turned on now than I think I've ever been in my life. It's difficult to think coherently, much less speak. All I want is to come. For one or all of them to take me over the edge I've been teetering on.

"You want to get off, don't you?" Reid asks, but I'm sure he already knows the answer to that question.

"*Yes*," I breathe.

"Then what are you waiting for? Start begging and maybe we'll think about letting you."

His words send a current racing through me, an electric charge that goes right to my pussy. I'm already wet, but a fresh gush of arousal seeps from me as I realize what they're all waiting for.

"Please," I whisper. "Please..."

He smirks. "Good start. You look so fucking pretty when you beg. Keep going."

I swallow hard, my breath coming in sharp gasps. I've never talked dirty in the bedroom, since Dylan preferred for me to stay quiet. He never talked dirty either, rolling his eyes every time I asked him to try. I feel a little awkward, unsure of what to say, but the intense need coursing through my veins is like a spark of inspiration.

In this moment, I feel like there's nothing I *wouldn't* say if it would get these men to give me what I need.

"Fuck me," I breathe, my cheeks heating even as my pussy clenches. "Make me come. I want it so badly. I need it."

"Even better, shortcake. But we're gonna need a bit more than that," Sebastian rasps and takes another teasing swipe at my clit, making me jump. They're teasing me, denying me what I want, but that only makes it hotter.

"Sebastian's right." Reid nods, trailing his finger over the curve of my breast. "That's not gonna cut it. We already know from your little list that you're a filthy little slut, deep down. But if you want us to fuck you like one, then you'll need to tell us exactly what you want."

I suck in a breath, shocked at the visceral way my body responds to his words. I've never been called a slut before, and I don't know why the hell I find it so hot, but I'm practically panting. It's like his degrading words have unlocked something in me, something I've been hiding for far too long.

But I'm done hiding. And I'm beyond giving a shit that these are my brother's best friends. All I know right now is that I need to come so badly that I can't think of anything else.

My eyes snap to Reid's, and I draw in a deep breath before speaking rapidly.

"I want all three of you to pound me until I'm sore and begging you to stop. I want to feel your hot, sticky cum dripping out of my pussy. And I want you to shut the fuck up and make me come already."

19

REID

My cock, already hard as hell, pulses as I listen to the filthy words pouring from Hailey's lips. And when she tacks on that last sentence, her eyes flashing with a challenge, I nearly lose whatever threads of control I had left.

Fucking hell. I should've known this girl could ruin me.

She's so fucking feisty, bratty and sassy in a way that drives me wild.

Naked and spread out on the bed like this, totally vulnerable and willing, she's fucking gorgeous. It's wrong to be thinking about my best friend's sister like this, to be talking to and treating her the way I am. I'll probably go to hell for this, but I don't care.

I've wanted Hailey for years, but I could never act on it. I knew better. Lucas would kill me if he found out the thought had ever even crossed my mind, and I don't blame him. If the roles were reversed and he was going after my sister, I'd beat his ass to a pulp too.

But judging from the way Sebastian and Nick are eating Hailey up like she's the best thing they've ever tasted, I know I'm not the only one who's been craving her. I sensed my brothers were into her before now, even though we never talked about it, and this just confirms it.

And clearly, Hailey's been hiding some feelings of her own. She's always had a bit of an edge to her, despite her soft exterior, but I had no idea it ran this deep. I'm almost shocked at the demanding way she just ordered us to make her come.

And I'd be lying if I said it didn't drive me crazy. So if that's what this filthy little fiend wants, who am I to say no?

I slide my hand through her hair, palming the back of her head as I kiss her deeply, then pull back to stroke her cheek with my thumb. "Good girl. You did a very good job telling us what you want."

"And yet here I lie, still waiting," she sasses me, a smirk tugging at her lips even as her cheeks flush. I'd never tell her this, but I love the brattier side of her because it brings out my most dominant instincts. There's nothing hotter than a sassy little vixen who's just begging to be tamed.

"Then get on all fours," I order, and her eyes flame.

"Oh, now you're gonna make me do all the work?" she banters back, although she does what she's told.

Sebastian and Nick lean back to give her room to maneuver, and as soon as she's on her hands and knees with her beautiful, perky little ass pointing up in the air, I bring a hand back and clap it hard against one of her perfectly round cheeks. She yelps in surprise but moans as she glances over her shoulder at me with a glint in her wide, expressive green eyes.

"Do it again," she breathes quietly, so I bring my hand down against the other cheek.

"I'm sorry, I couldn't hear you," I say over the cry that pours from her lips. My cock pulses at the sight of her wet, glistening pussy and the bright red handprints blooming on both of her ass cheeks.

"I said do it again," she begs, her voice louder this time.

Fuck. She's gonna kill me.

I share a look with my brothers, who are both clearly thinking something along the same lines. Then I lift my hand and spank her right ass cheek three times in quick succession. She cries out, her arms wobbling and giving way. Her upper body drops lower as she buries her face in the sheets, arching her back like she's silently begging for more. She's so wet now that it's running down the inside of her leg.

Her ass is so red that it looks like a perfect, fresh strawberry, and I brush my fingertips across the marks I've left on her, imagining how good it would feel to sink my teeth into that plump flesh. Goosebumps spread across her skin as she shivers under my touch.

"Fuck," she mewls into the sheets. "God, *fuck*, Reid."

Hearing my name on her lips like that makes me feel almost primal, nearly out of control. All the desire for her that I've been holding back for years is rising like a tidal wave inside me, and I don't think I can hold it back anymore. It'll tear me apart if I try, and I can't resist her. Not when she's kneeling, soaked, and begging for my cock like this.

I can't wait. I need to be inside her.

I've never shared a girl like this with my brothers before, but it feels right with Hailey. If ever there was the perfect woman for us to do it with, it's her. We all know her better than almost anyone else, and that's probably why we were all fighting so hard to win her over even though the whole thing was supposed to be fake.

None of us could ever just sit back and let the others have her. I can't speak for Nick and Sebastian, but seeing her with either of them would've eaten me alive with jealousy. But working together to get her off? Shit, that's easy.

"Quit torturing me and fuck me already," Hailey mumbles into the sheets, rocking her hips back as if searching for a cock to fill her up.

I have to show her who's really in charge here, so I thrust a finger all the way inside her, filling her up until she cries out, her head lifting off the mattress as her back arches.

Nick takes the opportunity to reach under her for her nipple, working it between two fingers while I roughly add a second finger and drive them both in and out of her. If she wants me to fuck her like a hungry little whore, then that's exactly what I'll do.

"Condoms?" I grunt, moving into place behind her as Sebastian tucks a lock of Hailey's wavy honey blonde hair behind her ear.

"I'm on the pill." Hailey shakes her head as she rocks forward and backward on my fingers, squeezing and pulling them deeper into her like she can't get enough. "Are you all clean?"

"Yeah. We get tested regularly. Everything's clear," Nick says as he keeps working her nipple. Hailey whimpers and looks over her shoulder at me.

"Then we don't need protection. I don't want to use condoms. I want to feel everything. Please..."

I can't fight the groan that wells in my chest, and it rumbles past my lips as I withdraw my fingers and start pressing my swollen cock into her. "I don't want anything between us either. You feel so damn good, trouble. It would kill me not to be able to feel every exquisite inch of you choking my cock."

"Yesss..."

Hailey exhales, long and slow, as I work my way inside. My shaft disappears into her tight pussy inch by inch, and when I finally bottom out inside her, she shudders, her entire body trembling.

"Fuck! Oh my god, Reid. Please, fuck me. I need... I need..."

"I know," I rasp, drawing out and driving back in. "Touch yourself for me, baby. You've done such a good job holding on. Now it's time for you to come like we promised. Get yourself off while you take my cock."

I fuck her in a hard, steady pace, and she turns her head to one side, resting her cheek against the sheets as she reaches between her legs for her clit.

Her fingers are a blur on the little nub as she chases her climax, and I grit my teeth, trying to keep a tight rein on my own pleasure.

When she finally falls apart on my cock, clenching and spasming around it, it feels fucking incredible. Hailey gasps for air and whimpers as she falls to pieces, and combined with the way she's gripping my shaft like a vise, it's almost too much for me to take. But somehow, I manage to keep it together until she finishes, burying myself inside her and going still as the tremors work through her body.

I take a second to gather myself and to give her a chance to catch her breath in the aftermath of her orgasm, then slowly start dragging my cock out of her. She inhales sharply, her body jolting with the sensation, but when she exhales, she relaxes just a bit, and I drive all the way back into her.

"Holy shit," she hisses. "It feels so... so intense."

"Can you take more?"

"Yes," she answers immediately, her blonde hair spreading out around her head as she gives a messy nod. She presses back up onto her hands, holding herself on all fours despite the way her arms still shake.

"Good, because you're about to get a *lot* fucking more."

"From all of us," Nick adds.

He reaches down to grip his cock, giving it a long stroke, and Hailey lets out the sexiest, dirtiest little growl of approval. I had no idea she could be this responsive, this eager, but I fucking love it, and I can't wait to see what other sides of herself she's been keeping from us.

"Give it to me. I want it all," she whispers, reaching for Nick.

He lets her stroke him while I keep driving into her from

behind, and something about the sight of her so desperate for all of us makes heat surge in my veins. Sharing a woman with my brothers like this wasn't exactly on my bucket list, but now that we're here, now that I'm watching her stroke his cock while taking mine? It's fucking perfect.

Sebastian settles his back against the headboard, jerking himself off deliberately as he watches the scene play out in front of him, and when Hailey's gaze shifts to him, I can only imagine the hungry look in her eyes. He smirks, squeezing the head of his dick before spreading precum over his pierced shaft.

"Don't worry, shortcake," he promises, his gaze locked with hers. "There's plenty more to go around."

"And it's all for you," Nick says, shifting his position beside us a bit so that he can reach between her legs for her clit. He toys with her, and I watch her ribs expand with each breath as I slide in and out of her. She's so wet from her first orgasm that there's barely any friction, but she's so tight that it makes white light cloud my vision every time I bottom out. "We're gonna make you come over and over."

"Don't let your mouth write checks your cocks can't cash," Hailey shoots back, and Nick chuckles darkly at her before he pinches her clit between his fingers.

She whimpers and spasms around my cock. Her back arches and she stops breathing, so I pick up the pace, my hips slapping against her ass as I fuck her roughly, until finally she releases the breath she's been holding and dissolves into an orgasm all over again.

It's about to push me over the edge too, but before she finishes her climax and takes me with her, I stop moving. I want to come, but not like this. She stays on her hands and knees, heaving for breath with her ass pointed in the air as her body slowly comes down from the high.

"We're gonna cross off another item from your list," I tell her in a low voice, and she glances over her shoulder at me.

"What do you mean?" she whispers.

"You're gonna suck me off while Nick fucks you."

Hailey's warm, wet pussy tightens around me, making it clear just how into the idea she is, so I smirk at her and spank her ass once more before I pull out. Nick moves around behind her as we trade places. As he settles between her legs, I kneel next to Hailey on the bed and take a fistful of her hair to direct her mouth to my dick while Nick grips her hips, making her eyelids flutter.

"Open wide, trouble," I command.

I drag the tip of my cock against her lips to prompt her, my blood heating at the little whimper that leaks out of her mouth.

"If it's too much, tap my thigh," I say, dropping my head to catch her gaze. "I'm not gonna take it easy on you, but you're still in control. Got it?"

She nods, her eyes wide and luminous. When her mouth drops open, I slide my cock between her full lips, and she groans around me. I have no idea how many times she's done this, but the way she starts bobbing on my length immediately makes her look filthy and eager in the best way.

"Fuck, that's it. Suck my fucking cock," I grunt, keeping her hair locked in my fist so I can guide her movements. "You wanted to see how bossy I can be? Here you go."

I thrust my cock deeper, hitting the back of her throat, and she whimpers as Nick presses into her at the same time.

"Goddamn, you got this pussy nice and warmed up for me, Reid," Nick grunts, his gaze locked on the place where he's sliding in and out of Hailey.

"Maybe I'll get her mouth good and ready for you next." I drag Hailey off my cock for a moment to look her in the eyes. "Would you like that?"

In answer, she lunges for me again, taking my length all the way down her throat until her nose brushes my lower abs. Nick is rougher with the way he fucks her, more intense, just like he is about pretty much everything, but Hailey doesn't seem to mind. In fact, it only seems to unleash her inner vixen even more. She seems completely lost to the pleasure of it as she rocks between us.

"God, I can't wait to feel you work my cock like that," Sebastian tells Hailey as he keeps stroking himself. "But I'm in no hurry. We all know you're saving the best for last."

That gets a chuckle out of me. "I dunno about that. Looks like she's having the time of her life to me."

"She's taking us so damn well," Nick tells him, and Hailey groans again around my shaft. The vibration travels right to my balls, and I know I'm getting close. Hell, I was right on the edge before Nick and I traded, but her mouth feels just as good as her pussy did.

"See? Just like I told you, we're going to fuck you like you deserve," I tell her hoarsely, and she sucks me faster in response, gagging on my cock.

"*Fuck*," I grunt, my head tipping back. "You're gonna make me come if you keep that up, trouble. Is that what you want?"

"Yes. *Yes*. Give it to me. Let me taste you," she begs, her words coming out in short gasps as she draws back for a second. Her hand wraps around my shaft and squeezes, and she follows her mouth up and down my length.

"You've got to earn it first. I want to see you come again. Give Nick the same ride you gave me," I tell her. "Let him feel how tight you get when you fall apart."

I pull her off my cock again, since I know I won't be able to last with her mouth on me. She stares up into my eyes, her deep green irises flashing in the light, before she narrows them and bites her lower lip.

With a determined expression, she starts throwing her hips backward to meet Nick's hard thrusts. Her face contorts with each pump, and little groans and whimpers spill out of her until their rhythm gets so fast that she can't control herself anymore.

"There you go, give in to it. When you do, I'll give you something to keep you quiet," I tell her, gripping my cock at the base. She tries to take it in her mouth, but I don't let her, and her whimper sounds like a mixture of frustration and arousal. She really does want it badly, and that drives me fucking crazy.

Truth is, I could come at any second just from watching Nick take her from behind like this. And that intense look she's giving me isn't helping. I squeeze my cock again while I watch to keep myself right on the edge, my heart thumping hard against my ribs, until finally her jaw drops and her brows stitch together.

"Oh my god," she whimpers as Nick's thrusts turn erratic.

I know she's about to come, so I grip her chin and slide my cock back down her throat. She sputters around it, sliding her tongue along my shaft and swallowing over and over as I hit my peak right along with her. She sucks me hungrily, hollowing her cheeks, and I feel like she's drawing a piece of my soul out through my cock.

It's intense and easily the hardest I've come in my whole life, but somehow, she swallows it all and keeps sucking me through the aftershocks as my hips jerk and buck.

"So fucking good," Nick groans, baring his teeth as he stills inside her. "Jesus, I'm not ready to come yet."

She shudders between us, filled completely by the two of us until my cock finally starts to soften and slips from her mouth. I release Hailey's hair and massage her scalp, worried I might have been too rough with her, but she grips my semi-hard cock in one hand and laps at it softly, cleaning me up while Nick gives her a break.

I tip her chin up to meet my gaze, then lean over to kiss her. I taste my cum on her tongue, and it makes my spent cock twitch like it's trying to rise again already.

"Fuck, that's so hot," I whisper when we part, and she grins at me like the little sex demon she is. "Do you think you can still take more?"

A flash of trepidation passes through her expression, reminding me that despite how well she's been doing, this is all new for her.

But there's not a hint of doubt in her voice as she nods and whispers, "I don't want this to ever end."

20

HAILEY

Nick lets out a low noise behind me, his grip on my hips tightening as his cock pulses. I'm so sensitive from how many times I've come already that he feels even bigger than he is—and he's fucking huge.

Both he and Reid have been giving me so much pleasure that it's impossible to focus on just one particular part of it. It's overwhelming in the best way, so I'm thankful for the breather, even though I meant it when I told Reid that I didn't want this to end.

I can't get enough. I'm not sure I'll ever be able to.

Reid grins down at me, his blue-gray eyes flashing with something that almost looks like pride, and wipes the corner of my mouth with his thumb.

"Good," he says, then turns to Sebastian. "Get over here and see how fucking good this mouth feels."

My heart pounds in my chest as Sebastian takes Reid's place, his swollen, pierced cock jutting out from his body. I lick my lips, staring at it. Ever since I learned about his piercings, I've been dying to know what they'd feel like inside me, and knowing that I'm about to find out makes me whine softly with desire.

I fist his cock gently, then tilt it up a bit more to admire the studs lining the underside of it. There are at least ten of them, and I can't stop myself from dragging my tongue up the line of piercings, lingering on each stud.

"Don't be scared. Suck it."

Sebastian's voice is rough, and I realize in a rush that it's because of me. His cock pulses against my palm, a dribble of precum leaking from the tip as if it's begging me to take it into my mouth.

"I'm not scared," I whisper, and it's the truth. "I think it's hot."

"Good." He swallows. "Because like I told you, I got them for you."

I can't help the way my body reacts to those words, and Nick grunts as I clench around him. Sebastian moves a little closer, allowing me to take him into my mouth, and I slowly work my way down his shaft, feeling the studs slide against my tongue on my way down.

"Mm," Sebastian groans. "That feels so fucking good, shortcake. Just wait until you feel them inside your pussy. You're gonna love it."

I draw back a bit, but Nick starts fucking me again before I can say anything in response, turning the start of my words into a moan. The image of riding Sebastian's cock, feeling his piercings rub against me in all the right ways, sends a shiver of arousal through me.

Nick must pick up on it, because he starts pounding away at me again, his powerful hands and fingers digging into my waist as he uses that grip to hold me steady. My entire body responds to his thrusting, deepening the arch in my back so I can take him even deeper.

"You were made for this," Sebastian murmurs, trailing his fingers lightly over my cheek. "Your mouth feels like heaven, wrapped around me."

"You have no fucking idea, Seb," Nick mutters, his voice a strained rasp. "Fuck, you're blowing my mind, songbird."

The praise makes my body sing, and it goes right to my head. This entire night has felt like something out of a dream—a filthy perfect dream—and I love how effortlessly they can go from talking to me like their dirty little whore to their prized princess. I want to be both of those things for them. I'd gladly do anything they ask, as long as they don't stop.

"I'm gonna fill you up. Gonna come inside this tight pussy. Can you handle that?" Nick asks, slowing down his movements. I don't answer, instead throwing my hips back onto his cock, and he lets out a sound somewhere between a laugh and a groan. "I'll take that as a yes."

With another grunt and a hard thrust into me, he erupts, and a moan gets trapped in my throat as I feel his warmth flooding me. I rock my hips back and forth, milking every last drop out of him while I keep sucking furiously on Sebastian's cock.

"Me too." Sebastian's jaw is tight, his eyes hooded. "Fuck, watching them fuck you got me so close to the edge. I can't last much longer. Come with us, baby. Come on. One more time."

I'm about to shake my head, since there's no way I should be able to finish again... but before I can, a tingling sensation starts to flood my veins, and I realize I was wrong.

Fuck. Fuck, fuck...

My final orgasm hits me like a comet, harder and faster than any of the times I've come before. I writhe between them, whimpering and drooling on Sebastian's cock as my body trembles like it has a fever it's trying to sweat out.

"Fuck, Hailey. Don't stop, don't stop, right there—"

Sebastian breaks off with a curse as he comes too, and I'm vaguely aware of swallowing his release as the pleasure wracking my body seems to go on and on. I lose track of time and space while the climax rocks me, and when I float back into my body and consciousness a few seconds later, I find Sebastian beaming down at me.

"Ho-ly shit," he drawls, gently brushing my sweat-soaked hair out of my face. "That was incredible to watch, shortcake. You're something else."

"You're fucking right about that," Nick agrees, pulling out slowly and slapping my ass with one hand.

I jump, but I can barely take in their words because I'm borderline delirious from all the orgasms I've had. I've never come this many times in a row before—but I can tell from the way Sebastian is looking at me that this won't be the last time either.

"You need a break, baby?" he asks, squeezing his slowly deflating cock before stroking it a few times. "It's been a lot. None of us would judge you for tapping out."

My eyes widen, a surge of the competitive drive that he always brings out in me flooding my chest.

There's never been a challenge Sebastian Cooper laid down that I didn't rise to, and this certainly isn't going to be the first.

"Are you worried you'll lose our bet?" I shoot back, although the sass I was going for is a bit ruined by the rasp in my voice from deep-throating two cocks.

He arches a brow, his cock thickening as he strokes it again. "Are you reconsidering my dare?"

"Fuck, no." I lunge forward a little, wrapping my lips around the head of his cock to prove it, and his chuckle morphs into a deep, guttural groan as his cock swells.

When I pop off him for air, he laughs again. "Okay, okay. I get it. You're not backing down from the dare."

"Definitely not."

"Good." He catches my chin and leans down to kiss me, then whispers against my lips. "Because you're gonna ride my pierced cock just like your bucket list says."

I fight back a shiver, turned on all over again just by the

thought. "Are you really ready to go again? I thought guys usually needed longer than that to recover."

He chuckles, glancing down at his cock, which is fully hard again. "I guess my body makes an exception to that rule when there's a goddess in my bed."

I know he's probably just being his usual flirtatious self, but that doesn't stop my heart from thudding against my ribs as he straightens up and turns to his brothers.

"I want her to ride me. Help her up."

Nick and Reid grab me under each arm, lifting me carefully. Sebastian lies down underneath me, and his brothers lower me down onto his cock like a queen on her throne.

He's a lot to take, unlike anything I've ever felt before, and I'm not sure if I can do it. It's hot as hell, but it feels a little weird and uncomfortable. Sebastian rubs my thighs.

"It's okay, just breathe. You can do this, baby." I wince as Reid and Nick let me go and Sebastian slides deeper into me. He reaches up and cups my cheek with one hand. "You trust me, right? You know I'd never hurt you."

"None of us would. And if any of us tried, the other two would kill him," Reid says, his eyes flashing possessively as he watches his brother's pierced cock disappear inside me.

"I trust all three of you," I say firmly, pressing down another inch. I've been fantasizing about this ever since we crossed naked paths in the hallway, and now that the moment's finally here, I'm not about to let anything ruin it.

"Then breathe, shortcake," Sebastian says, still holding my face in one of his hands. I nod and take a deep breath, then let it out slowly. "There you go. Just like that. I'm halfway in. Before you know it, you'll have all of me inside you."

That makes me want him even more than I already do, so I repeat the breathing several times until Sebastian lets out a shuddering groan.

"Look down, shortcake," he murmurs. "Look how fucking well you take me."

I glance down to the place where I'm stretched around him, and my breath catches as I realize I've done it. Every inch of his pierced cock is inside me. It's a filthy sight, my pussy flushed and swollen, my wetness and Nick's cum smeared across my thighs—but somehow, it's perfect too. It's a visceral reminder that all of this isn't just a dream. It's messy, and it's *real*.

"Fuck me," I whisper, the words coming easier than they did the first time I begged these men. "Fuck me, Sebastian. Show me what it's like."

A determined look passes across his face, and he bucks his hips upward, splitting me open with his cock. I gasp in surprise, falling forward a bit and bracing my hands on his chest. It feels incredible, and I swear I can feel each of the studs of his piercings inside me.

"Oh my god," I hiss. Those are the only words I can manage to speak. I've never felt anything like this before, and I love it. It's better than anything my fantasies could've ever cooked up, and Sebastian must know it, because the smile that spreads across his face is ravenous.

"Everything okay?"

"It's fucking perfect," I breathe.

"Just like you." He bucks up into me again. "Work your clit for me, baby. I want to see you get yourself off while you ride my dick."

I do it immediately, somehow forgetting that I wasn't sure I could come even *once* more several minutes ago. Now I feel desperate for another orgasm, for a release to all the pleasure building inside me.

"Holy fuck," I gasp as Sebastian settles into a rhythm beneath me. One of my hands slides down to circle my clit, and my free hand flails until Reid catches it and links his fingers between mine, squeezing tight. Nick strokes one of my shoulders and rests his other hand on top of mine above my clit like he wants me to show him how to please me. Like he wants to help.

"We've got you, songbird," he murmurs into my ear, his lips whispering against my lobe and turning my skin into a battlefield of sensations fighting for my focus. Determination flares somewhere inside me, and I use Reid's hand to steady myself as I start bouncing on Sebastian's cock, my fingers and Nick's working my clit together.

"Never knew it would be like this," Sebastian says intensely, staring into my eyes. "Better than I ever could've imagined."

His words, combined with the pierced cock driving in and out of me steadily, are almost too much for me to handle. My body and brain feel like they're on overload, and every time his studs slide against my walls, massaging my pussy lips, my breath catches.

My head falls back as a moan starts working its way up my throat. Sebastian's thrusts take on a new tone, faster and more desperate, like he's racing me to the finish line.

"Fuck! *Fuck*, don't stop," I mewl as I grind my fingers in harsh circles against my clit and crash into the most intense orgasm I've had so far.

Reid helps me stay upright, and Nick keeps massaging my clit as every nerve ending in my body catches fire. Sebastian fucks me through it, taking deep, hard strokes. Our bodies clap together, and I feel myself soaking him, squeezing and flexing around his cock, until finally he bucks into me one last time and lets out a shuddering groan.

I keep bouncing on him, working him over with my pussy, while he floods me with his cum, and he never takes his blazing blue-green eyes off mine. It's like he can see into my soul, like he can see the exact moment when I fall apart for him.

It goes on for what feels like forever, and when my muscles finally start to relax, I wilt against Reid, who catches me against his chest and helps lower me off Sebastian onto the bed. I snuggle up against Sebastian's toned, sweat-slicked chest, and Reid lies down behind me, sandwiching me between the two of them.

Nick looks down at the three of us for a moment, his thick dark brows drawn together as he takes in the sight of us. Unabashedly naked, he strides from the room, his tree trunk thighs and muscled ass flexing with each step. I hear the faucet running down the hall before he returns with a wet, warm wash cloth. Reid rolls me onto my back, and he and Sebastian work together to spread my cum-soaked legs apart so Nick can kneel between them and gently wipe my thighs and pussy.

I'm sex-dazed and already feeling sore in muscles I didn't know I had, but it's still one of the most tender, surprising things I've ever had a guy do for me. It never would've crossed Dylan's mind, that's for sure.

"Thank you," I murmur, struggling to keep my eyes open, and Nick raises an eyebrow at me. "You don't have to do that. It feels nice, though."

He frowns. "What? You've never had a guy take care of you like this after sex?"

"No," I admit sheepishly.

Reid grunts, anger clear in his tone. "Are you fucking serious? That piece of shit ex-fiancé of yours never did this?"

My face flushes, because they're making me feel like I've been accepting scraps for my entire life. *Maybe I have.*

I shake my head, shrugging one shoulder. "No. Like you said, he was a piece of shit."

"He's worse than that. He's a fucking parasite."

Sebastian nods in agreement, bringing my hand to his mouth to kiss it gently. "You deserve so much better than him and what he did to you, shortcake."

A sudden wave of emotion tightens my throat and steals my breath. How are these men all so good to me? I'm not sure if I believe them that I deserve it, and I have no idea what will happen next, but I'm so grateful that they gave me this night.

That they showed me how good things can be.

"Thanks," I whisper, blinking quickly to banish the tears that burn in my eyes. I'm not sure I trust my voice enough to say anything else, so I snuggle back up against Sebastian's chest, his heart beating softly in my ear.

Reid settles on our other side again, with Nick on that side too. The brothers keep talking to each other, and I catch bits of their conversation, but it's hard to keep my eyes open with three warm bodies surrounding mine and Sebastian's steady heartbeat lulling me to sleep.

My eyelids flutter until I can't fight their heaviness, and they fall closed.

21

HAILEY

IN THE MORNING, I emerge slowly from one of the deepest sleeps I've ever experienced. I was so tired, both mentally and physically, that I don't think I moved an inch or twitched a muscle all night.

As I blink a few times to clear my vision, I realize I'm sandwiched between Reid and Sebastian on the bed. I'm facing Sebastian, with my chin nearly resting against his chest. His body is curled around mine, his arm thrown over my torso. Behind me, Reid is cuddled up close, his large hand resting on my hip.

I feel like I'm wrapped in a protective little cocoon, and I let myself stay in a dreamy state for a few minutes, breathing in the scent of the two men and nestling into the comfort of being surrounded by their warm bodies.

But just as I'm starting to drift back to sleep, I feel something cool and wet against my foot.

"*Ah!*" I hiss, squirming a little at the ticklish feeling.

I lift up my head and see Bruno standing by the foot of the bed, licking my foot.

As happy as I am that he seems to be getting used to me, I'm so ticklish that I'm afraid I'm going to accidentally kick him in the face—and I'm pretty sure that would set us all the way back to square one. So I slowly pull my foot away, slipping it back beneath the covers.

The big hound dog looks up at me with plaintive, disappointed eyes for a second. Then he perks up his ears a little, swinging his head away from me as his attention shifts to something on the floor. His head bobs down and out of sight for a second, and then he pops back up with a pair of my panties between his teeth.

"Bruno, *no*," I whisper, trying not to wake the brothers. "Bad dog! No more panties!"

I flick my foot at him, but he just stands there showing off the fact that he's gotten ahold of my panties again, like it's worthy of praise. I try to hook the edge of the panties with my toe, but as if he can sense that I'm attempting to steal them back, he darts away and barrels out of the bedroom door.

Shit.

He escaped, and he's once again taken my panties hostage.

I slump back against the pillows between Sebastian and Reid, listening to the soft thudding sound of Bruno's paws on the stairs. I hear the sound of a low male voice next, which must belong to Nick, since he isn't here in the bed with us.

A minute or so later, he comes to stand in the doorway.

He's wearing low slung sweats that cling to the bulge hanging between his thighs, and no shirt. The sight of him standing there shirtless, with muscles rippling and soft fabric outlining his massive cock, is enough to make a girl want for nothing else in life.

"Uh, I think these are yours," he says, holding up the pair of panties that he's holding delicately in his left hand.

I nod, then blink as I realize they aren't even the pair that the dog just ran out the door with. They're a different pair entirely that Bruno must've stolen some other time.

"Yeah. They are." I grin, keeping my voice low. "And if you

happen to see a light blue pair lying around somewhere, those are mine too. It would seem that your dog has a serious panty obsession."

Nick's face flushes deeply, and I laugh quietly as I sit up. Reid and Sebastian stir a little at the disturbance, each of them making low, muffled noises as they start to rouse from sleep.

"You can put those on the dresser," I tell Nick. "And honestly, I don't mind. It feels like a bit of a cheat to win my way to a dog's heart with underwear, but hey, if it works, I'll take it."

Nick smiles at that, although the color doesn't fade from his cheeks.

"He *does* like you," he confirms. "I've never seen him take to anyone this fast. Hell, he's still on the fence about my brothers."

As if his ears have been burning from all our talk about him, Bruno pads back into the room at that moment, sniffing around on the floor as his ears hang low.

"No, Bruno." Nick shakes his head, stepping into the room after his dog. "No more panties, you thief."

But instead of listening to him, the dog comes closer to the bed and buries his nose against my foot again.

I lean forward, stretching out my hand to reach down and pet him on the head. Bruno lays his chin against the mattress, his jowls spreading out and making him look adorably melty as I rub his ears.

"Good boy," I whisper. "That's a good boy. No panties, just scratches."

Beside me, Reid and Sebastian both sit up in the bed. Sebastian leans over and kisses me on the cheek, and Reid smiles, resting a hand on the top of my thigh. The feel of his warm palm against my skin ignites all of my nerve endings, which still feel hypersensitive from last night.

I was distracted by the dog when I first woke up, but now that everyone is awake, I'm suddenly very conscious of the fact that all three of the Cooper brothers fucked me mere hours ago.

Internally, I start to panic a bit, my mind racing.
Was that a mistake?
Do they regret it?
Do I regret it?
No, definitely not.
What happens now?

"Um, should we talk about this?" I squeak, glancing from one Cooper triplet to the next to the next. "I mean, about what happened? What exactly are we doing here?"

"We're doing exactly what we said we would." Reid's voice drops a little, his hand traveling higher up my thigh. "We're helping you with your bucket list. Was that not clear last night?"

Goosebumps spread over my skin, my clit throbbing immediately at the reminder of what they did to me.

"No, it was. But—"

I cut my sentence short because I'm not really sure how I want to finish it. Do I really want to tell them how I'm feeling about all of this? Hell, do I even *know* how I'm feeling about all of it?

"I can hear the gears grinding in your head, trouble," Reid says, a chuckle rumbling in his chest. "Don't overthink it. You had fun, didn't you?"

I swallow. "Yes."

"And do you want to keep working on your list?"

"Yes."

"Then there you go." Sebastian nudges my shoulder. "We're happy to keep going until every single item has been checked off."

My breath picks up a little at that. Reid is right. I'm totally overthinking this. I've somehow stumbled into an alternate reality where all three of my brother's best friends have made it their mission to work as a team to fulfill every one of my sexual fantasies. I should just be enjoying this, rather than letting my mind run wild with all the ways things could go wrong.

But still...

"I don't want things to get... weird," I admit. "You guys are Lucas's best friends, and you've become my friends too. I don't want to do anything to jeopardize that. I don't want to risk losing you."

"You won't." Nick is still standing at the foot of the bed, his arms crossed and his expression unreadable.

"But we can lay out a few ground rules if that would help," Reid offers, giving my leg a squeeze.

"Like what?"

He shrugs. "Well, we can call this a friends with benefits situation, if you want. Because you're right, you're our friend too. So we'll keep it light, no strings, nothing serious."

Something in my chest twinges a bit at those words, a spike of disappointment cutting through me. But I know that what he's saying is for the best. One wild night—or even several of them—is way less complicated than the reality of what it would be like if it turned into something more. I don't even know how that would work, and it's terrifying to think of losing these men from my life entirely. Or even worse, coming between them somehow and splintering the tight brotherly bond they have.

"Simple is good." I nod, glancing from Reid to Sebastian and then Nick. "And, um, I don't think we should tell my brother about this."

"Yeah." Nick sighs and sits down on the bed, running a hand over Bruno's floppy ears. "I hate lying to him. But it's probably for the best."

"I think it is." I pull my knees up a little. "I don't like lying to him either, but if he punched Reid when he saw him dancing with me, I can't imagine what he'd do if he knew... what else you guys had done to me."

I'm flushing all over again, as if I wasn't wantonly begging for their cocks last night. But I have *never* been fucked like that, and it's still a bit hard for me to wrap my mind around the fact that it actually happened to me. It feels like it must've been someone else—someone who got all of her Christmas wishes and then some.

"Besides," I add quickly. "Since we're just fooling around for a little while, there's no reason for you guys to risk your friendship with him. I don't plan to be in Chestnut Hill for long, so there's an end date to all of this. And then things will go back to the way they were, and he never has to know."

Sebastian rubs at the scar on his eyebrow, looking at me thoughtfully. "Well, he thinks that you're just fake dating all of us right now so that Dylan will leave you alone and the rest of the gossips in town will get off your back. So let's just leave it at that. It will explain away the time we're spending with you, and we can all just keep the fact that you're actually sleeping with us on the down low."

"Okay."

I nod in agreement, and Reid does too. Nick hesitates for a moment, indecision on his face, and I wonder if he's warring with himself over whether or not he's okay with lying to Lucas, or if there's something else holding him back. He doesn't exactly look happy about it, but he finally dips his chin in a quick nod as well.

"Agreed," he mutters.

We stay in bed and talk for a while longer, laying out a few more parameters of our arrangement and deciding whether this will change how we act when we're in public. We all agree that it shouldn't. The story around town is that all three of the triplets are competing for my affection, not that they're sharing me, so they'll still display some jealousy toward each other and mostly go out with me one-on-one in public.

Once I feel like I have my feet solidly under me, I feel a lot better. This thing we're doing seems less scary and dangerous and more fun and hot, and I'm incredibly relieved that we all seem to agree it's going to happen again. Last night wasn't nearly enough.

My list isn't done, and I need to accumulate a lifetime of memories in whatever time we have together, because I have a feeling I'll be returning to those memories time and time again.

"Good." Sebastian stretches his arms over his head. "Now that we've sorted all of that out, who's ready for some breakfast? I'm fucking starving."

"I am," I say fervently. Turns out, sex with three men works up quite an appetite.

We all clamber out of bed, but as my feet hit the floor and I stand up, I wince.

Nick looks over at me protectively. "You okay?"

"Yeah, I'm fine." I give him a quick smile, since I can already see the worry gathering in his eyes. "I think that I'm just a little sore from last night."

"Is it bad if I take that as a compliment?" Reid grins, and I can't help but laugh.

"No, it's not bad. You should definitely take it as a compliment. The three of you made my body do things I didn't even know I was capable of."

"And what's that you were saying about us not even being able to make it halfway through your list?" Sebastian teases as he pulls his pants on. "I'd say we made it almost halfway through that list in one go last night. Pretty impressive, isn't it?"

My sassy side rears its head, because I can't let these three men get *too* cocky. I grab a robe from the dresser and tug it on, then plant a hand on my hip. "Well, there are three of you and only one of me, so I'd say by default that means my stamina is more impressive than all of yours combined."

Reid reaches out in a flash, catching my hand and tugging me toward him so quickly that I collide with his chest. His arm bands around me, his blue-gray eyes glinting as he murmurs, "I think you're being a brat. Maybe you need another spanking?

Or should I fuck your smart mouth again? Is that what you need?"

My blood heats at his words. I've always enjoyed pushing his buttons and sassing him back when he gets too bossy, but this takes it to a whole new level. It's even more fun to get under his skin when I know that the consequences will be very, very enjoyable.

"Maybe I need both," I murmur, arching a brow in silent challenge.

He hauls me closer against his body, one hand sliding down to grope my ass—but before he can do either of the things he just promised, Nick tugs me out of his arms, insisting on feeding me before anything else happens.

I'm not going to argue with that, despite the fact that the arousal flooding my pussy is definitely helping to banish some of the soreness. My stomach is rumbling, and I could use some coffee. None of us got a lot of sleep last night.

"I'll meet you guys downstairs," I tell them. "I'm just gonna hop in the shower really quick first."

"Are you sure?" Sebastian smirks. "We like you dirty, shortcake."

I blush and roll my eyes at him, grabbing some clothes from the dresser as they all head out of the room.

"Oh, and you should sing while you're in the shower," Sebastian calls over his shoulder as they go. "I want to hear you belting it out. Your voice is fucking beautiful."

Normally, I would shy away from anyone asking me to sing. I have too many bad memories of Dylan talking down to me and constantly telling me how my voice was "too shrill" or "off key." The reservation and self-doubt have piled up so high that I always get nervous if I know that anyone is listening. But for some reason, I feel like giving Sebastian exactly what he requested this morning. Even though they're probably not the most objective judges, the

Cooper brothers really seem to mean it when they say they enjoy my singing.

And I like that. A lot.

I grin at the spot where they disappeared, then finish grabbing stuff to change into and snatch up my phone before padding down the hall.

When I step into the bathroom, I set my clothes down on the closed toilet lid. Despite the fact that three guys live alone here, the bathroom is actually really nice. I take a moment to admire the custom cabinets that Reid must've built, and chuckle softly at the fact that even though Nick's whole job is to put *out* fires, there are a few delicious smelling candles lining the bathroom shelves and window ledge. I wonder if Addison got those for them, although it wouldn't surprise me if she didn't. I could be way off, but I can picture Reid being a bath guy, especially if he's sore from a long day of working in his shop.

Before I turn the water on, I decide to call Lorelai. I did, after all, promise to keep her apprised of all the juicy tidbits that happened while I'm here. And last night tops the charts of *juicy tidbits*.

"Hey, Hailey!" She answers exuberantly after two rings. "Oh god, *please* say you have something exciting to tell me, because I'm dying of boredom over here."

I lean against the bathroom wall, keeping my voice low. "I dunno, does letting the triplets read my naughty list, and then letting them *do* half of what's on the list to me last night count as exciting?"

There's silence on the other end for so long that I actually pull the phone away from my ear for a second, worried that we've gotten cut off. The call is still connected, so I put it back to my head, my brows furrowing.

"Lorelai? You there?"

"*What!?*"

Her scream is so loud that I definitely lose partial hearing on that side.

"Ow, ow, ow," I hiss, leaning my head away.

"Oh, sorry." Her voice drops to a more normal volume as she repeats, "Whaaaat?"

This time, she draws the word out, extending the single syllable into at least three. Knowing she won't be satisfied with anything less than every single detail, I quickly launch into the story, filling her in on the crawl space incident and everything it led to—including the revelation of my naughty list. She throws in a few comments or startled exclamations here and there, and when I finish the story by telling her how I woke up sandwiched between two of the men this morning, she lets out a long breath.

"Wow. So you really fucking did it! I'm in shock. I'm in awe." She chuckles, then adds, "So how were things this morning? What's the vibe? Is this a one-time thing, or…?"

"Not a one-time thing." I bite my bottom lip as a grin breaks out on my face. "We're not through the list yet. But we set some terms."

"Terms?"

"Yeah." I tell Lorelai what the guys and I agreed to—only temporary, no telling my brother, no strings attached.

"Huh." I can hear the slight hesitancy in her voice as she speaks. "Were these terms their idea, or yours?"

"Um, all of ours," I say with a shrug, trying to remember who exactly said what.

"And you really think you're gonna be able to abide by them?" she asks, skepticism in her tone.

"Yeah, of course. Why not?"

She laughs. "Because I know you, Hailey. You wear your heart on your sleeve. And as much as you like to act like your pussy is a sassy bitch, we both know you're led by your heart—not your head, and especially not your crotch."

She's not wrong. Sometimes my best friend knows me even

better than I'd like to admit. But it doesn't matter if Lorelai is right or not, because the guys and I agreed to those rules, so this is just how it's going to be. There's no point in overthinking it, and I honestly don't want to. I just want to enjoy it.

"It'll be fine," I promise her. "I'm having way more fun being back in Chestnut Hill than I thought I would. And I'm actually putting a dent in my list, which I was starting to think would never happen."

"Okay. If you're sure." Her tone lightens a bit. "And I want to hear which line items get knocked out next, so keep me posted! Some of us are going through a dry spell."

I chuckle sympathetically, because I know all about being in a dry spell. I've gone from one extreme to the other and I couldn't be happier about it.

After getting a quick update from her—she'll be sticking around LA for the holidays since she's a born and bred California girl—I promise to call again soon and hang up. Then I turn on the water and step into the shower.

At first, I stand under the gentle spray in silence, getting lost in my thoughts as I relive some of the highlights from last night. I don't even notice that I've started to hum until after I'm already doing it.

Despite the self-doubt Dylan left me with, music still comes naturally to me. But as soon as I become aware that I'm actually singing loudly enough for someone to hear, I start getting self-conscious again.

I wish that asshole hadn't left me with such lasting scars. I wish I could go back to being who I was before I met Dylan and became way too wrapped up in his narcissistic manipulation. I used to embrace life wholeheartedly and welcome any chance I got to sing in front of a crowd. I used to believe in myself and my abilities without question. And I didn't ever lessen myself or shrink myself down in order to fit into someone else's box.

Then Dylan Montgomery happened, and I let him stomp

around in my head and leave his dirty footprints there long after I left him.

No more. I'm done with that.

I shift from humming one of my favorite songs to opening my mouth and singing it. There's something about the acoustics in a running shower that make everything sound good, like having a backup singer made of raindrops that amplifies only the best parts of your voice.

Lathering shampoo into my hair, I start to really belt it out just like Sebastian told me to, closing my eyes and inhaling the wildflower scented steam all around me.

I sing the entire rest of the time I'm in the shower.

And it feels fucking amazing.

22

HAILEY

When I head down to the kitchen a while later, freshly showered and with slightly damp hair, I stop short in the doorway as I take in the sight of the enormous amount of food laid out on the table.

"How long was I up there?" I ask, my jaw dropping.

Reid chuckles. "Well, like you said, there are three of us and one of you. So the time it takes you to shower is the time it takes the three of us to do..." He gestures to all the food. "This."

"Wow." I grin. "You guys seem really committed to making sure I don't starve." Every place we've gone, they've practically ordered one of everything off the menu, and there's enough food here to feed a small army. "Is that a fake boyfriend thing?"

Sebastian strides toward me, taking my hand and tugging me into the room. "No. It's a real friends with benefits thing. We want to make sure you keep your strength up."

The look he gives me is so filthy that I flush instantly. It would be so easy to fall back into bed with them right now—*so* easy.

"Besides," he continues, settling me at the table. "I'm pretty sure we covered most of your faves."

I sit down and look at the spread, blinking as I realize that it is indeed an assortment of many of my favorite foods. Everything from eggs Benedict to French toast, to bacon and hash browns.

"How did you know I like all this stuff?"

Nick shrugs. "We know you."

He says it so simply, as if that's supposed to explain it all away. As if it's no big deal.

But it feels like a big deal, especially coming from this mountain of a man who so often used to barely even speak to me. I used to think it was because he didn't like me that much, but I'm pretty sure I was mistaken about that. Because even if he wasn't talking to me, he was paying *attention*, and that hits something in my chest that makes me smile softly at him.

He clears his throat and looks away, almost as if he's embarrassed by the admission that he knows me so well. I glance away too, because Lorelai is right. I do wear my heart on my sleeve, and I need to be careful about not getting too attached, especially now.

"Well, I'm not sure how much strength you think I'm gonna need," I joke lightly, turning my attention to the plates spread out before me. "But with this much food, I might need to make another list."

Reid's cloud gray eyes spark. "Or we could just keep working on the list you already created first." He inclines his head toward the window that sits right behind the table we're all at, taking a leisurely bite of bacon. "There's a window right there. Isn't that one of the items? Getting fucked against a window? The neighbors might even be around to watch, so you could kill two birds with one stone."

The piece of bacon I just picked up falls from my limp fingers as my stomach gives a little flip, and Sebastian laughs as Reid smirks at me. Bruno chimes in with a couple of random barks, as if he wants to join in the fun too.

The kitchen gets a little quieter as we all dig into the food, and we end up making a much bigger dent in it than I expected. The guys are so huge and muscular that they can really pack it away, and I like to think I hold my own with them. It turns out I really am ravenous after last night.

"Fuck, if only none of us had to work today." Sebastian groans in frustration as he gets up from the table a while later.

"All of you have to go in today?" I ask, polishing off the last bite of my French toast.

Part of me is disappointed, even though it's not a surprise that all of us have things to do today. Last night was a fantasy, and this morning, reality is back in full swing. Although it does still feel a bit like a dream to think about coming back here at the end of the day to all three of the Cooper brothers.

"Yeah." Sebastian puts his empty plate in the dishwasher, then comes back to the table to grab a few more. "I've got a few cars I need to work on today."

"And I've got a big carpentry project to finish," Reid adds, standing and gathering up the last of the dishes.

"Day shift at the station," Nick grunts, confirming that he'll be busy too.

Sebastian tugs me out of my seat, grinning at me as Nick scoots his chair back and rises too.

"Guess you lucked out this time, shortcake," he says.

"Lucked out? How?"

He smirks. "This buys you a little recovery time. If we didn't have to leave soon, you can bet your sweet ass you'd already be over my shoulder and halfway up the stairs right now. We'd have you back in that bedroom with your legs spread wide, trying to see which of us could make you scream the loudest."

Dammit. He cannot say things like that to me right before they're about to go.

My entire body lights up as if someone poured fire directly into my veins, and I must whimper softly, because his grin widens before he drops his head to give me a filthy kiss.

"To be continued," he promises, stepping away when we break apart.

The guys all have to head upstairs to shower and get ready themselves, and I spend a bit of time searching for the panties Bruno stole. I find them under his dog bed in the living room, and although he perks up as if he's hoping this will start another fun game of keep away, I quickly shove them into my pocket.

"Sorry, buddy," I tell him. "Not this time."

But even without the promise of a game, he pads closer, allowing me to give him a few gentle pets on his head before I run upstairs to throw the panties back into my room.

I head out shortly after the brothers all leave for their respective jobs, driving toward the center of town. I promised my parents and my sister that I'd stop by The Griddle House today. Since it's the weekend, my brother will be there too, and I haven't spent much time with Lucas since I got back into town.

When I get there, my parents and Pippa are already busy working. The diner is crowded with the end of the breakfast rush, and the three of them are racing around to keep up. Pippa is taking orders and practically dancing from table to table as she makes her way from one to the next in a practiced choreography. Our mom is behind the counter, taking the orders and handing them back through to our dad in the kitchen. A younger looking guy I don't recognize is behind the counter too, and I grin and wave at him as he looks my way.

"Hey, Hailey, over here!"

I glance over to see Lucas sitting in the booth at the back that's the unofficial 'family booth.' It's the one we always used to crowd in at when we would hang out at the diner after school, and even now, I'd bet that most of the diner regulars wouldn't sit in that booth unless the place was absolutely packed. They leave it open for me and my siblings, which I just love.

I greet my brother with a grin and slide onto the seat across from him.

"Want me to go grab you something from the kitchen?" he offers.

I shake my head since I already ate my bodyweight in bacon and French toast at the Cooper brothers' house. But I do still reach out and pluck a piece of toast off his plate. The guys were right—I'm hungrier than usual today. I can't even begin to figure out how many calories I must've burned last night.

"No, thanks," I say. "I just wanted to swing by to visit mom and dad and see you and Pippa for a bit. I already ate."

As I take a bite of the crispy toast, Lucas studies me.

"You look different this morning."

"Oh?" I freeze mid-chew. "Um, how so?"

"I don't know." He frowns. "You're a little flushed or something. Are you getting sick?"

Shit.

"I don't think so." I shrug, trying to ignore the sudden racing of my heart. "I parked a little farther away today. I probably should've worn a scarf."

I press a hand to my cheeks as if trying to warm them up, despite the fact that they're very warm already. But Lucas nods, leaning back in the booth as he glances over my shoulder.

"Oh yeah, it's really getting cold out there. It's supposed to snow again soon too, I think." He chuckles. "You've been in LA too long. You've gotta learn to bundle up."

"Right." I nod, grateful that he doesn't seem suspicious at all. "In LA, I barely ever need anything but a light jacket."

I press my fingers to my cheeks a few more times, trying to cool them down and banish the flush as I ask him about his plans for spring semester.

Once I finish my toast, I escape before Lucas can ask any more overly observant questions. The breakfast rush has died down by now, and the new guy is behind the counter, so I slip into the kitchen, assuming that's where my parents will be.

They're standing near the back fridge with their heads

together, having a low conversation, and the moment I look at their faces, I can tell something is wrong. My mother's features are crinkled with worry, and my father is rubbing the side of his head.

"Hey, what's going on?" I ask, stepping farther into the kitchen.

At the sound of my voice, my mother puts on her best "everything is fine" face. I can see right through it though, so I turn to my dad instead. He's usually better about being blunt and forthcoming.

"What's up? Is everything okay?"

He sighs, clearing his throat and glancing at my mom before looking back at me. "It's just been a hard month. We're a bit underwater financially, but we'll figure out how to turn it around."

"What?" My stomach drops. "How can that be? Every time I come in here, the place is packed to the brim."

"It's not that. We've got plenty of business." A look of pride crosses his face for a moment before his expression sinks again. "The problem is that our rent on the building has been raised too high. There's just no way we can keep afloat with things the way they are."

My jaw tightens.

I know exactly who they're talking about, and who raised the rent on them. *The Montgomery family*. They've always owned this building, just like they own a ton of other real estate in town. But as far as I know, they never used to overcharge my parents for rent.

"How long have they been jacking up the rent?" I ask, my voice going hard.

My mom shakes her head, clearly reading the direction my thoughts are going. "Hailey, it's not—"

"How long, Mom?"

She sighs. "About a year and a half."

So not that long after I left. Not long after I broke off my relationship with their son.

My hands clench into fists, and I glance around at the familiar walls of the kitchen, feeling a protective surge rise up inside me for this place. My parents love this diner. I love it too. It's a staple of the town, and now my parents might be forced out of business because a family that already has way too much money is demanding even more. And I can't believe that it isn't at least partially because of me.

Because I had the audacity to stand up for myself and leave him after he cheated on me.

"That's not fair," I mutter under my breath. "It's bullshit. They can't do that to you guys. They shouldn't take it out on you, just because—"

"This isn't your fault," my dad says firmly, cutting me off. "The Montgomerys have been trying to buy up this town and get rich off of it for years. It was inevitable that our turn for high rent was coming."

That doesn't make me feel much better. I'm still not convinced it was a coincidence that they jacked up the rent to unsustainable levels after it became clear that I wouldn't be becoming their daughter-in-law. But even if it is just random timing, that still doesn't make it right. My parents are so attached to this place, and the Montgomerys are basically bleeding them dry just because they know that my folks will work their asses off trying to keep it.

Pippa steps into the kitchen, stopping short when she sees us all. She bites her lip, and I turn to her, trying to get a read on her expression.

"Did you know about this?" I ask. "About the—"

"Yeah." She winces. "I knew. Sorry I didn't tell you before, but mom didn't want to ruin your Christmas."

A lump grows in my throat as I glance at my mother. She shrugs, looking a little guilty, but *I'm* the one who feels bad. She was trying to protect me, trying to keep my holidays happy and joyful, even as my dad struggled behind the scenes. But I don't want to be kept out of the loop. Not when it's my ex-boyfriend's family that's fucking with my parents.

"I want to help," I blurt. "At least let me do that. I can pull some shifts behind the counter while I'm in town. And if there's anything else I can do, count me in. Maybe I can drum up more business for the place or something. Whatever I can do. Anything."

"Thank you, sweetheart." My mom reaches out to give me a hug while my dad squeezes my shoulder.

"Hey, I know a way that you can help." Pippa comes closer, her face lighting up.

"How?" I ask as I step back from my parents.

"I signed you up for the Christmas parade."

My eyebrows shoot up. That was not what I was expecting her to say. "You signed *me* up?"

She lifts one shoulder. "Well, the diner. I talked Lex Camden into giving us a float this year. I thought it would be good publicity for the diner. And since you want to help so much, you could pitch in by riding on it."

Her grin is so broad it stretches across her entire face, and there's something mischievous in her expression that makes me certain she hasn't told me every detail yet. There's some catch I'm missing.

"Okay," I say slowly. "I can do that. Will it just be me?"

Somehow, her smile gets even wider. "Oh, no. The theme of the float is Santa and Mrs. Claus, so you'll need a guy up there too. And there are also two elf costumes, so it'd actually be even better if you had three guys..."

"Oh, no." I shake my head, realizing where she's going with this. "No way, Pip."

"What?" She turns to my parents as if looking for backup. "It's a great idea, isn't it? Come on, everybody loves the Cooper brothers! They'll definitely get a lot of attention, and since they're each apparently trying to date Hailey, I bet they'll agree to do it."

My mom's eyes widen a little at that. I don't know if she or my dad have heard the rumors around town about the Cooper brothers supposedly fighting over my affections, but if she didn't know before, she does now.

I flush, feeling a little awkward as I wonder what she thinks about all three of them trying to date me—and then feeling even more awkward as I refuse to think about what she'd say if she knew what they all did to me last night.

"Fine, okay. I'll do it," I say, just to move the conversation along from whatever's going on between me and the triplets. "I'll ride on the float, and I'll ask them if they'll do it too. But I can't *make* them, so I'm not responsible if they say no. Which they probably will."

Pippa just shrugs, shooting me a smug, little sisterly look. "We'll see."

I roll my eyes, although I have to appreciate the fact that my sister somehow managed to bring a little levity to the situation. Our parents don't look nearly as dejected as they did when I first entered the kitchen.

Now I just have to convince the guys to get on board with it.

23

SEBASTIAN

I HAVE my head buried beneath the hood of an old mustang when my phone starts to ping off the hook.

I wipe my hands off and go pick it up to see who is blowing up my text messages. It looks like there's a text thread that's been started between Hailey and my brothers. And based on her initial text, I can see why both Reid and Nick are blowing up the group chat.

HAILEY: *I've added an item to my naughty bucket list.*
NICK: *Oh?*
REID: *Do tell...*
I text back immediately.
ME: *I'm listening.*
HAILEY: *I want to ride on a holiday float in a parade with all three of you.*
REID: *Uhh, what? Is that some kind of sex euphemism I don't know about?*
NICK: *lol*

Honestly, I'm surprised that Nick even knows how to register humor over text messages. Apparently, Reid's comment hit him in just the right way. But I'm more curious about

Hailey's request. A holiday parade doesn't quite seem like the kind of thing that belongs on a kink-laden bucket list.

ME: *You want us to ride on a parade float with you? That seems like a step down from all the things you were riding on last night. ;-) Are you sure you're not just trying to trick us into doing you a favor?*

Little bubbles appear right away, indicating that someone is typing. But instead of sending back an immediate answer, Hailey replies with a chain of emojis that's so long it drops down into two lines of text.

HAILEY: *Okay, maybe I am trying to get you to help me out. A Christmas parade isn't exactly sexy. But if you do it, I'll pay you back in sexual favors.*

ME: *Now you have my attention.*

REID: *Go on.*

HAILEY: *If you guys do this for me, then we can do number fifteen from my list.*

NICK: *Number fifteen?*

REID: *We don't have the list committed to memory in numeric order, trouble. You're going to have to refresh our memory.*

I wait curiously to see which thing on her list is number fifteen, my imagination already running wild.

HAILEY: *I'll wear a vibrator that one of you controls.*

Holy fuck. I have an instant visceral reaction to those words as soon as I read them. Now that I know what Hailey's face looks like when she comes, I feel like I could get addicted to seeing that expression over and over. The way her eyebrows pinch together just a tiny bit, her mouth dropping open...

Fucking gorgeous.

But as fun as it is to watch her come, it might be even more fun to watch her try *not* to come. To be in control of a hidden vibrator, deciding when and how much to amp up the pleasure, all while she tries to act like everything is normal? Goddamn.

NICK: *During the parade??*
HAILEY: *I didn't say that.*

Since I'm already getting half hard just thinking about her being at the mercy of a vibrator that she can't control, I'm quick to answer for all of us.

ME: *Deal. We'll do the parade.*

She spams the group chat with a half dozen "thank you" messages and an emoji of a celebratory party hat. And just when I think that it's safe to put my phone down and get back to work, another message comes through.

HAILEY: *Also, this isn't on the naughty list, and I can't even pretend that it is... but there's a Christmas ball tonight, and I would love it if you guys would come with me.*

A Christmas ball? The only one I know of in Chestnut Hill is thrown by Dylan Montgomery's family. I grunt to myself, grimacing at the thought of going to an event that arrogant prick and his family are throwing. I'm honestly surprised that Hailey would even consider attending.

I start to type out a message, but before I can finish, another text comes through. My brother apparently read my mind, because it's the exact question I was about to ask.

NICK: *You mean the annual Christmas ball that Dylan's folks put on?*

HAILEY: *Yeah, that one. I'd understand if you guys didn't want to come. It's not exactly one of my top ten favorite things to do either.*

REID: *Then why go? You have nothing to prove to anyone, trouble.*

There's a long moment where she doesn't answer, and I keep my phone in my hand, gazing down at the screen. What could she be thinking? I know for a fact that she doesn't want to see that prick again—especially not at some fancy event that his rich parents are throwing, with her ex-best friend wrapped around his arm.

It doesn't make sense that Hailey would put herself in that position.

But after a moment or two, I find out why.

HAILEY: *My family is having some issues with the Montgomerys and their lease on the diner. We're all trying not to piss off his family and make things worse, so I pretty much have to go. I've already promised my parents I'll try to play nice.*

Dammit. I get what she's thinking now, but I hate the fact that Hailey feels like she has to do something she doesn't want to. Showing up to an event like that and having to act polite to her shitbag ex sounds awful.

The least we can do is make sure she's not alone.

ME: *I'm in.*

HAILEY: *Really?*

ME: *Yup, really. Can't let you have all the fun.*

NICK: *I'll go too.*

REID: *Looks like it's a party. Can't wait.*

HAILEY: *Thanks guys. It really means a lot to me that you're all coming.*

I hesitate, staring down at the screen, then tap out one last message.

ME: *We've got you, shortcake. Always.*

"Fuck. Dammit."

Standing in front of the mirror in my room, I mutter a few curses as my fingers fumble with the fancy buttons on the cuffs of my shirt. I still can't believe I'm going to a damn Christmas ball, of all things. I think I'd rather stick my head in a vise clamp on my workbench back at the garage.

I grumble under my breath about having to get dressed up and go somewhere so far out of my comfort zone. I'm a mechanic, after all, not a goddamn prince.

But then something in the mirror catches my eye, and I turn around to see Hailey standing in the open doorway of my bedroom. She looks like an ethereal vision—literally a *goddess* wrapped in a gold dress that hugs her body like a second skin.

She's fucking stunning.

I cross the room to her, wrapping my hand around her throat without saying a single word. Her pulse flutters against my palm as I drop my head to slant my lips against hers, and heat sparks between us as I kiss her hungrily.

When our lips break apart, I don't release my grip on her throat right away. She lets out a breath, looking up at me with those wide eyes that send an electrical surge through my entire body. Her chest is rising and falling faster, her pupils dilated.

"Wow. I should've had this on my list," she breathes. She swallows, and I can feel the movement against my palm. "A guy holding my throat like this."

"Do you like it?"

She nods, dragging her plush lower lip between her teeth.

"Duly noted. I'll remember that for later." I give a gentle squeeze, making her breath hitch, then release my grip and tilt her chin up with two fingers. "You look amazing."

"You clean up pretty good yourself." She grins as she reaches up to help me finish closing the buttons on my cuffs.

"Yeah, well, it's not exactly mechanic garb. I had to borrow the dress shirt from Reid."

I offer her my arm, which she takes, and then walk her down to the living room.

I can't help but glance at her intermittently as we make our way down the stairs. She's so fucking beautiful, and not just because of the dress. Her emerald eyes seem to pop against the gold and the glow she's putting off. She's let her hair down to flow against her bare shoulders and down her back, and the blonde strands look so soft that I want to wrap them around my fist.

As we walk into the living room where both of my brothers are waiting, Reid and Nick turn to face us.

"*Wow.*"

Reid's single-word reaction is more than Nick can apparently bring himself to say as he stands there staring speechless at her.

"Thanks." Hailey grins, looking almost shy. "I've actually never gotten a chance to wear this dress before. I bought it in LA, but a good opportunity never came up. So I guess that's one good thing about this ball."

"Hell fucking yes." Reid steps forward, pulling her into a kiss just like I did. When he releases her, he spins her to face Nick, like he's offering our brother a turn too.

Nick clears his throat, looking like he might still be a little dumbstruck. Fortunately, Hailey is learning exactly how to handle our stoic, slightly closed-off older brother. Instead of waiting for him to come to her, she goes to him, leaning up onto her tiptoes to press a kiss to his mouth.

The second their lips touch, it's like whatever was keeping him locked up breaks. His arms wrap around her, the kiss turning indecent in less than one point five seconds.

My cock twitches as I watch her arch against him, and I add this to the many, *many* reasons I hate Dylan Montgomery. If it weren't for his parents' stupid ass ball, we could stay right where we are and spend the rest of the night unwrapping Hailey like the delicious present she is.

Hailey finally steps back from Nick, who now looks a bit like he got hit by a truck.

Ha. You and me both, brother. And Reid too.

Bruno gives Nick and Hailey slobbery kisses goodbye, pointedly ignoring me and Reid, and then we all head out, piling into one car.

"When we get there, we probably shouldn't all walk in together," Reid suggests as we drive over, glancing between the rest of us. "It doesn't make sense for us to all show up together, since we're supposed to still be 'fighting' over Hailey."

"Good point." I almost forgot we're still trying to sell that story. "Maybe we should pick one of us for her to be officially attending the ball with, and the other two can walk in separately."

"I think it should be Nick," Reid offers up. "I mean, he's the least likely to fly off the handle and do something stupid, like giving Dylan a black eye."

Nick raises a brow at our brother's assessment of his self-control. I'm not so sure that *any* of us would manage to keep from flying off the handle if it was in defense of Hailey. But Nick doesn't protest the idea, so it's decided that he'll be her "official" date to the ball.

I don't really think much of it at first, until we get to the large event space where the party is being held. Reid and I head in first, and an unexpected feeling surges through me as I watch Nick walk in with Hailey at his side a short while later.

Instead of *pretending* to be jealous, I feel truly jealous—authentic, raw envy flooding my chest at the sight of my brother with Hailey on his arm. I find myself wishing I was the one by her side, and I feel a sense of possessive pride when I notice several of the people at the event glance in her direction.

Some of the guys let their gazes linger a little too long, and Nick pulls her a little closer, glaring them down. My hands twitch, itching to do the same. I know he's got this covered, and it's not that I don't trust him. I just wish I could be standing with her too, I guess.

It's weird, and I'm not quite sure what to do with the intensity of that feeling.

It doesn't help that this sort of event makes me feel uneasy in and of itself. I'm completely out of my element here, and I hate all the pomp and circumstance that the people attending things like this usually put on. The entire ball is over the top and ostentatious, and I don't like it at all.

"What a joke this all is," Reid mutters, echoing my thoughts. "It's all just a chance for the Montgomerys and all the other wealthy families of Chestnut Hill to show off. None of this is for anyone else's benefit but theirs."

"Agreed." I scowl, surveying the room to see if I can spot the bar. As soon as I see it, I tell Reid I'll go grab us some drinks, and then add, "Keep a close eye on our girl. There are a bunch of arrogant vultures in this place."

"You know I will."

He crosses his arms over his chest, looking almost as intimidating as Nick.

I turn away, and I'm making a beeline toward the bar when I catch sight of another face that brings me up short.

"Addison?" I blink at my sister, who's standing next to her husband and daughter. "What are you doing here?"

"Hey, Seb!" She gives me a hug, then grimaces as we separate. "I'm here to do a bit of schmoozing. There are some really good potential clients in this room, so I couldn't exactly turn down the invitation. I talked Michael and Iris into coming with me."

"Ah." That makes sense. She's an event planner, so I can see why she'd want to make connections with some of the people here.

"Hi, Uncle Sebastian!" My six-year-old niece, Iris, waves brightly from beside her mother.

"Hey, little munchkin." I reach down and swoop her into my arms, spinning her around once and making her laugh. When I set her down, her eyes are shining.

"Are Nick and Reid here too?" Addison asks.

"Yup. Over there." I point out to where Reid is watching the dance floor, and where Nick is standing just at the edge of it talking with Hailey.

"Is Nick actually going to *dance*?"

"I doubt it." I laugh. "You know him. Standing within five feet of the dance floor is probably as close as he'll get to dancing tonight."

Addison laughs, a sound that always reminds me of our mother. Our sister is only a few years older than me and my brothers, but her laugh sounds so much like our mom's. Maybe it's because she helped raise the three of us after our parents died, or maybe it's because she embodies all the best qualities that our mom had.

Addison is sweet as hell, but she also takes no shit. She's one of the strongest women I know.

"Well, you all clean up pretty well," she tells me with a smile. "Who knew I had such handsome brothers?"

"I hate wearing this shit." I fuck with my cufflinks, and Addison slaps my hand away.

I roll my eyes at her, and Michael laughs at the two of us. I like him. He's a good guy—down to earth, and he treats my sister well.

"I was just about to grab some drinks," I tell the two of them. "Can I get you anything?"

"Nah, let me go," Michael offers. "You and your sister can catch up a bit."

Addison gives him a kiss on the cheek, and once he strides away, my sister turns her attention back to me, her lips pursed to one side in an expression I recognize well.

"Sooo," she drawls, and I brace myself for the question I know is coming. "Nick and Hailey are looking pretty close over there together."

I nod. "Yup."

She eyes the two of them, who are still standing near the dance floor. Nick has his arm around Hailey, his hand resting on her lower back. Then she shoots me another look.

"I thought that I heard rumors that you were dating her.

And actually, I heard the same thing about Reid too. What's that about?"

Well, the rumor mill is definitely working.

I love my sister, and over the years, I've been able to confide all sorts of things to Addison that I haven't even told my brothers. But this is different. I definitely can't tell her the truth, so I'll have to feed her the same story we're telling everyone else.

"Nothing." I shrug. "We each realized we were interested in her, so we each asked her out. I went on a date with her, and so did Reid and Nick. It's nothing serious yet or anything. She'll pick one of us eventually. Or she won't, who knows? I don't think she's staying in town long anyway."

My answer is meant to be vague and slightly evasive, to give my sister enough to satisfy her without going into detail. But for some reason, with every word I speak, I find my mouth turning down into a deeper frown. I don't like the idea of Hailey picking one of us over the others, even if it's not real and I just made all of that up. The thought of it bothers me for some reason—almost as much as the idea of Hailey leaving Chestnut Hill again.

I clear my throat, trying to banish the sudden tightness in my chest. "Anyway, she's here with Nick tonight."

"Hm."

Addison doesn't say more than that, and she doesn't probe for more details, which is very unlike her. I worry a little that something I said might've tipped her off to the lie, but I'm saved from having to say anything else on the subject when Michael comes back with the drinks.

As soon as he hands me mine, I grimace. *Shit.* I forgot I was supposed to get one for Reid too.

"Actually, will you give this to Reid?" I ask my sister, passing it to her. "I'll go get another one for me."

"Oh, sure."

She, Michael, and Iris start making their way toward Reid, and I head off in the direction of the bar.

It takes a while to get my drink, and by the time I start heading back to join my sister, Michael, and Reid, Iris has wandered off to play with a couple of other kids her age. They're standing near one of the tables laden with beautiful centerpieces, and I watch Iris's face bloom with delight as she realizes that one of the flowers from the centerpiece has fallen onto the table.

She picks it up, bringing it to her nose to sniff it—but before she can, one of the other little girls standing next to her gives her a hard shove, snatching the flower out of her hand.

"Hey!"

My mouth opens, but the word doesn't come from me. Instead, it comes from Hailey, who swoops in like an avenging angel. Her face is angry as she stoops down beside them, plucking the flower back from the girl who stole it as she says something that makes the little girl flush guiltily.

Hailey stands up, offering the flower back to my niece before taking her hand. Iris beams up at her, looking as enamored as if she had just come face to face with Wonder Woman. I can see Iris chattering away happily as Hailey leads her back over to my sister and Michael, and I trail along behind them, unable to stop watching.

Once Hailey has deposited Iris safely back with her parents, she shares a look with Reid and then starts to walk away.

She's supposed to be here with Nick. I know that.

But goddammit, I need to kiss her.

Seeing her stand up for my niece was the hottest fucking thing I've ever seen, and I feel like I'll die if I don't get Hailey into my arms right now.

So I pivot to keep following her through the crowd, and when she skirts around to the edge of the large room, trying to get past a particularly loud group of people, I see an opportunity and take it.

Picking up my pace, I snag her wrist quickly and tug her

through a door leading to an adjacent hallway. We walk quickly down the hall, and when I see a door on our left, I test the knob. It opens, thank fuck, revealing what looks like a storage closet.

Good enough for me.

Not bothering to turn the light on, I pull Hailey into the little room after me, shutting the door behind us. The darkness in the space presses in around us as I turn around to face her, taking in her shadowy features by the light creeping in from under the door.

Hailey's wide green eyes flutter until they adjust to the dim light, then lock on mine, surprise clear in her expression.

"What's up?" she whispers. "Is everything okay?"

"I saw you with Iris just now."

"Oh. Is that why you brought me in here?"

I smirk, reaching up to trace the curve of her jaw. "No. I brought you here because it's been driving me crazy to not be able to kiss you all night."

I press my lips to hers to punctuate my words, and she moans as if the kiss is helping her let out some pent-up tension of her own. Her hands rest on my chest, and I can't stop myself from cradling the back of her head and pulling her deeper into the kiss.

Her hands snake down my back until they find the waistband of my pants, and she follows it around to the front and my belt buckle, which she fumbles with in the dark. I love the way she responds to my touch like this, how eager she is to reciprocate every time I put my lips on hers.

And the way she lights up when I brush kisses down her neck is intoxicating. But a flash of possessive anger flares inside me when I think about just how little that fucker Dylan appreciated what he had in Hailey.

I don't know how I'm ever going to let her go. This whole act we're putting on for the benefit of our nosy ass town has to stop at some point, but there's a part of me that can't stand the idea of seeing Hailey with anyone else. Or of any other man besides me or my brothers getting the chance to light her up like I am right now.

I kiss the soft, sensitive skin where her neck meets her collarbone and groan at the goosebumps that ripple across her shoulder. Without letting my lips leave her skin, I walk her backward a few steps until her back hits the door behind her.

Then I breathe into her ear, "One of your bucket list items was to have sex in a public place. Is this public enough for you?"

My eyes meet hers as I draw back, and her pupils dilate. The sight of it makes my cock twitch in my pants, straining toward her as she nods eagerly.

"Yes," she whispers, still nodding. "Fuck me. Please."

I grin at her through the darkness. "Good girl."

Our lips meet again, ratcheting up the heat raging between us even further. She wraps her arms around me, her fingertips digging into the skin at the back of my neck, desperate and clawing. I trail a hand up her bare thigh and slip it under the hem of her dress, stopping at her panty line.

Hailey pulls back, her eyes twinkling devilishly as she stares at me with her lip trapped between her teeth. It's almost like she's daring me, wanting to see how far I'll take things. I've always loved that daring, teasing side of her that isn't afraid to be a little bad.

"Should we see how wet you are for me already, shortcake?" I murmur.

My finger dips into her panties to find her pussy, and I grit my teeth at the realization that she's already soaked for me.

"God, you're fucking killing me," I grunt. "Is that all for me?"

She nods, her hair glinting softly in the darkness. "Yes..."

"Good."

And I mean it. I'm perfectly willing to share her with my

brothers—in fact, it's hot as hell watching them make her scream—but right now, I want her all to myself.

I torment her with my finger, dragging the tip across her clit and teasing her entrance. She moans and wraps a leg around me, pulling me closer so she can lunge for my lips again like a wild animal.

I'm definitely not the only one who's been going a little crazy with desire tonight, and the unrestrained way she's showing it awakens something in me too. I tug her panties aside roughly, and Hailey whimpers into my mouth. Her body is arching against mine, and her pussy is already so wet that I could fuck her right here and now if I wanted.

But not yet.

I circle around her entrance, making her squirm, before I push just the tip of my finger into her. Her breath catches, and she rolls her hips downward like she's trying to work my whole finger inside, so I let her. When I'm buried up to my knuckle in her warm wetness, she rests her forehead against mine, staring intently into my eyes.

"Sebastian. Please..."

She doesn't have to say anything else for me to know what she's thinking. She's sick of the teasing and she wants the real thing.

That makes two of us.

I pull my finger out of her slowly, drinking in the way she shivers in my arms from the feeling, then rip her panties off in one go, making her yelp as the delicate fabric tears away. She steps out of them and kicks them to the side without ever taking her eyes off mine.

"See? So fucking wet for me," I whisper as I hold my finger up between us to prove it. "Now the real question is, do you taste as sweet as you look?"

I start to bring my finger to my mouth to find out, but her

hand flies out to stop me, gripping my wrist as she bites her lower lip.

"Let me be the one to tell you," she whispers.

A groan rumbles in the back of my throat as she pulls my hand to her open mouth. She places my finger on the back of her tongue, then wraps her lips around it and slowly draws back.

"Mm," she moans around my finger, and I smirk at her.

"You keep finding ways to surprise me, my dirty little shortcake. So how do you taste?"

A sly smirk curves her plush lips as she releases my finger. "Like I'm not a good girl after all. Like I'm your dirty little slut."

My cock jumps. "Fuck."

Whatever control I thought I had a moment ago vanishes as heat floods my veins, and I spin her around forcefully. She catches herself on the door behind us, her hands splayed out across it, her tight little ass jutting out at me from under her dress. I hike the fabric up over her hips, exposing her bare cheeks and the glistening wetness of her pussy, and my cock aches so hard in my pants that it hurts.

"Fuck," I rasp. "I need to feel you."

I need to break the tension that's been building between us, just waiting for a spark to ignite it. My hands pull her hips toward me, grinding my clothed shaft against her ass. She moans breathlessly, her fingers clawing at the door, and the sound of her pleasure goes straight to my cock.

"Do you think you can be quiet?" I ask.

She glances over her shoulder to look me right in the eye, a hint of a smile at the corner of her lips as she answers me with one word.

"No."

My body floods with desire, and I grin back at her. "Good answer, baby. Because I like the idea of everyone at this party knowing exactly who's fucking you in this room."

"Then what are you waiting for?" she asks and balls her

dress in one hand to hold it up for me, showing off her perfect little pussy.

It drives me crazy, but as tempted as I am to give her what she's asking for right away, I want to drag this out a little longer. I want her to feel every little sensation, want to savor every sweet inch of her pussy as I slide inside.

I unzip and shove my pants down a bit, then slide my cock through her folds several times. She groans and arches her back even more, inviting me inside. She's totally fucking soaked, her wetness coating my cock, and I finally grip myself at the base and press just the head inside her perfect pussy, beginning to stretch her open.

"Oh my god," she hisses, her nails curling against the door and leaving tiny scrapes in the paint. The sight gives me an idea, so I lean forward, resting my lips just behind her ear.

"Count them," I tell her. "I want a mark on that door for each of my piercings as you take them."

She laughs, her voice thick with desire. "Oh my god, you're crazy."

"About you," I shoot back, ignoring the sudden jolt that shoots through my chest as I realize how true those words are.

Shoving those thoughts aside to consider more deeply later, I shift my hips forward a bit more, and she whimpers as the first stud of my Jacob's Ladder slips in. It takes her a second to follow my command, but then she slowly drags a nail across the paint.

"One," she says quietly. I kiss the back of her neck.

"Good girl. Keep going," I tell her and keep pushing until the next piercing slides in.

"Two." She scratches another mark in the paint next to the first, but it's even more jagged. "Don't stop. I want them all."

"Oh, you're gonna get them. Don't you worry," I say, clenching my jaw as I pitch my hips forward suddenly, sinking several more piercings into her and pulling a deep-throated groan out of her. About half my cock is inside her now, throbbing with arousal. "How many was that?"

Hailey doesn't answer. Instead, she drags her nail through the paint three more times. On the final one, she draws a line across the four previous tally marks. Then she turns to me, craning her neck to meet my gaze. "Three, four... five."

"That's right, shortcake. Well done."

I'm impressed. If she's so sensitive that she could count how many piercings went in with just one thrust, I can only imagine how good I must be making her feel. And the thought makes me want to give her even more pleasure. I can't wait to have her screaming my name in this room.

"More. Please," she begs, tapping her nail against the wall as if she's desperate to make another mark.

I laugh at her impatience, but I don't take pity on her, taking my sweet time as I slowly press the rest of the way inside, watching her gasp and squirm as she makes jagged tally marks on the door.

Finally, the final inch of my cock disappears into her tight pussy, and she drags in a breath as she makes the last mark.

"Ten," she whispers, her voice shaking.

I press a kiss to her neck, scraping my teeth across her skin before I whisper, "Well done. You did such a good job counting. I think it's time for me to give you what you want. What you need. Are you ready?"

"Yes." She nods, her palms flattening on the door. "Yes, yes, ye—"

The last word breaks off as I draw out and then plunge back inside, burying my cock to the hilt inside her. She cries out, her eyes going wide with surprise and arousal as she looks at me over her shoulder.

"Holy shit. *Yes*, Sebastian. Fuck. Me," she demands, and I don't think I could deny her anything when she says it like that.

I pull out and drive right back in, making her cry out again.

If she wants it hard and fast, that's exactly how I'll give it to her. I don't give her any time to adjust. I launch into a pounding rhythm, my hips slamming against hers, until she melts forward into the door, her cheek smashed against it.

"Oh my god. Oh my god!" she hisses as her free hand slips between her legs to work her clit. She's standing on her tiptoes, barely managing not to fall over, but she uses what little balance she has to rock herself backward in time with my thrusts, taking my cock even deeper. Fucking herself on my length.

"Go ahead. Say it. Scream my fucking name so everyone here knows who's got you so worked up," I mutter and wrap a fistful of her hair around my hand as I start thrusting even faster.

"Yes, Sebastian!" she cries softly, her voice somewhat muffled with her cheek against the door.

"Louder," I grunt and drive into her roughly again. Her pussy clenches around me, making my balls tighten. "Tell everyone how fucking good I'm making you feel."

"Oh... my... god. Sebastian!" I can tell she's still trying to keep her voice down, but it's a battle she's losing. Her sounds are getting louder and less controlled as she curls her fingers into fists against the door. "Keep going. Keep going, don't stop. Please, it feels so good. I'm gonna... gonna..."

Her breathing turns ragged, and I know she's about to fall apart, but I don't let up. Not until she takes one last sharp inhale, her muscles locking in a way that tells me her orgasm is cresting.

Just before she lets out the raw scream I can sense building in the back of her throat, I grip her jaw and tilt her face toward mine so I can smash my lips against hers, swallowing all of her perfect, addictive noises.

They're mine. All mine.

24

HAILEY

Sebastian kisses me through every little shudder of my orgasm, keeping his lips pressed firmly to mine until the last of the aftershocks course through me. When I finally stop pulsing around him, he releases his hold on my jaw but doesn't tear his dark gaze away from mine or stop fucking me.

"I changed my mind," he murmurs over the quiet, filthy sounds of our bodies clapping together. "Just for tonight, your noises belong only to me."

There's an intensity in his expression, a spark in his blue-green eyes that makes goosebumps spread over my skin. He picks up the pace again, slamming into me and making my eyelids fall shut. I melt against the door, letting it hold me up as my legs threaten to give out. I'm so sensitive from the earth-shattering orgasm he just gave me that every movement from him feels ten times more intense.

"There you go," he praises roughly. "That's my girl. Come for me again. I need it. I need to feel you clench around me."

"Then make me," I shoot back hoarsely, and he chuckles, fucking me harder and faster than ever. It's so intense that it overrides everything else in my brain, making it impossible to focus on anything other than his pierced cock driving in and out of me. It feels transcendent, like I'm about to float out of my body from the pleasure of it all.

"Is that what you want? For me to fuck you like my little slut?" he grunts through a series of thrusts, my hair still wound up in his fist. "Because that's what you are. My. Little. Slut."

He slams into me with each word, and I feel myself flying closer to a second orgasm, climbing to another level of ecstasy from each thrust.

"Yes," I moan. It's the only word I can manage to say.

"Sorry, I didn't hear you," Sebastian growls, then bottoms out in me and stays there, stretching me even more and forcing my eyes open in surprise and pleasure.

"Yes!" I cry. "I'm your little slut. Yours and your brothers'. Fuck me harder, Sebastian. *Please*. Make me come!"

"With pleasure."

Sebastian pulls all the way out, making me gasp, then plows back in before I realize what's happening. He does it over and over again, coming all the way out before slamming all the way in. And it feels so fucking good.

"Holy shit," I whisper as my body tenses, and Sebastian releases my hair to slap my ass.

"That's it. Give it to me but remember what I said: your noises are *mine*."

"Fuck," I groan and bite my lip to keep from screaming as my second orgasm tears through me. My eyes water from the pain in my lip and the pleasure he's giving me. His thrusting picks up, reaching a fever pitch, before he slams into me one last time and shudders. A beat later, I feel his cum flood me, hot and powerful.

"Jesus Christ," he rasps, his hips rolling against my ass with each wave of his orgasm until he's finally spent.

He collapses forward in the aftermath, his head resting against the back of mine. We stand there panting for breath, and after a long moment, Sebastian litters the back of my neck with kisses, sending chills racing across every inch of my body.

But he's not done with me yet. When he reaches the base of my neck, he pulls out of me abruptly and drops to his knees, spinning me around by my hips. Before I can ask what he's doing, he's shoving my dress up again as his mouth finds my pussy, lapping at the cum that's leaking out of me and down my inner thigh.

With his mouth full, he rises to his feet and presses his lips to mine, transferring the tangy cum from his tongue to mine. Heat blooms low inside me as I taste him, and I practically melt into a puddle as he sweeps his tongue inside my mouth, making sure I don't miss a drop. It's so fucking hot, so dirty and wrong, that my body shudders when he pulls away and smiles devilishly at me.

"I love knowing my cum will be inside you and on your tongue for the rest of the party," he says. "You like the way we taste together, baby?"

I swallow hard, my tongue darting out to lick my lips as I nod. "Yes. So fucking much."

"That's my good girl."

His grin, more than anything he's done to me so far tonight, is what truly threatens to make my knees buckle.

God, this man.

Sebastian picks up my shredded panties from where he dropped them on the floor, arching a brow at me before stuffing them possessively into his pocket.

"I think I'll keep these, to remember how this lame party turned into one of the hottest nights of my life," he tells me, sending a fresh spark of heat through my sated body.

"You know I didn't bring a pair of backup panties," I point out, biting back a grin as I adjust my dress, letting the skirt fall back down around my legs. "I won't have anything on under this."

"Oh, baby..." He palms the back of my head and kisses me again, his lips moving against mine as he murmurs, "That's the idea."

I laugh breathlessly against his lips, and after Sebastian tucks himself away and gets his pants zipped up, he helps me tame my mussed hair in the dim light of the closet. My eyes have adjusted enough that I can see the flash of tenderness in his eyes as he tucks a lock of hair behind my ear, his fingers brushing my cheek. I don't know what these men are doing to my heart, but I feel powerless to stop the feelings building inside me. And as foolhardy as it might be, I'm not sure I want to.

"You ready to head back out there?" Sebastian asks, trailing his knuckles along my jaw.

"Yes." I smile and nod, even though part of me wants to tell him 'no.'

Part of me wants to just call Reid and Nick and have them join us in here so that we can keep the *real* party going, away from Dylan and his family and the probing eyes of small-town neighbors. Where the four of us can just enjoy whatever this thing between us is, without having to think about playing our parts for our fake dating ruse or worry about what people would think if they found out the truth.

Where we could just *be*.

But I don't say any of that. Instead, I steal one last kiss from Sebastian's addictive lips and then whisper, "You go first. I'll slip out after you."

25

HAILEY

SEBASTIAN and I stagger our entrances, and when it's my turn to slip back into the main room where the party is being held, I work hard to temper my giddy smile, hoping I don't look as freshly fucked as I feel. He headed in before me, and I glance quickly at where he is standing off on the other side of the room by the bar where he's ordering a drink.

My head is filled with thoughts of him, thoughts about how much I liked the possessive way that he kissed me and talked to me. I liked how he whisked me off as if I was his without question.

And now it's not only my head that's filled with him.

I swallow hard, my thighs clenching as I feel a bit more of his cum leak out of me and coat my inner thighs. I can still taste him on my tongue, and it takes a bit of effort to bring myself back down to earth as I scan the large room, searching for Nick.

When I left the gruff, bearded Cooper brother, he was standing at the edge of the open space in the middle of the room where some people are dancing, but now I don't see him there anymore. He probably went to get a drink in order to tolerate listening to the gaggle of pretentious assholes while I was gone.

As I turn to head toward the bar, I spot Reid out of the corner of my eye.

He's not alone, and at first I think he's talking to Addison, who was standing near him earlier.

But it's not Addison.

It's Sutton.

His ex-girlfriend laughs at something he said, the sound light and airy, and my stomach twists with a sudden, uncomfortable rush of jealousy.

Sutton is beautiful. Stunning, really. Not only that, but she has a graceful air about her, almost like a ballerina, that always makes her seem elegant and ethereal. I don't know if they stayed friends after they broke up, and I guess it's not all that unusual for two people who used to date to say hi to each other at an event like this. But it's the way they're standing so close together, tucked away a little from the rest of the crowd, that makes me feel as if needles are prickling under my skin.

Sutton is standing a bit too close to him, her hand gently resting on the side of his arm as she leans in to speak in his ear. If I didn't already know that they aren't together anymore, I might even think they were a couple.

My footsteps slow, tension gathering in my shoulders.

It doesn't matter, I remind myself. *You're not even supposed to be here as his date tonight. And even if you were, none of this is real. So he can talk to whoever he wants.*

The words make logical sense, but my heart—and even my mind—refuse to fully process them. I know I can't look at them without my emotions being stamped all over my face, so I clench my jaw and quickly turn away, pretending I didn't even notice them.

Still, an ache spreads through my chest as I make my way across the room, deflating the balloon of post-orgasm bliss.

When I spot Nick in the crowd, towering over the people around him, relief surges through me. I pick up my pace, slipping through the well-dressed guests and stopping to say a quick hello to my family. I already said hi to the Montgomerys, grateful for Nick's steady presence at my back as I did. It felt awful having to look his mother in the eye and smile, but if it helps my family's business, I'll act nice with whoever I have to.

"There you are." Nick wraps his arm around my waist the second I stop beside him. "I thought I lost you."

He sounds genuinely concerned, and I wince. I know he wouldn't be upset about what happened between me and Sebastian, because the friends with benefits deal is between me and all three of the brothers. But I didn't mean to make him worry.

"Sorry," I tell him, leaning into his large frame. "I saw some girls bullying Iris on my way back from the restroom and stopped to help. And then Sebastian caught me and... wanted a moment alone."

Nick's eyebrows twitch upward. I wasn't trying to make that sound like an innuendo, but I think it did anyway. I grin guiltily, biting my lip.

"We snuck into a storage closet," I admit.

His midnight blue eyes darken, and he pulls me closer, wrapping his other arm around me too. His head drops as he buries his face in my hair, and I have to work hard to keep my mouth from dropping open on an audible moan. He's not even doing anything, just breathing me in, but it's enough to make my already shaky legs wobble.

"You smell like you just got fucked," he murmurs after a second, in a voice low enough for only me to hear. "Did you?"

God almighty. This man. He doesn't say a lot, but what he does say is usually enough to just about knock me on my ass.

"Yes," I whisper.

We're so close together that I can *feel* the small shudder that works through his body in response, and he drags in another breath before he finally releases me. He's looking at me like he's seriously considering dragging me back into that closet and taking his turn, but he must decide it would be too risky for the Cooper brothers to keep pulling me into secluded closets, because he just scrubs a hand over his bearded jaw and then turns back to watch the couples dancing.

I watch with him, sneaking glances over at Sutton and Reid every once in a while.

Between the possessive feelings and the heavy sexual tension between me and Nick, I'm a total mess, and I try to distract myself by providing a running commentary about the dancers. I speak in a low voice, telling Nick pieces of gossip about the people I recognize and making up stories about the ones I don't.

"Is that true?" he asks when I tell him that one of the women dancing with a short, stocky man moved to Chestnut Hill because she's in witness protection.

"No," I admit. "I have no idea. I was just making it up." I grin, turning to look up at him. "Should I call *Shadow's Edge* and see if they're looking for writers? I bet I'd be pretty good at it."

Nick looks startled for a second. Then he barks a laugh, and the sound does almost as much to me as the dirty words he whispered in my ear earlier.

"I like your laugh," I tell him. "It's nice."

He immediately starts to look self-conscious, and I can practically see him retreating into the shell he used to always slip into around me.

"You don't have to do that," I say before I can think better of it and stop myself.

His brow furrows. "Do what?"

"Hide from me." I nudge him with my shoulder, my heart thudding harder. Maybe I shouldn't be saying any of this, but I feel like I'll regret it if I don't. "I feel... I feel like you used to hold yourself back around me. Like you didn't want me to see all of you. But you don't have to do that. Because the truth is, every new piece of you that I get to know only makes me like you more."

A flush rises up from beneath his dark beard, and my stomach flips. *Fuck*. Did I make things awkward? I know this is all supposed to be just no strings attached fun, so maybe I just crossed a line by saying that.

"Sorry," I say quickly, backtracking. "I didn't mean to—"

"Hailey." Nick's gruff voice interrupts my babbling. My mouth snaps shut, and he turns toward me as our gazes meet. "The reason I was always so quiet around you was because... I like you too. And I was never sure how to act around you."

My heart skips a beat in my chest, stuttering once before starting to gallop like a runaway horse. For a long moment, I can't think of a single thing to say. Because unless I'm totally misinterpreting, Nick just admitted that he had a thing for me, even as far back as when we were kids.

The thudding of my heart intensifies as Nick and I stare at each other in silence.

Then I rest a hand on his chest, rising up onto my tiptoes to reach him as I press a soft kiss to his cheek. I'm tempted to kiss his lips, but I'm not sure Dylan's party is the best place for a big show of PDA—and besides, I worry that if I did that, I wouldn't be able to stop.

He leans into my touch a bit, like a flower seeking the sun, and butterflies fill my stomach when I finally draw back.

"I'm glad I know you, Nick Cooper," I whisper softly. "I'm glad you've let me get to know the *real* you."

His throat works as he swallows. "I am too."

I grin at him, the giddy feeling I felt when I snuck out of the closet after Sebastian returning tenfold. But then I hear laughter coming from the corner where Reid and his ex are standing, and it breaks through the happy, light feeling in my chest. I look over to see Sutton smiling broadly and giggling at something Reid just said.

My stomach drops out, a cold feeling rushing over me as if I've had a bucket of ice water dumped over my head.

"Hey. You okay, songbird?" Nick cocks his head, looking a bit concerned, and I realize I must be frowning unconsciously.

"Oh. Yeah." I do my best to find my smile again as I nod. "Everything is fine."

My lie sounds unconvincing even to me, but before Nick can ask me anything else, Sebastian walks up to us with my brother beside him.

"All right, I think we've put in enough time here, don't you think?" Sebastian tugs at his tie. "Let's get the fuck out of here and go somewhere more comfortable."

Lucas nods in agreement. My brother is usually pretty good at playing the part of polite diplomat at these sorts of functions. It's probably a skill that he's fine-tuned since becoming a football coach and having to manage a team of both players and their parents. But even he looks ready to go.

"Yeah." He scowls. "I made nice with the Montgomerys for a bit, and none of us punched Dylan in the face, so I'd say we've gone above and beyond. I checked with mom and dad, and they're heading out soon too."

Nick nods, stepping away from us. "I'll go grab Reid."

I head toward the door with Sebastian and Lucas, already looking forward to getting out of here.

When Nick returns to join us with his brother in tow, I can't help but stiffen a little as Reid's shoulder brushes against mine. I pull away from him, Sutton's laughter still echoing in my mind. I know it's stupid to be mad at him, and I'm not even sure anger is what I'm feeling. But I just need a second before I can act like everything is normal.

He glances over at me, his brows furrowing, but he doesn't

say anything as we all get our coats and leave the venue, stepping out into the snowy night.

"What do you say? The Old Oak?" Sebastian suggests, and everyone chimes in with agreement. "Lucas, you want a ride?"

"Yeah, thanks. I came with my folks, so I don't have a car here."

When we reach the car, Lucas climbs into the front passenger seat as Sebastian gets behind the wheel. Reid opens one of the back doors for me, ushering me into the car. But before I slide in, he takes the opportunity to catch my arm in a light grip, dropping his head to speak in a low voice.

"Hey, what's wrong? Did something happen at the party?"

"Nope, nothing at all." I bite my bottom lip, then blurt quietly, "Looks like you had fun though. I didn't realize that you and Sutton were still so close."

Reid's head jerks back a little, his hand freezing on the car door as he looks at me with a startled expression.

"Are you guys getting in or what?" my brother calls from inside the car.

I quickly slide in, and Reid climbs in after me, followed by Nick. I end up sitting by the window behind Lucas, with Reid in the middle of the back seat between me and Nick. Sebastian and Lucas fall into easy conversation, and I can feel Reid's gaze on me in the dim interior of the car as he studies me.

"Hey, how about some music?" he says suddenly, looking up toward the front.

"Sure." Lucas turns on the radio. He messes around with it for a bit until he finds a good song, then turns it up.

The sound fills the car, pouring through the speakers as Sebastian drives carefully down the snowy streets. I chew on my bottom lip, staring out the window to keep from looking over at Reid and having to explain why I'm so upset. Honestly, I'm not even sure that I *can* explain why I'm upset. It's all just a hot jumble of emotions, and none of it is very easily put into words.

After a moment, Reid rests a hand on my leg. I glance down at it for a second before I meet his eyes, and he leans a bit closer.

"Are you... jealous?" he whispers, his voice barely audible.

My face flames, both because he's calling me out on it and because it's true. He must be able to read the answer on my face, because he shakes his head, a slow smile spreading across his face.

"Trust me, trouble," he breathes. "I have no interest in my ex."

I lean back and lift an eyebrow at him. "Oh, really?" I whisper. "It sure seemed like you did."

His fingers trail up my leg, moving to the inside of my thigh and toying with the edge of my dress. I hate that it gives me chills, and I hate that he clearly notices. His lips curve even more, something burning in his eyes as he leans closer.

"It wasn't her I was thinking about all night." His breath stirs my hair as he speaks quietly. "It was this."

His hand disappears under my dress, and I'm suddenly hyper aware of the fact that my panties are still stuffed safely away in Sebastian's pocket. Reid's fingers find my pussy, and I stiffen, my eyes shooting to the rearview mirror. Is he really doing this? With my brother in the front seat?

Holy fuck.

My eyes drift back to Reid's, and he smirks at me. He clearly knows what he's doing is risky, but he doesn't seem to give a damn because his fingers are tracing my folds, teasing me. If Lucas catches us, I don't even want to think about what might happen... but I also don't want Reid to stop. Not after the way I saw his ex-girlfriend practically throwing herself at him tonight.

I steal another glance in the rearview mirror, but Lucas is totally absorbed by the conversation he's having with Sebastian in the front.

This is insane and I know it, but I can't stop myself. I spread my legs a fraction of an inch, silently inviting Reid to keep going. He smiles devilishly at me before he slips his fingers a little higher and drags them slowly up and down my slit before he presses one of them inside me.

My teeth clamp down on my lip to keep myself from making any noise, and I focus my eyes straight ahead, both to keep an eye on Lucas and because I know if I look at Reid, something is going to come out of my mouth and give us away.

Reid slides his finger in even deeper, then starts slowly working it in and out. His hand is thankfully covered by my dress, but I have to grip the cushion of the seat to hold back the moan that's bubbling in the back of my throat. Lucas's conversation with Sebastian and Nick definitely wouldn't be enough to cover it up.

"So, what did all you think of the ball?" Lucas asks the whole car, and I tense up. It takes everything I have to keep a straight face, to not betray any hint that one of his best friends has a finger buried in me as we speak.

But Reid must really be in the mood to torment me, because just as I open my mouth to answer Lucas, another finger slips into me, choking the words in my mouth.

"F-fine," I stammer.

Lucas nods, not seeming to catch on. *Thank fuck.*

"I can't speak for the rest of you, but I had a fucking great time," Sebastian says, glancing at me in the rearview mirror from the driver's seat.

His eyes glint at me for a moment—until he spots Reid's hand in my lap. I watch the comprehension play out on his face as he puts two and two together, and I silently beg him to be quiet. I give him the tiniest shake of my head I can manage, and he winks at me. I don't know whether that's a good or bad sign.

"It was all right," Nick says, thankfully taking the focus off me as Reid starts fucking me faster with his fingers and massaging my clit with his palm. My breath catches in my throat, and my eyes burn at the corners from the effort it's taking to hold in all the noises I'd love to be making right now. "But I'm glad we blew out of there early."

"Hah. Nick has never been one to get into the holiday spirit," Sebastian teases him, and Nick flips him off in the rearview, making the whole car laugh. Then Nick turns to face me, and his eyes land on the spot where Reid's hand is moving surreptitiously beneath my dress.

What the hell are you doing? he mouths silently at me.

I give him a look before darting my gaze to Reid, reminding him that *I'm* not the one who's doing this. A heated, amused look spreads across Nick's face, and instead of doing anything to rescue me from my current predicament—although I'm not sure I *want* to be rescued, no matter how risky what we're doing is—he settles back to watch, his eyes glinting in the lights that flash by outside the car.

"I've been feeling a little more cheerful than usual this holiday, honestly," Sebastian says, still looking at me in the rearview.

"Me too," Reid agrees as he pushes his fingers all the way inside me.

"Wow. That's a Christmas miracle," Lucas says, and the guys all laugh.

I appreciate that the triplets are doing their best to keep Lucas talking and distracted. God knows I need the help right now, because it's taking every ounce of willpower I have not to melt into a moaning puddle in the back seat with Reid's fingers working me over. Between the adrenaline rush of doing something like this and the way Reid seems to know my body even better than I do, I'm not going to be able to hold it together much longer.

"It's nice having you back in town though, sis," Lucas comments. "Just like old times, getting the whole gang back together. It's awesome."

"Yeah, it's great," I say stiffly with a forced smile, even

though he can't see my face from where he's sitting in front of me. I can barely get the words out around the moan that's burning in the back of my throat and threatening to give me away. Reid curls his fingers inside me, and I clench my thighs around his hand, my hands curling into fists as pleasure shoots through me.

Nick's nostrils flare as he watches my response, his eyes dark.

Lucas, bless him, is totally oblivious. He slumps back in his seat and looks out the window. "Are we there yet?"

"Almost," Sebastian answers, glancing up at me in the mirror as he makes a turn. My body weight shifts with it, driving Reid's fingers deeper into me. "Something tells me you aren't the only one in a hurry to get off this ride."

His words are thick with innuendo, and a shiver races down my spine because he's right. As good as Reid is making me feel, he's also driving me crazy, and I can't wait to come—the risk be damned. While Lucas is looking out the window at the streets of Chestnut Hill as the scenery slowly passes by, my eyes lock with Reid's. I nod at him shakily, silently pleading with him to bring me over the edge.

He smirks and starts to work my clit and my pussy at the same time, sliding his fingers in and out as his thumb circles my clit. Sebastian turns to Lucas, asking him a question even as he reaches out to turn the music up a bit, and a rush of gratitude fills me as pleasure spikes in my veins.

Reid glances at his brother, then shifts his expression back to me.

He subtly leans a bit closer to me, dropping his voice as he murmurs, "This is for thinking I still have any interest in Sutton, trouble. Remember this next time you feel jealous of her or any other woman. None of them could ever compare to you."

He drags his fingers out of me and pinches my clit gently, making me jolt and dig my nails into my palms. The rush of sensation sends me soaring closer to an orgasm, and when Reid repeats the action once more, a little harder this time, I fall to pieces.

I raise one hand to my mouth and bite down hard on my knuckles to keep from making a sound, my gaze still locked straight forward. Sebastian glances up, watching the scene play out in the rearview mirror without giving anything away or crashing the car, and somehow, he manages to keep up his conversation with my brother through it all. But although his tone is even and casual, I can feel the weight of his gaze like a physical touch.

Reid circles my clit with the pads of his fingers, working me through the end of my climax, and a tiny squeak escapes me.

"You okay, Hailey?" Lucas asks. "I can scoot my seat up if you don't have enough room."

"No!" I choke out, my pulse jumping. "No, I'm fine."

"There's plenty of room back here. We're good." Reid slowly pulls his fingers away from my clit as he speaks, leaving a smear of wetness on my inner thighs, then withdraws his hand from beneath my dress. My eyelids flutter as I watch him, and he stares at me intently as he lifts his fingers to his face.

Reid, I mouth, wishing I could whimper his name out loud as he sneakily licks the tips of his fingers, cleaning up my wetness.

"Yeah," he says, dropping his hand and leaning back in the seat, satisfaction radiating from him as I struggle to catch my breath, my entire body tingling. "We're doing just fine back here."

26

HAILEY

The car pulls into The Old Oak parking lot before I'm ready to get out. Hell, I don't even know if I'm actually going to be *able* to stand up when the time comes. I'm shaking from the orgasm, feeling flustered and unsteady.

"Looks like the place is hoppin' tonight," Lucas comments as Sebastian cuts the engine, surveying the crowded parking lot. "Hopefully we can get our usual table."

The fact that he's talking about tables and not about bloody murder makes it clear he has no idea what just happened, but my heart is still slamming hard against my ribs at the idea of how easily we could've gotten caught.

I glare over at Reid, who just arches a challenging brow at me as he slides across the seat and gets out of the car. Dammit, he's so fucking bossy and confident—and even though I secretly love it, there's no chance in hell that I'll ever admit that to him.

Thankfully, Nick comes around to open my door and takes my hand, helping to steady me as I step out. Sitting that close to us in the backseat means that he knows *exactly* what just happened, and he's doing his best to help me keep it under wraps. His calloused hands are rough against mine as he gives my hand a small squeeze, and the desire burning in his gaze is almost enough to make me come on the spot.

"You good?" he murmurs, his voice low.

"Yeah." I swallow, glancing across the car to where Reid is standing. "Reid was just... making a point."

Reid's gaze locks with mine, and he reaches down to subtly adjust himself. A surge of satisfaction rises inside me at the strained look that passes over his face—at least he was torturing himself even more than he was torturing me.

Nick chuckles as Sebastian slams the driver's side door next to us. "A point, huh? He seems to have made it well."

"Yeah." I clear my throat, hoping the blush on my cheeks will be mistaken for a flush from the cold. "He did."

"Come on!" Lucas slams his own door and jerks his chin toward the bar. "Let's get inside. I'm sure it's getting crowded."

Sure enough, it's packed in The Old Oak, and there aren't many available tables or seats at the bar when we enter the crowded space.

"I'll go get us some drinks. Bar service will be faster than waiting at a table. You guys find us a spot." Sebastian takes off toward the bar on a mission to hunt us all down some cocktails.

"I'm going to the bathroom," I say, raising my voice to be heard over the music. It will do me some good to splash cold water on my face, and I still need another minute to fully recover from the orgasm.

My brother nods, and he and the other guys head off to find us a table. I take my time in the restroom, gathering my scattered composure and sliding some gloss over my lips. Once I feel like I look a little less flushed and freshly fucked, I slip out of the ladies' room.

"Hailey? Hailey Bennett, is that you?"

I turn at the sound of my name to see a man emerging from the men's bathroom. He looks familiar, and I frown a little as I try to place him.

"Do you remember me?" He grins. "Ken Hayward. We had biology together junior year."

"Oh. Of course! How have you been?"

"I'm good. Wow, I didn't know you were back in town. I thought I heard through the grapevine that you were living out in LA now."

I dread thinking about what else this guy from my school days has heard. I feel like my reputation in Chestnut Hill is the stuff of legends—but not the good kind of legend.

"Yeah, I'm back home to see my family for a while."

"Nice, nice." He nods, stepping a little closer to me as we move out of the way of a few people heading to the bathrooms. "So what were you doing out in LA? Modeling?"

"Oh, no. I was—"

My words break off as the hairs on the back of my neck stand up. A second later, Ken glances over my shoulder, his eyes widening slightly. When I follow his gaze, I see the three Cooper triplets wearing identical expressions, standing nearly shoulder to shoulder in the hallway behind us. They glower so hard at Ken that he doesn't even bother to say goodbye to me. He just slips *back* into the bathroom, probably to avoid having to try to squeeze past them to get to the rest of the bar.

I huff a laugh, putting my hands on my hips as I turn to face the three men. "Honestly, you're just as bad now as you were back when I was in high school."

"What's that supposed to mean? We always had your back in high school." Reid isn't wrong, but that's not what I meant.

"Yeah, and you also always scared off practically any guy who wanted to date me. Even an innocent exchange like this one, a bit of harmless flirting, and you guys practically jumped down the throat of any man that looked at or spoke to me."

"It's not our fault." Sebastian smirks. "None of those clowns were good enough for you."

But Nick isn't laughing. He steps closer, his large body

looming over mine in the hallway as he boxes me in against the wall.

"We're going to be even worse now," he warns in a low voice. "Because now I know just how good it feels to be buried inside your sweet pussy. And I'm not in the mood to share with anyone but my brothers."

Holy shit. The bartender is gonna have to come mop me up off the floor, because I think I'm about to melt into a damn puddle.

Nick steps back, sliding his hand into mine and tugging me away from the wall. He leads me over to rejoin his brothers, and as we all head back through the crowded bar, Reid leans over and murmurs in my ear, "Nick is right. If you get to be jealous, then so do we. And I don't like anyone's hands on you but ours."

I swallow hard, remembering how his hand wasn't just *on* me during the car ride over here. It was inside me.

Fuck, I'm never gonna make it to the end of the night.

These men have already made me come three times, but despite that, I'm in a state of such high arousal that I feel like I'm a walking piece of tinder, just waiting to catch flame.

Lucas waves at us from the table where he's holding our spots, leaning back as we all take our seats around him. There aren't quite enough chairs, but Nick solves that problem by tugging me down onto his lap and wrapping an arm around my waist. I swear I can feel a bulge beneath my ass, and it takes every bit of restraint I have not to squirm against him.

Despite the constant distraction of Nick's proximity—and the way he seems bound and determined to take advantage of the fact that the two of us are technically the ones on a 'date' tonight by keeping his hands on me at all times—it's actually really nice to be out with my brother and the three triplets.

It doesn't take long before we're reminiscing about old times, joking and laughing about stupid shit the guys got up to when they were younger, and the different memories we all seem to have of certain events.

I swear that it was Lucas's idea to sneak onto the Brewer family's property and rig up a massive slip-and-slide with a tarp, a hose, and some dish soap. He shakes his head and laughs, shooting back that *I'm* the one who forgot to turn off the hose, accidentally leaving the water running all night and flooding the field. That leads us into reminiscing about the time all five of us made a mini ice skating rink in our backyard, and more stories spiral out from there, leaving us all laughing.

About thirty minutes after our arrival, the noise in the bar dips a little as the music cuts out, and the bartender announces that karaoke night is about to start.

Lucas perks up. "Oh shit. I forgot it's karaoke night. Hailey! You should sign up to sing!"

"No, thanks." I shake my head, my heart skipping a beat. "I'm not really in the mood."

My brother frowns but lets it go. As someone takes the stage to start the first song, I can't help but watch them, a strange feeling of longing tugging at my chest.

I wish I could do that. I wish it was still easy for me.

As if he can read my thoughts, Nick's arms tighten around me a little. The others have resumed their conversation around the table, but he ignores them for the moment, tucking my hair behind my ear before murmuring, "Just imagine you're singing in the shower. Close your eyes and pretend that's where you are."

I bite my lower lip, my gaze dropping to the pocked wooden table. I'm torn between fear and an almost bone-deep desire to sing, the two sides of me warring in my head.

"You have such a beautiful voice, songbird," he whispers. "You don't have to hide it."

I look up at him, surprised by his choice of words, and his blue eyes meet mine. He's still got his arms wrapped around me, his chest solid and warm against my body. I know he won't *make* me go up there, but the look of confidence and pride in his face makes me want to be the person he sees when he looks at me.

Someone brave.

Someone talented.

Someone free and uninhibited.

My pulse starts to race faster, but I nod. "Okay."

Nick smiles, releasing me as I slip off his lap and make my way toward the signup sheet at the bar. I can barely believe I'm doing this, even as I pick out my song and then return to the table to wait for my turn. We keep talking and drinking, but I'm barely aware of any of it anymore, my mind totally focused on what I know is coming.

And then the bartender calls my name, and I feel like I might pass out on the spot.

"You've got this," Sebastian tells me, giving me an encouraging look. Reid echoes that sentiment, and Nick and Lucas chime in too.

Okay. Okay, I've got this.

I'm still terrified, but even though my nerves are on fire, Nick's calm words help to put out the blaze. I guess he has a knack for that, and for encouraging people to be the best versions of themselves. It's why I know he's going to be a great fire chief at the station someday.

I make my way up to the small, makeshift stage slowly. The song plays, and I close my eyes and start to sing. I do just what Nick said and pretend that it's just me, alone in the shower under the running water with the excellent makeshift bathroom acoustics, instead of a crowded bar filled to the brim with people watching and listening to me.

It goes okay at first—but then I make the mistake of opening my eyes.

As soon as I see the audience staring back at me, the words to the song fly right out of my head.

I stop singing mid-verse, holding the microphone in a tight grip as my heart tries to pound its way out of my chest.

Then a voice cuts through the bar, deep and masculine.

It's Sebastian, and he's singing.

Reid's voice joins his brother's a second later as they pick up where I left off, reminding me of the lyrics. My brother figures out what they're doing quickly and starts to sing too, and I swear I can even see Nick's lips moving as he adds his voice.

A few other people in the bar start to belt out the song too, and I laugh, a giddy sort of feeling rushing through me as I gaze out at all of them. They're all still watching me, but it's no longer quite as terrifying as it was a moment ago, and I join back in with them as we start the third verse.

My voice picks up strength as I go, and I keep my eyes open as I lose myself in the music again, no longer worry about performing and just enjoying the pure act of singing.

By the time the song ends, my voice is the only one in the bar. Everyone else has gone quiet, and as the last note fades out, there's a moment of silence.

Then applause breaks out, along with a few whistles and stomping boots.

I don't even care if they're applauding my singing or just the fact that I stumbled and didn't give up. Either way, I'll take it.

The Cooper triplets and my brother are all on their feet, clapping the loudest, and the looks on their faces make my heart swell. I give a little bow and hand the microphone off to the next person, then scamper back toward the table, feeling almost high from the exhilaration of the moment.

It might not have been the world's best performance, but I did it.

And I'm so fucking proud of myself.

27

HAILEY

Waking up surrounded by male bodies is something that I'm quickly getting used to. When we got home after singing karaoke, Nick was the first one to fuck me, bending me over and letting his brothers watch as he made me scream his name. Then Sebastian and Reid shared me, taking turns fucking me until I was shaking like a leaf between them, before coming on my stomach and marking me up with a possessiveness that made me shiver.

The next night was more of the same. And the night after that.

After several more nights of sleeping nestled between all of the brothers, passing out after being fucked by all of them, I'm falling down a rabbit hole and becoming more and more certain that I never want to leave Wonderland.

It's been a wild few days—hedonistic and perfect—as the guys have helped me explore my bucket list. And as if that wasn't enough, they've also added a few items that I never even thought to put on my naughty list in the first place. I've loved every minute of it.

I'm sore, but in a good way. I think my body is finally

starting to adjust to the constant sex, and my recovery time is a lot faster than it was after our first night together.

Yawning quietly, I try to stretch my arms, but there are limbs tangled up everywhere. I'm sandwiched in between Nick and Reid, with Sebastian on Reid's other side, his arm draped along the base of the headboard and his fingers threaded through my hair. They're all still dead asleep. I think they might have underestimated my sex drive, because I've definitely been wearing them out too.

Treating it sort of like a game of Tetris, I slide out strategically without waking up any of them and walk to the bathroom.

As I catch a glimpse of myself in the mirror, I can see that I have a rocking case of sex hair. The back of it is so teased from rubbing against the pillow that I could pass as an eighties rockstar.

I strip down and start the water for the shower. After it gets warm enough, I step under the spray and stand there for a few minutes with my eyes closed, thinking about the last few days and how the four of us have fallen into such a comfortable rhythm together. It's going to feel strange when it's not like this anymore, as if there's a chord missing in a song, and nothing hits quite right anymore.

When I open my eyes to reach for my shampoo, I come up short. It's not on the shelf I've claimed as my own in the shower caddy.

"What the...?"

I frown, glancing around in confusion for a second before realizing that my shampoo bottle is on Reid's shelf instead. Before I can question what it's doing there, I hear the bathroom door open, and I open the shower curtain to peek out and see who it is.

My eyes are met with the tantalizing sight of Reid, fully

naked as he pads across the small bathroom. I grin and pull the curtain open wider, inviting him inside.

"I thought you were asleep," I say as he steps beneath the water with me.

He nods. "I was. I woke up and noticed you were gone, so I came to find you."

"I'm glad you did. Now you can tell me why you stole my shampoo."

Reid laughs as he takes the shampoo and squirts some onto his palm. I watch the inked lines on his chest move as he rubs his hands together to get a good lather.

"I might've used it the other day," he admits, looking slightly sheepish.

"Really? Did you run out of your own?"

"No. I just..." He shrugs, and I raise an eyebrow.

"You just like the way it smells?" I finish for him, guessing where he was going with that.

His eyes flick down, catching with mine. The blue-gray color looks soft and warm in the morning light. "I like the way *you* smell."

My heart gives a flutter. Sometimes the simplest little things he says knock me on my ass, leaving me feeling breathless and a little off-balance and completely unsure of how to respond. Before I can say anything, Reid grins, jerking his chin in a circular motion.

"Turn around so I can wash your hair."

"Bossy," I mutter.

I turn around just like he ordered, although I take my sweet time doing it.

"Sassy," he shoots back, giving my ass a little slap with a shampoo covered palm when I move too slowly for him.

I chuckle, feeling more at ease as we slip into the comfortable dynamic that's sprung up between us over the past week or so. It's a lot like how we used to interact, but with a new undercurrent beneath it that makes sassing him and riling up his bossy side even more fun.

"Are you gonna sing for me?" he asks as he starts to wash my hair.

The sensation of having my scalp massaged by his strong fingers is so divine that I almost melt into a puddle. I've never had anyone wash my hair before, except at the hair salon. And this is so much better than that.

"Mm, maybe," I murmur, letting my eyes drift closed. "But I think today might be an out of the shower singing day."

"Good." He chuckles. "I like those."

Ever since my karaoke experience, I've been getting a bit bolder. I haven't sung in front of a crowd again, but I've started singing around the house. Not just in the shower, but while I'm doing dishes or cooking in the kitchen, or playing with Bruno in front of the fireplace. The guys seem to love it, and I do too. I feel like I'm getting back a piece of myself that I lost for too long.

We stand together in silence for a few minutes, Reid gently lathering the shampoo through my hair, and as my mind wanders back to that night at The Old Oak and everything that came before it at the Christmas ball, I bite my lip, a question burning on the tip of my tongue.

"Can I ask you something?" I say quietly.

"Sure."

"Why didn't things work out with you and Sutton? I mean, you guys were together for a while, weren't you?"

"Yes, we were."

"So why did you break up? What ended it?"

He turns me around to rinse the shampoo out of my hair, his gaze a little out of focus and his expression thoughtful as he considers his answer. It's a long moment before he speaks, and then he sighs.

"My parents were so in love with each other. I always loved the strength of connection that they had. I never wanted to be in a relationship that was anything less than that, especially after we lost them. I wanted to find a love like they had... and I realized that Sutton and I weren't really like that. It wasn't how I felt about her."

I nod, resting my hands on his chest as I mull his answer over in my mind. I feel like I can relate to that, at least a bit.

"I don't think that I ever had that kind of love with Dylan either," I admit.

"Of course you didn't." He scowls, smoothing my wet hair back from my face. "You're too good for that fucker. You always have been."

"I wish I'd realized that sooner." I blow out a breath, tracing the lines of his tattoos idly with my fingers. "If Dylan is trying to punish me for our break-up by getting his parents to raise the rent on my family's diner, I'll never forgive him. My family's whole livelihood could be in jeopardy. It's fucking awful."

I've been stopping by the diner every day since I found out what was going on, doing my best to lend a hand and help out. But there's nothing I can do to fix the rent situation, and I hate that feeling of powerlessness.

Reid leans down to press a kiss to the top of my head. "I'm sorry, trouble. That fucking sucks."

"Thanks."

I let out a breath, gazing at his chest as he straightens. My fingers follow the lines of the intricate design that covers his entire left pec and the meaty part of his shoulder. I've seen it dozens of times by now, but I've never really studied it this closely before.

"Are these daisies?" I ask, cocking my head to one side as I notice what looks like a twisting chain of flowers woven into a broader pattern of sharp lines and bold curves. The daisies are subtly hidden among the stronger elements, which include barbed wire coiling around a compass with the arrow pointing north.

"Yeah."

"I never noticed them before." I glance up at him, blinking water droplets out of my eyelashes. "I love daisies. They're my favorite flower."

"I know."

Just like a few moments ago, his words are simple, but the effect they have on me is dizzying and complicated.

I swallow hard, licking my lips as he holds my gaze in the steamy little cocoon of the shower. He doesn't say anything else about the tattoo, and I don't ask if he knew that daisies were my favorite when he got it—or if that's why he incorporated them.

I think I'm a little scared to ask, honestly. I'm scared to know the truth, whatever it might be, and even asking a probing question like that feels like it breaks the 'casual, no-strings' rule we implemented. It opens a door that I'm terrified to open, because on the other side of that door, everything could fall apart.

What's happening between me and the Cooper brothers right now is simple and easy. As wild and debauched as it is, it still feels *safe*.

I'm not sure my heart could take anything more.

But even though I don't say anything, I can't stop my fingers from sliding over his wet skin, tracing the daisies woven into his tattoo. He drops his gaze to watch my fingers, then rests his hand over mine, flattening my palm against his chest. I can feel the heavy thud of his heartbeat as he leans down and—

The shower curtain is ripped back as Sebastian pokes his head into the shower.

I let out a startled squeak at his sudden appearance, and Reid mutters a curse under his breath, dropping his hand away from mine.

"Dammit, Sebastian. We've been over this. You can't just barge into the fucking bathroom when someone is showering."

"Oh yeah?" Sebastian smirks. "Then how did you get in here?"

Reid snaps his mouth shut, glowering at his brother, and the youngest Cooper triplet laughs.

"You two sure look nice and cozy," he observes, arching a brow.

"Yeah, so shut the curtain, you're letting out our steam." Reid tries to pull the curtain closed on him, but Sebastian just pushes it open again.

"Hey, shortcake." He gives me a playful wink. "How about another dare?"

Reid looks like he's about to strangle Sebastian, which I'm sure is at least half the reason his brother is still in here. I'm not the only one who enjoys pushing Reid's buttons. "What the fuck are you talking about?"

"Yeah, what kind of dare?" I ask, intrigued.

"I dare you to streak through the woods behind the house. You're already naked, and you're nice and warm from the shower. So the cold air and fresh snow will be invigorating." He grins. "Kind of like the polar plunge."

Reid grimaces, but I'm already trying to guess whether this will be easier or harder than jumping into a freezing cold lake. My guess is easier, since nothing could be as cold as that water—and just like when we were kids and Sebastian would throw down a dare, there's no way I'm going to back down.

"Okay, fine." I shoot Sebastian a sweet smile. "I'll do it... if all of you do it with me."

"Done," he agrees instantly, at the exact same moment that Reid says, "No fucking way."

"Well, now you're just being a party pooper like Nick," Sebastian chides his brother just as the man in question walks into the bathroom to see what we're all doing in here.

"Are you guys talking about me?" He frowns, his eyes groggy and his hair still messy from sleep. Nick is fucking adorable first thing in the morning, half mountain man and half teddy bear. "What are you all doing in here anyway?"

"We *were* enjoying a nice, relaxing shower," Reid points out, irritation coloring his tone. But he clearly knows his brothers well enough to realize that the quiet moment is long gone, because he turns off the water and grabs me a towel from the rack, helping me wrap it around myself.

Sebastian laughs and explains the dare to Nick, who surprises me by nodding.

"The guys at the fire station did something similar on my first day," he tells us. "So sure, I'm in."

That leaves Reid as the only holdout, and he finally agrees—either because of the pleading look I give him or just because his pride won't allow him to be the only brother who isn't up to the challenge.

"Worried about shrinkage?" Sebastian teases as we all head downstairs and walk naked toward the back door of the house.

Reid snorts. "Even if there were shrinkage, I'd still be fine. I'd be more worried about all those metal piercings freezing your impaled dick."

Sebastian howls with laughter, and even Nick chuckles at that. I can't help but join in, amused by their banter.

At the back door, Nick lays out the rules: one lap around the entire wooded area behind the house, not taking shortcuts, and no covering up your naughty bits. There aren't any neighbors too close by, and the chances of someone walking by at this time of morning are slim, so the risk of being spotted by anyone is negligible.

"The winner is the one who completes the whole streak without breaking any of the rules and makes it back to the house first."

"That's easy, I'm the smallest and the fastest." I probably just jinxed myself by bragging, but I don't even care.

Sebastian opens the back door to count us down. "Three... two... one..."

A gust of chilly air sweeps into the house, and I'm already anticipating frostbite.

"Go!"

All four of us take off running.

I make it out of the door first, followed by Sebastian. I glance quickly over my shoulder and see Reid and Nick get stuck trying to squeeze through the door at the same time. They struggle for a few seconds before pushing through and making a beeline after us.

As my bare feet pound through the snow, the cold makes me gasp and sucks my breath away. The frigid air burns my lungs as I run, and my toes go numb almost instantly. As much as I've never been a huge fan of running, I embrace it now because the physical exertion is the only thing keeping me warm.

For a few seconds, I'm in the lead. I wasn't wrong about being the smallest, most agile, and lightest on my feet. But the loop around the back of the yard is studded with so many trees that there's more weaving in and out than I expected. I can tell the men are coming up fast behind me, and as I put on a burst of speed, I trip over a tree root hidden under the white drifts and fall face first into a mound of snow.

"Hailey! Oh shit!" Sebastian laughs as he stops to help me up, brushing the snow out of my hair. "Are you okay?"

The other two men catch up to us and stop to make sure I'm all right.

I laugh breathlessly, my teeth chattering a little. "Other than my nipples being frozen solid, yes, I'm fine."

"I'm happy to kiss them if that would help." Reid smirks, giving me a filthy look, and Nick bends down to gather up a mound of snow in his hands.

Before anyone can ask what he's doing, he molds the snow into a ball and pitches it at Reid's head.

"Motherfucker!" Reid retaliates instantly, not even bothering to form the snow into a ball, just grabbing a handful and pitching it at Nick.

Within seconds, things have escalated into a full-blown snowball fight. And as cold as I was a moment ago, I can barely feel it anymore as I join in. We scream and shout and run around the yard, stopping to collect snow and throw snowballs at each other. The guys go lighter on me—except for the one that Reid hurls at my ass, which leaves a solid red welt.

"That's for being a brat," he tells me, his voice husky.

I smirk at him and get him back with two snowballs at once while Sebastian has him distracted with a snowball strike to the shoulder.

Just as I'm reaching down to scoop up another handful of snow, someone snatches me up by the waist. I'm thrown over a muscled shoulder, and I yelp as the world tilts around me.

"Nick! What are you—"

"Someone is coming," he informs me, striding quickly around the side of the house to get us out of sight. "And no one gets to see you like this, flushed and beautiful and naked. No one but us."

Butterflies take off in my stomach, and I laugh at how much he acts like a guardian grizzly bear sometimes. From my upside down view, I catch sight of Sebastian and Reid as they join us to walk back inside. I can only imagine what we look like—three big, burly, naked men with their cocks hanging out, carrying a naked woman back to their house.

This would definitely be a good bit of juicy gossip—*if* anyone had actually seen us.

28

HAILEY

After a change of clothes and a hot cup of cocoa, I sit all curled up on the couch beneath a blanket that Nick pulled out of the closet for me. It's extra thick and warm and feels homemade. I wonder if it's something that perhaps Mrs. Cooper made for her kids years ago.

Bruno is curled up on the couch beside me, openly snoring with one paw on my lap as if we've suddenly become best friends.

"Jesus, they really do make 'em different in Montana," Lorelai says, her voice coming through the speaker on my phone. "Butt ass naked? All three of them? And you too?"

I chuckle. "Yup."

"Yeah, there's no fucking way you could *pay* me to run around in the snow naked like that. I get cold when it drops into the fifties here." She snorts. "Not even the promise of three dicks could get me to willingly go streaking in a frozen tundra, no matter how good the sex was."

Leaning deeper into the couch cushions, I adjust the phone at my ear. Bruno gives me a slightly put out look as I disturb his slumber, then rests his head on my lap alongside his paw.

I smile down at him, scratching his ear as I say, "Well, the sex is *really* good, so that helps. But that's not why I did it. It was just... fun."

"*Just* fun?" Lorelai's voice shifts a little, and I hear the unspoken question in her words.

"Yes, *just* fun." I nod firmly, trying to cut her off before she can get started. "I told you, I can do this without getting too attached. Yes, I like them a lot. Yes, it's been amazing getting to see all these new sides of them."

And I'm going to miss them so much when I leave again that I don't know how I'm going to breathe.

That thought hits me hard, nearly knocking the wind out of me, and I take a second to recover my voice before I speak.

"I'm not gonna lie and pretend these guys don't mean something to me," I tell my best friend. "But they've *always* meant something to me. Nothing has changed, and nothing has to change. We've still got the rules in place."

"Right." She laughs softly. "The *rules*."

"What?" I ask, because I know there's something else she wants to say.

I can almost hear her shrug over the phone. "I'm just saying, not everything in life fits into a neat little box. Not everything follows the rules."

I pick at a loose thread on the blanket, biting my lip. "I know. But this has to. It's the only way to make sure no one gets hurt."

"Okay." Lorelai hesitates, and I wish she was here with me right now so we could be having this conversation face to face. When she speaks again, her voice is a little quieter. "I just want to make sure you don't let the past hold you back from what you want in the present, or even the future. You ran from your past once, but you don't always have to keep running."

"I know," I whisper, thinking back to the bar the other night, and how amazing it felt to sing in front of people, despite the utter terror of it too. It felt like shedding a piece of that past I've been running away from, but I know that parts of it are still clinging to me, weighing me down like anchors.

"Shit, I've gotta go." Lorelai makes an annoyed noise. "Derek just sent me an SOS message, he needs me to run to West Hollywood to pick something up for him. Sorry!"

"That's okay." I roll my eyes, knowing what a nightmare her boss can be. "Tell him I said 'fuck you.'"

"Oh, I will. And I'll throw in one from myself while I'm at it." She makes a kissing noise through the phone. "Love you! Talk soon, okay? Bye!"

"Bye."

I hang up, grinning at the way I can already hear her rushing out the door. She has a sort of love/hate relationship with her boss, with maybe a tiny bit of lust thrown in there too. I'm honestly waiting for the two of them to just hate fuck once to get it out of their systems.

When my phone rings again a second later, I figure that Lorelai forgot to tell me something. But as I swipe across the screen to answer, I realize it's my mom calling instead.

"Hey, Mom."

"Hi, sweetheart. I have a favor to ask you. Any chance that you can cover a shift at the diner this evening? Your father and I have to get some paperwork done, and Pippa can't work tonight. We're applying for a grant, although it feels like a bit of a long shot. But it's worth trying, I guess. Anyway, I know you've been helping out a lot, but this would be a full shift, with closing duties and everything. Would you feel comfortable—"

"Of course," I say immediately. "Yeah, I can do that. No problem."

"Oh thank you. You're a lifesaver! Jacob will be here too, but he's just not fast enough to be able to work on his own yet. So I'd feel better having two people here in case it gets busy."

"I get that. I can totally come in. Just let me know what time."

She does, and I promise to be there before we hang up.

It's not how I was planning on spending my evening, but I know how hard my parents have been working, and I really meant it when I said I wanted to help in any way I can. I'm still really worried about their business going under. The least I can do is pick up a few shifts as needed—especially if it gives them a chance to look for ways to save the diner.

It's late afternoon by now, so I don't have a ton of time before I'll need to head out. I reluctantly peel myself off the comfy couch, earning a sad look from Bruno, which I soothe by rubbing his scruff. Then I head upstairs, singing under my breath as I put away some laundry I started earlier. It feels oddly domestic, folding up my clothes and putting them away after grabbing them from the guys' dryer, and I try to ignore the fact that I kind of like it.

Sebastian is the first and only one of the three brothers to get home before I leave to head out to the diner. I didn't expect any of them to be back yet and am pleasantly surprised when I walk downstairs and see him coming in through the front door.

"Hey!" I grin as he stomps a little snow off his boots on the mat. "Early day for you? Not enough broken cars to fix?"

"Nah. I got all my work done, and I could've stayed late to start another project but decided not to. Instead of servicing cars, I figured I'd much rather come home and spend my time servicing other things... like *you*." He winks, then shrugs. "Besides, after dicking around all morning and getting a late start, I honestly just wasn't in the mood to work."

"Me neither." I scrunch up my face. "But unfortunately, I won't be able to stay here and hang out with you tonight. My mom called, and they need me to come in and help cover a shift at the diner tonight. Apparently, she and my dad are working on applying for some grant, and Pippa is unavailable to cover the shift. They have the new guy working tonight, but my mom says he needs my help."

"New guy?"

"Yeah. You've probably seen him around. He's younger, kind of tall, maybe early twenties. Blond hair, cute smile."

Recognition flashes in Sebastian's eyes, and then he frowns. "So it's just going to be the two of you working at the diner tonight? Alone?"

"Yup."

He was just starting to take off his boots, but now he bends down and laces them back up. "I'll go with you."

My eyebrows pop upward. "Really?"

I'm surprised he wants to come do a shift at my parents' diner with me, especially since he just said he doesn't really feel like working. But he nods decisively.

"Yeah, I'll go. Actually…" A slow smile spreads across his face. "Wait here a second."

He turns on his heel and strides out of the room, heading upstairs for a few moments. I do what he asked, waiting for him with curiosity burning in my chest.

When he returns, there's a glint in his eye that I don't quite recognize, and he walks toward me without breaking stride. As soon as he reaches me, Sebastian boxes me up against the wall, and a thrill races through me as the heat of his body radiates into mine. His starving eyes rake over me, and I feel like he's already stripped me naked, even though we're both fully clothed.

He reaches around to his back pocket and holds something up between us, and when I realize what it is, my breath catches.

"A wearable vibrator?" I arch a brow, keeping my tone teasing even though my heart is racing. "I wouldn't have pegged you as the type, but if that's what you're into…"

Sebastian chuckles and shakes his head. "Oh no, don't get it twisted. This is all for you, shortcake."

Desire rushes through me at his words, my stomach fluttering at the thought of walking around with the vibrator inside me and it being our dirty little secret.

Maybe I'm reading into this all wrong, but I feel like this is his way of claiming me. Of making sure that even if I'm working with another man all night, I'll be thinking of Sebastian every second of the evening. The possessiveness of it touches something primal inside me, making goosebumps spread over my skin as arousal floods my veins.

As if he can smell it radiating off me, Sebastian reaches down and unzips my pants before working them down my hips.

"Spread your legs a little for me," he commands.

"Fuck," I whisper, biting my lip. But I do as I'm told, and Sebastian kneels in front of me with the vibrator already humming in one hand. He smiles up at me for a second, then teases my pussy lips with the vibration. If I wasn't already worked up, I damn sure am now.

But he switches it off a moment later and starts pushing it into me slowly. It's shaped in such a way that while the majority of the silicone toy is buried inside my pussy, there's a small curved part of it that nestles right against my clit. When Sebastian is satisfied with the way it's placed, he presses a light kiss to my lower abdomen and stands up.

"You're going to wear that all evening at the diner. And I'm going to keep this with me while you work," he tells me, holding up a little remote control.

Excitement and nerves tangle inside my stomach, and my tongue darts out to wet my lips. "Are you serious about this?"

"Of course. It's on your bucket list, remember?" Sebastian grins as he pockets the remote. He gives me a kiss, then his expression turns more serious as he runs this thumb along my jaw gently. "Do you trust me, shortcake?"

"Of course," I say instantly, echoing his words.

"Good. Because I promise I'll always take care of you. I'll always look out for you, and I'll never let anything bad happen to you... even if I might tease you a bit first. So do you want to do this?"

I hesitate for only a fraction of a second before nodding. Because the truth is, even if I'm a little nervous, I *do* want this. And I trust him completely.

"Yes," I breathe.

He kisses me again, his tongue sliding hungrily against mine, and it melts away any lingering nerves. "Good. Then let's get going."

He offers me a hand, so I take it, and he walks me to the car to drive me to the diner.

I'm hyper aware of the vibrator inside me, especially when we drive across a particularly bad pothole, making me squirm. Sebastian keeps one hand on my leg for the entire drive, his thumb stroking my knee, and I can't stop thinking about when that same thumb is going to flip the vibrator's switch and make me fall apart.

Or about how excited the idea makes me.

As we pull into a parking spot toward the back of the diner's lot a few minutes later, I spot Mom and Dad emerging from the front door, so I hurry out of the car and stride over to them.

"Hey! Where are you off to in such a hurry?" I ask.

Dad smiles. "I'm taking your mother out for dinner. We both need a bit of time to de-stress with everything that's been going on lately."

"Oh, that's great!" I beam at them both. "You deserve it. Have a good time!"

"Thanks, sweetie. Jacob is already inside. Go easy on him tonight. The customers seem to like him a lot, and he's been doing well so far, but he's still learning the ropes."

"Okay. I'll be nice," I promise.

I give them both a hug, then head into the diner with Sebastian trailing behind me.

"You're really staying?" I ask as we stomp the snow off our shoes inside The Griddle House.

He chuckles and nods, then leans closer so that only I can hear him.

"Turns out our little friend doesn't have the greatest range," he whispers, and his words race down my spine and right to my clit. I jolt when the vibrator briefly hums to life inside me before Sebastian quickly switches it back off. "Seems like it's working well at this range. Guess that just means I'll have to stay close."

This is torture, and he knows it, I think, my heart pounding. *How the hell am I going to make it through an entire shift with him sitting there watching and literally fucking with me?*

"I'll let you get to work. Let me know if there's anything I can do to help," he says.

I shake my head, a breathless laugh falling from my lips. "Oh, I think you'll be helping plenty."

His eyes gleam with amusement, and he kisses my cheek before he strides toward a booth at the back of the diner and sinks down onto the seat. He winks at me, and I huff out a breath before I head into the back to get ready for my shift.

"Oh, hi. You're Hailey, right?" Jacob, the new guy, greets me from the sink where he's washing dishes as soon as he spots me. "Thanks for coming in tonight. I was a little nervous about the idea of working a shift on my own."

"Yup, that's me. And no problem. My mom said you've been doing great, but it's always nice to have a bit of backup, especially if things get busy."

"Yeah." He nods, the relief clear on his face. "Anyway, I think everything's all set up and ready to go for the shift. I already filled all the condiment baskets and I'm finishing up the dishes now. Is there anything I missed?"

"Let me give the place a little once-over and I'll let you know."

"Roger," he says, flashing me a grateful grin. I can see why the customers like him. He's cute, and he's got a friendly, golden retriever kind of energy.

I stride through the swinging doors that connect the kitchen to the dining room and breeze through the space to do a few quick checks. There are a few small things Jacob missed, but for the most part, everything looks perfect.

Not bad for a new guy. They usually start off on way worse footing than—

My thoughts catch in my brain when the vibrator flares to life inside me, and I have to bite my lip so hard it hurts to keep from making any noise. My head twists toward Sebastian, who's sitting with the remote held loosely in one hand and smirking devilishly at me, as if silently daring me to say or do anything to give away our little secret.

But the bell on the front door dings as a couple walks in, and I have to pull myself back together quickly, putting on my best forced smile.

"Hi, welcome to The Griddle House. Sit anywhere you'd like."

The vibrator turns off as the couple settles in at one of the tables near the large front windows, and I drop menus at their table before making my way to the booth where Sebastian is lounging like a predator waiting for its prey.

"Can I get you anything?" I ask, my gaze darting to the vibrator remote in his hand.

"Thanks, shortcake. Could I get a black coffee, please?"

"Coming right up."

A slow smile spreads across his face. "Oh, I sure hope so."

My cheeks flame at the double meaning in his words, and I walk away on wobbly legs to grab his coffee.

The diner starts to pick up for the dinner rush a short while later, and although Sebastian takes pity on me and leaves the vibrator off while I'm speaking directly to customers, he teases me relentlessly anytime I'm not taking orders or delivering food. I don't know if it's better or worse that he never lets the little vibe stay on long enough to make me come, but my body is flushed all over from the constant peaks and valleys of pleasure.

At one point, he turns the vibrations up so high that I have to lean against the large refrigerator in the kitchen to stay upright, and Jacob gives me a curious look.

"You okay?" he asks, his puppy dog face scrunched up a little with worry.

"Y-yes," I say quickly, pressing away from the fridge. "I think I just got a little, um, overheated. I'm fine now."

"All right. Let me know if you need a break," he says, offering me a sympathetic look.

I nod, swallowing hard, then head back out onto the floor. Sebastian turns off the vibrator as I emerge from the back, an innocent, satisfied look playing across his handsome features.

"You're going to pay for this," I whisper when I reach his table. It's taking everything I have not to melt, even though the vibrations are no longer teasing my clit.

"Well, of course I am. This is a diner. I'm not the dine and dash type." Sebastian chuckles, gazing up at me with a wicked gleam in his eye.

That's not what I mean, and he knows it, but before I can say anything in return, Jacob emerges from the kitchen. He starts to walk toward us, probably planning to try to lighten my workload by taking Sebastian's order. I wave him off, then turn back to Sebastian, pretending that's why I came to his table in the first place.

"Can I get you anything to eat?" I ask, my voice a bit hoarse.

"Hm, I don't know." He tilts his head to one side as if considering. "I'm feeling pretty full. What about you?"

"Absolutely. Stuffed."

Sebastian chuckles. "Hm, well sometimes an appetizer is better than the full meal. Don't you think?"

Oh my god. He's driving me fucking crazy. And I hate how much I love it.

"I prefer both."

Sebastian's expression shifts, turning hungry. "That makes two of us. But I think I'll be fine with my coffee for now, thanks."

He lifts his mug to his lips, smirking at me over the rim, and I glare back. He's having the time of his life edging me like this...

And I don't know how long I'm going to be able to keep it together.

29

HAILEY

The rest of the night passes in a blur as I take orders and drop off plates, all the while trying to ignore the desperate, burning arousal in my core. Just like he promised, Sebastian stays for the entirety of my shift and eventually orders a burger before the kitchen closes.

"You should probably get something too," he says, giving me a playful look.

"Why is that?"

"You're going to need the energy. Trust me."

Need spikes through my veins at that, so I take his menu and retreat to the kitchen to put in an order for two burgers, one for each of us. Jacob is washing dishes from one of the last tables to leave.

"Just the one guy left?" he asks over his shoulder.

"Yeah, but he's leaving soon. Why don't you go ahead and call it a night?"

Jacob's brows pinch together. "Are you sure? There's still a lot to do."

"This isn't my first closing shift at this diner," I reassure him. "I could do it all in my sleep by this point. You did great tonight, but I can take care of things from here."

He shoots me a grateful look, then nods. After finishing a few more closing tasks, he heads out, and the cooks clean up their stations and leave a short while later. I make sure all the doors are locked before I carry the two plated burgers out to Sebastian and set one in front of him.

"So, what are you going to eat first?" I ask, resting a hand on my hip and arching a brow at him. "This burger or me?"

"Fuck, shortcake." Sebastian groans. "You can't tease me like that."

"*I'm* teasing *you?*"

He chuckles and gestures across the booth. "Point taken. But you really should eat something. I'm sure you've worked up an appetite tonight."

He's not wrong, so I sit across from him and tuck into my burger. It's cooked perfectly, like always, and I'm just going for another bite when the vibrator comes alive again, sending a jolt through me and turning my bite into a drawn-out moan.

"Oh, my fucking god," I whimper, swallowing. "You're evil."

Sebastian switches the vibe off, then rests his elbows on the table, his gaze locked on my face. "It's been so much fun watching you squirm tonight, baby. I have to admit, I'm impressed with how well you held it together."

I shrug, panting for breath. "What can I say? I do well under pressure."

He lifts a brow. "How much pressure?"

His thumb swipes across the vibrator remote, turning it to its maximum setting, and I drop the burger on my plate in surprise. The vibration is so strong that it makes my thighs clench, my clit throbbing wildly. After hours of agonizing stimulation, the shock of it is enough to send me careening into a powerful climax.

My head falls back against the booth cushion, and my hands grip the edges of the table as a hoarse cry pours from my throat.

"That's it," Sebastian praises, his gaze devouring me. "Let yourself go. I've been dying to hear those sounds all night."

After all this teasing and edging, the orgasm he's finally allowing me to have is easily one of the most intense I've ever felt. My eyes squeeze shut so hard it hurts, and it's a good thing there isn't anyone else in the diner with all the noises coming out of me.

As the last aftershocks shoot through my veins, Sebastian rises to his feet suddenly, sliding out of the booth and hoisting me into his arms. He carries me toward the kitchen with long strides, kicking open the swinging doors. He sets me down and kneels in front of me as he undoes my pants and tugs them down my legs along with my soaked, messy panties.

Gripping my hips, he presses kisses to my thighs, working his way up toward my aching, throbbing pussy, giving me chills and filling me with desire all over again.

He slowly drags the vibrator out, and I hiss out a breath as my inner walls clench around the sudden emptiness.

"You looked so fucking gorgeous tonight, all flushed and needy. I loved seeing it," he growls, then lifts the vibrator to his mouth and sucks my wetness off it. My jaw drops open as I watch him, my chest rising and falling fast.

"Shut up and fuck me," I beg, past the point of teasing or dragging this out. I can't wait any longer.

Something flashes in Sebastian's eyes, primal and wild.

He rises to his feet and shoves down his pants enough to free his cock, then spins me around to face the large metal refrigerators. My hands slap against the smooth metal, bracing myself as he yanks my hips backward and plunges into me. My breath catches in my throat as he opens me up, and the studs of his piercings drag against my sensitive skin on their way in. My fingers curl against the fridge, my head drooping a little as sensations overwhelm me.

He pulls my hips back and slams into me again, rough and desperate.

"Fuck," he mutters. "So good, shortcake. So. Fucking. Good."

He seems just as turned on as I am, his breathing harsh and ragged as he thrusts so deep and so fast that my hands slide against the refrigerator as I try to steady myself. As crazy as the teasing with the vibrator drove me tonight, it must have done something to him too, and I wonder how long he's been thinking about this very moment.

"That's it, open up for me, shortcake. This pussy was made for me, and I'm gonna fucking take it," he grunts, his fingers digging into my hips as he drops his head to nip at my neck.

"Oh god, I'm close," I whimper.

"Come for me," Sebastian demands, but I shake my head, trying to stave off the rising pleasure.

"You come too," I breathe. "Come with me. I want to feel you fill me up."

"Jesus fuck."

I will myself to hold it together as he picks up the pace, making unintelligible noises pour from my lips. I'm trying so fucking hard to wait for him, to make this last longer, but it's hopeless. His cock feels too incredible sliding in and out of me, his piercing studs rubbing against my walls and ratcheting up the pleasure until I can't hold back the storm raging inside me.

"Sebastian," I warn, my voice rising. "I'm... I'm... oh god!"

Just as I let myself go, flying over the edge, he groans with me and fills me with his release. His cock pulses over and over, his hips grinding against my ass as he groans my name, murmuring it under his breath like a prayer.

His fingers lace with mine where my hands are braced on the fridge, and we stay like that for a while as our breathing finally starts to slow. Then Sebastian peppers kisses to the back of my neck and finally pulls out, grabbing several paper towels to help me clean up.

I watch him work with careful focus as he wipes away his cum from my thighs and tosses the paper towels in the trash, and he helps me fix my own clothes before taking care of his. Fortunately, this part of the kitchen is completely hidden from the front part of the diner, so no one passing by could've seen anything through the windows.

"I'm starving," I admit as I lean back against one of the fridges, thinking of my unfinished burger that's still sitting on the table of the booth where Sebastian was camped out all night.

Sebastian laughs. "Yeah, me too, actually. I never ate that food you brought me. I was a little distracted."

"Huh." I chuckle, arching a brow at him. "So was I. Luckily for us, we're still at a diner, because this place has a *lot* of food."

He nods, then opens one of the other fridges. "What are you in the mood for?"

"Something cold and refreshing, and maybe sweet." I glance at him with slight embarrassment over my perpetual sweet tooth, but he grins, clearly finding it endearing.

"Something sweet, coming right up."

Sebastian disappears into the fridge for a moment and then re-emerges with a pie pan containing several pieces of leftover apple pie, stuffed to the brim with cinnamon filling.

It's *perfection*. Sex and pie—a combination definitely heaven-sent.

I slide down to sit on the floor, resting my back against the fridge, and he takes a seat next to me, handing me a fork as we both dig into the pie.

"That was incredible," I murmur after swallowing a bite. "And now I can tick one more item off my list."

"Told you my brothers and I would get through the whole thing," he says, leaning closer to nuzzle his nose against the sensitive skin of my neck. It makes me squirm, a little spark of arousal lighting inside me. "We don't back down from dares, remember?"

I laugh, and as he takes another bite of pie, my mind drifts back to my conversation with my best friend earlier.

"I told Lorelai about your dare this morning, and how we all ran naked through the snow," I tell him, grinning lazily as I lick whipped cream off my fork. "Pretty sure she thinks we're all crazy."

"Eh." He shrugs. "I saw a video once of a surfer who got attacked by a shark and *kept* surfing. So I think Californians are their own brand of crazy."

That makes me laugh, and I lean my head against his shoulder. It feels good to sit with him like this, just lounging and talking like we used to back in his garage sometimes. Although it's even better now, with our bodies still flushed and warm from sex and the taste of whipped cream and cinnamon on my tongue.

"I told her about what we're doing," I admit. "The fake dating, and the... bucket list thing. I figured it would be okay, since she's miles away from Chestnut Hill and couldn't spill the beans to anyone. Not that she would—she's ride or die for me, so she'd take the secret to her grave."

"Yeah?" Sebastian twists his neck a little to look down at me, then feeds me another bite of pie. "What did she have to say about all of it?"

"I believe her exact words were 'get it, girl.'" I smirk, leaving out the part where my bestie warned me not to get my heart broken. I'm heeding her warning, or at least trying my best to, but I don't need to share all of that with Sebastian.

He chuckles, making his shoulder shift a little beneath my cheek. "That's a good friend."

"Yeah." I grin, staring at the wall opposite us. I hesitate, mulling over my next words, then add, "She also told me to stop running from my past."

Sebastian sets down the plate, sitting up a little straighter as he cranes his neck to try to see my face. I lift my head, not wanting him to get a crick in his neck.

"What does that mean?" he asks.

Picking up the fork, I drag it through the slowly melting remnants of whipped cream on the plate. "I'm not quite sure what she meant. We had to cut our call short so she could run an errand for her boss. But I can guess what she was getting at." I sigh. "I ran away from Chestnut Hill after what happened with Dylan. I just couldn't stand to be here anymore, with the looks and the whispers and the constant reminders of him. And I *thought* I was running toward something when I left, but now... I'm not so sure."

I chew my lip, staring down at the plate. My thoughts feel a little jumbled, and I don't really know how to express what I'm trying to say.

"I think we're all running from something, shortcake." Sebastian's voice is unusually serious, and when I look back up, his blue-green eyes are fixed on me. "Even those of us who didn't leave town like you did are running in our own ways."

"What are you running from?" I ask quietly.

He pauses before he answers, a contemplative look entering his expression. Then he lets out a quiet breath. "The same thing you are, I guess. The past. Who I was. Who people still see me as."

"What do you mean?"

He swallows, a look of pain entering his eyes. "Sometimes I feel like my life has stood still ever since my parents died. I took over our dad's shop, and that gave me something to focus on, something to do. And don't get me wrong, I fucking love working with cars. I love being a mechanic. But I feel like... I dunno. I guess I feel like I'm always walking in my father's shoes, and I never quite measure up."

There's something so vulnerable in his expression that I

can't stop myself from scooting a little closer to him. I rest my hand on his upper arm, feeling the hard muscles just beneath the skin.

"Of course you measure up. Sebastian, if your dad could see you now, he'd be so proud."

"Thanks." He reaches up to put his hand over mine. "I hope he would be. And I'm proud to carry on his legacy. It just feels like everyone has an expectation of me that I'll never live up to."

"I don't," I say firmly. "You're an incredible guy. You can always make me laugh, and you keep both of your brothers from getting too lost in their own heads. You're amazing with cars, and even if you say you're not a gentleman, you're something better. You're a *good* man. If anyone else doesn't see how amazing you are—as your own person, not as a reflection of your father—then that's their loss."

His eyes soften, something warm passing through them.

"Damn, shortcake. You're gonna give me a big head."

I chuckle, but the humor fades from his eyes as he lifts his hand and brushes his thumb over my lip. He leans forward and kisses me, this time slowly and with a sort of deliberation that I can feel all the way down to my toes.

When our kiss finally breaks, he tucks a lock of hair behind my ear, trailing his fingertips along the curve of my jaw.

"You know," he murmurs. "Maybe we should stop caring so much about what everyone else around us thinks and just start embracing what we really want."

"I couldn't agree more," I say, grinning as his featherlight touch makes goosebumps scatter down my neck.

But as we finally clamber to our feet and get back to doing the last few closing tasks before leaving the diner, a little thought keeps pricking at the back of my mind.

What if the thing I want is something I can never have?

30

NICK

Our niece is pure and absolute *chaos*.

"Wait, wait! Hang on before you do that." I reach out to grab the sprinkle jar from her hand, but it's too late. Iris has already dumped a small truckload of sprinkles into a messy pile atop a Christmas cookie.

"Uncle Nick, *look!*" Iris beams, clearly proud of her handiwork. "That one's mine," she declares, eyeing the sprinkle covered cookie with the look of a child who's anticipating a major sugar high.

"Well, so much for that container of sprinkles," Sebastian comments wryly. "We've got backups, right?"

"Yeah, right here."

Reid brings out a few more of the small plastic containers while Hailey indulgently oohs and aahs over our niece's decorating skills.

The kitchen is a total mess, Bruno keeps getting underfoot because he's trying to lick up any spilled sprinkles, there are cookie cutters everywhere, and... I'm actually having a great time.

When Addison called yesterday to see if we could watch Iris for a bit today, we all agreed quickly. My brothers and I adore our niece, even though she's a bit like a tiny walking tornado sometimes. Actually, that might be the exact reason *why* we love her so much.

"This is so fun! I love Christmas cookies!" Iris exclaims, kneeling on a stool by the counter and watching as Hailey rolls out more dough. She beams.

I hide a grin, my gaze shifting from my niece to Hailey. The Christmas cookies were her idea, and she seems to be having a great time with Iris. And for Iris's part, every time she looks at Hailey, I swear she has stars in her eyes.

I don't blame her for that one bit.

Hailey finishes rolling out the dough, and I watch as she, Iris, Reid, and Sebastian all gather around and start using the cookie cutters to cut out shapes. I snort when Seb tries to wad a bunch of extra dough into a cutter to get one last cookie out of the scraps of rolled-out dough.

"You're not using it right," I tell him. "I don't think the cookies are supposed to look all irregular like that."

"What are you talking about?" He shrugs, continuing right on with his mission. "They're cutouts—they're supposed to be all different shapes."

He places a cookie that looks like a dangerously deformed reindeer on the tray, then dabs a splotch of frosting on Hailey's nose. She grins, trying to lick it away, but she can't quite reach it.

With a quick glance at Iris to make sure she's not watching, Sebastian pulls Hailey away and licks the frosting off for her, following it up with a kiss on her lips.

"More sprinkles please!" Iris calls, holding out her hand like a doctor asking for a scalpel.

Reid shakes his head wryly, opening up a container and handing it to her.

"I blame you for this, you know," he tells Hailey as she and Sebastian return to rejoin the cookie decorating. "You put all those sprinkles on that test cookie we made, and it gave her ideas."

Hailey sticks out her tongue at him. "Maybe you just don't understand art. Stop trying to stifle my creative expression."

He smirks at her. "Sassy."

"Bossy."

The two of them share a look, amusement and attraction clear in their expressions, and another smile twitches at the corners of my lips.

"Come on, Nick!" Hailey glances over at me, gesturing me closer. "You haven't made a single cookie yet. You have to try doing at least *one*. Maybe Reid will approve of your decorating techniques more than ours."

She nudges Iris, who giggles.

I'm standing a little apart from all the action, and I hesitate. Although I love having Iris over, it's not really in my nature to just throw myself into the hustle and bustle of activities like this. Normally, I feel more comfortable on the sidelines, but as Hailey raises a cookie cutter invitingly, I find myself stepping forward.

The movement is automatic, almost instinctive, and I can't quite tell if it's because a part of me has been itching to join in or because I'd do pretty much anything this woman asked me to.

I cram my large frame in around the counter with the rest of them, taking my time cutting out and decorating one perfect cookie as the rest of the batch gets made and decorated in a flurry of activity.

Once the tray is full and the last of the dough has been used up, Sebastian leans over to inspect my cookie.

"Wow, Nick." He chuckles. "If you ever get sick of being a firefighter, I could see pastry chef as a viable alternative career."

"Let me see." Hailey leans over, and her jaw drops. She spins the tray around to give Iris a better look. "See that? Isn't it so pretty?"

Iris's eyes get big. "I *love* it. Uncle Nick, you're so good at this!"

Even though it's just a dumb cookie, I feel a flush of pride in my chest, and when Hailey looks up at me, she gives me a secret little smile.

"All right," I announce, stepping back and clearing my throat. "We should get these in the oven now so they have time to cook before we have to head to the parade."

"Good thinking." Hailey nods. "Iris, do you want to help me?"

Iris hops off the stool and traipses over to the oven with Hailey, who makes sure the exuberant little girl stands well clear before she opens the oven door. Hailey explains to her how the heat will make the sugar crystals melt a bit, and I gaze at them as Sebastian and Reid start filling up the sink and dumping used cookie cutters in to clean them. I should help too, but I can't seem to move.

I can't look away.

Normally, I like to keep things well-organized and under control. I don't like flying by the seat of my pants like Sebastian does or putting myself out there like Reid. But with Hailey, I feel like I'm drawn to her unbridled desire to just live life with everything she's got.

I always had a crush on the *idea* of her when we were younger, and I never told anyone about my secret obsession with her. But even though I watched her back then too, always aware of her anytime we were in a room together, I never got a chance to experience this side of Hailey. The adult, impassioned, and unequivocally gorgeous version of the girl that I secretly held a torch for all those years ago.

But this? The real thing? This messy, lively woman making cookies with Iris and filling the house with joy and moving comfortably around our space as if she belongs here? This is even better. The real Hailey Bennett is so much better than the version of her that I thought I already adored.

I don't even realize that I'm lost in thought and have been staring at Hailey until Sebastian walks up beside me and nudges my shoulder. I jerk a little in surprise, and when I glance over at him, he smirks.

"I know," he says in a low voice.

Almost at the same time, we both turn our heads to look back at Hailey, and a sudden realization falls over me, as quick and certain as dusk coating the evening sky.

I'm not the only one who feels this way.

I don't know if either of my brothers used to pine over Hailey the way I did, but I can tell they're both fucking enamored with her now.

Reid turns to watch her too, crouched in front of the oven with Iris as they watch the cookies slowly start to puff up, and she glances over at us, probably feeling the weight of our gazes on her.

"What?" She frowns, swiping at her face and accidentally leaving a streak of flour on her forehead. "Do I have something on my face?"

"*Now* you do." Reid chuckles, standing up and gesturing for her to join him at the sink. "Come here. I'll get it."

He dusts the flour off her forehead, and we finish cleaning up while the cookies bake. By the time they're done, we have to hurry out of the house to make it to the parade on time. We have to get there early, since we're going to be on a float—something I still can't quite believe I agreed to.

The annual Christmas parade is a big event in Chestnut Hill. A lot of people look forward to it every winter, dressing up and gathering by the side of the road to watch the procession go by.

My brothers and I rarely go though, and we've *definitely* never volunteered to ride on a float.

"Are you sure we can't back out of this?" Reid grumbles as we make our way to the coffee shop where we promised to meet up with Addison to deliver Iris. "I think maybe running around in the snow the other day gave me a cold."

Hailey calls his bluff immediately. "Oh no, are you getting sick?" She gives an exaggerated sigh. "I guess that means you won't be able to join the rest of us in any *activities* for a few days. Bummer."

Reid picks up on her insinuation and changes his tune. "Nah, I'll be fine."

Sebastian chuckles, punching him in the arm.

Addison is waiting for us outside Deja Brew, and she waves as we approach. She's got a few bags with her, which means her Christmas shopping must have been successful.

"How'd it go?" she asks, and Iris beams.

"I made *sooo* many cookies."

"And ate so many too, I bet." Addison chuckles, shifting her gaze from her daughter to us. Her gaze flicks over Hailey where she stands between Reid and Sebastian, a look of curiosity crossing her face, but she doesn't comment. Instead, she just gives us all hugs, thanking us again.

As Addison leads Iris to where Michael is holding a spot for them along the parade route, Sebastian, Reid, and I follow Hailey toward the staging area for the parade. They have a sort of makeshift tent set up for people who will be riding on the floats.

"Wow," Sebastian mutters as we near the tent. "That thing sure is a spectacle, isn't it?"

I follow his gaze to see a float advertising the Montgomery family's real estate business, which is bigger than all the other floats in the lineup. It's also the very first one in the parade.

I snort under my breath, then tense up a little as Dylan steps around the side of the float, coming into view. He has Brielle on his arm, and a few people who are probably employees of his family's company trail behind them. He glances in our direction, his gaze landing straight on Hailey.

Without thinking, I reach out and put an arm around her, pulling her against my side possessively as I glare him down.

She's mine, jackass.

For a brief second, Dylan's face looks like he's swallowed something sour, and a fierce satisfaction wells within me. Then we reach the tent, and Reid holds it open for us all to enter.

"Come on." Hailey gives my hand a squeeze and then slips out of my grasp, walking quickly toward one corner of the tent. We're the only ones in it, but I can tell other people have already been in here. There are little stations set up around the tent for each group that will be riding a float. "Our stuff is over here."

She gestures to several costumes dangling from plastic hangers, and I freeze mid-step.

What the hell?

"Santa, Mrs. Claus, and the elves?" Sebastian flips through the hanging costumes, then gives Hailey a look. "Really?"

"We're supposed to wear those?" I grunt.

She shrugs, putting on an innocent expression. "Yeah. Did I forget to mention we'd be dressing up? You didn't think we'd just be wearing our street clothes, did you?"

I frown. "Honestly, I'm not sure *what* I thought this whole thing entailed."

"I should be Santa because I'm the sexiest." Sebastian winks at Hailey, who laughs and rolls her eyes.

"Okay, first off, no you're not." Reid snorts, shoving Seb's shoulder. "Second, this is a family parade, so I don't think anyone's really looking for a 'sexy Santa.' You wouldn't be able to handle the role, so I'll do it."

"What? No fucking way!"

Sebastian sounds like he's ready to go to war over the Santa suit, and I don't really blame him. I'm not thrilled about trying to squeeze my thighs into those tights that the elves are supposed to wear—which is why I'm glad that I have the obvious advantage here.

"I'm the only one with a beard," I throw in. "Santa has to have a beard."

Sebastian throws up his arms. "There's a beard with the costume, and your beard isn't even white."

I'm just about to argue that point when Hailey steps in.

"Actually," she says with a grimace. "The beard part of the costume is missing." Her smile breaks out like a ray of sunshine as she turns to me. "So Nick gets to be Santa."

I nod in satisfaction, unable to contain my grin as I watch my brothers struggling into their elf costumes. This is gonna be fucking great. I might need to take a few pictures to hang on to for future blackmailing purposes.

But when Hailey steps out from behind the little partition that blocks off the changing area, I forget about elves and parades and practically everything else in existence.

She's wearing a pair of black boots, white tights, and a red fur-trimmed dress with a black belt wrapped around the middle. There's a Santa hat perched on her head, and although nothing about the costume is particularly scandalous—Reid is right, it's a family event—the overall effect makes her look so damn good that my cock twitches at the sight.

"Damn, songbird," I choke out, my voice hoarse.

"Is it okay?" She spins around, trying to get a better look at herself since there's no mirror in here, and I catch her hand to stop her.

"It's perfect," I tell her simply.

A flush paints her cheeks, perfectly complementing the deep red of the dress, and I have to subtly adjust my pants as I slip behind the partition to change too.

Fortunately, the Santa costume fits my large size, and

although there's some bitching and moaning, it doesn't take Reid and Sebastian long to get dressed after I emerge.

"This isn't the kind of elf I was hoping to be," Sebastian grumbles as we leave the tent and head toward our designated float. "I was hoping for a more subtly sexy Middle-Earth type vibe. You know, with the long ponytail and the crossbow."

"What the hell are you talking about? You're a Christmas workshop elf." Reid shakes his head, adjusting his pointed hat. "What kind of Santa's elf have you ever heard of having a crossbow?"

"To be fair," I interject. "I don't think they had crossbows in Middle-Earth either."

Although she's trying to hide it, I can see Hailey's shoulders shaking with suppressed laughter. "I think you all look amazing. Sebastian, you're sexier than Legolas."

As we climb onto our float, I see a few guys from the station sitting in the firetruck, which is two vehicles ahead of us. Wilson, one of our newer hires, does a double-take when he glances over at me, then slaps Carter on the chest and gestures in my direction. I lift a hand in greeting, flushing slightly.

I've never once volunteered to ride on the firetruck in the parade, and that only involves wearing our usual gear—so I'm sure they're a little surprised that I volunteered to dress up like Santa today.

Hailey rests her small hand on my shoulder and points to the Christmas throne on top of the float where I am supposed to sit. "That's your spot, Santa."

Dutifully, I go take my assigned seat. At least I know I'll bring a few smiles to people's faces, and I think riding around on the firetruck at Christmas time might become a new tradition once I hopefully attain fire chief status.

But when Hailey steps forward to sit on my lap, all thoughts of my future plans fly out of my head. My gaze snaps to her when she rocks a bit on my lap, working to keep her balance as the float lurches into motion.

"You're riding with me?" I can't contain my smile as I ask.

She gives me one of her radiant smiles. "Of course. Where did you think I would sit? There's only one chair on the float."

"I guess I thought you'd be standing with my brothers."

She chuckles lightly as she glances over at Sebastian and Reid standing at the edge of the platform in their elf costumes. They both look a bit awkward, but I can tell they're putting on a game face for the crowd.

"Mrs. Claus sticks with Santa on the float," Hailey tells me with a decisive nod. "Otherwise, the elves might start to talk."

A grin tugs at my lips. "Well, we can't have any rumors flying around the North Pole."

The float trundles down the street, and I wrap my arm around her waist to hold her securely against me as the parade begins—but we haven't even made it a full block before I realize that our seating arrangement might've been a big mistake. The combination of her firm ass against my lap and the bouncing movement of the float on the bumpy road are nearly more than I can take.

She's so close, all nestled up on my lap with the wildflower and honeysuckle scent of her hair tickling my nostrils and her beaming smile next to my cheek while she waves out at the crowd. The proximity of this gorgeous, perfect woman has a visceral effect on me, even though I try not to let it.

I smile and wave at the people of Chestnut Hill who've gathered to watch the parade, trying not to think about how good Hailey smells and feels in my lap, and how with my arm around her like this, if there were no clothes between us and no audience, I could be fucking her from below right now.

But as much as I try to shake the thoughts from my head and concentrate on the fact that we're supposed to be playing the roles of Mr. and Mrs. Claus, Hailey is impossible to ignore.

Hell, she's *always* been impossible to ignore, and it's even more difficult in this moment.

My cock twitches, swelling against her ass even as I will it to deflate.

Hailey stiffens as she notices it, and before I can murmur an apology in her ear, she shifts her weight, grinding her ass against my thickening length. I suck in a breath, trying to control my body's response to her accidental movement—but then she does it again.

Although she keeps her gaze focused on the crowd, not looking at me, she starts to squirm on my lap, teasing me into getting harder and making it more difficult for me to maintain a shaky grasp on my self-control.

Fuck. She knows just what she's doing to me. And she's doing it on purpose.

31

HAILEY

I CAN ONLY SEE Nick's face out of my peripheral vision, but it's enough for me to notice the lines of tension tightening on his face as I wriggle my ass against him in a subtle movement. Butterflies are going wild in my stomach as I keep my gaze focused forward, waving to the crowd. I'm vaguely aware of the cheering faces and the sounds of the gathered spectators, but all of my focus is on Nick, and the rapidly growing evidence of what I'm doing to him.

My pulse trips along at a fast pace, wetness gathering in the crotch of my panties as I grind against his cock again.

Nick growls low in his throat, tightening his grip on my waist.

"If you keep doing that, I'm not gonna be able to stay in control," he rumbles in my ear, his voice strained.

I know he means it, but instead of stopping, I shift my weight so that I'm sitting more fully on his cock, making him grunt softly.

"And what would you do if you lost control?" I whisper.

He turns to look at me, his dark blue eyes roiling when they meet mine. "I'd make you come right here and now for taunting me with your perfect fucking ass."

Oh my god.

A smirk tugs at my lips, even as my stomach flutters with a rush of arousal. If he thinks the threat of that "punishment" is going to stop me, he's dead wrong.

I don't take my eyes off his, and instead of letting up, I put all my weight into grinding against the lump of coal in his Santa pants. He growls in my ear, the sound hungry and strained.

"I warned you," he murmurs roughly.

Shifting his weight a little, he reaches for one of the red-and-white striped blankets on the float for us to use in case we get cold. He throws it over our legs, covering us from the crowd, and a second later, I feel one of his calloused hands sliding up the inside of my leg.

"I don't remember asking for this for Christmas, Saint Nick," I tease, my pulse kicking into overdrive.

"Maybe not with your mouth," he shoots back with a feral grin. "But even Santa has to take care of his wife's needs when her body is so clearly screaming to be touched."

His fingers slip under my costume to find my pussy and brush across it, making me squirm on his lap. He tightens his grip around my waist again with his free hand.

"Be still," he whispers, his voice low, "or you'll give us away."

I know this is crazy, and there's a real risk that we could get caught, but I can't help myself. I spread my legs to give him better access, because the truth is, the recklessness of what we're doing just turns me on even more. I keep one hand raised high, waving to the crowd of excited townspeople as the float rolls by, but when one of Nick's fingers slips inside me, it takes everything I have not to let my reaction show on my face.

"Look at you, songbird," Nick says in my ear, his bristly beard brushing against my neck and making me shudder. "No one out there knows how bad you're being for me. They don't know how filthy and greedy you are, opening your legs and begging me for more, do they?"

He shoves his finger all the way inside me, holding me close against him, and my back arches against his chest.

"Oh my god, Nick," I hiss, my toes curling inside my shoes. "You're gonna make me—"

"Make you what? Make you come on my lap? Make you fall apart with all these people watching, none of them knowing what a dirty slut Mrs. Claus is?"

"I..."

I can't say anything else. I don't trust myself to speak without letting out an embarrassing moan, so I press my lips firmly together instead, and Nick chuckles.

"Do you want another finger, my dirty little songbird?" he whispers. "You want me to stretch you out? It won't be as good as my cock, but I bet I can make you come in less than five minutes."

God, it won't even take one minute.

I'm so turned on by everything he's doing and saying that I feel like I could shatter already. But even though I know I'm playing with fire, I nod, answering his question silently.

I can't see his smile, but I can practically feel it as he presses a second finger into me, grinding against my clit with his palm.

I let out the smallest whimper and bite down hard on the inside of my cheek to keep it to myself. There's Christmas music blaring from the float, but that wouldn't be enough to explain away the strained look on my face if I don't keep it under control. Even if the spectators don't figure out what's really going on, I don't want anyone in the audience to think Mrs. Claus is having a stroke or something.

Reid and Sebastian are still standing in front of us, looking silly but hot in their green elf tights as they wave to the crowd, clueless about what's going on behind them. They provide some distraction from what Nick is doing to me under the blanket, but most of the eyes in the crowd are understandably locked on me and Nick. After all, as Santa and Mrs. Claus, we're the power couple everyone is here to see.

Knowing that—and feeling Nick's thick fingers pumping slowly in and out of me—is a wild rush like no other. Any little thing could give us away right now. If I can't keep my mouth shut or my face composed, or if a winter breeze strikes up and lifts up the blanket that's draped over my legs, we could expose ourselves to hundreds of people.

"You've been a *very* naughty girl this year," Nick whispers, curling both fingers inside me. I clamp down around him in surprise and pleasure and grind against his hand, desperate to get him deeper.

"And the year... isn't even over," I whisper raggedly before locking my lower lip between my teeth again to keep from crying out.

"Exactly. Plenty of time to get yourself into more trouble."

His thumb finds my clit, and he drags its rough pad around the sensitive bud while his fingers keep teasing my g-spot, torturous and slow. My breath hitches in my throat, my thighs clenching. I feel like I'm going to spontaneously combust on his lap.

"That's it," he urges in a low voice. "Come on, Mrs. Claus. Give Santa his gift."

"Fuck," I gasp, my brows stitching together as I struggle to keep my expression neutral.

I can't let myself fall apart in an obvious way. Not here. I'm determined to get through the parade without being busted for public indecency, so I straighten up and wave more aggressively. I have to let all the energy building up inside me out somehow before I scream, so it might as well be by egging on the crowd.

I get a roar of applause in response, so I beam at them, despite the fact that there's a voice screaming in my head that I'm seconds away from coming.

When Nick slides his fingers out of me abruptly to bring their wetness to my clit, pinching just hard enough to send a burst of pleasure and pain shooting through me, a plaintive moan slips out of my mouth.

Fuck, I'm about to lose it. I'm going to fall apart here in his lap with hundreds of people watching.

Reid must hear the tiny noise I make beneath the music, because he glances over his shoulder toward us. His eyes widen, shock and heat sparking in his eyes, and my stomach flutters. I might have the rest of the crowd fooled, but he clearly knows me well enough by now that all it takes is one look at my face for him to figure out what's going on.

For a half-second, his gaze stays locked with mine, as if he's wrestling down the impulse to stride over and drop to his knees in front of me so he can join Nick in pushing me toward an earth-shattering orgasm. But then he clears his throat, turning back to face the crowd.

"Merry Christmas, everyone!" he bellows, cupping both hands around his mouth to make the sound louder, drowning out the barely contained whimpers pouring out of me.

Sebastian looks at him quizzically for a second, then flicks his gaze to me.

If I weren't so overwhelmed by pleasure and the need to stay quiet, I'd laugh at how quickly he picks up on what's going on too. Just like Reid, he locks eyes with me for one scorching moment, and the heated look on his face is almost enough to incinerate the float from the ground up.

Then he turns back to the crowd, joining his brother in providing a distraction by getting the crowd to clap along with him to whatever song is blaring from the speakers. They take turns glancing back at me, their eyes flashing, and I can almost feel the burn of their jealousy and arousal at what's happening between me and Nick.

"They've got you," Nick breathes in my ear, his fingers

working faster. "I've got you too, songbird. Come for me. No one will know, I promise."

I don't see how he can promise that when I'm pretty sure I'm about to scream his name in a decidedly *not* family friendly way. But as Nick's words sink in, it strikes me in a rush that even though he's the only one touching me, all three of them are working together to take care of me—and that knowledge warms something in my soul.

It makes me feel safe, cared for... and more deeply desired than I ever thought possible.

I fight against the urge to roll my hips against Nick's hand, not wanting to risk drawing attention to what he's doing to me. Instead, I clench tightly around the intrusion of his thick fingers, milking them the same way I would his cock.

"Please," I breathe. "Oh fuck. Oh *fuck*, god, Nick..."

When the orgasm hits, it rolls through me slowly, and I grip the blanket as stars dance in my vision, joining the lights sparkling on the nearby floats. I suck in ragged breaths through my nose, doing my best to keep my eyes from rolling back as pleasure fills me, expanding outward from my core and filling my limbs. Nick's arm stays locked around my waist, helping keep me upright and holding me steady until the wave crests and then starts to ebb away.

I release a shuddering breath, melting slowly against him, and when he hums in satisfaction, I can feel the vibration of it against my back.

"I guess that's another tick in the naughty column," he murmurs, teasing my clit with gentle strokes of his fingers and sending little jolts through my veins. "Good thing I like it when you're a bad girl, songbird."

32

HAILEY

My heart doesn't stop racing as we make the final turn that leads us back to the beginning of the parade route. Nick's fingers ease away from my clit, but I can still feel the hot press of his cock against my ass, and it's all I can do not to grind down against it.

But I've already teased him enough, and since the parade is almost over, we'll have to stand up soon. I'll have to figure out how to walk on legs that feel like jelly, and Nick will probably need a minute to adjust himself.

I know that Sebastian and Reid could both tell what was happening, and the fact that they covered for the small noises that escaped me is yet another sign of how well all four of us seem to work in sync without even needing to talk or ask for anything. It's as if we're all connected by some sort of crazy chemistry.

Nick slides his fingers out from between my legs just as the parade is about to end. That timing couldn't have worked out any better if I tried.

The end of the parade route is right on Main Street, and a crowd of people gather around the floats, clapping and cheering. Nick slides the blanket off of our laps and gallantly offers me his hand, helping me stand up. I suppress a grin at the gentlemanly gesture—especially since *he's* the reason my legs are shaking like a fawn's.

"Did you have a good ride, trouble?" Reid asks as he and Sebastian join us in trooping off the large float.

I flush, prickles of awareness rushing over my skin at the undertone of heat in his voice. "Yes. It was amazing."

"Fucking hell," Sebastian groans under his breath, his voice strained. "I can't wait to get you back home. Standing up on the float, knowing you were about to fall apart right behind me? Pure torture."

"He's right," Reid adds. "And it's not easy hiding a hard-on when you're wearing tights. I think we need to punish you for being such a bad girl."

A delicious shiver runs down my spine as we join the townspeople drinking hot chocolate and eating holiday goodies at the parade's end. I'm feeling so good that not even the sight of Dylan gazing dourly at me and the three Cooper brothers can knock the smile off my face. He looks like he just tasted something sour, his face scrunched up and his eyes a bit narrowed. But I just give him a little wave and then turn my back to him, ignoring him completely.

"Hailey! Guys!"

My sister's voice rises up above the hubbub of the crowd, and I glance around to see her leading my parents and Lucas through the throng of people, waving wildly at me.

They reach us a moment later, and my mother pulls me into a hug.

"You looked lovely up there," she tells me. "Thank you for representing the diner, it means so much."

"That was the best Christmas parade in years." My dad beams. "You all did a great job! And you and Nick made a great Mr. and Mrs. Claus."

Little does he know what I was actually doing while riding

on that float. I feel my cheeks start to flush a little, but thankfully Reid comes to the rescue by immediately turning the conversation toward talking about all the publicity that the float will hopefully bring in for the diner.

My parents excitedly tell him about a few new additions to the menu, and Lucas chats with Nick a bit about the upcoming football season. Sebastian floats in and out of everyone's conversations while I give my sister a quick report about the new guy at the diner and how he could probably take on a few more shifts to help balance out her schedule.

But beneath all the excited talk, the sexual tension that started building up between me and the three Cooper brothers back on the float keeps simmering. Instead of dissipating now that the parade is over, it only seems to be winding tighter and tighter, making my body hum like a live wire.

It's a dangerous thing, considering that my brother is standing just a few feet away, and so are my parents. I try my best to ignore the triplets' close proximity and the ravenous glances they keep shooting me out of the corners of their eyes.

Thankfully, my brother gets drawn into a conversation with a colleague of his from the high school, and my parents head off to greet a couple of friends they spotted in the crowd earlier. But Pippa—well, she's never been as easy for me to fool.

The moment our brother and parents are out of earshot, she grabs my arm, tugging me to one side.

"Ohhhh shit!" she hisses in a low voice. "You're with the Cooper brothers for *real!* All of them?"

My stomach drops. *Oh fuck.*

"What?" I shake my head, my eyes widening. "No, don't be absurd. It's all just acting, like I said before. Something to keep the town gossips from rehashing me and Dylan and that whole mess."

I give a strained laugh, trying to brush it off, but fail

miserably. My sister can always read me when I'm trying to deny stuff. I'm honestly not a very good liar—at least, not when it comes to her.

Pippa arches one brow at me and rests one hand on her hip. She doesn't say anything, just stands there staring at me with a knowing look until my resolve crumbles.

"All right, *fine*," I whisper, glancing around to make sure no one is eavesdropping on us. We're standing far enough from the Cooper brothers that they can't hear us, but I can feel them watching us, heat and curiosity still lingering in their eyes. "It's true. But you have to swear that you won't tell anyone!"

Her jaw drops open, her eyes flashing with excitement. "Why would I tell anyone? This is amazing! Holy shit! Lucas doesn't know, does he?"

"God, of course not." I shake my head emphatically. "He would absolutely flip. Swear to me that you won't utter a word of this to anyone, especially not him."

"Cross my heart and hope to die." Pippa makes a crossing motion with her fingers over her chest, and I check to make sure that I can see both of her hands and that she's not crossing fingers anywhere. It's a trick she used to use when we were kids.

But this time, she seems to really mean it.

"You can trust me," she promises, her expression turning a bit more serious as she drops her head, leaning in closer. "I won't say anything. I promise on our sisterhood. How long has it been going on?"

I shake my head. "I don't really know exactly. It feels like it's been going on forever, at least in my head. I'm not sure when it started getting real."

Wait, what am I saying? None of this is actually "real."

I clear my throat, quickly correcting myself.

"I mean, it's not real. Not really. It's not like we're all in love or anything. We're just, um... having some fun. We agreed to mess around a bit while they help me rewrite the story of me being Dylan's jilted bride."

"Holy shit." Her eyes are like saucers. "So you and... all three of them? Like—*together?*"

My cheeks flame, but I know there's no point in starting to lie now. She's already seen through me, so it's a little late for that.

"Yes," I admit, and she squeals quietly. "But it's only temporary!" I quickly add. "I wasn't anticipating this at all. I had no idea it would ever happen, and definitely not with all of them."

Only temporary.

The words stick in my throat a little as I say them, echoing in my head like a clock chiming down the hours.

I keep trying desperately to remember that this is just a bit of temporary fun, nothing more.

The only problem is that every time I tell myself that, it feels less and less true. Now, not only do I feel like I'm lying to everyone else, but I also feel like I'm starting to lie to myself as well.

"All right." My dad's deep voice interrupts our conversation as he makes his way back over to us. "Who's up for some food? Should we all go grab something?"

I see Reid and Sebastian shoot me a look, and I can practically feel the tension crackling between us. Honestly, ever since Sebastian said that he couldn't wait to get me back home, I've been dying to be alone with these men, to finish what Nick and I started on the float.

"Um..." I swallow, turning to my dad. "Well, I guess we could—"

"You must be pretty wiped out after riding in the parade, Hailey," my sister interjects, giving me a pointed look. "I bet you and the guys are pretty cold too. It must've been a bit windy up there on the float, and you're probably anxious to get out of those costumes. So if you're not up for going out for food, we totally understand. We wouldn't want you getting sick right before the holidays."

"Oh, yes." My mom, who's rejoined us as well, nods. "We definitely don't want you getting sick. You four should go warm up and get changed."

A burst of love for Pippa swells in my chest. She knew *exactly* what to say to get us out of having to join everyone for food, appealing to my mother's protective instincts and constant worry about any of her children catching a cold.

She's being my wing-woman, and I fucking love her for that.

"Yeah," I say, latching on to the opening that Pippa has given me. "We should probably just head home today. But I'll see you guys again really soon—I'll pop over to the house or come by the diner."

"Okay, sweetie." My mother gives me a hug. "That sounds good."

Lucas, my parents, and Pippa head out a few minutes later, and the Cooper brothers and I finally get out of our silly parade costumes and head home. The car is quiet on the drive, and the air seems to thicken with each passing moment. I don't know about the three men, but I'm definitely replaying every single second of the parade.

As soon as we get back to their place, Sebastian holds the door for me as we pile out of the car. Reid walks into the house first, with Sebastian and Nick behind him and me bringing up the rear.

I close the door behind me and move to follow them into the living room, but stop short when I realize that all three of them are standing shoulder to shoulder, gazing at me with ravenous, expectant expressions.

"What?" I whisper.

Reid doesn't smile, but a spark of amusement flashes in his

eyes. "I told you that we'd have to punish you for being such a bad girl on the float. Did you think I was kidding?"

My thighs clench, anticipation twisting in my stomach. "No."

"Good." He lifts his chin, gesturing to me. "Then strip off everything except your panties."

33

HAILEY

Goosebumps race across my skin at Reid's order. I strip everything but my panties off quickly and stand there nearly naked for a second, reveling in the way three pairs of eyes rake me like a pride of lions waiting to pounce.

"Look down, trouble," Reid tells me, his voice still low and commanding.

I do what he says without question, and my eyes widen at the sight of a pair of gorgeous Louboutin heels set beside the door. I've never seen them before in my life, and it strikes me in a rush that the guys must've bought them—for me.

"Put them on," Sebastian says, arching a brow.

Biting my lip and resting a hand against the wall to steady myself, I slip one foot and then the other into the beautiful stilettos, amazed at how perfectly they hug my feet. The men got the exact right size.

"Good. Now get on your knees," Reid says firmly, and although my breath hitches, I'm not about to disobey. I sink down to them slowly, and he smiles at me when I'm done. "Good girl. Now crawl to us."

Again, my skin surges to life with a tingling heat. I gingerly put both hands on the floor, then move one in front of the other, crawling across the living room toward the three of them.

"Stop," Reid barks, and I obey instantly. "Eyes up here. Unless I tell you otherwise."

I tilt my chin up to lock eyes with him and nod as a shiver tingles down the length of my spine. He knows exactly what to say and what to do to push my submissive buttons, to get me right into that space where I know he's in control and I can just let go and *feel*.

And I love it.

"Goddamn, you look so fucking good on your knees," Reid says as he admires me. He beckons me forward with two fingers, and I obediently start crawling toward them again, adding a slink to my movements as my hips sway back and forth. "Fuck, you love being shared by us, don't you?"

I nod without breaking eye contact, my heart hammering against my ribs.

"Yes," I whisper as I reach the three of them and come to a stop in front of Reid, who's at the center. "I love it more than anything."

"Of course you do. Because you're a good little slut for us, aren't you?" he asks, his voice a low rasp. "Just for us."

"Yes," I repeat with more emphasis, and Reid's jaw clenches as he unzips his pants and reaches inside to retrieve his hard, leaking cock. He grips the base, giving it a squeeze, and my clit throbs.

"Then why don't you show us just what a filthy, perfect girl you are?"

"Mm," I moan and rise up off my hands to take his cock in one of them, guiding it into my mouth. Nick chuckles hoarsely as he shoves his pants down as well, palming and stroking his cock.

"Look how fucking hungry she is for it," he murmurs. "Even after I got her off at the parade."

"Like I said, she needs all of us. Because you're a greedy little thing, aren't you, trouble?" Reid asks as my lips glide across the swollen shaft of his cock. All I can do is groan eagerly around him. "Fuck yeah, you are. Tap if it's too much."

With that warning, he grabs my head and thrusts his cock hard and fast in and out of my mouth, almost making me gag. But I relax the back of my throat, suppressing my gag reflex as I stare up at him through my lashes, heat coursing through my veins at the rough way he's using me.

He slides in and out several more times before finally dragging me off his cock, both of us breathing hard. His shaft is slick and shiny with my saliva, the vein running along the top pulsing angrily. He's so hard it looks almost painful, but instead of pressing back inside my mouth, he smiles down at me, tipping his chin toward his brothers.

"I know what you need," he tells me softly. "So take it, trouble. Suck them both, just like you want to. Let us share you, the way we fucking love to."

A flood of wetness soaks my panties, and I lunge for Nick first, taking him all the way down to the base.

"Fuck," he curses, his spine curling a bit as his cock pulses against my tongue. He grips the back of my skull, holding me in place until I'm coughing and sputtering on him, then finally lets me go.

I come up gasping, dragging in a deep lungful of air before sliding back down his length. My nose brushes against the hair at the base of his cock as I deep throat him over and over, moaning around him.

By the time I finally pull away, I feel like my entire body is flushed with arousal. I switch over to Sebastian and moan at the familiar, metallic taste of his piercings as they glide over my tongue. But all I can think about, hunger for, is to feel them inside my aching, soaked pussy instead.

"Such a good girl," Reid praises as he and Nick watch. "Open wide for him."

The three of them take turns with my mouth, each man fucking my face until he's right up to the edge before pulling me off his shaft and passing me to the next one. The wet, sloppy sounds of my mouth on their cocks and their hands stroking themselves fill the room, and I close my eyes as Nick palms the back of my head, lost in a fantasy of the three of them coating my face in their cum at the same time.

Then Nick's hand tightens on my hair as he tugs me off his cock, sending tingles spreading across my scalp.

"Get up," he orders, pulling me up to my feet so he can look me in the eye. His dark blue irises are on fire with desire. I reach for his cock to stroke it, but he brushes my hand away, smirking as he shakes his head. "No more of that, songbird. It's your turn. Take off your panties, then go to the window and brace your hands on the glass."

"Yes, sir," I say, my voice breathy.

He drops my hair, leaving behind a tingle like an ice cube on bare skin, and I kick off my soaked panties and stride over to the window, my new high heels clicking across the floor. I can't see their faces, but I feel their gazes burning into my back, watching my every move.

I know they can see how wet I am from the way they've been using me. I feel it, hot and slick between my legs, with every step I take. My clit is throbbing with arousal, so much that I feel like I could come just from the friction of walking like this.

But I reach the window before that happens, so I bend slightly to rest my hands on the glass and jut my ass out at the three of them. Without glancing over my shoulder, I slip a hand between my legs, intending to finger myself and really give them a show, but this time, Reid's hand pushes it away. A second later, I cry out when his palm collides with my ass cheek.

"Nice try." He chuckles roughly. "I love the initiative, trouble. But that's for my brothers and me to do."

"Then what are you waiting for?" I shoot back, being a brat just because I know it will bring out his dominant side even more. "This pussy isn't going to fuck itself."

He chuckles darkly. "Oh, baby. You have no idea what you're in for. Nick, you want to take her first? You're the one who got her all worked up and needy at the parade."

"With pleasure," Nick rumbles, stepping closer. "We're gonna make your whole body sing, songbird."

Without warning, he grips my hips and slides his cock into me, forcing my mouth open and my body up against the window. He grabs me by the neck, gripping just tightly enough to make my pulse race without coming close to cutting off my air, and my forehead rests against the window pane. He's not holding anything back, and with each powerful thrust into me, my breath spills out and fogs the window.

"Fuck, look at you taking him like a champ," Reid groans. "Is this what you were wishing for while he made you come on that float? Is this what you wanted?"

I nod, my cheek pressed against the window, but he shakes his head.

"Use your words, trouble."

"Yes! Fuck, yes!"

Satisfaction flashes through his eyes where he stands beside us, and he rests his fingers on my collarbone, then drags them down my body, teasing my nipples lightly before moving lower to find my clit. With his eyes locked on mine, he circles it hard and fast, and I cry out, my eyes squeezing shut.

"There you go," Sebastian murmurs, moving in on my other side and joining Reid in touching me. "Scream for us. Scream so loud that all of Chestnut Hill will hear you."

"Fuck," I gasp, my heart racing in my ears and almost

drowning out the wet, slapping sounds of Nick fucking me like a wild man.

"That's not very ladylike, trouble," Reid scolds in a deep voice, then draws back and gives my clit a light slap.

"Oh my god!" I gasp. The sensation combined with Nick's cock pounding into me, is almost overwhelming. My legs start to tremble as the rest of my body tenses, and stars dance in the edges of my vision as my orgasm builds closer and closer to the crest. There's no way I could hold it back even if I wanted.

Reid's intense gaze shifts to Nick. "She's going to come. Fuck her harder, just the way she likes it."

Nick grunts and nods, then turns up the intensity even further. He's slamming so hard and fast into me now that I'm sliding up the glass, but all I can focus on is the wave of pleasure welling inside me.

I take one last desperate breath and hold it for several seconds as I hurtle into an orgasm, my body trembling underneath Nick's thrusts and Reid's palm as he continues working my clit. When the breath I've been holding comes shuddering out of me, I feel like my soul goes rushing out alongside it for a moment. Then I snap back into my body as all my senses come roaring back, and I realize I've been screaming the whole time.

"I told you we'd make you sing," Nick grunts as he continues fucking me mercilessly, but his words barely pierce through the blood rushing in my ears. When I finally start to come down from the high, he slows down enough that he can lower his lips to my ear. "Before I fill you up, do you want my brothers to fuck you like this too?"

A lightning bolt of heat streaks down my spine.

"No," I rasp, and Nick's thrusts stutter. Reid's brows jerk upward, surprise flashing through his expression. It brings a grin to my face, and I chew my lip as I stare back at him, working up the nerve to ask for what I need most right now.

"I want all three of you to fuck me," I breathe.

Reid smirks, his features relaxing as he keeps toying with my clit, bringing out a few aftershocks from my climax. "I had a feeling you'd say that. Do you want me or Sebastian next?"

"Neither. I want all three of you... at the same time."

His eyes widen, and his hand freezes on my clit. Nick chuckles behind me as Sebastian lets out a rough groan. The temperature in the room seems to gradually climb with each heavy second that passes, as all three of them absorb my words.

Finally, Reid rests the fingers of his free hand on my chin. "Are you sure you know what you're asking for?"

"As sure as I've ever been."

"Then say it. Tell us exactly what you want and how you want it."

Keeping my palms braced on the window, I glance over at Sebastian, who's standing on my other side. "I want you to fuck me, all at the same time. I want a cock in all three of my holes. One in my mouth," I breathe, holding Sebastian's gaze so that he gets the message. Then I crane my neck to meet Nick's eyes. "One in my pussy." Finally, I look back to Reid. "And one in my ass."

All three of them groan at once, making me shudder. Without a word, Sebastian nods and disappears up the stairs, and Nick pulls out of me slowly before lifting me up by my legs to carry me to the spot in front of the fireplace with Reid right behind us. Nick gently lays me down on the floor on my back, sprawled out in front of them, and Sebastian returns a second later carrying a bottle of lube.

Holy shit. We're really doing this.

My stomach flutters with anticipation as the three of them strip off their remaining clothes and join me on the floor, their hands and mouths exploring every inch of my body and lighting me up with desire all over again.

Nick lies on the floor beside me, still rock hard.

"Ride him," Reid breathes into my ear as he kisses my neck, so I spin onto my hands and knees, still in my heels, and climb on top of Nick, guiding his cock back into me.

"Fuck," Nick groans as his hands find my hips and his cock disappears up to the hilt.

"Good. Now lean forward," Reid instructs, pressing gently on the small of my back.

I drop both hands on either side of Nick's head to brace myself and present my ass to him. Reid kneels behind me, his chest pressed against my back, and teases my asshole with his fingers. My breath catches at the unfamiliar sensation, my body clenching involuntarily.

"Breathe deep now, trouble," he tells me, his voice soothing. "Nice and deep, in and out."

I do as I'm told, and Reid runs his fingers around and across my hole, slowly getting me used to the feeling of it and relaxing me while he kisses my neck and shoulder. Sebastian stands in front of me, his pierced cock bobbing in front of my face, and pops open the bottle of lube. Reid reaches out, and Sebastian turns the bottle over to drizzle out a healthy amount into Reid's palm. Reid works it into his fingers to warm it up.

"Are you ready?" he asks as he lowers his hand back to my ass.

"Fuck yes," I whimper, but my breath still catches when his slick fingers find my asshole again. My pussy clamps around Nick's cock, pulling a groan out of him, but it's nothing compared to how tightly I squeeze him when one of Reid's knuckles slips past the tight ring of muscles.

"Goddamn, you're gonna make me come like this," Nick groans as my pussy spasms around him.

"You're gonna make me come first," I say, shaking my head a little jerkily. I can feel sensations building inside me, pleasure already burning so hot in my veins that I know it won't take long.

Hunger flashes in his irises, and his fingers dig into my hips like he can't wait to start fucking me again. That makes two of us.

"That's one finger," Reid says as he pushes it all the way into me, then starts slowly dragging it back out. Both my holes squeeze, and I can't fight the groan that bubbles at the back of my throat. "Keep breathing. I'm going to work another finger in."

I take another deep, long inhale, and on the exhale, two of Reid's fingers start pushing against my hole, making my toes curl. The stretching feels amazing, and with Nick's firm cock still buried in me, it's already almost enough to make me come. But Reid applies more pressure, shoving his thick fingers into me and opening me up more, and I know I'm going to lose it.

"Fuck, I can't hold it," I whimper and hold on to Nick's shoulders as another orgasm tears through me. Reid's fingers fuck me faster, working me through it as Nick thrusts up into me and I soak his cock in response.

"Good girl. Give in to it," Reid encourages, twisting his fingers up to the knuckle inside me and making me cry out as wave after wave of pleasure pulses through me. I fall forward onto Nick, my elbows and wrists resting on his chest, and Reid chuckles. "I think you're ready for the real deal now."

"Shit," I whisper as the last of the orgasm works its way out of me. But Sebastian tips my head up by my chin, his dribbling cock beckoning me, and I take it into my mouth without a second thought, working his piercings with my tongue.

"Oh, she's definitely ready," he says with a laugh as he passes Reid the bottle of lube. I hear the cap pop and the wet crackle as Reid coats his cock with it. His greased cock head finds my hole, teasing it, and I moan around Sebastian's cock.

"Deep breaths now, trouble. Just like before," Reid says, stroking my lower back as he starts pushing into me. My eyes flutter shut, but I keep breathing and bobbing on Sebastian as

Reid stretches me out. His head presses past the tight ring of muscles a few seconds later, and the breath leaves my lungs, my cry muffled around Sebastian's shaft.

It's a good thing I have Sebastian's cock in my mouth to keep me quiet, otherwise the whole neighborhood would hear me screaming in pleasure.

"Is that okay?" Reid asks, pausing. "How does it feel, trouble?"

I draw back a little so that I can speak, my voice raspy. "It feels... oh god, it's so much. But I need... I need more."

"That's our girl."

Reid keeps working his way inside, murmuring praise and encouragement as he tells me to open for him, to let him in, telling me he knows I can do it. Nick lies still to give me the chance to adjust, and after what feels like a long time, I hear Reid exhale in pleasure when the base of his cock meets my body.

"It's in," he rasps. "You're taking all of me. All of *us*. Are you all right?"

A moan is all I can manage to answer with, and the three of them chuckle. Reid stays still for a few moments before he starts to very slowly drag his cock out of me, and I feel like I might pass out from the sheer amount of pleasure rushing to my brain. But it's nothing compared to the way every nerve ending in my body lights up when he starts driving back into me again.

"Fuck!" I hiss, Sebastian's cock falling out of my mouth. But he lifts me by the chin and presses back in, muffling the rest of my noises.

"This is what you wanted, isn't it, shortcake?" he asks as I hollow my cheeks around him.

And he's so fucking right about that. This is every one of my filthiest fantasies come to life.

I've forgotten how to speak, all rational thought replaced by the wavelike rhythm of the three of their cocks sliding in and out of me in alternating movements, completely in sync. Sebastian slides down my throat while Reid thrusts into my ass and Nick draws out of my pussy.

It's fucking ecstasy. The men murmur filthy things to me, punctuating their words with snaps of their hips, filling me up even more as the tempo increases.

Sebastian's cock leaks precum onto my tongue, flooding my senses with the salty tang of him, and I hum in delight. His head drops back while his hands wrap around the back of my neck, holding me still so he can use my mouth at his own pace.

I'm completely lost in the thrill of it all—until somewhere across the room, my phone starts ringing in the clothes I left behind. I ignore it, too lost in the moment to care. But almost as soon as it stops ringing, it starts up again.

"Fuck," Sebastian mutters, his teeth bared with annoyance. "Hang on."

He takes his cock from my mouth and then strides quickly over to my pile of clothes to fish my phone out. He stares at the screen for a moment, a look I can't quite read passing across his face.

Then he shocks the hell out of me by swiping across the screen to answer.

"Oh, hi, Dylan," he says, bringing the phone to his ear. "Sorry, Hailey's a little preoccupied and can't come to the phone right now."

34

HAILEY

My heart thunders in my chest as both Reid and Nick go still inside me, the three of us freezing in place.

I can't believe my ex just called me—or that Sebastian answered.

His eyes glint with mischief and a kind of possessive heat as he turns and strides back toward us. Kneeling in front of me, he arches a brow, the silent dare clear in his expression.

Oh my god, does he want me to...?

My stomach flips over with nerves as I realize what he's getting at, and my arms shake as I lean forward, wrapping my lips around his cock. Sebastian clenches his jaw, his stomach muscles tensing as I run my tongue over him.

Then he presses a button on my phone's screen, and suddenly, I can hear Dylan's voice coming through, loud and clear.

Holy shit. He put it on speaker.

"Well, where is she? And why the hell are *you* answering her phone?" Dylan's irritated voice fills the living room, and Reid pulls back and then drives his cock deep into my ass before anyone can answer. It shocks a moan out of me, muffled and low around Sebastian's cock, and the phone goes silent for a second.

"Hailey? Is that you?"

I can't say anything intelligible with Sebastian's shaft filling my mouth, but Nick pinches my clit, making me whimper loudly enough that the whole county can probably hear it.

"Good girl," Sebastian murmurs, pride flashing in his blue-green eyes. "Let him hear you."

"What the fuck is..." Realization dawns in Dylan's voice. "Are you...?"

"Are we what?" There's a possessive rasp in Nick's voice as he drives up into me from below, his fingers digging into my hips. "Are we taking care of her in a way you never could? Yes, we fucking are."

"Wanna show him, baby?" Reid murmurs, dropping his head so that his lips brush my ear but still speaking loudly enough for Dylan to hear. "Wanna let him hear how loud we make you scream? Go ahead, let him know how good you are at taking three cocks at once. Tell him what it takes to satisfy a woman as fucking perfect as you."

Reid and Nick take turns slamming into me as he speaks, and my moan is louder this time, totally unrepressed and desperate.

I pop off of Sebastian's cock, and he takes over where I left off, stroking himself as I gasp out, "Fuck. Oh fuck, oh my god. I'm gonna..."

"She's gonna come for us," Sebastian growls into the phone, his gaze locked on me as he slides back into my mouth. "Over and over and over again."

"What the *fuck?*" Outrage colors Dylan's voice, and I can practically hear him sputtering through the phone. "This is insane. Are you fucking serious? You can't just—"

"We can, and we are." Sebastian holds the phone closer to my mouth so Dylan can hear the full extent of my moans and whimpers, then brings it back to his face. "Hear that? I'd say she's more than satisfied."

Maybe it's the worst timing, or maybe it's the best—but either way, I feel another orgasm starting to build low inside me, desperate to get out.

Every nerve is white hot with sensation, and Sebastian's cock slips out of my mouth again as every muscle in my body contracts, tightening and tensing, until all at once they release and I scream my pleasure. Sebastian holds the phone by my mouth for the entirety of it, and I'm sure I'm blowing Dylan's ear out with all the noise I'm making, but I don't give a damn.

He deserves it and worse for what he did to me.

"That's right, shortcake," Sebastian praises. "You look like a fucking goddess right now, being worshipped the way you deserve." He lifts the phone closer to his face. "And as for you, you piece of shit? You can lose her fucking number. Because you had your chance with her, and you fucking wasted it."

With that, he taps to end the call, then tosses my phone onto the couch. Before my climax even ends, I feel another one surging up to take its place in a rolling boil. It spills out of me in a flood as wetness gushes from me, soaking Nick's cock.

He and Reid start pounding into me in response, one man slamming into me as the other pulls out, and there's so much stimulation that I feel like my brain is short-circuiting.

"That's it. Lose yourself in it. God, you look so fucking beautiful like this," he groans.

"Keep going," Reid encourages, reaching around to trace circles around my clit while Nick drives his hips upward into mine.

"I-I don't know if I can. It's *so* intense," I gasp. My voice is husky, my body still trembling with the aftershocks of the earth-shaking orgasms I've already had.

"Yes, you can. You can do fucking *anything*. You can come for us again."

He drives his cock into my ass up to the hilt to make his

point, and my back arches as another hoarse cry works its way up my throat.

Despite the exhaustion burning through my muscles, I still feel insatiably hungry. So even though I feel as if my body is being pushed to its limits, I brace myself on Nick's chest and use my hips to drive down on both his and Reid's cocks, clenching around them as I drag myself upward again.

"Fuck yeah. Take what's yours, songbird," Nick grunts, staring up into my eyes. His irises flash with a heady mixture of heat and awe, and it only makes me want him more. Reid peppers my neck and shoulder with kisses as I ride the two of them with wild abandon, my mouth wrapping around Sebastian's cock again.

What feels like hours pass as they push me to a place I've never been before, riding a wave of sensation that feels like its infusing my entire body. I come again, and then again, so many orgasms rocking through me that I lose count.

Finally, after one last climax licks through my veins, I truly can't take anymore. I fall forward onto Nick's chest, gasping and boneless, and as if they can read my mind through my body, Reid and Nick race each other to the finish line. They alternate desperate thrusts, their cock heads each hitting my g-spot from different angles, until Nick's face contorts, his neck muscles straining.

"Fuck!" he growls and bucks beneath me, flooding me with his cum.

Reid isn't far behind. He slams into me one last time and grunts in my ear, kissing and biting at my neck as his cock swells inside me.

"Eyes up here," Sebastian orders, stroking himself as Reid fills me up.

Still breathing hard, I glance up at him, biting my lip in anticipation.

He wraps my hair around his fist, tilting my head back. "Open wide."

"Yes. Please, yes."

I whimper and drop my jaw as he jerks himself off quickly, his strokes rough and fast. Hot spurts of his cum land on my tongue, making me moan, and I hold my mouth open, letting him see his release held in my mouth before I finally swallow it all. He stands over me, gasping as he squeezes out the last few drops, then holds out his hand for me to clean it.

My tongue traces eagerly over each of his fingers, and he smiles with heated tenderness. "That's my girl."

Satiated and utterly spent, I slump against Nick's chest. He and Reid gently pull out of me, then lower me down onto the rug between them. The three of them sandwich me between their hot, sweaty bodies, kissing and touching every inch of me they can get their hands and lips on.

"That was fucking incredible, songbird. You did good."

"Better than good." Sebastian presses a kiss to my wrist. "You're perfect."

I feel completely boneless, limp and exhausted from the intensity of it all. For a long moment, I just float, my eyes half closed, as I bask in the post-orgasmic bliss.

Then the realization of what just happened zaps through me like a bolt of lightning.

My eyes fly wide open, and I sit up so suddenly that I almost make myself dizzy. "Oh, shit!"

"What's the matter, shortcake?" Sebastian asks. He and his brothers all sit up as well, concerned looks on their faces.

"Dylan knows." I swallow, glancing quickly between each of them. "He knows you're all sharing me. Not that you're fighting over me, or that I'm dating each of you separately. He knows about..." I gesture to our naked bodies. "This!"

"Right." Reid frowns, running a hand through his hair.

Sebastian grimaces. "Fuck, shortcake. I'm sorry. I didn't

really think it through. I just saw his name flashing on your screen, and I wanted to make sure he knew that you were doing great without him."

A flush of warmth fills my chest, and I smile softly at him. "I know. And it meant a lot to me. But... what if he tells Lucas?" I bite my lip. "He could sabotage your friendship with my brother. He could—"

"Hold on there, songbird." Nick pulls me onto his lap, stroking my hair. "Don't let your worry run away with you. We don't know if he's gonna do anything at all yet."

Reid nods, looking thoughtful. "Honestly, I highly doubt this is something Dylan will want to shoot his mouth off about. He might not want everyone in town knowing that the woman he let go now has three men in her bed. You know what I mean?"

Sebastian snorts. "Agreed. His ego couldn't take people knowing that."

"And besides," Nick adds, pressing a kiss to my temple, "even if he were to tell people, and even if word were to get back to Lucas, we can always tell your brother that we just said all of that to fuck with Dylan."

Reid takes my hand, rubbing his thumb over my knuckles. "Lucas already knows we're pretending to date you to put Dylan in his place."

"Right." Sebastian nods, tilting my chin up so that our gazes meet. "So it's not a huge stretch for him to believe that we answered the phone and pretended to all be sharing you to get in Dylan's head even more. We'll just tell him it was a prank. A lie."

I think it over for a minute, trying to extinguish the flicker of worry in my chest. It's true that the groundwork has already been laid with my brother for him to think the guys are just helping me make Dylan jealous and get him to back off. I guess this is no different. It's not like Dylan has actual photographic evidence. Anything can be said over the phone, but that doesn't necessarily make it true.

My stomach sinks a little at the idea of calling what just happened between us a prank or a lie when it felt like so much more than that, but I shove that thought away.

Hopefully, we won't have to make up an explanation for it at all, if the guys are right and Dylan keeps it to himself.

I nod, blowing out a breath. "Okay. We'll go with that story if it ever gets back to Lucas."

"All right." Sebastian presses a kiss to my hair, sighing softly against the strands. "Fuck, I'm sorry, shortcake. We weren't trying to make shit more complicated. I just got carried away. I fucking hate that guy, and I wanted him to know you've got people who appreciate you. That you don't spend a single fucking second crying over that sad sack of shit."

In spite of the worry and the messy, complicated emotions crowding my chest, I can't help but smile at that.

"Well, I think he got the message."

"He'd better fucking have," Nick grumbles, sounding like he'd be perfectly happy to call Dylan back up and fuck me on speakerphone again just to prove a point.

My smile widens a little, the tension finally draining from my shoulders. I turn my head to kiss Sebastian, then pull Nick and Reid close and kiss them too.

"That was amazing. One of the best experiences of my entire life," I whisper, sliding my fingers through the hair at the nape of Reid's neck as we break apart. I glance at the other two, making sure they see the truth in my eyes as I add, "And no matter what happens, I'll never regret it."

"Good," Reid growls. "Neither will we."

It's dark outside by now, and although Bruno evacuated the area when we were making a racket, he comes padding back into the room as we all clean up and tug on some clothes.

It's cozy and warm, and when Sebastian and Nick go to raid

the fridge for something to eat, I end up curling up against the couch with Reid after he gets a fire going.

He wraps an arm around me, tucking me close against his body as the sound of his brothers talking in the kitchen filters into the living room.

"I love Christmas time so much," I murmur, feeling sleepy and lazy again now that the panic has subsided. "It's like every holiday food and drink is a little slice of bliss—cookies, eggnog, pumpkin pie. And it all tastes better when it's cold outside, for some reason. It was never as good in LA."

Reid chuckles. "Yeah, some things go better with snow, I guess."

He hasn't put a shirt on, and I trace his tattoo with my fingers. I would ask if he's cold, but I'm sure he isn't. All I've got on is his brother's shirt, and I feel fine. The fireplace is crackling, and I can see a light snow falling through the darkness outside the living room window. It's so cozy in here that even Bruno is contentedly snoring away. Of course, my panties are nowhere in sight, which means he probably buried them somewhere before he sprawled out for a nap.

I glance around the room, taking in the familiar space. It's comfortable and warm, and if I really let myself think about it, this house feels more like *home* than anyplace has in a while.

"Have you ever thought about leaving Chestnut Hill?" I ask Reid idly.

He shakes his head. "Not really. I mean, I've thought about how I could maybe expand my business if I moved. But for the most part, I'm pretty satisfied with how it is."

I nod, feeling almost envious of his simple, straightforward response. "I wish it worked that way for all people and all careers."

He rests one hand on my leg, staring into the fireplace. "I think it can."

"How so?"

I glance up at his face, watching the firelight dance across his handsome features. He takes a moment before he answers, his fingers stroking back and forth against my thigh.

"I don't think it matters whether you're in a small town or a big city, no matter what your dreams and goals are. If it's where the people you care about are, then that's home, and you can make anything work."

His words hit my heart like a ton of bricks. I know Reid isn't wrong about that sentiment, but I still think that Chestnut Hill might not be the place for me. How could I ever launch a singing career in such a tiny place with no big label studios and no crowd-drawing venues? Then again, I'm still struggling with even getting myself to sing without freezing up, so maybe that's not a question I'll ever have to grapple with.

My mind drifts back to the way the three Cooper brothers supported me from the crowd at karaoke. Just having them there helped me overcome my nerves and sing in front of an audience for the first time in ages. It literally plays into the point that Reid is making.

I spent two whole years in Los Angeles trying to make it as a singer and carve out a career for myself in the music industry. And what do I have to show for it?

Absolutely nothing.

Not unless you count crippling self-doubt every time my feet hit the stage.

But when I'm around these men, I don't feel like a failure. I don't feel like the only measure of my success is in whether I built a successful career.

I feel amazing. I feel treasured.

Just as I am.

"Okay, this is by far the biggest plate of cookies you've ever seen." Sebastian strides back into the room, interrupting our quiet conversation as he shows off the large plate piled high with the Christmas cookies we made when Iris was here.

After the workout we all just had, the cookies look and smell delicious. So does the eggnog that Nick carries in a moment later, and I can already smell the spices and whiskey that they must've doctored it up with.

"What? We *had* to spike it at least a little." Sebastian notices me eying the eggnog and smirks as Nick passes out the cups. "That's what Christmas is all about."

Reid snorts. "Funny, I thought Christmas was about peace and love for your fellow man, and maybe even the magic of Santa Claus. I had no idea it was about spiked eggnog."

"Oh. Well, then, I'll drink yours."

Sebastian reaches out to take the cup from his brother's hands in response to Reid's sarcasm, but Reid snatches it back quickly, making me laugh. Nick and Sebastian settle in close by, and I sigh contentedly.

This is perfection—all four of us lounging in the living room, munching on Christmas cookies and eggnog after a completely mind-blowing night of sex. The fact that it's framed by falling snow and a crackling fire is definitely something that seems like it goes along with what Reid was saying. This kind of thing wouldn't be happening if I was still in LA right now.

This is a Chestnut Hill, Montana thing. More than that, it's a Cooper brothers thing.

I sip my eggnog and listen as the guys talk and banter with each other. It's so easy, sliding back and forth between hot sexual fantasies and the feeling as if we all just belong together. And I honestly don't know which part of this I love the most. Is it living out every sexual fantasy I've ever had with three of the hottest guys in all of Montana? Or is it this feeling of being safe and at ease with these guys who make me feel like I'm at home with them?

I'm lost in that thought when Bruno suddenly pads across the floor and comes to stand directly in front of me, showing off my slobbered-on panties, which are hanging from his mouth.

"Hey, give those back!" I reach out to grab them, but he takes off, obviously wanting me to chase him around and turn it into a game.

But I'm too exhausted from all the sex, too cozy where I'm sitting with the guys by the fireplace, and too distracted by all of my conflicting emotions, to want to run around chasing the dog right now.

"Fine," I grumble as I sink back down between Reid and Nick, resigning myself to the fact that I'm going to need to buy some new panties that haven't been chewed up or drooled all over. "Just keep them. It's the least of my worries."

I watch as Bruno gives a shake of his head, splaying out his front paws like he's trying to tempt me into running after him.

"What are you doing?" I say with a wry chuckle. "You won. You won the panties. They're all yours, you naughty dog."

All three of the Cooper triplets glance between me and the dog—and to my surprise, Bruno looks almost *guilty* at the slight scolding that I gave him. He turns slowly around, as if he doesn't like the fact that I called him a "naughty dog."

He walks toward me, panties still firmly clenched in his teeth, and sits down as if he's come to talk. Then, without me even having to say anything, the dog drops the panties in front of me and lowers his head for pets.

I'm stunned. Hell, we all are. Out of the corner of my eye, I can see Nick and Reid staring at Bruno with open mouths.

"Holy shit. I've never seen him do that before," Nick murmurs, shock clear in his tone.

"Do what?" I blink. "Return a pair of stolen panties?"

He shakes his head. "No, I've never seen him give something back like that. Even with me, he never brings back any of the things that he grabs and runs off with. I swear, in the springtime after the snow thaws, I'm going to find a pile of my stuff half-buried in the yard."

I reach out to pet Bruno's head, taking my panties and

setting them up on the top of the couch so that they won't tempt him again.

Bruno presses his head against my palm, so I rub him some more until he curls up in front of my feet and lies down.

"Wow. I'd say that the dog has officially adopted you." Sebastian stares at Bruno, then laughs. "Who knew that the big, drooling pooch could ever like anyone other than Nick?"

Reid nudges my shoulder with his. "Guess you can never leave now. Not after you've won over Bruno and all."

I know he's just teasing, making a joke because it's so funny and odd that the dog seems to have totally attached itself to me now. Especially since Bruno seemed to despise me when I first arrived.

But still, his words make something tighten in my chest. Because it feels like yet another thing that's going to make walking away from all of this really fucking hard to do.

35

SEBASTIAN

IT'S DEFINITELY STARTING to feel like Hailey just *belongs* here with us—especially when she wanders into the living room a few days after the holiday parade, wearing my clothes like it's second nature.

I glance up at her from where I'm sprawled out on the couch, unable to suppress my grin. "Damn. My flannel shirt has never looked so good before."

It's the truth. The shirt she's got on is one of my oldest, softest flannels. It's one of my favorite shirts, actually, and I fucking love seeing her in it. Especially when the only other item of clothing that she's wearing is a pair of panties.

"Hope you don't mind." She's only done up the middle buttons, and she tugs at the hem of the shirt a little. "I wasn't quite ready to get all the way dressed yet, and I saw it sitting on the back of your chair. I just wanted to lounge around in something soft and comfortable for a bit before I need to get ready."

"I don't mind one bit, shortcake." My gaze roams over the way the baggy shirt falls over her soft curves, tracing the long line of her legs where they emerge from beneath it. She's fucking stunning. "You can keep it. I don't ever want it back. That shirt has never been so happy."

She blushes, laughing lightly as she walks closer. Then she sighs, plopping down onto the couch beside me.

"I sort of wish I didn't have to get dressed up at all tonight. There are always a million things to do around the holidays. It seems like we were just at that Christmas parade."

"That was a few days ago." I immediately regret pointing that out, because it reminds me that everything is happening so fast. The days are passing too damn quickly, and the Christmas season will be over soon. I wonder if that's when this whole arrangement of having Hailey here with us will end too.

I don't really want to think about it.

Bruno perks up in his bed by the window, glancing our way. As soon as he sees Hailey, he hauls himself to his feet and lumbers over. He practically follows her around the house these days, and every time he sees her, his houndish face lights up.

"Hey, Bruno. Who's a good boy? You are! Such a sweet boy." She leans down to pet him, flopping his ears around and making him practically shiver with delight.

Great. Now I'm jealous of both a shirt and a dog.

After sending Bruno to doggie heaven with several minutes of attention and scratches, Hailey plants a kiss on the top of his head and stands up.

"I'd better go get dressed soon," she tells me. "I want to get there early so I can help out."

The Bennetts are throwing their annual Christmas party tonight. It's actually one of my favorite holiday events, nothing at all like the stuffy ball that the Montgomerys threw.

"We can come early and help too," I offer, volunteering my brothers along with myself. I doubt they'll mind.

"Really?" She lights up a little. "Thanks. I'm sure my parents would appreciate the help."

"Of course. Your family is like our family too. And we take care of what's ours."

An expression I can't quite decipher passes across her face at my words.

She blinks at me and swallows, then leans down quickly and gives me a kiss before disappearing back upstairs. I watch her go, curious what was on her mind just now.

I don't have a lot of time to think about it though, since I need to get ready myself. I trail after her, throwing on a long-sleeved shirt that looks nice without sacrificing comfort and a pair of dark jeans. I pop into Nick's and Reid's rooms to let them know what's going on, and when my brothers and I are all dressed and ready to go, the three of us head down to the living room to wait for Hailey.

She appears just a few minutes later, and as she descends the stairs, my stomach feels like it drops about a foot and a half.

The dress she's wearing tonight isn't as fancy as the one she wore to the Montgomerys' ball, but it's definitely more *her*, and that makes it even better. The hem hits just above her knees, and she has a pair of leggings on beneath it. The dress itself is made of a sweater material that hugs her curves like it was made just for her, and the green color is a perfect complement to her emerald eyes.

"Wow."

Nick is the one who breathes the word, but I'm pretty sure we were all thinking it.

"Thanks." She grins. "You guys don't look half bad yourselves."

I walk over and tilt her chin up, leaning down to press a kiss to her lips. "You clean up pretty good, shortcake." I move my head to one side a little, nipping at her earlobe before adding in a low voice, "But I still stand by the fact that you look sexiest of all wearing nothing but my shirt."

She shivers slightly, biting her lip as I straighten.

Nick and Reid fall in on either side of her as I lead her toward the door, and all four of us head out. We're able to play things a little more relaxed tonight, since there's no one we're trying to impress the way we were at the ball. So despite the fact that we're still outwardly supposed to be competing for her affections, we all arrive at her parents' house together, not bothering to stagger our entrances.

We're early, so no guests are here yet. Mr. and Mrs. Bennet welcome each of us with a hug, and Grandma Dee gives a special warm welcome to Nick. He's her favorite. And it takes less than a minute for the two of them to start talking about some show that they've been watching together.

"Thank goodness you're here." Mr. Bennett chuckles, gesturing out to the front walkway. "Would you strapping young lads mind helping me shovel the drive and clear out a few parking spaces along the street? I don't want any of our guests slipping on the ice or getting their heels stuck in the snow."

"Sure thing, Mr. Bennett." Nick is the first one out the door to grab a shovel, with me and Reid close behind.

When Lucas joins us, it feels like old times again.

We switch off between shoveling and chipping away at some ice that's accumulated, and with the five of us working together, it doesn't take long for us to clear space for people to park.

After we finish, Mr. Bennett takes Reid and Nick into the garage to show off his new workbench setup. I wander back into the house and head toward the kitchen, hoping that maybe Mrs. Bennett has some homemade hot chocolate brewing, or a few hot toddies. I could really go for something to warm me up from the inside out after that shoveling.

But as I near the kitchen doorway, the sound of voices stops me.

"I just don't want you to get hurt, that's all." Mrs. Bennett's voice is slightly muffled, as if she's got her head in the fridge or something. It grows clearer as she continues, and I hear the fridge door shut. "It just... seems like a bad idea. Those boys have been like family for years, and they're your brother's best friends."

"I know." Hailey's voice is quiet.

"Aren't you worried it will end badly?" Her mom sighs. "It seems like they're getting along fine now, but if you get serious with one of them, what do you think will happen then?"

"It's okay, Mom. I know what I'm doing."

"Do you?" There's the sound of something being set down on the counter. "Because I've seen the way they look at you. All three of them."

"What do you mean?"

"Oh, come on Hailey." Her mother chuckles, although I can still hear the worry in her tone. "It's clear as day to anyone with eyes. They're head over heels for you. And I see the way you look at them too. All of them."

My heart gives a heavy thud, pounding against my sternum so hard that it startles me out of my frozen state. I turn away from the door quickly, forgetting about hot chocolate and hot toddies and everything else.

The entire conversation replays in my mind as I make my way blindly through the Bennetts' house, barely paying attention to where I'm going. But one phrase keeps getting stuck on repeat, echoing over and over.

I see the way you look at them too.

"Shit! Whoa, man. Where's the fire?"

Lucas jerks back as I round a corner heading toward the back door of the house, holding up his hands as I almost plow into him.

"Oh, sorry." I clear my throat, trying to wrestle my thoughts back into submission. "Uh, I was just gonna go see if any snow needed to be cleared away out back."

He glances toward the door. "Good question. I'll check with

my dad." When he looks back at me, his brows furrow. "You okay?"

"Yeah." I force a smile onto my face. "All good. Just ready for some of your mom's famous eggnog."

"Oh Jesus, don't fucking remind me," he groans.

Mrs. Bennett, god love her, made the most disgusting batch of eggnog one Christmas about five years ago, and it knocked out about half of us with food poisoning on Christmas day. Since then, she's refused to make it from scratch, but the memory still haunts us.

Lucas shakes his head, still looking a little queasy, and to be honest, I do too—although not for the same reasons.

A knot of guilt is twisting in my stomach, and I don't know what the fuck to do about it.

My brothers and I are more than just friends with Lucas. We used to joke that he was our long-lost quadruplet. And I hate the fact that I'm keeping a secret from him.

I see the way you look at them too.

Mrs. Bennett's words flash through my mind again, making my jaw clench.

This was all just supposed to be something fun, something to help Hailey out against the town bullies and her douchebag ex. But now it's all spiraling away from what it was originally intended to be. It's turning into something more, something... deeper.

Something a hell of a lot more complicated.

36

HAILEY

By seven-thirty, the party is in full swing, and I'm slowly nursing my second glass of mulled wine.

The first glass, I drank so fast that I practically scalded my mouth after my mother basically told me she thinks all three of the Cooper brothers are falling for me... and that I'm falling for them too.

Oh god.

My stomach pitches like I'm on a rollercoaster, and I take another quick sip of the spicy, sweet wine.

I make my way through the living room, greeting a few friends of the family who haven't seen me since I got back. Several of them exclaim at how happy I look, and no one mentions Dylan or his family at all, which I appreciate. I'm sure they know that shit wouldn't fly in this house. And besides, my parents' true friends aren't the types to take pleasure in gossiping about painful moments in my life.

Once I escape a small group of people who want to know if I had any fun celebrity sightings in LA, I make a beeline for the couch, where Grandma Dee and Pippa are sitting with their heads together, laughing quietly.

"What's so funny?" I ask, sitting down on Grandma Dee's other side.

"We're playing 'never have I ever.'" Pippa grins, her eyes sparking with mischief. "Turns out Grandma Dee has a very sordid past."

"Oh, hush, you." Our grandmother swats at her, but she's laughing, her cheeks flushed.

"All right." I grin. "I'm in. Who's turn is it?"

"Grandma's," Pippa informs me, and we both turn to our grandmother expectantly.

"Hmm." Grandma Dee purses her lips. "Never have I ever... jumped out of an airplane."

Pippa smirks and takes a sip of her drink. She and a friend of hers went skydiving last year. She sent me a video of it while I was in LA, and just watching the recording made me feel a little queasy. Definitely not for me.

We keep playing as the party continues around us, laughing and joking in our little corner of the room. I glance up after a while and see all three of the Cooper brothers talking to Lucas and another teacher from his school. As if he's somehow sensed my gaze, Nick looks over, meeting my eyes.

I smile, giving him a little wave, even as butterflies burst to life in my stomach.

After that conversation with my mom in the kitchen, my thoughts have been churning over and over. I can't stop thinking about what Sebastian said earlier, when he offered to come help get ready for the party.

We take care of what's ours.

What would it be like if I was actually theirs? Not just pretend, and not just shared in their beds, but theirs in all ways?

What if we made this thing between us real?

Is that even possible?

"Earth to Hailey! Are you even listening?"

I'm so lost inside my head that I don't notice my sister trying to get my attention until she jabs me in the side with her elbow.

"Sorry." I yank my gaze away from the Cooper brothers before anyone can notice me staring. "I was just thinking. Must be the mulled wine. What did you say?"

"I just prompted us with a never have I ever. Want me to repeat it?"

"Yes, please."

My sister flashes me a shit-eating grin, then says, "Never have I ever had a four-way."

My heart stops. *Oh, no she fucking didn't.*

"A four-way?" Grandma Dee looks slightly confused. "Like a four-way radio? Do they even make such a thing?"

Pippa stifles a giggle and waits for me to respond, looking pointedly at the glass of mulled wine in my hand.

But instead of taking a drink, I pick up one of the little throw pillows on the couch and whack her with it. She yelps, dissolving into laughter, and Grandma Dee looks at both of us like we'd lost our damn minds.

"No, Grandma," Pippa informs her, blocking another blow from the throw pillow as a few people glance our way. "It's not a radio. Let's see..." She ducks again, pursing her lips and shooting me a look. "How would you describe a four-way, Hailey?"

"You little brat." I drop the pillow and roll my eyes. "Grandma, it's not a radio. It's something dirty."

It suddenly dawns on Grandma Dee what Pippa was talking about, and her eyebrows shoot up, her mouth forming a little 'o' shape. I flush, but I can't stop myself from chuckling a little as Pippa cackles. Grandma Dee starts to laugh too, and it isn't long before the three of us are giggling like children.

It actually feels good to laugh like this, a moment of normalcy and levity that actually does manage to break me out of my thoughts for a while.

I poke Pippa in the side when we finally get ourselves back

under control, but she just gives me an innocent look and throws her arms around me, pulling me in close for a hug.

"Love you, sis," she singsongs, and I grudgingly hug her back.

"Love you too. Brat."

The game continues, and after a few more raucous rounds—during which my sister behaves, thank goodness—I tell them to go on without me while I get a refill of wine.

I walk past the Cooper brothers, flashing Reid a quick smile, then head into the kitchen. But I stop short as I enter.

My mom is standing near the stove, and my dad has one arm around her as he speaks to her in a low voice. I have a sudden flashback to when I walked in on my parents in the kitchen at the diner, and just like then, my stomach drops.

"Oh my gosh, what's wrong?"

I race into the room, and they both look up. My mom wipes at her eyes, a guilty look flashing across her face, as if she feels bad for crying at her own holiday party when she'd normally be playing the happy hostess.

But I don't care about that. I care about what's got her so upset—especially because I'm pretty sure I know what it is.

"It's the Montgomerys, isn't it?" I demand. "What did they do now?"

My mom shakes her head, fluttering one hand toward the door. "Sweetheart, everything is fine. Go back out and enjoy the party. Your father and I were just getting a few things to bring out to the refreshments table."

"Bullshit." I don't budge. "You can tell me. This involves me too, and I want to save the diner as much as you do. Please."

My voice drops a little on the last word, and my mom sighs, her shoulders sinking as she seems to deflate a little.

"The grant isn't going to work out," she admits quietly. "And it's looking like the Montgomerys are going to raise our rent again in the new year."

"We think they're trying to force us out," my dad tells me, anger coloring his voice. I don't think I've ever seen him this pissed off. "They want to develop that block, and they probably think they could get a more lucrative deal if they tore down the diner and replaced it with something else. So they're squeezing us."

"Can you just move the diner?" I ask, crossing my arms as my mind races. That building has been the location of the diner for years, and I hate the idea of them losing it, but they could try to start over somewhere else. "Find another location?"

"We're looking into it." My dad isn't crying like my mom, but he looks beaten down and grim, the friendly ease he greeted us all with earlier gone. "But the Montgomerys own a lot of the prime real estate around town, so it won't be easy."

My mom reaches out, brushing her thumb over my cheek, and I realize a tear has slipped through my lashes too.

"Don't worry about it for tonight, okay?" she says softly, giving me a little smile. "I don't want it to ruin your holidays. And no matter what, Hailey, we'll be okay. I promise. We'll figure something out."

I can tell she's trying to reassure me, but although I give her a weak smile and a nod, it does nothing to banish the tight knot in my gut.

There's literally no way that we can fight against the Montgomerys. They've got a tight grip on this town, and with all of their money, they can outspend us for the rest of our lives.

But no matter how powerful they are, that doesn't mean I'm going to back down and let them destroy my parents' business.

I'll just have to find some other way to fix this.

37

HAILEY

A FEW DAYS after my family's Christmas party, I offer to run some errands for the diner to help take some stress off my parents' minds. It's the least I can do, considering that I don't have the money to just buy a way out of this mess, and I also don't have any brilliant strategy for how to fix it yet.

But I'm committed to helping them save the diner somehow.

I just need to figure out *how*.

As I'm walking out of the hardware store, my phone rings in my purse. When I dig it out, I almost drop it on the sidewalk as I see the name on the screen.

Dylan.

What the fuck does he want?

I stare at the screen as it continues to ring, mentally debating whether to answer it or not. When I do pick up the call, I *don't* say what I really want to say, which would be something along the lines of calling him a selfish prick who's unjustly targeting my parents' business. Instead, I grimace and try to shove all of my anger into a tight little box in my chest. I can't really afford to piss him off, not when his family has so much power over mine. It would make things worse for my parents if I aggravated an already shitty situation.

"Hi, Dylan," I say, forcing my voice to sound pleasant.

"Hailey, how are you?"

"Fine."

"Good, I'm glad to hear it." His voice has that smooth, charming quality that fooled me for a long time when we first started dating. "Listen, I'd love to talk to you about something."

I frown, stepping aside when I realize I'm blocking the door to the hardware store. "What do you want to talk about?"

"It's not really a conversation for over the phone. Could we speak in person? You could swing by my house. I'll be here most of the day."

I hesitate, because the last place I want to go is Dylan's house. I used to spend a lot of time there, but like everything else that got tainted when he cheated on me, I don't have any good memories from that place that I want to hold on to now.

But all I can think about is the tears in my mother's eyes the other night at the party, and the hopeless look on my dad's face. Running errands for them might take a tiny bit of pressure off them in the short term, but in the long term, it's not really fixing anything.

If I have a one-on-one conversation with Dylan, maybe I can convince him to talk to his parents, to get them to ease up on my folks and back off the diner.

It's worth a shot anyway, even if it means completely swallowing my pride.

"Yeah, okay," I say, my voice a little stiff. "I've got some stuff to do today, so I can come by in the late afternoon, if that works."

"That's great." I can hear the smile in his voice. "I'll see you soon."

We hang up, and I spend the rest of the day finishing up the stuff I promised to do for my parents. The guys are all at work, and I don't text them to let them know I'm going to be meeting up with Dylan. As long as our meetup is quick, I should be able to make it home before they get back, and I know they'd all want to come with me if I told them where I was going.

But with the three of them glowering at him from over my shoulder, I know there'd be no chance at all of convincing him to spare the diner.

When I get to Dylan's house, I pause on the front step.

The place is a bit bigger than the Cooper brothers' house, even though Dylan lives here alone. Unless Brielle has moved in, which I suppose is a possibility. They're engaged, after all, so if she hasn't yet, she probably will soon.

"Unless he decides to build them a brand new mansion for their happily ever after," I mutter under my breath, snorting derisively.

I don't feel jealous thinking about that possibility. I know I dodged a bullet by walking away from our wedding, and I also know that there's no house big enough that it could've made me happy in a marriage with Dylan.

Taking a deep breath, I ring the bell.

When the door swings open, Dylan stands in the wide entryway with his designer shirt unbuttoned a few buttons and his expensive shoes shined to perfection.

"Oh, Hailey. Thanks for coming."

"Sure."

I nod, keeping my expression schooled into something neutral, even as I privately wonder how I ever found this man all that attractive. Everything about him seems so artificial now. The way that his hair is so perfectly styled without a single strand out of place, and the way his lips always tilt upward just a little, like he's smirking at the world.

Sure, he's good looking in a conventional sort of way, but I'd take Sebastian's messy after-sex hair, or Reid's crooked dimples, or Nick's scruffy beard any day of the week. The Cooper brothers are so imperfectly and authentically masculine that it makes Dylan seem like a cardboard cutout.

Maybe that's why he was always putting me down so much —because he knew that, at the end of the day, he didn't measure up.

"Come on in," he tells me, sweeping his arm out and holding the door open wider.

I follow him inside, and he leads me into the living room and gestures for me to have a seat on the couch. He sits down beside me, and I cringe internally, wishing he'd sat down first so that I could've taken a chair or something. Sitting on the same piece of furniture with the guy who fucked my ex-best friend makes my skin crawl.

"So how have you been enjoying your time since coming back home?" he asks, cocking his head a little. "Does it feel weird being back again? Or have you settled into a new normal? It seems like you've been keeping busy."

I get the feeling that he isn't just asking me how I'm liking the Montana winter or enjoying holiday time back home with my family. He's talking about me and the triplets.

"It's been nice being back."

My answer is plain and simple, purposefully keeping things vague as I opt for a non-answer to his implied interrogation.

Dylan studies me for a second, as if he's trying to figure out some hidden meaning behind my answer. Then he clears his throat, shaking his head.

"Listen, I called you because I wanted to talk about something a bit... sensitive. That's why I didn't want to speak on the phone."

I nod, tensing a little. "Okay. Well, I'm here. So let's talk."

"I know that my family has had to raise the rent on The Griddle House by quite a bit. It's unfortunate."

He makes a sympathetic face as he says that last word, and I tap my fingers on my thighs to keep from curling my hands into fists. Unfortunate is one word for it. Extortion is another.

"Yeah, I'm well aware of that," I tell him coolly. "What about it?"

"Well, I know what a staple of the community the diner is. And I know how much it means to you. So I'd like to discuss some possibilities with you. I want to find a solution."

In spite of myself, I can't help the little ray of hope that bursts in my chest.

"I would appreciate that," I say carefully. "What kind of solution are you thinking of?"

He smiles. "Well, I think I could get my parents to drop the rent back down to what it was a few years ago."

My eyebrows shoot up. A few years ago, business at the diner was great and my parents were bringing in a healthy profit after all of their expenses. Everything was great, and if they could go back to that...

"That would be amazing," I say, torn between excitement and wariness. "What would you need from them?"

"Nothing." He waves a hand. "I'm not doing it for them, Hailey. To be honest, I'd be doing it for you. For old time's sake."

My stomach tightens a little. "What do you mean?"

"Don't you remember?" His eyes warm a little. "We met at The Griddle House. So that right there makes it worth saving."

Oh fuck.

Something in his eyes is tripping all the alarm bells in my head, and when he reaches up to cup my jaw, I jerk backward.

"What are you doing?" I ask, my voice sharp.

He reaches for me again, sliding his hand around the back of my neck and through my hair. "I want you back, Hailey. Ever since you came back to Chestnut Hill, I haven't been able to stop thinking about you. Every time I see you with one of those damn Cooper brothers, it gets under my skin. Because you don't belong with any of them. You belong with me."

He leans in as if he's going to kiss me, and I shoot to my feet, backing away several steps.

"What the fuck?" I stare at him in shocked disbelief. "Are you fucking serious?"

"Oh, please." He stands up too, shaking his head. "Are you going to try to tell me you don't feel it? That you don't feel the connection between us? I know you're only parading around town with the three of them to make me jealous. It's so fucking obvious."

"*What?*" My hands curl into fists. I'm so stunned that I feel like I'm having an out-of-body experience, adrenaline flooding my veins. "The connection between us? I left you, you asshole. You cheated on me, and I left this whole fucking town just to get the hell away from you. Why the hell would I ever want to get back together with you?"

He stares at me, unblinking. "Oh, come on. Don't you think you're being a bit melodramatic? All couples have their ups and downs."

"We didn't have ups and downs, Dylan. You were the *down*. I don't want you. I don't want to ever be with you again. And there isn't anything in the whole, entire world that you can dangle over my head that will make me forget what you did. You cheated on me with Brielle and now you're trying to cheat on Brielle with me. That's seriously fucked up. What kind of lowlife scumbag are you?"

"Are you... rejecting me?" Dylan's voice makes it very clear that he's in shock over the fact that I'm turning him down.

Whether he thinks that he is god's gift to women, or simply that he can force anyone to do whatever he wants if he throws enough money and power their way, he was definitely not expecting me to stand up to him like this.

"Yes," I bite out.

He blinks again, the shock in his expression turning to anger. "You're making a big mistake, Hailey. You really think that you're too good for me? What, do you think those Cooper brothers are better? Are you really fucking all *three* of them?"

My jaw clenches. "That's none of your business."

Dylan's nostrils flare, and his face twists with jealousy, as if he can't bear the thought that I've moved on to not only one other man but *three*. We've all played our parts so well that Dylan is practically seething with envy. He can't stand that he's lost and the triplets have won.

"I don't even know why you're acting like this," I say quietly. "It's not like you ever even wanted me when we were together. You treated me like shit."

I shake my head even as I speak. I shouldn't even be arguing with him because he'll never see outside himself. He's incapable of it.

"And you think that those orphaned brutes are going to treat you any better? None of them are half the man that I am. None of the three of them have the money, status, or power that I do. They can't give you any of the things that I could have. You've really messed up, Hailey."

His words hit me hard in the chest—not because he's right, but because of how fucking wrong he is. Maybe none of the Cooper brothers can give me what my shitty, rich ex can—but they can give me the things that *matter*, and they already have.

I stand up and march toward the front door of the huge, sterile mansion with my emotions roiling.

Just as I put my hand on the doorknob, I whip around to say one last thing. Dylan stands in the hallway, looking as if he's going to double down on his efforts to make things difficult for me and my family now. But as much as I want to do anything I can to help my parents save the diner, this is one thing that I can't do.

"I will never *ever* get back together with you, Dylan. So you can go fuck yourself—or Brielle, or whoever else you're going to use next."

With that, I wrench open the door and stride outside.

My hands shake as I grip the steering wheel on the drive home. I'm so strung out and upset over my interaction with Dylan—and more than that, I'm worried about what he'll do now that I've angered him even further.

When I walk into the Cooper brothers' house, Bruno comes right up to greet me, and I drop down to my knees to hug him. I pet his head and feel my emotions welling up as I bury my face in his fur. He lets me, and I feel like it's a sign that our bond has solidified. Animals have a sixth sense when their humans are upset, and Bruno is more sensitive than anyone has given him credit for.

The guys must've heard me get back, because they come walking toward the door altogether. It takes them less than a second to realize that I'm upset.

"What's wrong? Did something happen?" Nick's voice has a hard, protective edge.

"Nothing."

"Don't lie to us, Hailey," Reid scolds me gently. "You know we can tell when you're upset, and you look pretty damn shaken up right now. What is it?"

As much as I want comfort, I don't want to tell them that I went to meet with Dylan alone. And I don't want to tell them what he said and did, because they'll likely want to go beat the shit out of him, and that will make matters even worse than they already are. I also don't want to tell them how I've probably just escalated the bad situation my parents are in with the diner.

"I don't want to talk right now."

My voice is trembling as I stand up from petting the dog and look at all three of the brothers, suddenly filled with the intense desire to be held by all of them.

"I just... want you to kiss me," I whisper. "Please."

Sebastian steps forward and pulls me into his arms, embracing me and planting a soft kiss on the side of my temple.

The other two men follow suit, and within moments, I'm encased between the three of them as they take turns kissing me over and over.

I cling to them, letting their touch and their closeness soothe the raw parts of my heart.

This is where I feel safe. This is where I feel at *home*.

38

HAILEY

Since Dylan's offer was obviously contingent on me getting back together with him, my parents still desperately need my help at the diner. So when I wake up the following day, I offer to pick up another shift.

I figure it will give me something to put my mind into since I'm still reeling emotionally from my interaction with Dylan. I haven't mentioned it to my parents or even Lucas or Pippa. Mostly because I still feel guilty about the fact that Dylan is essentially punishing our family over my choice to break up with him.

Not only is it wrong and childish, but I don't know how to handle it at all. Dylan did so much damage to my heart and to my ability to let love in again without waiting for the other shoe to drop, that it sometimes feels like I have crippling anxiety anytime I'm around him. I hate that he still is able to rouse any reaction out of me at all. I just want to forget about him and that whole shitty time of my life.

It sure isn't easy when he's got a chokehold on the diner though.

When I get to The Griddle House, I try to just forget about all of it and focus on working my shift. It's funny how there's an easy rhythm of being here, even though the diner is currently buried under a stressful predicament. This place will always bring me comfort, no matter what. At the end of my shift, I take my time cleaning up. I actually enjoyed working here today more than I thought I would, and it helped to give my troubled mind a break for a few hours. But just as I'm finishing up and getting ready to go home, I notice a few of Brielle's stuck up friends walk past me and sit down at a table.

I plan to simply ignore them since my shift is over and I'm almost out of here anyway. But I can't help noticing the way they start to stare at me and whisper amongst themselves. They snicker and giggle and then turn up their noses as if I'm garbage compared to them with their designer handbags and people like Dylan Montgomery on speed dial.

One of them says something that unmistakably sounds like juicy gossip, but I can't quite make out what it is. I can hear my name mentioned though, which is no surprise since the Divas seem to love using my life as fodder for their rumor mill.

I scowl at them and dismiss it. I'm used to them being rude to me, and it's honestly not even worth my time.

I walk into the back to get my phone, remembering not to leave it behind at the last moment before I head home. But as soon as I reach for it, the screen lights up and I see a ton of missed messages and calls, and I get immediately anxious. Normally, no one blows up my phone unless there's been some sort of emergency.

What the hell is going on?

It takes me only a few seconds to realize that it's not just texts and missed phone calls that are slamming my notifications feed—it's all of my social media channels too.

Even as I stand here holding the phone in my hand, the notifications are popping up faster than I can read them. Every single one of my social media outlets are blowing up. And everyone I know is trying to get hold of me.

I click on the first notification that my finger touches and it pulls up a social media story that was posted to my story and just commented on again a few seconds ago. When I see what it is and read the title of the post, I feel like everything in the room starts to spin.

Ho, Ho, Hoe—it's a Merry Christmas for Hailey Bennett. Imagine sucking on those three candy canes this season. #ChestnutHillSlut.

The picture is a photograph taken of me and the three Cooper brothers at the Christmas Parade. It must have been taken right after we got off the float. I'm standing at the side of the street looking disheveled in my sexy Mrs. Claus dress, after just having orgasmed on Nick's lap. And all three of the guys are standing around me with hungry looks in their eyes—looks that most definitely translate into the picture. The three guys look as if they want to each ravage me on the spot.

I remember that moment clearly. I just thought that we had done a pretty good job of covering it up. And I don't remember anyone being around us at that exact time that could have taken a—

Dylan.

Oh fuck.

Dylan Montgomery walked right past us while me and the guys were standing there after we had just gotten off the float. I remember how he glared at me and looked as if he was fuming with jealousy as he walked past us. He must have taken this picture and just happened to have lucked out that it depicts the perfect expression on all of our faces to imply there's something going on between me and all three of the guys.

My feed is exploding faster than I can look at it, with both strangers and people who actually know me weighing in on my personal life. Several of the Divas are coming up with creative synonyms for slut, shaming my relationship with the Cooper brothers and calling it disgusting. People I've never even met are making jokes at my expense, labeling our relationship immoral and taboo.

Dylan's name pops up in the comment thread several times, egging people on and planting the seeds that this "debauchery" has been going on ever since I set foot back in town. He even points out innocent moments that I've been seen around Chestnut Hill and implying a sexual undertone to everything, even when there wasn't one there to begin with. He's trying to trash my reputation, and it's working.

I flip from one social media feed to another, but it's been posted on all of them. My phone is getting hot in my hands as it tries to keep up with the deluge of comments and alerts.

Fuck.

Panic rises within me as I start to freak out.

"No, no, no, this can't be happening." I grimace and shake my phone like a Magic 8 Ball, as if that could somehow erase all of the posts and comments.

This is bad. *Really* bad. This is going to completely tank my family's reputation. In a small town like this, all it takes is one tarnishing remark to sink someone's career or their chances of future success. And this isn't just one remark, it's hundreds, maybe even thousands.

This was never supposed to get out. This was a secret game that the triplets and I were playing, and it was never supposed to turn into something real that could be paraded around in front of the town as if we're a circus on display.

And even though my brain has been toying with the idea of not wanting to keep it a secret anymore, it was certainly not supposed to get out like this. Dylan is painting it all as something disgusting and improper. He's making the guys out to be some sort of predators, and me out to be a slut with an insatiable sex addiction. He's ruining all of the good things that have been building between us and skewing them into a nightmare.

I should have seen something like this coming. I should have known that my ex is so vindictive that of course he wouldn't just let it go. Not after that phone call, and not after he got a glimpse of how happy and fulfilled Sebastian, Nick, and Reid have been making me. Dylan wants nothing more than to ruin things for me, and all because I left his cheating ass behind.

His bruised ego is going to be the end of me.

I don't know what to do. I can't read anymore. I can't even look at the messages and missed calls on my phone because I don't want to see my family's reaction to all of this.

Pippa might have already known, and maybe my mom had a clue too, but none of them knew that it was like *this*.

Fuck, this means that Lucas knows now too.

How in the world am I ever going to face him now that he knows I've been having sex with all three of his best friends and lying about it straight to his face? He'll never talk to me again. He'll never trust me again.

He'll probably want to kill Reid, Sebastian, and Nick too.

This is all turning into a terrible mess.

I shove my phone into my pocket and push out the kitchen doors back into the main area of the diner.

Everyone looks up as I enter the room, and my heart stutters in my chest at the sudden feeling of so much attention directed my way.

The post that Dylan made is going viral, and all of my private business is being spread all across town—hell, it's gone far beyond the town limits by this point. That's how things work when they go viral, and that means I'll never be able to outrun this like I tried to outrun Dylan years ago.

I try not to look at anyone as I stride out of the diner and head straight for my car. I just need to get out of here and away from all of these prying eyes for a bit. I need to recover somewhere where I'm not under scrutiny and figure out what the hell I'm going to do about this and how I'm going to face my family.

I race toward my car, fumbling with my keys and dropping them once in the snow piled up at my heels. When I finally manage to get inside my car, I lock my doors and try to take a deep breath to calm myself. My hands are shaking against the steering wheel and it's cold as fuck in here.

I try to think for a second about where to go.

Part of me wants to drive right back to Dylan's fancy ass house and lay into him for what he's done. He's a coward at heart, and I want to read him the riot act for being such an asshole and demand that he take down the posts.

But then I realize it won't do any good. The damage has already been done. Even if he takes the stuff down now, it's already out in the open public space. All that going to his house is likely to do is result in an argument that makes things even worse. If that was even possible.

Maybe I should just drive straight out of town, just like I did the last time. I feel like I just need to get away from everyone and all of the rumors that are going to crush me like a pummeling tsunami. I need time to think and figure out damage control measures before my relationships with everyone that I care about start to fall apart before my very eyes.

If I go see Lorelai in person, then she could help me work through this and stave off the panic attack that is quickly threatening to engulf me.

But I know that I can't just leave town. Not only because running away won't fix any of this, but also because the one place that I feel the most like going to right now is home to Sebastian, Reid, and Nick. I feel safe with those guys, and they always seem to have a level head about figuring out what to do, especially Nick.

I start the engine, resolved that going back to their house is the right thing to do. I'm sure they've already seen what's happening. Most of the missed calls and texts are probably from them. They're probably worried about my reaction and might even be trying to reach me to get me to come straight home so that they can help.

I just need to get back to them and then we can figure all of this out together.

I start to drive, simultaneously trying to wipe my eyes, calm my nerves, and see the road through the falling snow.

The weather is intensifying and there's a winter storm coming in, the kind of storm that would be perfect if I was curled up near the fireplace surrounded by the Cooper brothers.

I drive faster, just wanting to get there and get back to their arms where I feel safe and protected. I want to be cocooned in their embrace and listen to Reid tell me that everything is going to be fine as Sebastian strokes my hair with the broad palm of his hand.

I'm not even looking at the speedometer when I feel the car spin out from beneath me.

Here in Montana, it's the black ice that is the most dangerous. They call it that because the ice blends in with the black of the pavement, making it impossible to see until it's too late.

In the instantaneous moments that I lose control of the car and feel it spinning out from beneath me, I try to remember what to do. There's some sort of rule to follow in order to counteract the movement—is it to turn into the direction of the spin, or out of it?

I can't remember because my head is too filled with other nonsense and my mind and body are both panicking. The car careens off the road and tumbles over itself as it falls into a deep ditch.

I black out almost as soon as the hood hits the giant wall of snow that forms the side wall of the ditch and feels as if it's made of bricks instead of snow.

It all happens so fast that I can't even dissect the seconds leading up to the crash. And when the car smashes to a halt, I don't even feel anything.

I don't feel cold or pain or even scared.

For a second, not even enough time to comprehend, there's a blur of images that play across the inside of my eyelids. Maybe this is what it's like when they talk about our life flashing before your eyes right before you die. I've read about it before, and they say that you see the things that mean the most to you in your final moments before you leave this earth. I guess that explains why I see a momentary flash of Sebastian, Nick, and Reid's faces all staring back at me before everything goes black.

39

HAILEY

When I wake up, my eyelids feel heavy, and for a few minutes, I just let them stay closed.

There's a dull ache in my head, and my muscles feel stiff. Then I start to remember what happened.

I pull my eyelids slowly open and have to squint to block out the bright fluorescent lights above me. I'm groggy and disoriented, and waking up inside what looks like a hospital room doesn't do anything to ease my stress.

I get ready to look around for a button to call the nurse, but then I hear deep voices calling my name from down the hall.

It's the triplets, and from the sound of urgency in their tones, they are all demanding to be let in to see me. They sound panicked as they argue with the nurse outside my closed hospital room door.

"I'm sorry, sir, but you can't go in. Only immediate family members are allowed into the room to see her. She still hasn't woken up and—"

The nurse's frustrated explanation is interrupted by the sound of Nick's gruff voice.

"I'm a firefighter and in line to be fire chief someday. I'm here at this hospital every time there's a fire or ambulance run, saving lives and working with your staff on a daily basis. And if you don't let us into that room right now to see Hailey Bennett, I'll—"

"But sir, this has nothing to do with your role as a firefighter, or emergency services. It's a standard hospital rule that only immediate family members are allowed inside the room of a patient who is still unconscious. When she wakes up, I will be happy to ask her if she would like visitors."

"Not good enough." Sebastian's voice is harsh. "We need to see her *now*."

I quickly gather my voice and call out of the room before the guys wind up doing something that will get them in trouble.

"I'm awake! It's okay, you can let them in. I'm awake now!"

There's a slight sound of confusion and some shuffling around outside my door, and I really hope that Sebastian hasn't knocked the nurse down and caused a scene.

When the door opens, I'm relieved to see all three of them standing in the doorway right behind the nurse, who thankfully still looks to be in one piece.

"Ah, Hailey." She smiles at me through tight lips. I can tell that the Cooper brothers have been a thorn in her side, and something flickers through my chest at the realization that they would've done anything to get to me. "You gave everyone quite a scare, but you're going to be just fine. The doctor will be in to see you soon. Are you feeling up for any visitors? These three men have been *really* wanting to see you."

I nod my head eagerly, ignoring the fact that it still aches.

Without waiting for her to move out of the way, the guys push past her from both sides and surround my hospital bed. Their gazes are a bit wild and panicked as they scan me up and down to make sure I'm okay.

Reid bends down and places a gentle kiss to my cheek while Sebastian takes one of my hands to hold in his. Nick looks over all of the medical charts hanging on a hook at the foot of my bed, clearly trying to decipher what the doctor's notes say.

"This all looks good. It seems like you're going to be just fine, no lasting damage." His voice is audibly relieved.

"Fucking hell, Hailey, we were so worried about you. I'm so damn glad you're okay."

Reid takes my other hand as he speaks, and I squeeze his fingers softly, the worry that twisted my gut when I woke up draining away just from having them all here with me.

It's everything I need.

It washes away everything else.

But then another burst of noise in the hallway yanks my attention away from the Cooper brothers and the little bubble we seem to be in. My parents rush into the room, speaking over each other and crowding around me as the triplets take a step back to let them in.

Pippa pauses at the foot of my bed, her eyes widening as she glances around at the triplets. She shoots me an empathetic look, and then her gaze darts toward the door where Lucas is standing.

As soon as my brother walks into the room, everything becomes immediately tense.

Lucas is *pissed*.

I can see the steam practically wafting from his ears, and I don't think I've ever seen him so mad before. He glares at each of the Cooper brothers with a look that could kill as he strides up to my bed. He doesn't say a word to any of them, clearly not wanting to have it out with them here inside the hospital.

"How are you feeling?" Lucas asks me. His voice is strained, and I can see the muscles in his jaw clench. His entire body seems tense, and I get the feeling that he's only one ill-timed remark away from exploding at all three of his best friends—assuming that he still even considers them that.

A sick feeling grows in my stomach when I think about all the damage that Dylan's bullshit has caused.

"I'm fine," I tell my brother. "It wasn't a bad accident. It could've been worse."

Before I can say more, a doctor walks in, raising his brows at how crowded the room has become.

"Ms. Bennett, I'm glad to see that you're awake. I know you gave everyone quite a scare, but I have good news for you. You're just fine." The doctor smiles warmly at me, but it doesn't really help matters. I think even *he* can sense the tension in the room. "We're going to keep you another night or two, just to err on the side of caution and make sure that you're perfectly okay before releasing you. After that, you'll be free to go. You've got a minor concussion and some bruising, but no major injuries."

"Thank you, Doctor." My father nods, his expression drawn.

The doctor does a few checks on my condition, then tells me that he'll send the nurse in with some water before leaving the room.

I almost wish he would stay, just to keep the awkward tension from returning after he closes the door behind him.

But the moment he's gone, it all comes rushing back.

"You can go now," Lucas says coldly as he turns to the triplets.

Sebastian crosses his arms and plants his feet, lifting his chin. "You can try and make us."

My heart sinks, a pit forming in my stomach as I see the beginnings of a standoff forming.

"Come on, Mom and Dad," Pippa whispers as she hooks her arm around our mother's arm and starts to pull both of our parents out of the room. "Let's go get a few snacks to temper all of these guys' hangry attitudes."

My father looks back over his shoulder as if he's wondering whether or not he should stay and try to keep the guys from killing each other. But Pippa is great at getting people to go along with her, and she successfully manages to remove my parents from the room.

That's when the real fireworks begin.

"What the *fuck*?" Lucas rounds on the Cooper brothers as soon as we're alone. "I've heard the rumors about how you're *all* with my sister. I've seen the pictures on social media. And before you go trying to tell me that it's all some fake charade, you can save it. I'm sick of being lied to."

"Calm down, Lucas," Reid says, lifting a hand.

"You want me to calm down when I find out that my three best friends are fucking my sister? And sneaking around and lying to me about it too? How about instead of calming down, we all go outside, and I beat the shit out of each of you? I can't believe Hailey would ever—"

"Hey, watch what you say about her," Sebastian growls protectively, his hands curling into fists.

I sit straight up in the bed, horrified at the thought that the triplets and my brother all seem ready to throw down.

"Lucas, stop! You don't even know what you're talking about."

My brother turns to look at me, but he clearly doesn't want to listen. He's got his mind made up that his three best friends have gone behind his back and taken advantage of his little sister, and he's just as hurt and angry as I was afraid he would be.

But I can't have them all fighting. I care too much about all of them to watch their friendship fracture. I need to do something to try to calm him down and de-escalate this whole situation.

"Lucas, *listen*," I say, my voice as strong as I can make it, even though I still feel a bit woozy. "You can't just go around believing rumors and gossip that you see on social media. You know better. It was nothing. We were all just... having a bit of fun together. It started out as fake dating, like we said, and it still is. We just hooked up once or twice—it's nothing serious and nothing that's going to continue. It's not even worth being mad about."

All three of the Cooper brothers turn to look at me, expressions I can't quite read on their faces. I'm downplaying all of this to my brother to keep things from escalating, but it feels like I'm lying more *now* than I was before, when we were keeping all of this from him.

Still, I let my words stand. I can't have all of this ruin my brother's friendship with his best friends.

"You know how Dylan is," I continue desperately. "He has it out for me. He's holding on to a grudge over my leaving him because he has a bruised ego. He's just trying to drag me through the mud and ruin my reputation. The triplets and I were just trying to get him to back off from giving me a hard time, and things got a bit carried away. There's... there's nothing else going on."

Silence falls in the wake of my words as the triplets keep staring at me and my brother seems to process what I said.

The door opens a moment later, and the nurse comes in to hook something up to my IV. She glances around the room at the four men who are all standing there silently staring at her. The tension thickening the air is enough to make her leave quickly before I think to ask her what she put in the drip.

The achiness in my head is still there, compounded by the confrontation that I'm trying to defuse. I try to search the faces of the men as I wait to see what Lucas is going to do now.

Nick has a pained look in his eyes, Sebastian looks hurt and confused, and Reid looks almost angry. Something feels wrong in my chest, and the expressions on their faces just make it even harder to breathe.

I feel like I just took a hammer and broke something fragile, and it makes tears burn the backs of my eyes.

But it's better that I keep things at peace between the four of them, even if it means betraying my own heart, and possibly even risking hurting theirs.

I want to say something else, to fix this and smooth things over between all of us. But the more I try to think of the right words to say, the more my brain starts to feel fuzzy. I listen as Nick starts to say something to my brother, but I can't quite make out the words. His tone sounds tightly civil, like he's trying to call a truce.

My head starts to feel heavy, and I lay it back against my pillow.

"Hailey, are you okay?"

"F...ine."

I hear my brother's question, but when I try to answer him, my words sound slower than they should.

I watch Nick walk around to where the nurse had been messing with the drip. His motion leaves a blur in my field of vision as my eyelids droop.

"They gave her some pain meds," he informs the others. "Probably to combat the headache of her concussion."

The wooziness from earlier gets more intense, and I'm struck by the sudden overwhelming urge to just tell all the people in this room that I love them—Lucas, the triplets, all of them. I blame it on the drugs kicking in, and the sleepy haze that makes me want to be more honest than I probably should.

Fortunately, sleep wins out before I can form any more words, and I feel myself sinking against the pillow as my eyes close and the sound of their voices accompanies me as I drift off.

I wish I could hold on to my lucid thoughts for just a bit longer—but maybe it's for the best that I can't.

40

HAILEY

When I come fully awake again, I can tell that it's the next day by the bright, early morning sunlight coming through the window blinds in long golden streaks.

I look around me and blink in surprise as I realize that all three of the Cooper brothers are still here.

Did they stay with me all night?

There's only one chair in the room, which Reid is sprawled out on, sound asleep and breathing deeply. Both Sebastian and Nick are on the floor, leaning up against the wall. Sebastian has his head tilted back, his dark brown hair messy and tousled, and Nick's bearded chin is tucked against his chest as if he's a hibernating bear.

None of them look particularly comfortable, but they all stayed. They stayed for *me*.

I lie still, staring at the three of them as they sleep and feeling my heart swell. I wish I could have read their expressions better when I lied to my brother about this being "nothing." And I wish I could have somehow conveyed with a glance to them that my words couldn't have been further from the truth. To me, this feels like *everything*.

After several minutes, there's a very soft knock at the door before it opens and my sister walks in.

A smile spreads across my face at the sight of Pippa. I could use a little girl talk after all of the elevated testosterone from yesterday.

"Hey," she whispers, keeping her voice low when she sees that the guys are all still asleep. "I came by to visit with you for a bit."

She walks over and sits on the side of my skinny hospital bed, and I scootch over to make room for her.

"The doctor says that you're perfectly fine and that you'll be discharged today. That's good news, right?"

I nod, but Pippa can clearly tell that there's still something on my mind. She rests a hand on my leg and smiles.

"I know there's a lot of bullshit online right now," she adds quietly. "But try not to let stuff get to you."

That's definitely easier said than done.

"Is it still going on? The social media stuff?" I brace myself for an answer that I already know I don't want to hear.

She grimaces, wrinkling her nose. "Yeah, unfortunately. It's just so odd how it managed to go viral so quickly. Like, it's spreading around so fast that people in other states are now leaving comments about your relationship with three guys and your sex life."

I lift my hands to my face. This is so much worse than I ever thought it could get. I know my mom tried to warn me, but even *she* didn't see something like this coming. Who could have ever guessed that my sex life would be plastered on the internet nationwide for random strangers to comment on and judge?

I groan through my fingers. "How could this have happened? And why did I ever have to get involved with a prick like Dylan Montgomery? I thought he'd already done as much damage to my self-esteem as he possibly could, but I guess he still found a new way to try to ruin my life."

"Yeah, assholes have a way of asshole-ing." Pippa reaches out to pull my hands away from my face, then pulls me into a hug. "But don't worry, sis. I promise I've got your back, no matter what."

I smile at her as she draws back, bolstered a little by her reassuring words. I know Lucas is probably still furious, but it feels good to have my sister on my side.

"How are Mom and Dad taking it?" I ask.

She shrugs. "You know they love you."

I do know that they love me—they love all three of their kids beyond measure. But I also know that they already had a lot on their plate to deal with even before this whole scandal came out that I'm at the root of yet again.

"Can I ask you something?" Pippa blurts suddenly.

My brows draw together as I nod. "Sure."

"What's really going on with you and the Coopers? Is it just sex, or is it something more than that? I mean, I'll support you no matter what. I just want to know what it is that you're going through so that I know how to help. Dylan is painting you out to be, like, some kind of wild sexaholic or something, and Lucas feels like they took advantage of you when you were in a vulnerable place. But what do *you* think? Do you really care about all three of the Cooper brothers, or is it just a fling? A bit of holiday experimentation?"

I chuckle at her phrasing, but my stomach twists as I contemplate her question. I want to spill my guts, to tell her the whole truth. I'm sick of keeping stuff a secret from my family, but I can't quite find the words to answer right now. I have too many unsettled emotions in my head and heart, not to mention the unreadable emotions that I picked up on the men's faces yesterday, and Lucas's feelings about all of this.

"Because if it's just about sex," Pippa continues when I don't speak, "then I get it. There's nothing wrong with that, especially since you've been single for a while now and—"

"Yeah, it's something along those lines," I interrupt her just so we can stop talking about it. Even though my answer isn't really truthful, it's similar to what I told my brother, so at least I'm staying consistent until I can figure things out.

Pippa nods, dropping it for the moment.

"Well, however things end up playing out, we're sisters, and that means we always need to stick together. We may be kind of opposites in some ways, but I love you to death. You know that, right?"

I reach out and hug her again, smiling against her shoulder. "Yeah," I whisper. "I know, and I love you too. Thanks for being my wing-woman."

Pippa grins as I let go of her. "Always. Although next time, if you're going to get involved in something as scandalous as screwing our brother's three best friends, please give me a heads up first."

She laughs lightly, then pats the bed and gets up to leave.

"There won't be a next time," I say as she heads toward the door. "Trust me, this is enough drama to last a lifetime."

After Pippa is gone, I look back at the men and startle with surprise when I realize that Reid's eyes are open. He's awake, his gaze locked on me.

My chest squeezes, a knot growing in my stomach. *Did he overhear my entire conversation with my sister?*

Just like I did with Lucas yesterday, I told Pippa that it was basically just sex and downplayed all of my feelings for the Cooper triplets. If Reid heard that, then it's the second time in less than twenty-four hours that I've flat-out lied about how much all of this means to me—how much *they* mean to me.

Everything feels wrong. Everything is spiraling out of control faster than I can figure out how to rein it back in.

I want to say something to him to explain myself, but I hesitate, because I don't even know what I *can* say to make this all better.

Before I can get my sluggish tongue to work, Sebastian and Nick wake up too. Nick makes a noise in his chest as he stretches his muscled limbs, and he and Sebastian both turn their focus to me as if their gazes are drawn by a magnetic force.

"Good news, Hailey." The doctor who was overseeing my care yesterday walks into the room, breaking the tension. "I'll be signing your discharge paperwork shortly. You'll be released within a couple of hours."

Sebastian and Nick stand up from the floor as the doctor asks me how I'm feeling, checks my vitals, and tells me to monitor my symptoms. He signs a few papers, tells me to have a nice day and be mindful of that black ice on the roads, and then leaves.

Within the hour, the nurses have unhooked me from all of the invasive monitors and the IV, and I'm climbing out of the hospital bed, watched closely by the Cooper brothers.

None of us have spoken much since I woke up, but all of the *un*spoken words between us are like a cacophony in my brain.

That feeling of *wrongness* pervades everything as they help me gather my things. Their movements and postures seem stiff and awkward, but they're all still as attentive and protective as always. None of them say more than a few words to me, but I can see them watching to make sure that I'm okay.

Nick gives the room a once-over to make sure I have everything before we leave and folds up a copy of the discharge papers and doctor's orders to stuff in his pocket.

Sebastian asks me if I want to ride a wheelchair out, and I'm tempted to laugh at what I think is a joke—but then I notice his serious, worried expression, so I just quietly shake my head.

"No, I'll be okay. I can walk."

All three of the brothers surround me as they escort me out of the hospital. It's strange to feel as if there's a rift between us, as if the conversation that usually flows so freely amongst all four of us has been stunted somehow. But it's also reassuring to realize that even when things are so messed up between the four of us, their devoutly protective nature stays the same.

I blink in the bright light as we step out of the small regional hospital, heading toward the parking lot. But we don't get far before a voice I don't recognize calls out my name.

"Hailey Bennet?" A man strides up to us. "Hi, I'm Leonard Shaw, a reporter for the *Frontline Journal*, an online paper. I'm interested in covering your story as a special interest piece. Since your story went viral, it's sparked a lot of conversations about non-traditional relationships and polyamory, and I'd love to get a quote or two from you."

Leonard holds up his press badge to show me. He's middle-aged, with a friendly smile, and although his demeanor isn't confrontational or judgmental at all, I flush with embarrassment all over again.

As if my sex life hasn't already been made public enough? Now an online newspaper wants to ask me questions about it? When is this going to end?

I open my mouth to tell him I'm not interested, but before I can get a word out, all three Cooper brothers step up in front of me.

"You need to back the fuck off," Sebastian growls at the reporter as he sweeps his hair from his eyes, looming over the shorter man. "It's fucking stupid to judge people for their consensual choices in this day and age."

"Hailey Bennett has a lot more important things to be known for than this," Nick chimes in. "She's an incredible singer, and a devoted daughter who's trying to help her family's diner stay afloat."

"Yeah. She's funny and smart and ten times the woman that all those Diva princesses who've been talking shit on social media are," Reid chimes in. "If you were a decent reporter, then you'd be reporting on all of that, instead of looking for fifty shades of gossip to use as clickbait."

All three men are standing shoulder to shoulder in front of me, clearly trying to make it impossible for the reporter to snap a photo of me leaving the hospital. As I stand behind the protective wall they've made, I blink away the tears that well in my eyes.

Even after what I said to Pippa this morning, and what I told Lucas yesterday, they're all still defending me. I don't feel like I deserve it, but I tuck their sweet words away in my mind, wanting to remember them forever.

Surprisingly, Leonard doesn't try to push harder. From a small gap between Reid and Nick's arms, I see his eyebrows shoot up. He actually seems intrigued by the way the guys all defended me, and he holds up his hands, nodding to all of them.

"Okay. I understand. If she changes her mind, she can call the *Frontline Journal* offices and ask to speak to me. Take care," he adds, lifting his voice a little to address me. "I was sorry to hear about your accident. I'm glad you're all right."

The moment the reporter turns to leave, the men relax slightly. Keeping a wary eye out, they escort me straight to Nick's car.

"I'm glad to be heading home," I murmur with a sigh of relief once I'm settled in the front passenger seat.

But none of them say anything to me, and I can feel tension building in the car as the silence grows heavier. Despite all the nice things that they just said about me to that reporter, it's clear that the mess between us still hasn't been resolved.

I don't say anything else for the entire ride back, because I don't know where to begin or how to sort through all of my emotions. But as soon as we walk into the house and Bruno lifts his head from where he's sprawled out in the living room, the awkward and uncomfortable feeling lingering between the four of us is more than I can bear.

"Thank you for the hospitality, and for giving me a place to say. But, um... I should probably go," I say with a lump in my throat. "I can crash on my sister's couch, and we can be done with all of this. I really appreciate everything that you've done for me, and I don't want to keep making things any more difficult than they already are."

Reid stares at me, his expression unreadable and his jaw tight. "Is that really it? You're just gonna let it end like this?"

I fight back the tears that have been threatening to fall all morning, reminding myself that this is how it was always going to go. This was always going to come to an end and there's no sense in dragging it out any longer. It's just going to make it harder on everyone.

"This was just a fling." I steady my voice to keep it from shaking. "But we'll always be fr—"

He interrupts me with a growling voice.

"Go ahead. Say friends. I'd love to put you on your knees and fuck the lies right out of that gorgeous mouth."

My heart jolts inside my chest, and my body warms all over, heat blooming between my thighs and my breath sticking in my throat.

"What?" I whisper.

He doesn't look away, his challenging gaze locked on mine. "You heard me."

I want to be brave enough to say the words, to ask the question that's been at the tip of my tongue and the front of my mind for weeks now. And even though my stomach is churning with nerves, I force myself to spit it out or risk never knowing.

"Was it *more* than just a fling?" I breathe. My heart threatens to pound out of my chest as the words pass my lips.

It takes only a second or two for Sebastian to answer me, but it feels like I'm hanging on for an eternity.

"You fucking know it was."

I stare at him with my mouth hanging open as his words wash over me. I think a part of me always knew—or at least hoped—that they felt like this was real too, but hearing Sebastian say it makes it feel undeniable.

"Ever since the moment you first came into the garage to talk with me after school, this has been real to me." Sebastian pauses as if he wants to make sure that I understand the gravity of what he's saying. "Hailey, it's always been you."

A hiccupping sob pours from my mouth as the emotions that have been roiling inside me since yesterday finally crystallize, expanding in my chest until it feels like there's no room for anything else.

"For me too," Nick murmurs gruffly as he takes a step forward and sweeps a strand of hair away from my cheek. "I started falling for you the first time I met you, and that feeling only gets stronger with each passing day. Hell, I can't breathe sometimes when you're around me, because I crave you so badly."

Reid is the last to speak, and I can still see the flash of anger in his eyes from earlier, although it's tempered by something warmer and softer now.

"Trouble," he says, tilting my chin up. "How could you ever think that none of this was real? It's been the realest thing in my life. A once-in-a-lifetime thing that most people only dream of finding. You mean the world to me, and the thought of having you leave and losing you is the one thing that could literally hurt me the most. We should never have let the lie go on as long as it did—not the lie that we were telling everyone else, but the lie we were telling *ourselves* when we claimed this was fake. Because it's not. It never has been. Don't you see how much we care about you?"

I stand like a statue in the foyer, my gaze bouncing between the three of them as my mind struggles to process the declarations they just made. It feels too good to be true, and some part of me is panicking, trying to brace myself for the fall back down to earth when I wake up from this dream.

All this time, it really hasn't been in my imagination. It hasn't just been me being a fool and falling for three men I could never have.

The Cooper brothers have fallen for me too.

41

REID

Although Hailey's hair is mussed from being in the hospital overnight, her cheeks a bit more pale than usual in the aftermath of her accident, she's never looked more beautiful to me than she does in this moment.

I can see the hope that rises in her eyes as she processes my words, and the words that Nick and Sebastian spoke. For a moment, her lips start to curve up in a heart-stopping smile—but then she shakes her head, her face crumbling.

"But how could this ever work?" she whispers. "It *can't*. People will talk. If we think the gossiping and rumors are bad now, can you even imagine how much worse it could get? People will judge us. The Divas, Dylan, the town gossips. Everyone will condemn the four of us being together. They'll say it's scandalous and taboo and—"

"We don't care about any of that," I say, and my brothers nod in agreement, their expressions serious.

"But what about Lucas?" She blinks away the tears in her eyes, still shaking her head. "You can't say that you don't care about your best friend. I know all three of you love Lucas. I can't come between all of you."

"He'll get over it," Nick tells her, conviction in his voice.

"The three of us and Lucas have been best friends for years. I have faith that our friendship can withstand this."

"And even if he doesn't forgive us," Sebastian adds, "we're still not willing to give you up just because of him. We'll do everything we can to make things right with him, to apologize for lying to him. But I think I speak for all of us when I say that we won't apologize for how we feel about you. Because there's nothing wrong with that."

"That's not what the world will say," Hailey whispers, biting her lip. "There will always be people who will judge us. Even if he can get over the fact that we lied and snuck around without telling him, he might not be able to accept all four of us together."

"Your brother loves you," I tell her gently, staring into her gorgeous green eyes. "He wants you to be happy—and if this is what makes you happy, do you really think he'd try to stop you? I think you need to give him a chance to surprise you. He was pissed and surprised when he found out, but he's not an asshole. He's one of the best people I know."

Hailey lets out a breath, her lips quavering at the corners as emotions churn in her eyes. She glances between me and my brothers again, her delicate throat moving as she swallows.

"Are you sure you really want me? That you want this?" She turns toward Nick. "I'm so messy and chaotic, and you like things to be simple and organized. Won't I drive you crazy?"

He chuckles, arching a brow at her. "You *do* drive me crazy, songbird, but not like that. You drive me crazy in the best way—in a way I never even knew I needed until now. You're like a breath of fresh air, a whirlwind that swept through our lives, and I need your kind of chaos to keep me from getting too lost in my own head. I need *you*."

Her chest rises as she drags in a breath, and I can feel the way her walls around her heart are starting to come down. I fucking hate that her shitty ex made those walls a necessary defense, and I hate that we didn't do a good enough job of letting her know the true depth of our feelings until now. I was too afraid to rock the boat, afraid of what would happen if I admitted to myself that this was never a lie... but I should've come clean to Hailey a long time ago.

She shifts her gaze to Sebastian, her brows drawing together a bit as she breathes, "What about you? You said yourself that you want people in Chestnut Hill to see you as more than your bad boy reputation. How do you think that will work when everyone knows that you're sharing me with your brothers?"

Sebastian flashes her a wicked grin, taking her hand in his. "I think I don't give a fuck. You taught me that, shortcake—to not care so much about what people say about me. You showed me that I'm worth more than my reputation, whatever it may be, and that the only people's opinions that matter are the ones I love."

"A-fucking-men to that," I murmur, and my voice draws Hailey's attention back to me.

She stares into my eyes, still holding Sebastian's hand as she gazes at me as if she's searching for something—one final word to convince her that this really could work between all of us, maybe.

"You of all people must realize how many things could go wrong with this," she says, her emerald eyes shining. "I'm always gonna be a brat, you know. I'm never gonna make things easy on you. It's one thing to say you like that side of me when this was supposed to be temporary, but can you honestly see yourself wanting that forever?"

I don't even need to think about it before giving her my answer.

"Hell, yes. I fucking love it when you sass me, baby. And I guarantee I'll never get tired of it."

That draws a small smile out of her, her expression radiant with growing hope, and I can tell she's starting to believe me. To believe us. I know she's had her heart guarded for a long time, thanks to that pathetic excuse for a man she once called a fiancé. But now she has *real* men in her life.

I step closer to her and lower my voice.

"It makes me hard as hell when you act like a brat, trouble. I love it when you argue with me, because I enjoy giving you something else to do with that gorgeous mouth of yours."

Hailey's tentative smile grows with that remark, a spark of heat glinting in her eyes.

"Well, what about the times when you're a bossy dick?" Her lips twitch at the corners. "What about when you piss *me* off?"

I can feel an answering grin spread across my face.

"Then I'll get on my knees to apologize. Baby, I'll get on my knees and beg you to stay here with us if I have to. We don't want you to leave. None of us do. We want this."

Her breath hitches, her body swaying toward me. "I do too. I just don't know if—"

Before she can finish that sentence, I drop down to my knees. I'll do this right here and now in order to prove to Hailey that I'd do anything for her.

"Reid, what are you doing? Whatever this big, dramatic gesture is, you... you don't need to do it."

I can hear the trembling in her voice, and I don't move from where I'm kneeling in front of her.

"This isn't just a gesture," I tell her honestly. "It's real. And you might not think that you need us, but we sure as hell need you."

Something is beating at the inside of my chest, keeping time with my racing heart. Every part of me feels like it's straining toward Hailey, desperate to banish any shred of doubt from her mind. I want to break down and crash through all of the walls that she's built around her heart. I want to show her that real men won't hurt her, that *we* won't hurt her—ever.

And if the way to do that is to lay my own soul bare for her to see how desperately the three of us need her? Then that's what I'll do.

"The flowers in my tattoo are because of you," I murmur, tilting my head up to meet her gaze. "It's not just a coincidence that they're your favorite flower. I got them because you were always on my mind, and because I felt like I had to have a part of you with me in some way. I guess a part of me always knew that things between us were meant to be more. I just didn't realize how much more."

Hailey's lower lip trembles, and she reaches out to take Nick's hand in her free one, as if she needs that connection to both of my brothers right now. Something to ground her, to hold her steady.

Good. That's what we should always be for her.

"Everything about this feels right," I say, my throat clenching as I swallow. "I don't just want you, Hailey. I want to share you with the two people I've known and loved for my entire life. I want us to work together to take care of you, to keep finding new ways to make you scream our names. I want us to be your *home*. Because you're ours."

Beside me, Nick sinks down to his knees, kneeling on her left side. Sebastian, who's standing on her other side, drops down as well so that the three of us are all looking up at her.

"Ours," Nick echoes, kissing her hand as tears slip down Hailey's cheeks.

"Ours." Sebastian murmurs the word like a prayer, pressing his lips to her other hand.

Hailey drags in a shuddering breath, nodding as she meets each of our gazes in turn. When my brothers release her hands, she runs her fingers through Sebastian's messy dark hair and strokes Nick's scruffy beard. Yearning shines in her eyes as she looks at me, and I forget how to breathe momentarily.

"I didn't mean the things that I said at the hospital—the things I said to Lucas and Pippa. I just didn't know how to handle it, and I wanted to make everything okay for everyone. I thought I was making things better, but I just made them worse." She pauses, taking in a slow breath and letting it out. "I didn't want to get my hopes up and have my heart broken, especially not after how hard I've tried to protect it."

"You don't need to protect your heart from us," I promise, hoping that she already knows that by now.

"I know." She nods, her expression soft. "And as much as I tried to push down my feelings and remind myself of all the reasons that this could never work, I still can't convince myself that it isn't what I want. I can't remember a time in my life when I felt as happy as I've been since I moved in with the three of you. No one makes me feel like you do."

The bright winter light streaming in through the windows catches the strands of her honey blonde hair, making it gleam like gold. She looks like an ethereal goddess, *our* goddess, filled with a radiance that shines into every corner of our lives.

As I gaze up at her, the mistletoe I convinced Nick to help me hang in the entryway the other day catches my eye. She's standing right beneath it, and a smile tugs at my lips.

"Look, baby."

I point above her head, and Hailey glances up to see the tiny piece of greenery dangling there.

"You came back into our lives because of Christmas, so I guess it's only fitting that we should show you just what you mean to us by kissing you under the mistletoe," I murmur.

Her shy, happy smile hits me right in the chest. "I like the sound of that. Now get up here."

I grin, shaking my head as she reaches for me. "Oh, I don't think we need to *stand up* to kiss you."

For a second, she looks confused, and then starts to bend her knees as if she's going to come down to our level by kneeling too. But as if he's read my mind, Nick quickly puts a hand on her thigh to keep her upright.

"You're going to stand right there, trouble," I tell her, reaching up to deftly undo the button of her pants, "while we stay on our knees and kiss you under the mistletoe. After all, no one said that mistletoe kisses need to stay above the waist."

Hailey laughs softly at my words, her breath quickening.

Holding her gaze, I unzip her pants. She traps her lower lip between her teeth in that sexy way it always does when she's turned on, and she shimmies her hips a little to help me as I gently tug her pants and panties down her hips and legs, careful not to aggravate any of her bruises.

Her pretty pink folds are already glistening with arousal, and I can't stop myself from dragging my tongue up her slit, savoring her taste. She gasps, and her hands fly to my shoulders, her nails pressing through my shirt and into my skin. But I don't want to get too carried away too fast, so instead, I place a gentle kiss on her pussy.

"You're next," I tell Nick, who's kneeling to my right, and turn her carefully to face him. He swipes his tongue over her too, then kisses her clit. The shudder that wracks her delicate body makes my dick strain against my pants.

"God, every inch of you is beautiful, songbird," Nick groans, stealing another kiss before he turns her toward Sebastian.

"More than beautiful. Perfect," Sebastian murmurs as he rests one hand on each of her thighs and kisses her pussy, teasing her entrance with his tongue and eliciting a protracted moan from her.

The sound does something to me, and it must affect my brothers the same way, because all three of us descend on her like a pack of hungry animals. Sebastian eats her out while Nick and I kiss and lick at the tender, sensitive skin of her thighs until she's shivering.

"Oh, my fucking god," she whimpers as Sebastian's tongue parts her folds and flicks at her clit. We alternate going down on her, making sure that she never goes more than a few seconds without one of our mouths on her flawless little pussy.

Angry purple and blue bruises, big and small, litter her legs from the crash, and I kiss each one I can find, my lips barely more than a whisper on her skin. It kills me to think about how much worse things could've been, how we could've lost her, and how lucky we all are that the worst didn't happen.

It's a Christmas miracle.

That thought awakens something in me—a need to show her how much she means to me.

Suddenly filled with a fierce determination, I nudge Sebastian out of the way and bury my face in her pussy, my tongue driving into her. She shudders against my mouth, her fingers sliding through my hair.

"So good," I groan. "We're never letting you go, trouble. Never."

Nick isn't about to let me have her all to myself, so he pushes me out of the way and starts eating Hailey out like he's afraid he'll never get the chance again.

We keep passing her between the three of us, taking turns feasting on her and letting our bodies say all the things our words can't express adequately. We share her just like we always have, one of us working her pussy while the others tongue her clit or play with her breasts, until she's clawing at our hair and begging us with incoherent words.

"Please," she gasps. "Please, I need to come. Oh god, I'm so close..."

Finally, Sebastian stands to kiss her mouth, holding her gently by the back of her head, while Nick flicks at and sucks on her clit, and I hungrily plunge my tongue in and out of her.

"Come for us," I beg, needing to feel it. To remind myself that she's still here, that she's alive, and that this connection between us still burns just as bright as it always has. "For all of us. Right now."

Her body starts to tremble, and her fingers dig into my scalp as she turns as rigid as a board and then shudders against my face. Nick keeps working her clit, and the gush of arousal that accompanies her climax soaks my lips and chin, turning me on even more as I fuck her with my tongue.

As the orgasm finally subsides, she slumps a bit, resting more of her weight against us. Nick leans back, and I carefully scoop her up into my arms and kiss her forehead repeatedly as she nuzzles against me.

"More," she whispers, already sounding sleepy, and I chuckle.

"Not yet, baby. Fuck, I want nothing more than to carry you to bed to show you just how badly we all need you, but we don't want to hurt you. You need time to recover first."

"Okay." She sighs, and the fact that she gave in so quickly lets me know that she really must be exhausted. "But... will you lie with me?" she asks, gazing up into my eyes.

I stroke her cheek and smile, my chest aching. "Of course we will, trouble. Always."

She beams at me, and I carry her to the bedroom and lay her down like she's the most precious jewel in the world.

The three of us help her get under the covers, then carefully climb into bed with her. I can't keep my hands off her, so I pull her to my chest, where she rests her head against my shoulder and sighs contentedly. Sebastian presses his chest against her back, tenderly kissing down her neck and shoulder, while Nick sits at the edge of the bed and reaches under the covers for one of her feet to massage it.

Hailey's gaze moves between us all, emotions roiling behind her eyes as she takes a deep breath.

"So this is... real?" she whispers. "We're really doing this—the four of us, together? Are you in?"

"For as long as you'll have us," I say immediately, at the

same time Sebastian answers, "Fuck, yes," and Nick nods and grunts, "Definitely."

All three of our voices blend into one, and tears shimmer in Hailey's eyes as a shaky smile curves her lips.

"Good," she whispers. "Because I'm in too."

I grin back at her, my heart thudding against my ribs.

I swear, those are the best words I've ever heard in my life.

42

HAILEY

"I really can't thank you enough for everything you've done over the past few days," I say, cradling my phone by my ear.

"Eh, it's nothing."

Lorelai laughs, casually downplaying her skills as a keyboard warrior who's been coming to my defense in the comment threads of nearly all the social media channels where people have been talking about me online.

"Someone had to get on there and talk some sense into all these ignorant, backward fools," she adds, indignation clear in her voice. "Whatever happened to open-mindedness? Besides, nobody trashes my bestie and gets away with it."

A grimace twists my lips. "So... has it been really bad? Is it getting even worse?"

I haven't allowed myself to look at any of it, choosing to preserve my peace and the happiness I've found with my men.

"Actually..." Lorelai's voice perks up a little, and I can imagine her grinning. "I've been pleasantly surprised by the number of supportive comments I've seen lately. I think that's sort of taking the wind out of the sails of the haters. And do you remember that reporter who you said tried to talk to you?"

I groan, wondering what kind of article he might have published, even though he seemed a lot better than some of the other people who have tried to pick apart my personal life since Dylan blasted all of this into the public eye.

"Well, he published a big piece in the *Frontline Journal* talking about how more and more people these days are choosing to explore supposedly 'non-traditional' romantic situations, and how it's redefining the way people think about relationships."

"Really?" I blink.

"Yup. He agreed with what the Cooper brothers said, that shaming people for consensual sex is outdated and stupid. It was a really well-written article, honestly. I'll send you the link."

"Thanks." I grin, resting my head on the back of the couch as I idly pet Bruno. Then I let out a quiet sigh. "I'm still worried about the fallout in Chestnut Hill," I admit. "It's different in person and *inside* a small town. It's more personal here, and there are people who would love to make my life hell."

"Like your ex?"

"Yeah, he's definitely at the top of the list. And the Divas."

But even as I speak, I don't feel the same worry churning in my gut that I used to. I feel more settled and certain about all of this—partially thanks to the guys and their unwavering support, and partially thanks to my talks with Lorelai. I've changed a lot in the weeks since I arrived back in Chestnut Hill. I'm neither as timid nor as guarded as I once was.

"So what are you going to do?"

Lorelai asks the big question, and I take a moment to gather my thoughts before answering her.

"I'm not going to let anything hold me back anymore," I say simply. There's a confidence in my voice that isn't faked this time. "I've decided to stop letting anyone else influence my decisions. I've spent too long letting people's opinions get to me.

Hell, I fled this town the last time because I was part of a scandal that wasn't even my fault. But I don't want to run away this time. I'm all done feeling lost and holding my heart behind a wall of armor. I want to reclaim who I want to be and who I want to be with. I've finally found something really good here, and I don't want to lose it."

"Yesss! That's my girl!" Lorelai's voice is full of happiness, and it makes me smile.

She's been there for me for a long time now, keeping me sane ever since I moved out to LA and always ready to show up with a bottle of wine and a pint of ice cream... or a shovel to bury a body. I owe her a lot.

We talk for a bit longer, and Lorelai catches me up on everything that's been going on in LA. I love my bestie, and love hearing about her life—but as I listen to her, it strikes me suddenly that I have no desire to return to California at all. It's funny how easily I've settled back into Montana life. The winter here at the holiday time feels magical, and even though I was apprehensive about returning to Chestnut Hill and facing the small-town drama that I left behind... now I find myself not wanting to leave.

Obviously, the triplets have a whole lot to do with that, but I've also come to recognize that there are parts of my hometown that I truly do love—and I refuse to let Dylan or Brielle or the Divas ruin that for me anymore.

After Lorelai and I catch each other up on all the minutia of our lives, we finally say goodbye, and I set the phone down, nestling deeper into the comfy cushions of the couch.

I'm scratching the spot behind Bruno's ear that I've discovered he likes best when Nick walks into the room. He freezes in the doorway, his gaze locked on me for a long moment as he stands there in silence.

"What?" I ask, scrunching up my nose. "What is it?"

Nick clears his throat, as if he didn't even realize he was staring. He smiles sheepishly, looking boyish despite his thick, dark beard. "Nothing. I'm just still getting used to the idea that you're actually mine. That you're *ours*."

I like that. I like it so much that I get up and walk right over to him. I love how I can knock this big, gruff mountain of a man on his ass and make him vulnerable despite himself. I love seeing those rare smiles of his become less and less rare, and I love being able to get up every day and kiss him, just because I can.

When I reach him, I wrap my arms around his neck, leaning into his solid frame as I press my lips to his.

"I like the sound of that," I say against his mouth as his beard tickles my cheek. "As long as you're mine too."

He makes a low, hungry noise, wrapping both thick arms tightly around me and holding me close. He kisses the life out of me, lifting my feet off the ground before setting me back down.

"You know," he murmurs thoughtfully, "I've never really been one to be super nostalgic about the holiday season, but I can't help feeling like you're the very best thing that the magic of Christmas has ever brought me."

I plant several kisses all along the side of his cheek and down his scruffy jaw.

"Wait, wait," I tease him. "You're telling me that Nick Cooper has a soft spot for Christmas? Baking holiday cookies, riding on parade floats—pretty soon, you'll be putting up Christmas decorations all over, and your brothers won't be able to tease you about being a grumpy scrooge anymore."

Nick raises an eyebrow at me, his dark blue eyes glinting with amusement. "Who do you think helped Reid hang up that mistletoe?"

My thighs clench at the memory of that moment after we got back from the hospital. It will forever remain one of the best moments of my life—not just because of how good it felt to be eaten out and shared by all three of them, but because it was the moment we finally all admitted that we wanted this thing between us to last.

I never stopped to think about who had placed the mistletoe there, although I have to admit I'm slightly surprised that Nick was in on it with Reid.

"Well, Nick Cooper." I arch a brow. "I guess that puts you on the naughty list."

He laughs, then shows me why he *really* deserves to be on the naughty list, his hands roaming possessively over me as he kisses me again. When we finally break apart, I'm breathless and a little unsteady on my legs.

"We should head out soon," I say, glancing at the clock on the wall. I talked to Lorelai longer than I realized, and it's getting to be late in the day.

"Are you sure that you want to do this?" Nick asks, a protective edge to his voice.

I nod. "Yeah. I do."

Going to a party in the town square tonight feels a bit intimidating—but like I told Lorelai, I'm done hiding or letting other people dictate my life. The Christmas Eve Bash is the biggest and most celebrated of all the holiday events in Chestnut Hill. Most of the townspeople attend it. And I've decided to go with the guys, not pretending to be with just one of them, but acknowledging that I'm with *all* of them.

"Okay." Nick nods, kissing me tenderly again. "We'll be by your side the whole night. Whatever happens, you're with us."

His reassuring words cloak me in comfort, and I reluctantly leave the haven of his arms to go upstairs and get ready. I've just gotten my dress on and am rummaging around for my heels when Reid knocks on the door frame, stepping into the room.

"Fuck, you look gorgeous, trouble." He smiles, his gaze roaming over me before he meets my eyes. "Are you nervous?"

"A little," I answer honestly. "Mostly just because my

brother will be there. I couldn't care less about the rest of the town, but I do want to try to smooth things over with Lucas. I want you three to mend your friendship with him."

"And we will," Reid promises.

He strides across the room and wraps me in a protective embrace, kissing the top of my head. I nuzzle my cheek against his chest where I know the flowers that were meant for me are inked onto his skin.

The two of us head downstairs, where Sebastian and Nick are waiting, looking handsome as hell. Sebastian, never to be outdone by his brothers, tugs me away from Reid and smudges my lipstick with a breath-stealing kiss before drawing back and helping me fix my makeup. Then we all pile into the car together, heading downtown for the Christmas Eve Bash.

I can feel people glancing over at us and hear the undercurrent of their whispers the moment I walk into the square with all three men, but I keep my head high.

Nick is on one side of me, and Sebastian on the other. Reid is slightly behind me, and I can feel the warmth of their body heat enveloping me in a sort of protective encasement as they all gather close.

When I catch sight of my brother through the growing crowd, my stomach flutters with nerves.

Here we go.

He notices us too, and a hard look settles over his face as he approaches us. With every step he takes, the butterflies in my stomach flap harder. I hate that my relationship with the Cooper brothers caused this rift between them and Lucas, but the truth is, I was hiding things from him too. If he's mad at them, he should be just as mad at me.

"Lucas," I say when he reaches us, trying to keep my voice steady. "We were hoping to see you here."

"Oh really?" He narrows his eyes, glancing at the three men

who are flanking me. "You were *all* hoping to see me? Got any more lies to come clean about?"

My shoulders tense, but Sebastian gives my hand a reassuring squeeze before he steps forward.

"No," he says simply. "No more lies. Lucas, you know we love you, man. You've been our best friend ever since we were kids, and none of us want that to change. We all respect you and feel like shit about having kept this from you for as long as we did. But in our defense, everything we told you was true at the beginning. It *was* all meant to be fake. Then, when things started to change and we realized our feelings were real, we weren't sure how you'd react."

"Can you blame me?" Lucas's voice is gruff.

"No," Nick says, his hand settling on my lower back. "You've always protected your sister, and you always will. But we've always protected her too. And we always will. We're not letting this go. Hailey means the world to all of us, and I hope you'll come to accept that."

My brother's face is unreadable, but I can practically see the thoughts churning through his mind as he weighs their words.

"Remember that time she drew lines all over her face to connect her freckles?" Reid says, fond amusement coloring his tone. "Remember what I told you that day after we all made sure no one in school would make fun of her? I said I wouldn't let anyone hurt her. I meant it then, and I mean it now. So do Sebastian and Nick. All we want—all we've ever wanted—is to take care of Hailey. We'll treat her the way she deserves to be treated, I promise."

Lucas's eyes widen a little, and my heart thumps at the reminder of that day.

"Please, Lucas," I whisper. "They make me happy. This makes me happy. I want to be with all of them, and we'd really love your blessing."

His throat works as he swallows, but before he has a chance to say anything, a chipper voice rises above the hum of the gathered revelers.

"Oh, there you are!"

Pippa pushes her way through the crowd to join us, a broad grin on her face.

True to her usual form, she glances between the five of us and seems to immediately pick up on the vibe of what's going on. Sidling up to Lucas, she drapes an arm around him, giving him an exuberant side hug.

"Hey, big brother. Hi, Hailey. Hi, guys!" She grins broadly at the Cooper triplets before nudging our brother. "You know, it's really great to see Hailey so happy again, isn't it? For a while there, I thought she would never open up her heart to anyone else, and just look how things have ended up. Not only has she found happiness again, but she found it *three times over!*"

Her words, and her genuine display of happiness for me, seem to land hard with Lucas. He grimaces, as if he's feeling a bit like an asshole for not being as supportive as Pippa has been. He glances down at her, then back to me and the guys.

"Fuck," he mutters, blowing out a breath. "I'm sorry, Hailey. I didn't mean to... I was just worried about you, you know?"

"I do know," I say softly, emotions forming a lump in my throat. "But you don't need to be. Not anymore. I'm happy, Lucas, just like Pippa said. I haven't been this happy in—well, forever. I feel like I've finally found myself. And this..." I glance around at the Cooper triplets and then rest a hand on my heart. "This is who I want to be. Who I want to be *with*."

He nods, the remaining tension draining from his face.

"That's all I want for you. And I guess... I guess it's a good thing that you have three people standing up for you. Especially three people I trust as much as them." He narrows his eyes, glancing at his friends. "But no more lying. No more sneaking around. That's not how best friends operate."

"You're right." Reid nods seriously. "Never again."

I bite back a smile as the air around us seems to thaw a bit, despite the winter chill. Giving my men a quick grin, I pull Pippa aside to allow them to talk to Lucas a bit, giving them the chance to bury the hatchet once and for all.

As their deep voices float over to us, I lean in to whisper to Pippa. "Thanks."

"For what?"

"For always having my back. And for helping Lucas see the light."

"Of course!" She beams with a satisfied smile. "I like you and the triplets together. It just makes sense. More sense than you and Dylan *ever* made together. I always thought that maybe the three of them had a thing for you, and the fact that you didn't have to choose just one? Well..." She fans herself in an exaggerated motion. "I'd say that makes you the luckiest girl in the damn world."

I grin, because it's starting to sink in that this is my reality now and not just a fantasy. The men that I crushed on and daydreamed about throughout nearly my entire adolescence are now my boyfriends.

It might not be a traditional fairytale ending, but it's the perfect one for me.

Pippa and I talk for a while longer before she catches sight of a few friends of hers and gives me a quick hug, promising to meet up with us again later. Then I head back to rejoin Lucas and the Cooper brothers, and we move through the crowd in search of my parents.

I'm just starting to think that this night will go off without a hitch—until Dylan steps into my path.

"Well, well, well. If it isn't the woman of the hour." His words slur a bit as if he's been drinking. My stomach tightens into a knot, and I glance around to see if he's here with Brielle, but I don't see her here anywhere.

"Just keep moving," Reid murmurs in my ear, his hand gripping my arm gently to steady me.

We try to walk around Dylan, but he steps sideways, blocking our path again.

"You've definitely changed Hailey," he says, his voice full of condescending derision. "At least the old you would've been too embarrassed to make a spectacle of yourself by showing up here with the three men who are passing you around like a cold."

I glare at him, the knot of anxiety in my stomach dissolving into a ball of anger.

"You know what, Dylan? I'm not the spectacle here—*you* are," I shoot back. "I didn't cheat on my fiancée with her best friend. I didn't try to trash my ex's reputation just because I was being a jealous, petty little bitch. I didn't launch a social media campaign to smear someone because I couldn't stand the fact that they might be happier without me. That was all *you*."

The Cooper brothers are all standing so close to me that I can feel the strength and solidity of their bodies, but none of them speak, allowing me to be the one to tell Dylan off.

It makes me feel powerful and supported, giving me the strength to stand up against the asshole who put me down for years and crumbled my self-worth. Dylan made me feel hopeless, both about my dreams of becoming a singer and my chances of ever finding real love and happiness.

But not anymore.

"I don't care what you or anyone else thinks of me or my relationship. And the fact that you seem so obsessed with my personal life honestly just makes you look like the pathetic one."

Dylan's face turns three shades of red, drunken fury filling his features. "The only reason I'm obsessed with it is because it reflects badly on me now that everyone in Chestnut Hill knows my ex-fiancée is nothing but a trashy whore who'll spread her legs for any—"

"Watch your fucking mouth, Montgomery." Sebastian's voice is low and full of warning.

"If you say another goddamn word about her, you'll regret it," Reid adds.

"Now move the fuck along before we land you on your ass." Nick jerks his chin, looking just as pissed as his brothers as all three of them square off with Dylan.

43

NICK

I'M NEARLY VIBRATING, ready to snap this motherfucker in half if he says another word to, or even *about*, Hailey. It takes everything I have, every last thread of self-restraint, for me not to knock him down where he stands.

Dylan blinks, clearly a bit cowed by the combined force of our anger. His face shifts color, the drunken flush replaced by a sickly pallor that makes him look even more like the weasel he's always been. But then he puffs out his chest, affixing a smug smirk to his face as he glances back at Hailey.

"You really think these three cavemen are your best option?" he asks, snorting a laugh. "You really think they can protect you? I'm going to absolutely *ruin* your family, Hailey. Their diner is toast. I'll make sure that The Griddle House is closed up within the month, and your family will have *you* to thank for it."

Sebastian makes a noise in his throat. "Fuck it," he grunts, his hands curling into fists.

But before he can take a swing at Dylan, I'm already moving, my body following the impulse before I'm even consciously aware of having it. My fist draws back as I take a step toward Dylan, then land a punch squarely on his jaw.

Dylan reels backward from the blow as he tries to steady himself on his feet. If it weren't for the people that he stumbles into, grabbing on to for support, he'd probably go down like a sack of potatoes. There's a ripple through the crowd as the townspeople around us realize what's happening, and Dylan wipes his mouth with the back of his hand as he straightens, glaring at me.

I can tell that he's both scared and pissed off, just like a cornered animal, and I can't help the primal feeling of satisfaction that rushes through me.

Good.

Maybe now he'll think twice before talking shit about Hailey.

"You're going to regret that," Dylan hisses like a petulant child. "I'll take you down too. I'll use every bit of my family's influence to ruin you and destroy your career at the fire department." He tugs at his jacket, glaring at me. "My parents make a sizable donation to the fire department. You can be sure that you'll never become fire chief now. Hell, you'll be lucky if anyone lets you even clean the toilets at the station after this stunt."

Fucking asshole.

Blood rushes in my ears as I step forward again, grabbing Dylan by the throat to pull his face to mine.

"You're nothing but a shit stain and a bully, hiding behind your money and threatening people by abusing your status. Without your parents' resources, you'd have nothing. You already lost the best thing you ever had—and trust me, you're never getting Hailey back. So I don't give a fuck what you threaten to do to me. You can't use blackmail to get your way this time."

Dylan shoves at my arm, his eyes a bit wild, and I release my grip on his throat—only because I'm afraid I won't be able to fight down the urge to squeeze much longer. As soon as I'm no longer touching him, he seems to regain some of his bluster, letting out a derisive laugh as he lifts his chin.

"I would never stoop to blackmail. My family just uses the connections they have, and unlike you, people in this town actually respect me."

"Well now, I respect the Coopers." A gruff voice from the crowd catches my attention. "They've always done right by me. And I respect the Bennetts too."

I glance around to realize that we've drawn an audience. Everyone at the Christmas Eve Bash seems to be focused on us. The man who spoke—Jasper Williams—steps forward, giving me a little nod before glaring at Dylan.

"*You're* the rotten part of this town, Dylan Montgomery. You and your corrupt parents have done nothing but hurt people and their businesses here." Jasper's white hair sticks out from beneath his winter hat, his breath clouding the air in front of his face as he shakes his head. "And as for blackmail, I don't know what else to call the awful terms of the business deal your family pushed me into—except for extortion, maybe."

I rock back on my heels a little, surprised as hell to hear someone from this town actually stand up to Dylan or his family. It's been an open secret in Chestnut Hill for years that they've been taking advantage of small businesses and family-run operations, abusing their wealth and power. But no one ever stood up to them or confronted them about it, because they'd make sure to pull strings and punish anyone who tried.

"He's right—they're all right." Meredith Jenson, a woman with thick brown hair and a straight nose, narrows her eyes at Dylan while coming to stand beside Hailey. "My father went into business with you, and then you and your parents snuck all sorts of shady terms into the contract that cost him his antique shop. You preyed on an old man's livelihood just to line your own pockets even more."

"They did that to us too!" someone else shouts from the crowd. "Put my family through hell!"

I glance at Reid and Sebastian, who both look as surprised as I am at this sudden outpouring of support. The murmurs rising up from the crowd grow louder as several more people step forward to reveal that they too have had to endure Dylan's manipulation and abuses of power over them and their family businesses.

Hailey isn't alone. Her family isn't alone.

Dylan and his parents have tried to take advantage of almost everyone here, abusing their power in Chestnut Hill and threatening people to stay quiet about it so that they would feel like they were in a vulnerable position against the Montgomerys.

Within moments, the amassed crowd begins to turn on Dylan and his parents, finding courage in their collective strength and calling them out for what they've done. Hailey's parents come to stand with us, and Mr. Bennett speaks out in a sterner voice than I've ever heard him use before.

"You've bullied this whole town with your family's money for a long time. The way that you engage in business practices is shady at best, and illegal at worst. And now you're trying to blackmail my daughter simply because you think you can." He gestures to the people gathered around us—people he's known for his whole life, neighbors, patrons of their diner, and friends. "Well, I have news for you: you *can't*. We're done letting you get away with that kind of nonsense."

A savage smile spreads across my face as I watch Dylan flounder in the face of so many people all confronting him at once.

"Oh, *please.*" He scoffs, his eyes darting from side to side. "The work that my family does here is more than this town deserves. You are all lucky to have my family's money propping up your businesses. You'd have nothing without our investments." He gestures to Meredith. "Your father's antique shop failed because he couldn't turn a profit. Simple as that."

"That's not true!" Meredith shoots back, clearly undaunted. "And I can prove it. I still have all the threatening messages you sent him."

Reid snorts a laugh from beside me. "Looks like you aren't very good at covering your tracks, Dylan. You're not a good man, or a good boyfriend, and it would seem that you don't even make a good liar."

The noise of the crowd swells as everyone around us starts to talk about the threatening messages, rewritten leases, and exploitative contracts that the Montgomerys forced on them. Dylan holds up his hands, trying to speak over their words, to defend himself again—but his voice is drowned out by the wave of condemnation rushing his way.

His cheeks flush, and he glances around, clearly looking for some support. His parents don't seem to be here tonight, but I catch sight of Brielle standing a short distance away. He gestures sharply for her to come stand beside him, but Brielle doesn't move.

Maybe Hailey's backstabbing ex-best friend has finally realized that Dylan hasn't been loyal to her either, and she isn't willing to let her reputation tank right alongside his.

For an awkward few seconds, Dylan stands like a deer in headlights amidst the crowd, stuttering more useless words to try to defend himself against their accusations—but then he seems to shrink in on himself, turning and slinking away into the crisp winter night.

The cheer that goes up as he leaves the town square makes me grin broadly.

Good fucking riddance, you asshole.

I turn and glance at Hailey, who seems stunned as she stares after Dylan.

"You okay?" I reach out to brush my fingers over her cheek.

"Yeah, I... I am. I just can't believe everyone came to my defense like that." She licks her lips, her green eyes shining as she meets my gaze.

"I can," I tell her softly. "You're worth sticking up for, Hailey Bennett. And you're not the only one Dylan took advantage of. You were the lightning rod—the one who gave all of these people the courage to stand up to him too."

I lean down, unable to resist the urge to press my lips to hers. When Sebastian and Reid pull her into their arms to kiss her too, she kisses them back without hesitation, making pride swell in my chest.

That's our girl.

I'm vaguely aware of Hailey's parents talking to several of the people who confronted Dylan, all of them making plans to form a coalition to stand up to him and his family, fighting back against their ruthless business practices, and I make a mental note to see what my brothers and I can do to help.

The tension in the air starts to dissipate as someone cranks up the holiday music playing from the speakers arrayed around the area. We're in the middle of the town square, with strands of colorful Christmas lights strung above our heads and a giant tree waiting to be lit.

This is supposed to be a party, a festive event of holiday cheer and merriment, and now that Dylan is gone, it's definitely time to get the party started.

A short while later, Pippa and Lucas head over with their parents to unwrap the trays of Christmas cookies and cocoa that they've brought, courtesy of the family's diner. Drinks start to flow, and people start to dance near the towering, unlit tree. Snow begins to fall gently, filling the air with glittering tufts of white.

Hailey holds out her hand to catch a few snowflakes, looking enchanted, and when I step closer to her, she shoots me a beaming smile.

"Now do you believe in the magic of Christmas?" she asks.

I chuckle, inclining my head. "I'm starting to."

She tugs her bottom lip between her teeth, pressing her hand to my chest. "I can't believe that you did that."

"Did what?"

"You *punched* Dylan in the face!"

Sebastian chuckles, stepping up beside us. "You'd better believe it, shortcake." He winks. "Guess I'm not the only bad boy in Chestnut Hill. Glad to see someone else taking the title for a change."

Hailey tips her head back and laughs, then goes up onto her tiptoes and kisses me.

"Thank you," she whispers against my mouth.

I hold her close, never wanting to let go. "You don't need to thank me. The only thing I regret is not doing it a long time ago."

As the words leave my mouth, the music playing from the speakers switches from an upbeat tune to a slower, sweeter one. Nearby, people are still dancing beneath the falling snow and twinkling lights. It's romantic and magical, and Hailey deserves to enjoy every bit of it.

Taking her hand, I pull her out onto the makeshift dance floor, and her eyebrows shoot up as we join the other couples swaying to the music.

"What are you doing? You don't dance." Her gentle reminder is laced with curiosity.

"Yeah, I do, songbird—for you."

I would do anything at all for her. Even punch a guy out in front of the entire town. Even dance.

Sebastian and Reid follow us out onto the floor, and the four of us find space among everyone else already dancing. My brothers and I all dance with her in turn, passing Hailey back and forth between us, making no bones about the fact that we're all together.

Most of the fuss about our relationship seems to be dying down, especially now that Dylan has shown his ass in front of the entire town. No one will pay any attention to him anymore if he tries to spread rumors about us.

When Sebastian passes Hailey back to me on the dance floor, I pull her close against my body and drop my head to brush my lips against her ear.

"You know," I murmur, "there are still a few items on your bucket list that need to be checked off."

I can feel her body shiver with anticipation as she melts against me, and my cock swells in response.

Time to take this gorgeous woman home.

44

HAILEY

We burst through the front door of the Cooper brothers' house, our hands and mouths all over each other in a whirlwind as we tear off our clothes, leaving a trail halfway up the stairs. The men pass me between them so often and quickly that I lose track of who I'm kissing, but it doesn't matter. I can't get enough of all three of them, of their hard bodies and firm hands on me.

But when Nick kneels in front of me halfway up the stairs, pressing my back against the banister, I realize there's no way we're making it to the bedroom before the real fun begins.

And that's just fine with me.

He drags his beard across my pussy, teasing me and making my skin flash with goosebumps, while Reid takes me by the chin and pulls me in for a deep, powerful kiss, and Sebastian's mouth closes around one of my nipples. He drags the tip of his tongue in circles a few times, then gently clamps down on my nipple with his teeth to hold it in place so he can flick his tongue against it.

"Fuck," I moan into Reid's mouth as Nick's tongue explores my pussy at the same time.

I feel like I could totally lose myself in the three of them. There's so much arousal, so much raw passion, sparking between the four of us that it lights up my nerves in all the best ways.

But it's hotter than ever now—because it's not just about sex anymore. We're beyond that, beyond pretending this is just a simple hookup. There's meaning to it, and the way each of them is working me over makes that crystal clear. They *care* about me, so much more than I ever realized, and that makes me feel like the luckiest girl in the world. Plenty of women would kill for this kind of connection with *one* man, let alone three.

"Everything okay?" Reid asks when our mouths finally part, his eyes searching mine.

"Flawless."

"Just like you," he says with a warm smile, and I lunge to kiss him again, basking in the feeling of his mouth on mine, Sebastian's teeth on my nipples, and Nick's tongue on my pussy.

But Nick catches me off guard when he hoists both of my legs up onto his shoulders with my back braced against the banister, suspending me in space. With a groan, he buries his face deeper between my legs, his tongue dragging over every inch of me. My head falls back, and Reid palms the nape of my neck, supporting me as he holds my gaze intently.

"I love this look on your face. When you're lost in the feelings my brothers give you," he says as Sebastian moves up to my neck, kissing it and dragging a moan out of me.

"It's one of the most beautiful sights I've ever seen," Sebastian agrees, his voice barely more than a whisper in my ear.

I mewl and shudder beneath their touch, trying my best to hold off my climax a little longer as Nick devours me. It's a good thing he's holding me up with his broad shoulders, because if I were still standing, I think my knees might give out.

"You know what else I love? I fucking love how sensitive you are, trouble," Reid says, his eyes burning as his fingers trail down my chest toward my clit. He brushes a fingertip against it, lighting me up from the inside, and smirks at the reaction it draws out of me. "God, I can't wait to get you to bed."

"I can't wait either. So why should we?" I whisper and swing one leg off Nick's shoulder, catching him by surprise. My heart races as I turn around, resting my stomach against the banister and leaning over it a bit to expose my ass and pussy to them all.

"Fuck," Reid growls and claps a hand against one of my ass cheeks, giving me an intensely pleasurable sting.

Nick takes a swipe at my pussy with his tongue from behind before standing up and teasing my entrance with his cock head. Then he pushes inside. I grip the banister and bite my lip as I adjust, and Nick only gives me a few seconds to catch my breath before he starts thrusting.

"You take me so well," Nick grunts. "I'll never get tired of this. Fucking *never*."

My legs shake with each thrust, and Reid and Sebastian watch their brother fuck my brains out until their control finally snaps.

"My turn." Reid steps closer, nudging Nick's shoulder.

Nick groans and pulls out, and Reid takes his place immediately. He grips a fistful of my hair tightly, using it to gently pull my head backward as he teases my entrance with his cock.

"Ready for more?" he asks.

"God, yes. Fuck me. All of you."

It's been hell waiting for them all to feel comfortable enough to fuck me again since the crash, and the way that Reid is manhandling me right now has opened the floodgates of my arousal. With his cock notched against me, I pitch my hips backward and feel him slide inside where he belongs until his body meets mine.

"Mm, so greedy." He chuckles. "Fine. I'll give you what you want, my beautiful little brat."

With that, he draws back slowly, then slams all the way back inside. I cry out, and the banister squeaks from the force.

"Look how wet she is already. It's been a long wait, huh, shortcake?" Sebastian asks with a sympathetic look as he tilts my chin up with his hand to face him. "Don't worry. We'll make it worth it."

I nod and rock backward again to meet Reid's next thrust. His cock hits my g-spot, making me moan, and Sebastian smiles and nods encouragingly.

"There you go. Take what you need. But make sure you save some of that energy for me."

Reid pounds into me several more times, each stroke hard and demanding, then abruptly pulls out and slaps my ass again before he steps back to make room for Sebastian. "Your turn."

Sebastian's cock rests against my stinging ass, and the coldness of his metal piercings, along with the thought of getting them back inside me, makes a shiver run through me. I'm expecting him to take me just like his brothers did, but instead, he spins me by the hips to face him.

"That's better," he murmurs, his eyes gleaming with desire. "I want to see your beautiful face when I fuck you."

He lifts me up, resting my ass against the banister, and I lock my legs around his waist and my arms around his neck. He presses a kiss to my lips, his fingers digging into my thighs.

"There you go. Let me take care of you."

He begins pressing into me, his pierced length stretching me and making it difficult to concentrate on anything else as I silently count each stud. He never takes his blue-green eyes off my face, watching each little shift in my expression, until he's all the way inside me. Then he kisses me again.

"Fuck, baby. You look so good when you're taking my cock. I fucking love the way I can read it all on your face."

I don't have the mental bandwidth for words right now, so in response, I attack his lips with my own. He growls, his tongue sliding against mine, and lifts me farther up the banister to let me fall back down on his cock. I gasp into his mouth when our bodies meet.

"That's it. Get fucking loud for me," he growls and does it again, pulling a shuddering moan out of me. His brothers stand on either side of him, stroking themselves and watching with expressions that are nearly feral with lust.

It's almost too much to take, and Sebastian must be able to sense how close I'm getting, because he hoists me off the banister after another moment. Without ever pulling out of me, he carries me up the rest of the stairs toward my bedroom, with Nick and Reid right behind him.

Every step Sebastian takes moves him in and out of me a little, inching me closer and closer to my orgasm, and I'm sure I'm going to lose it before we get to the bed—but somehow, I'm able to fight it back.

Sebastian climbs onto the bed with me still clinging to him, then lays me back on the pillows and gently pulls out to hover over me, admiring my spread legs. My hand instinctively reaches for my clit, but Reid catches me by the wrist and shakes his head.

"Uh uh, baby. Not so fast." He turns to Sebastian. "Lie down." Sebastian flops down next to me on his back, and Reid's eyes drift back to mine. "Get on top of him."

I heard him loud and clear, but my arousal-addled brain is slow to respond, so he and Nick both lift me up like I weigh nothing. I'm expecting them to lower me down onto their brother's cock, but instead, they move me higher until my pussy is hovering over his face, then set my knees down on the mattress.

"Good." Reid nods in satisfaction. "Now grab the headboard."

"Why?" I ask breathlessly.

"Because it'll give you something to hold yourself steady while you ride my brother's face."

My body hums at his words, even as my stomach flutters with nerves. This is another one of the few remaining things on my bucket list, and Reid knows it. We've done way more adventurous stuff than this already, so it's not like I have anything to be nervous about. But still, I can't help but be anxious.

"Are you sure?" I ask, glancing down at Sebastian's face where he looks up at me from between my legs. "I won't suffocate you?"

"I wouldn't give a shit if you did, shortcake," he answers with a chuckle. "Being smothered by your pussy is literally my dream way to die."

That makes me laugh, and I finally work up the courage to nod. "Okay."

I grip the headboard like Reid told me to and shift my weight on my knees, which are resting on either side of Sebastian's head.

"Mm, fuck yes. There, just like that." Sebastian hums in approval, reaching around to grip my ass cheeks and using that hold to pull me closer to him. His tongue darts out to lick my clit, making me jump, and he chuckles. "Don't be afraid to put your whole weight down on me. Reid told you to ride me, and that's what I need you to do. I want to bury my face between these gorgeous thighs and never come up for air."

His words burn away any reservations I still have. I lower my pussy down against his waiting tongue, rocking backward and forward against him, and he groans in approval. My nails dig into the headboard because it feels *amazing*, way better than I thought it would when Reid first told me what to do.

Sebastian holds me in place for a moment to work his tongue inside me, then gently pats my ass to encourage me.

Without a word, I know exactly what he wants me to do, so I start bouncing up and down on his thick, muscular tongue like it's his cock instead.

"Fuck yeah, ride his face," Nick says, leaning closer to watch Sebastian's tongue driving in and out of me as he strokes himself. "How's she taste, Seb?"

"As sweet as ever," Sebastian's muffled voice answers as his tongue works me over. "So fucking good."

Reid's hand reaches for one of my stiffened nipples and gives it a sharp twist, making me cry out and clamp down on Sebastian's tongue.

"I know you've been waiting a long time for this, trouble. I bet you're getting close already, aren't you, dirty girl?"

"Yes," I breathe because it's all I can manage and he's one thousand percent right.

Between this and the three of them sharing me on the stairs after days of not being able to have sex with them, I'm teetering on a knife's edge, and even the slightest sensation could send me hurtling over it.

But I don't want them to stop.

"So if I did this, would it be too much?" Reid asks as he reaches with his free hand for my clit. He slaps it lightly before pinching it, and my breathing turns ragged.

"Oh my god," I groan, bouncing harder on Sebastian's tongue.

Reid chuckles. "I'll take that as a yes. Why don't you help me out here, Nick? Let's see how far we can push her. I want to know just how much our girl can take."

"Thought you'd never ask," Nick says, his smirk clear behind his beard.

He and Reid each take charge of one of my nipples, pinching and twisting them. My head falls back, and my eyes start to water from the sheer sensation of it all. When both their hands also find my clit and their rough, calloused fingers take turns working it while Sebastian stiffens his tongue and drives it in and out of me, I know I'm lost.

"That's right," Reid urges, his voice low. "Fall apart for us, trouble. We've got you. I want to see you fucking lose it."

As if in response to his command, I come hard, screaming. My hands grip the headboard so hard that it hurts. But that hold is the only thing keeping me grounded, the only thing stopping me from completely leaving my body. The three of them don't stop working over my body, not until the final shockwaves fade away and the spell breaks.

"Holy shit," I gasp, shuddering each time Sebastian's tongue laps against me, cleaning up every bit of the mess I've made.

Reid and Nick help me climb off their brother's face, and I melt onto the mattress, exhausted and glowing. Sebastian's head rolls to face mine, his chin still glistening with my arousal.

"That was absolutely fucking perfect," he murmurs and kisses me, his lips slick and sweet with my taste.

A fresh wave of desire surges inside me as Nick lifts one of my arms in both hands. He turns it to expose the tender skin on the underside and drags his lips and beard down the length of my limb until he reaches my wrist.

"Everything about her is perfect. Every. Single. Goddamned. Thing," he says, kissing my wrist between each word before reaching for my other arm and kissing that wrist too.

"One more bucket list item down," Reid says as he brushes my hair out of my face. "But there's at least one more I think we can take care of."

My heart skips a beat at the suggestion, and my eyes snap to his. "What are you going to do?"

His smile deepens, and he shares a look with his brothers before nodding at me. "Let's just keep it a surprise. It's more fun that way, don't you think?"

He leaves me hanging and disappears out of the room for a

few seconds. I have no idea what's about to happen until he returns with a blindfold dangling from one finger and a few feet of rope thrown over his shoulder.

"Where did you...?"

He shrugs. "After I read your bucket list, I had a feeling we might be needing some supplies, so I picked some up. I like to be prepared."

My skin erupts in goosebumps as Nick and Sebastian kneel on either side of me, each man holding one of my arms in their hands. They position me just how they want me while Reid approaches and fits the blindfold over my eyes, then loops the rope around each of my wrists and ties them both to the bed posts.

"Is everything okay?" Sebastian asks, temporarily lifting the blindfold so I can see his face. "The ropes aren't too tight?"

"No, they're fine."

"Good." He drops the blindfold again and checks the tie in the back. "Can you see anything through this?"

I shake my head, and the bed creaks as someone climbs off the mattress. A second later, I jump when a hand meets my rib cage and fingers tickle down it like a set of piano keys.

"She's telling the truth," Sebastian informs Reid and Nick, so it must have been him testing me.

"Oh, this is gonna be fun," Nick says, and I can hear the smile in his voice. It makes my nipples harden.

Tied up and blindfolded like this, I'm completely at their mercy. I won't know what's coming or from where, who's touching or fucking me. They can do whatever they want, and all I can do is lie back and enjoy the ride.

God, this is even better than my fantasies. Because it's with all of them.

The bed creaks as someone kneels on my right side, and I hold my breath in anticipation.

"If it's ever too much, just say so, and we'll stop, okay?" Reid asks. I nod quickly, although I don't see that happening. "Good girl."

His hand runs through my hair several times, relaxing me, and a second later, I jump again when I feel something brush against my lips.

I part them instinctively and feel Reid's hard cock slip inside. It's warm and firm, leaking salty pre-cum on my tongue, and I hum at the taste of it.

"Fuck, that's hot," Reid groans quietly as I work my tongue across the underside of his shaft and then circle his crown.

A hand finds my thigh and trails downward, all the way to my foot, but I can't tell whose it is, not even when it starts massaging the sole. I groan around Reid's cock, and he gently rocks his hips forward and back, guiding his length in and out of my mouth.

"Let's play a little game," he says as he continues fucking my mouth. "A guessing game. We're going to take turns touching you or fucking you, and you're going to try to figure out who it is."

I draw back a little, popping off his shaft to speak. "What if I get it wrong?"

He just chuckles in response, his fingers tracing the line of my jaw. Then he kisses me before the mattress shifts as he moves to one side. I shiver as the hands massaging my foot set it gently back on the bed, and the mystery man moves upward over me.

A cock head presses against my entrance, and my hips instinctively rise to meet it.

Everything feels more powerful like this. Maybe it's because I can't see, so my body is trying to compensate, but I swear I can feel each electric little movement as whoever it is starts to press inside me, opening me up. I can't feel any piercings, so it's safe to rule out Sebastian.

"Sebastian?" I guess in a whisper.

"Wrong," Reid answers for whoever is fucking me, and when I open my mouth, another cock slides between my lips. He's not gentle, hitting the back of my throat on the first thrust, and when I gag a little, he pulls back and strokes my cheek. "Too rough?"

"Not rough enough," I gasp back, my body buzzing.

Reid chuckles. "That's our filthy girl. Every time you get it wrong, you'll pay for it."

"Fuck," I whimper.

"Oh, trust me, there will be fucking," he promises, and whoever's inside me takes a hard thrust out and in, making my breath catch in my throat.

God. If this is the punishment, I can't wait to find out what the reward is.

Honestly, I can't believe how much *both* ideas turn me on. I never thought I'd get to do even half of the things on my bucket list, and there's no one I'd rather be doing something like this with than the three of them. There's no one else I'd ever trust even remotely enough to make myself this vulnerable with, mentally or physically.

Do they have any idea how much this means to me?

"Guess again," Reid orders. It wasn't him, and it can't be Sebastian, so that only leaves one other option.

"Nick?"

Nick groans in confirmation and takes several deep, needy strokes into me. My hands twist and writhe against the ropes holding them in place, and I try to wrap my legs around him to keep him going, but he abruptly stops and pulls out, leaving me panting and begging for more.

"Please, keep going. *Please.*"

"That was only the first round, songbird," Nick says over the shuffling of the three of them moving around the bed, taking different positions. "You're gonna have to work harder than that to get your reward."

Several seconds pass without any of them talking or touching me, and my head instinctively tosses side to side, hopelessly trying to get some sense of what's happening or coming next. There's a hunger inside me only they can sate, and every second that passes without one of them fucking me drives me crazier.

"Someone fucking touch me," I whine, tugging against the ropes desperately and making the headboard creak a bit. As if on command, a hot mouth lands on my clit, and I cry out in surprise and arousal as a tongue laps against it, sending electric currents charging through every nerve in my body.

My feet brace against the mattress, driving my pussy against their mouth. But just as I'm breathing into the relief of the stimulation, they pull away, edging me and denying me what I want the most. It's maddening, but it's also one of the most intimate things I've ever done—because I've completely given up control, putting myself and my pleasure in their hands.

Another cock brushes against my entrance, snapping me out of my thoughts and back into my electrified body. Because of the blindfold and the ropes holding my hands, my other senses feel more awake and alive than ever, and the familiar scent of cognac and amber floods my nose.

"Sebastian," I whisper automatically, and he chuckles for a second before he slaps the head of his cock lightly against my pussy lips, making me squirm.

"How did you guess already?"

"Your scent. I'd recognize it anywhere."

"Fuck, baby."

Sebastian lowers himself down on top of me, pushing his cock into me as he does. My legs wrap around his waist, holding him there and pulling him closer. But he doesn't move, not yet. Instead, he strokes my cheek and drops a gentle kiss to my parted lips.

"I love that you know us well enough to recognize me by the

way I smell," he says quietly, still stroking my cheek. "It's amazing, Hailey. Just like the rest of you."

Unexpected tears burn in the corners of my eyes beneath the blindfold, but I forget all about them when Sebastian draws back, the studs of his piercings sliding across my inner walls.

"Here's your reward for guessing correctly," he murmurs. "We're gonna make you feel so good."

"You already have," I breathe, whimpering as he drives back into me.

Someone else's cock glides across my lips, offering me something to hold in my mouth while Sebastian fucks me, and I take it without a second thought. Their cocks work in unison, driving me right up to the edge when Sebastian pulls out abruptly.

"Not yet, shortcake," he says and pulls away as the cock I've been sucking withdraws.

"Please, I need more," I beg. "I'm so close. Fuck, please!"

I feel like I'm coming unglued from all this sensory deprivation and stimulation, like my nerves will fray if one of them doesn't get me over the edge immediately.

But I don't have to wait long. Someone hikes me up by my waist, sliding their legs under me and resting me on them before driving their cock into me.

"Reid," I breathe, my back arching.

"Damn right," he says possessively and works my clit as he pounds away at me. "Gonna make you come until the only thing you remember is our names."

Someone pinches my clit as Reid fucks me, and I writhe as I come hard.

He follows me over the edge a moment later, and then Nick takes his place again. I don't even have to guess who it is this time, because I can hear Nick's deep voice murmuring how beautiful I am and how good I feel as he slides into my wet, cum-soaked pussy.

When Nick comes inside me, grunting out his release, it pushes me over the edge again, and I can feel their combined releases slipping down my inner thighs as Sebastian grips my knees and spreads them wider.

"Look at you," he groans. "So messy for us. You're so fucking wet, but goddamn, you're squeezing me like a vise. I won't last long, shortcake. *Fuck.*"

His hips collide with mine over and over as he holds my legs beneath the knees, keeping me right where he wants me. My ass shakes with each thrust, my lower back lifting off the bed. The breathless cries I've been trying to hold back bubble up out of me along with my orgasm, and I can feel Sebastian hitting his peak at the same time I do, his cock jerking inside me.

I gasp out his name as pleasure spikes, but as the waves of sensation slowly start to ebb away, they're replaced by a new wave of emotion.

The tears I felt burning my eyes earlier streak down my cheeks as a rush of feelings rises up like a tidal wave.

Sebastian must notice, because he draws out quickly, releasing his grip on my legs. He shoves the blindfold up my forehead, his expression worried as he stares into my watering eyes.

"What's wrong?" he murmurs. "Was it too much?"

Without waiting for an answer, he and his brothers hurriedly untie my arms and cradle me between their warm, sweaty bodies.

"Hailey? Are you okay?" Reid asks, pulling my gaze to his by my chin. "Talk to us, baby."

I laugh through a sob, wiping my eyes quickly with the backs of my hands as I nod.

"I'm fine. Better than fine. I just... I love all three of you so much."

45

HAILEY

All three of the Cooper brothers stare at me, the air heavy with the weight of what I just said.

For a suspended moment, no one moves or says a word—until Sebastian leans in and cups my face in both his hands.

"Say that again."

I swallow down my nerves that this will scare them away, licking my lips before I whisper, "I love you. Maybe it's fast, but that's how I feel. I think I've always loved you, in a way."

A broad smile lights up Sebastian's face. "Fuck, baby. I love you too."

He gives me a deep, powerful kiss that's just as intense as any of the others we've shared, but this one is different. It's loaded with meaning. When we part, he's still beaming.

"It's usually up to me to fix things, being the mechanic and all," he says, his voice low as he brushes my lip with his thumb. "But I think you fixed me this time. I'm a better man for knowing you, Hailey. You make me want to be the best version of myself."

"I didn't fix anything. You were already perfect just the way you are, inside and out. And you have so much to offer in here," I tell him as I rest my hand on his chest above his heart.

His blue-green eyes burn, and the scar that cuts through his eyebrow shifts as his brows draw together with emotion. "I think you're the only person who's ever really seen that in me."

"Well, it's true. I've seen it over and over again. You're an amazing man, Sebastian."

"And you're an incredible woman, shortcake. I love you so damn much," he says, his lips finding mine again.

While we kiss, Reid reaches for one of my hands, squeezing it hard. My eyes drift to his when Sebastian and I part, and I'm shocked to see Reid has tears in his eyes.

"Are you okay?" I whisper, squeezing his hand back, but all he does is smile and shake his head at me.

"Honestly, I didn't think I'd ever find this kind of love in my life," he starts, his voice quiet.

"Why not? You're the kind of guy everyone knows and wants to be friends with."

Reid chuckles. "Friends, sure. But to love? That's a whole different thing. In a small town like this, people come and go, but they rarely stay. Even *you* left... but you came back. And you brought my heart back with you."

He pauses, his blue-gray eyes locked on mine. He gives my hand another squeeze, then lifts it to his mouth to kiss the back of it.

"I fucking love you, Hailey. You were always the one I was waiting for. I was always holding out for it, even when I couldn't see it. But I see it now, as clear as day. You're what I want. Now and forever."

"Reid..." I swallow, my heart thudding so hard in my chest that it almost hurts. "You're what I want too. I love you so much."

I throw my arms around him, and he kisses me hard and almost desperately, like he's afraid I might disappear if he lets me go. But I'm not going anywhere. Not now, not ever. Right here with these three amazing men, the loves of my life, is where

I belong, so I kiss him as deeply as I can, hoping it will do the convincing for me.

When we break part, Reid looks like the happiest man on earth. Well, second maybe to Sebastian, whose eyes are shining with joy as he watches the two of us. But my gaze drifts to Nick, who's lying beside me, staring off into the distance and looking shellshocked, like he's in some kind of emotional overload.

I reach for him, running my hand through his scruffy beard, and that seems to bring him back into the present. His head turns to face me.

"Are you okay?" I whisper. "You look like you've seen a ghost."

"I just..." Nick clears his throat, staring at me like he can see right through me. "I feel like I just keep waiting for the other shoe to drop or something. To wake up and realize this was just a dream. I've wanted you for so long. For as long as I can remember, honestly."

It's incredibly rare for Nick to open up like this about his emotions to anyone, and that's exactly how I know how much he means it—how deep his feelings run.

Resting my hand on his chest, I murmur,

"I'm not going anywhere, Nick. You can stop worrying. I'm yours for as long as you'll have me."

"Forever," Nick blurts quickly, sitting up so his eyes meet mine. "I want you forever, songbird. I don't ever want to be without you."

He pulls me toward him to kiss me, as wild and forceful as he always is, but with a new urgency, like he's trying to show me just how badly he needs me.

"Do you feel that?" he asks when our tongues untangle, leaving me gasping. I nod. "Good. Never forget it. I know I hid it for a long time, but I'm fucking tired of pretending I'm not fucking obsessed with you. I'm absolutely crazy about you, Hailey. Always have been."

"Me too," I breathe and fall into another kiss with him, losing myself in it and the feelings surging between us.

It must be contagious, because Reid's and Sebastian's hands start exploring my body, responding to the spark.

Nick climbs on top of me, pushing my legs apart with his knees, and presses into me, already hard for me again. It's rough and possessive, but that's exactly what I love about him. His dark blue eyes bore into mine like two endless oceans I could lose myself in.

I nod, my throat tight as I tell him, "Take me, Nick. I'm yours. Completely."

He grunts and thrusts into me, hitting a spot so deep that I see stars. Reid and Sebastian kneel on either side of the bed, watching us and stroking themselves, and I make eye contact with both before reaching for their hands. They take one in each of theirs, squeezing them, and I feel like I'm soaring. I've never felt as bonded with the three of them as I do in this moment, and I never want it to end.

"I'm yours too," I whisper to Reid, pleasure and love filling my chest as his fingers lace with mine.

Then I turn to Sebastian. The final piece to this puzzle. The other man who owns my heart.

"And yours," I breathe, my eyes hooded as I hold his gaze.

"And you're ours," Sebastian rasps, his words echoed by his brothers.

Their hot, hard bodies envelop me, cocooning me between the three of them, and I feel high on happiness, boneless and weightless, as if I might actually drift away if I dare to close my eyes.

But I'm not going anywhere.

And neither are they.

46

HAILEY

As warm sunlight streams through the window, my eyes pop open with an enthusiasm that I haven't felt in years.

It's Christmas Day, and I'm waking up in bed with all three of the Cooper brothers surrounding me. If this isn't the very best Christmas gift a girl could ask for, then I don't know what is.

But just as I go to roll back over and sink back into a slow morning of snuggling with the men before I get up, I realize that my feet are buried under something heavy. I look down, expecting to see that one of the guys has their legs draped over mine—but instead, I'm surprised to see a big, furry body.

Bruno is on the bed with us, his big head draped across my calves and half his body lying on my ankles. I've never seen him sleep on *anyone's* bed before, not even Nick's, but here he is, all passed out and snoring and curled up on my feet. He's so heavy that I have to put a bit of effort behind pulling my feet out from under him, and when I do, Bruno stirs, waking the guys.

"Is that... the dog?" Reid looks down groggily toward the foot of the bed.

"What the hell is he doing here?" Sebastian wriggles his feet against Bruno's side to try to get him to jump off the bed, but the dog doesn't budge.

Nick chuckles. "I guess he's so attached to Hailey by now that he doesn't want to wait until morning to follow her around."

"Aww." I pout out my lower lip, strangely touched by the idea.

"We need a bigger bed," Reid groans, flopping an arm over his face.

"Either that, or Nick needs to teach his dog some manners."

Nick rolls his eyes at Sebastian. "As if he listens to me anymore. Hailey has him wrapped around her little finger."

I grin at my successful attempts to win over the dog's affections. Little did I know that our relationship would begin with a pair of stolen panties.

"I can't help it if Bruno loves me the most," I tease. "And he knows I love him too."

Nick grunts, rolling toward me and sliding an arm beneath me as he pulls my body against his. He kisses me on the side of the face, then down my neck and around my collarbone as if he's possessively marking his territory everywhere that his lips touch.

I start to giggle, both because it tickles and because he's clearly feeling a little competitive with a dog.

"Are you jealous?" I ask, still laughing.

Nick's eyes narrow playfully as he draws back to find my gaze. "Of Bruno? Never. But I'll be happy to remind you of who you belong to anytime you need a reminder."

I shiver in response. I *really* like possessive Nick.

We all take a few more moments in bed, and then Nick manages to coax Bruno off the bed. The disgruntled dog shakes his head and rests his chin on the blanket, staring at me with adoring eyes, and I make sure to give him extra pets when we all get up.

It's a bit chilly in the house, so Nick starts a fire and Reid makes a fresh pot of hot coffee that smells like hazelnut wafting from the pot.

The guys all have on low slung pajama pants and bare chests that make them look like carved Grecian sculptures as they walk around the house, comfortable and at ease. I pull one of their oversized flannels around me and borrow a thick pair of socks to keep my feet warm against the chilly floorboards.

Once the coffee has been poured and the fire in the hearth is stoked and crackling, the whole house takes on a cozy Christmas morning vibe.

When we walk into the living room together to sit by the Christmas tree and enjoy our coffee, I stop in my tracks in the doorway.

A small gasp falls from my lips, my eyes widening.

Set up right beside the sparkling lit tree is a beautiful electric keyboard. It's something I've always wanted—but I've never mentioned that to the Cooper brothers, I'm sure of it.

My eyes dart between the lovely instrument and all three of the guys in astonishment.

"What's that for?"

"It's for Christmas, *obviously*." Sebastian laughs and kisses me on the tip of my nose before walking into the room to sit down on the couch.

Nick takes my hand, and we follow Sebastian in.

"It's for you, songbird. It's our gift to you, so that you can compose songs and play music while you sing."

"I... I don't know what to say."

I'm speechless, moved to joyful tears by both the gift and the gesture. It means so much to me that they would think to get me something as special as this.

"We want to support your music," Reid chimes in. "You're so fucking talented, trouble, and we want you to be able to explore that. We want to see you soar."

Tears start to fall from the corners of my eyes as I pull them close to kiss each of them.

"Thank you," I whisper past the emotions clogging my throat. "Thank you so much. I love it!"

I walk over and run my fingers over the instrument, feeling the smooth, cool keys beneath my hands. Then a rush of excitement floods me as I remember that I have a surprise for them too. I reach around behind the tree to take out the three small packages that I hid there last night.

"I got each of you presents too."

I can't contain my smile as I hand them their gifts. It's not much, definitely not as extravagant as a new keyboard, but I wanted to give each of them something special and meaningful.

Reid opens his gift first, and as soon as he pulls out the frame and looks at it, his blue-gray eyes warm.

"Hailey, this is *perfect*. Thank you."

He holds up the picture, one of the four of us that my sister managed to snap on the downlow when we were all at my family's Christmas party together.

"I know it's not a very elaborate gift, but I wanted to give you this picture because I know it will be the first of many. This is just the start of our collection of memories together," I tell him softly.

He gazes at the photograph for a long moment, love and adoration playing across his features. Then he tugs me onto his lap and kisses me, his lips warm and hungry. I lose myself in it for a moment, allowing myself to bask in his affection unhurriedly. After all, we don't just have all day to spend together—we have a lot longer than that.

"Okay, Sebastian," I say once we break apart. "You're next."

I watch as he opens his package, hoping that I didn't miss the mark with this gift.

For a few seconds, Sebastian just stares at the small plaque I got him without saying a word. His brows are furrowed, and I can't read his expression. But then he pulls me into a hug and buries his face against my neck.

"It's fucking perfect, shortcake," he breathes. "God, I love you."

"What is it?" Nick asks, wanting to see the gift that is still in Sebastian's hands and partially obscured by our bodies.

When Sebastian lets me go, he holds up the sign that I had made for the front door of his garage.

Cooper Automotive
Sebastian Cooper, Owner, and best damn mechanic in all of Chestnut Hill

"It's just that the garage never really had *your* name on it after your father passed away. And I know how much that place means to you, so I—"

I shrug, breaking off, and Sebastian cradles my jaw, kissing me deeply.

"I can't wait for you to come visit me there like you used to," he murmurs. "I'll set up a spot just for you."

"It's a date," I tell him, my heart fluttering.

Nick is the last to open his gift, and when he pulls out the shirt that has the word *Chief* embroidered on the back of it, he immediately pulls it over his head, tugging it on. It fits him perfectly.

"I know you're not fire chief *yet*, but you will be someday." I grin. "I figured you should start looking the part."

He chuckles. "I like the way you think, songbird."

"I know the presents aren't anything big." I lift a shoulder, feeling my face flush. "I wish I could do even more, but—"

"Are you kidding me?" Nick tugs me closer, drawing me into his arms. "*You're* our present. And that's the best fucking gift I've ever gotten."

My heart flip flops as they all kiss me, sparks dancing across my skin everywhere their hands wander.

This could all easily heat up, with me nestled between them

in nothing but a flannel shirt, socks, and panties, and two of the men still shirtless—but we manage to pry ourselves apart several minutes later, breathless and mussed. As much as I'd love to spend the entire day naked with them, Christmas only comes around once a year, and there will be plenty of time for that later.

Once we've untangled ourselves from each other, we carefully set our gifts by the tree and go get ready for the festivities we have planned with my family.

When we arrive at my parents' house an hour later, my mom and dad greet us all warmly. I can tell they're still adjusting to the new dynamic between me and the guys, but they were never really upset about it the way Lucas was. And Pippa and Grandma Dee? They're all in.

Grandma Dee gives me a hug first, and then dotes on each of the guys. She gives Nick an extra long squeeze as she compares him to one of the characters on *Shadow's Edge* and calls him a "real life Romeo" for snagging her granddaughter. Nick banters back with her easily, and watching the two of them joke around brings a smile to my face.

My sister waggles her brows at me, smiling from ear to ear as she glances between me and the guys. When I go to give her a hug, she sticks her finger on my arm and makes a sizzling sound, causing me to burst out laughing.

"Glad you're here." Lucas steps out from behind our sister to give me a hug before nodding to his friends, his lips tilting into an easy grin. "Pippa wouldn't let us touch the cookies until everyone arrived."

He rolls his eyes, and Pippa gives him a playful smack on the shoulder as the Cooper brothers laugh.

"Well, we still have to wait a bit," my mother interjects. "Addison and her family aren't here yet."

I blink, glancing over at my parents. The fact that they invited the triplets' older sister and her family warms my heart.

Now it really will be like we're all one big happy family together on Christmas Day.

When Addison finally arrives with her husband, Michael, and Iris, I brace myself for a bit of awkwardness. I haven't seen Addison since the news broke about me dating all three of her brothers—but fortunately, she doesn't bat an eye as she steps up to give me a big hug.

"Thanks for including us in your celebrations," she murmurs. "We're so glad to be here. And I have to say, I've never seen my brothers happier. That's got to be your influence."

I swallow, giving her another squeeze before releasing her and stepping back. "Well, they make me happy too."

"Good." She beams at me.

"Hi, Hailey!" Iris chirps. "Merry Christmas!"

"Hey, Iris. Merry Christmas to you too!"

I give my cookie baking companion a wave, and she looks up at me with a wide-eyed expression as she asks, "Are you going to be my new aunt?"

Her question catches me completely off-guard, and I choke on my next breath, my jaw dropping open.

"Please say that you are!" she adds. "You'd be the coolest aunt ever! We could bake cookies all the time, and play games, and—"

I glance over at the triplets as Iris rambles on excitedly, trying to hide the flush that I know is creeping up my face. I expect to see them looking a bit awkward or uncomfortable, but all I see in their eyes is banked heat—which only makes me blush harder.

Thankfully, my sister comes to the rescue before I have to come up with an answer for Iris.

"Okay, everyone's finally here! Who wants Christmas cookies?"

As we settle in with our cookies and eggnog, the smell of my mother's homemade Christmas dinner wafting out of the kitchen, I can't seem to stop smiling. It feels like I've gotten everything I never knew I wanted for Christmas this year—and to think, I was dreading coming to Chestnut Hill.

Thankfully, the universe knew what I needed even better than I did.

47

HAILEY

The more I smooth down my dress in front of the mirror, the more the palms of my hands start to sweat.

If anyone had told me a week ago as we were celebrating Christmas with my family that I would be getting ready to do this soon, I would have said they were nuts.

"If you keep doing that, you'll rub all the sparkles off. And it's New Year's Eve, so you definitely want to be as sparkly as possible."

I turn to see Sebastian standing in the doorway. He takes a step forward and kisses me softly.

"You're nervous. I can tell."

"Of course I am." I sigh. "I don't know if I can do this."

"You can most definitely do it." He grins and turns me back around to look at myself in the mirror again. "You shouldn't be nervous, shortcake. You're a badass. You're the woman who helped break the Montgomerys' hold on this town. You can do anything."

I can't help but smile at that, pride rising in my chest—not just for myself, but for everyone else in Chestnut Hill too.

After so many people stood up to Dylan that night, the sentiment in town started to shift against him and his family.

Now his parents are having to work extra hard to keep the contracts that they have with business partners in town, many of whom have already been stepping away and cutting ties with the Montgomerys altogether.

Public opinion has turned against them, which means that they won't be able to rule the whole town like they used to. Since the Christmas Eve Bash, more and more things about their shady practices came to light, and their reputation in Chestnut Hill is shot.

They ended up offering my parents a better deal on the rent for the diner, just to try to salvage what they could—but my parents turned them down.

Another small investor group in town have offered my folks a business partnership, deciding to buy out the building where the diner is located and expand it. They'll own the building, and my parents won't be subject to Dylan's family or his whims anymore.

"Are you two ready?"

Nick's voice startles me as he and Reid step into my bedroom, dressed and ready to go themselves. All of a sudden, my nerves return in a dizzying rush, my heart thudding against my ribs.

"How on earth did I let you all talk me into this?" I groan, making a face.

"Multiple orgasms?" Reid jokes, and I can't help but laugh.

That eases a bit of my anxiety, but I still feel like there's a small army of ants marching beneath my skin.

The New Year's celebration is on the east side of town, in the hippest little pub that Chestnut Hill has. It's not a huge venue, but it's big enough that anyone who wants to attend can, as long as they pack in pretty tightly. And since New Year's Eve is one of the biggest events this town celebrates, second only to Christmas, that means it's likely to be a full house.

I don't know what I was thinking when I let the guys talk

me into singing for the event. I guess I just got swept up in the excitement of the holidays and was overwhelmed by how much their gift of the keyboard meant to me. That, and a few holiday cocktails, had me agreeing without stopping to consider how nervous I would be when the time came.

And yes, the Christmas night orgasms helped too.

When we get to the venue, I have to give myself a mental pep talk just to get out of the car. I spent hours picking out the perfect dress to pair with the Louboutin heels, but still, I'm tempted to flee back home and put on my pajamas so I can watch the ball drop in the privacy of my bedroom *without* having to get onstage in front of a crowd of people.

The Cooper brothers, always my biggest cheerleaders, urge me gently into the pub. Reid has one arm wrapped around my waist, and Sebastian keeps looking at me with a "you can do this" expression in his eyes. Nick keeps telling me how lovely I look in my silver dress, with my hair swept over one shoulder.

But all I can think about is the fact that I'm going to be opening my mouth and singing in front of an entire pub filled with people.

Not in the shower, not in the comfortable safe space of the house with the guys and Bruno—but in front of a real, live crowd of people, where I could freeze onstage and humiliate myself.

When we walk inside, I try not to look around, because I don't want to see how many people are here. But just when I feel like my stomach is about to do somersaults, I hear a familiar voice call out from across the room.

"Hailey! Heyyy! Over here!"

I glance over and catch sight of Lorelai, and my eyes widen as shock and joy shoot through me.

"Oh my god! You're here! What are you doing here?"

I can't help but squeal as I let go of my men's hands and run toward my best friend to give her a hug.

"Please, girl. I wouldn't miss your debut performance for the world!" She looks over and gives the guys a wink. "They told me you were singing tonight and even bought my plane ticket, so *of course* I had to come spend New Year's Eve with my bestie!"

I had no idea she would be here, and I'm so grateful for her support—and to the guys, for reaching out to bring her here. I truly do have the most wonderful people in my life.

We all sit down together, and Sebastian orders a round of drinks. At this point, I feel like I could drink the whole bottle of whatever the bartender brings just to calm the butterflies in my stomach.

"She's nervous, huh?" Lorelai says in a low voice as she nudges Nick in the side.

"She doesn't have any reason to be." Pride fills his expression. "She's incredible and she's going to do great."

"See? This is why I like these guys." Lorelai laughs as the drinks are set down in front of us on the table. "They've got your back, babe, and so do I. You're going to kill it tonight, so get out of your own way and knock their socks off!"

Her enthusiasm is overflowing. It always is, which is one of my favorite things about her.

I smile and take a long swallow of my drink, hoping to calm my nerves a bit. After a while, someone steps up to the mic on stage to talk, and my pulse immediately jumps into overdrive.

I only vaguely hear the man welcome everyone to the New Year's Eve event and then introduce me by name. Lorelai has to poke me in the ribs to get me to stand up, and when I walk toward the stage, my legs feel as if they might give out from beneath me at any moment.

As I step onto the stage, I feel almost ready to faint. But then I see all three of the triplets right there at the front of the pub, supporting me. And beside them, my best friend is cheering me on, joined by my sister and Lucas.

I can't let them down. And more than that, I can't let *myself* down.

So when the music starts... I sing.

I sing for Reid, Sebastian, and Nick. I sing for Lucas and my sister. And I sing for my best friend, who came all the way here just to show me that she believes in me.

Letting go, I lose myself in the song as I belt out the tune. It feels good. It feels fucking *amazing*. By the second song, I'm really starting to find my footing, and by the third and fourth songs, I'm actually able to look out at the rest of the crowd, my hips swaying to the beat.

By the time I finish the final song, the crowd applauds with wild enthusiasm.

I'm flushed with happiness and excitement as I step down from the stage. The Cooper brothers are waiting, and I run toward them to hug each of them in turn.

"You were so great!" Lorelai says.

Nick rubs at his beard, his eyes gleaming. "You were. Beyond great, even. You were astounding."

"Like we knew you would be," Reid adds. "You're fucking incredible."

"And just look at the response from this crowd!" Sebastian grins as he waves his hand to motion to the still-clapping audience. "They loved you!"

I'm delirious from the rush of it when someone comes up beside me and taps me on the shoulder. I turn around in surprise, frowning in confusion as a man I don't recognize smiles at me and gives a little nod.

Normally, the guys tend to get a bit protective and possessive if another man approaches me, but right now, they're grinning at each other as if they know a secret that I don't.

What the hell? What's going on?

"Miss Bennett, my name is Clarence McConnell. I'm an agent with Sky Talent. Your, um, boyfriends invited me here to see you sing this evening." The tall, middle-aged man chuckles. "They were quite convincing, in fact."

He holds his hand out for me to shake, but I just gape at him for a moment, floored by his words.

The guys invited a talent scout to this event just for me? Holy shit.

"There's been some interest in you and your story already," Clarence continues as I finally snap myself out of my daze and shake his hand. "The viral video and accompanying article about you has made you an internet darling. And once we get your music out there, I think the world is going to fall in love with you."

"I'm sorry..." I grip Nick's arm to steady myself, my mouth going dry. "What... what are you saying?"

Clarence chuckles, smoothing his perfectly styled hair. "I'm saying that I'm very glad these men convinced me to come and listen to you sing. You're quite talented, Miss Bennett. My agency has been looking for smaller artists to represent—undiscovered talent, as it were—and I think you'd be a perfect fit. I'd love to sign you to Sky Talent, if that would be of interest to you."

He hands me his card, and my fingers shake as I take it.

"I... yes, I'm definitely interested," I say, my voice shaking.

"Great." He nods, looking satisfied. "That card has my number. Give me a call on Monday, and we can discuss things. I'll be happy to answer any questions you may have and tell you more about our agency. We're based in Los Angeles, and we have a fairly small roster, so you'll get a lot of personal attention."

I nod. "Okay. Thank you. I'll be in touch."

Clarence shakes my hand again, then does the same with each of the men before heading out. Once he's gone, I turn to them all in shock.

"You invited a talent agent here tonight to hear me sing?" I blurt. "But what if I froze on stage? What if I didn't do a good job?"

"Impossible." Reid smiles at me, tucking a lock of hair behind my ear. "We knew you'd fucking kill it, trouble."

I throw my arms around him and kiss him, melting into his embrace before moving to kiss Sebastian too.

"Thank you," I whisper as I press my cheek against his chest.

I kiss Nick last and linger in his arms as I try to soak all of this in. But then it hits me in a rush what "this" is, and I draw back suddenly, my smile melting away.

"What's wrong?" Nick's brows pinch together.

"Once we decided to date for real, I was thinking I would stay in Chestnut Hill. But if I sign with Sky Talent, what if I end up having to travel for singing gigs or whatnot? What if they want me to move back to LA? Won't that derail things between all of us? I don't want to ruin what we have."

Reid's hand settles on my lower back, warm and soothing. "Nothing will come between us, shortcake. We'll go wherever you are." He catches my chin between his thumb and finger, tipping my head up to meet his gaze as he smiles softly. "After all, home is where the people you love are, not a physical place on a map."

EPILOGUE

HAILEY

One Year Later

"Hey, Pippa, can you cover for me? I want to duck out a bit early."

My sister peeks her head through the doors leading from the kitchen to the main room of the diner, raising an eyebrow at me. "How come? Do you have a hot date or something?" she teases before laughing. "Of course I will. Tell the guys I said hi."

I thank her, then grab my bag to slip into the restroom to change.

I can't believe it's almost Christmas again. And I really can't believe that it's been almost a year since my life was turned upside down in the best way.

Over the past several months, I've been splitting my time between helping out at my family's diner and pursuing my music career. The Griddle House has been recently expanded and is doing really well. I think it's surpassed my parents' expectations, and they both seem to have a bounce in their step these days that I love to see. Now that the Montgomerys' threats are no longer hanging over our heads, we can focus on other things. *Better* things.

And just like the men promised, the development of my singing career hasn't come between us at all. Fortunately, I've been able to remain based in Chestnut Hill, even though I travel for gigs sometimes. When I do, the guys come with me, and we make a whole fun trip out of it.

My heart races at the thought of the Cooper brothers as I lock the bathroom door and open my bag, pulling out the sexy lingerie that I bought the other day.

Moving quickly, I tug off my work clothes and slip into the lingerie set. Rather than putting my clothes back on over the skimpy, lacy items, I just wrap my coat around myself, then check the mirror to make sure that no one will be able to tell.

Fortunately, my coat is long enough that it ends just above my boots, so it's almost impossible to tell that I'm not fully dressed beneath the outer layer.

My hands shake with excitement as I tie the belt on my coat, then I shove everything else into my bag and head out.

"Bye, Pippa!" I wave at my sister as I leave the diner, the bell over the door chiming.

Anticipation flutters in my stomach as I drive home. I'm still living with the Cooper brothers, and Bruno leaps up to give me an exuberant greeting as soon as he sees me, but other than that, the house is empty.

I frown, glancing around.

"Where'd they go, boy?" I ask as I rub Bruno's head.

As my ever constant and faithful buddy, he pads over to the back door and snuffles loudly as he digs at the crack between the door and the floorboard.

Ah. The guys must be outside.

"Thanks, bud," I tell him, giving him another pet as I glance out the window.

In the large open area behind their house, the guys have been working on building a music studio for me. It's something so special and also so practical, and I adore them for putting all this effort into making it. It will allow me to rehearse and record music right here at home, and between all of their craftsmanship skills and ingenuity, it's going to be decked out with everything that I need.

I head outside, and my boots sink into the snow as I pull my coat tighter around me. It's cold out today, and I love the way it makes my bare skin feel against the inside of my warm coat. It feels as if every inch of me is alive.

As I walk toward the small building in the backyard, I can't help grinning at the sight.

Reid took the lead in designing it, and they've all been putting in lots of hours to build it. Sebastian has been engineering all the sound system mechanics, and Nick has been running the electrical wiring and lighting—up to fire code, of course.

It's all basically done.

I open the door to step inside, and all three of them look up when they see me come in. It looks like they were deep into working on something, but all it takes is one glance for me to have their full attention.

"You're home early." Nick smiles as he stands up.

Reid and Sebastian follow, and all three of them move in my direction. But before they can reach me, I pull off the belt on my coat, letting it fall open to reveal what's hidden beneath.

Their words of greeting choke off as three ravenous gazes suddenly rake over me.

"Holy fuck," Sebastian rasps.

The hoarseness in his voice gives me goosebumps, and I shuck my coat, letting it fall to the floor before I stride toward them with a sway in my hips.

As soon as I get within arm's reach, Nick yanks me against him. The other two step close, and within seconds I'm sandwiched between all three men.

"Jesus, Hailey." Reid's words are a fervent exhale as he

crushes his lips to mine and runs his hand down my body. "Are you *trying* to kill us?"

"No, definitely not." I draw back, giving them an innocent look as I flutter my eyelashes. "Is it too much? I can put my coat back on if—"

"Fuck, no," Sebastian growls, spinning me around to face him as he takes his turn kissing me, his hands cupping my breasts.

I tip my head back, whimpering softly as hands and mouths roam all over my body. The feeling of being worshipped by three men at once, three tongues tracing my skin and hands touching me everywhere, is an overwhelming sensation that I can't even put into words.

"This is stunningly sexy, songbird." Nick's teeth nip at my shoulder as he slips his fingers inside my delicate panties. "What's the occasion?"

"There isn't one," I whisper, hissing out a breath as he teases my clit with his fingertips. "I just wanted to surprise you."

"You definitely did that." Reid chuckles as he pinches my nipple lightly, making me moan. "The best kind of surprise."

"You know..." I trail off, my brain short circuiting for a moment as Sebastian sucks on my other nipple through my lacy bra. "I was thinking—since we already checked off every item on my list, I need to write a new bucket list of dirty things to do with all of you."

"Does that mean we won the bet?"

Sebastian glances up at me through his lashes, his mouth still teasing my breast. His eyes glint with heated amusement, because he knows full well that they did. They ticked off every single item on my first naughty list, and it was more fun than I ever imagined it could be.

"Yeah, you won," I tell him, tugging his hair to pull him up for a kiss. "But now that just means we have to start all over again with a new list. I dare you."

I arch a brow at him, expecting him to smirk as he meets my challenge. But instead, a serious, almost nervous look crosses his face, and he glances at his brothers.

"Actually..." He clears his throat. "We have a list of our own."

My brows shoot up. "You do? What's on it?"

He glances at Reid, then at Nick, and all three of them step away from me a bit. I immediately miss the warmth of their bodies, but I'm too intrigued by what they're talking about to be disappointed that our moment was interrupted.

Nick disappears for a moment, heading into what will be the actual recording booth before returning and nodding at his brothers.

Reid pulls a folded up piece of paper out of his back pocket, and Nick and Sebastian come to stand shoulder to shoulder with him as he hands it to me. It brings back memories of the time when I went upstairs to grab my bucket list and then came back down to the living room to show it to them. I was so nervous at the time, and honestly, they look just as nervous right now.

"Let's see..." I draw the words out as I slowly unfold the paper. "Just what kinds of dirty things do you all have on your lis—"

My voice breaks off, shock ricocheting through me.

There's only one item on the list, and tears well in my eyes as my gaze scans the words.

"Go on, songbird," Nick says quietly. "Read it out loud."

I swallow, licking my lips before I choke out, "It says, 'marry the woman we love.'"

As the last word leaves my lips, all three brothers move in sync. Nick pulls out the object that he must've retrieved from my recording booth, a small velvet ring box. He opens it, and each of the men plucks out a ring before dropping to their knees.

Sebastian, Nick, and Reid surround me, each on one knee

and each holding up a beautiful diamond ring. Each design is a little bit different, but I can already see how perfectly they'll overlap and complement each other when they're all on my finger.

"Oh my god," I whisper, lifting a shaking hand to my mouth.

Nick smiles at me from behind his beard, his dark blue eyes warm and deep as twin pools. "We weren't planning on doing it quite like this, but I don't think I can wait a second longer. We love you, Hailey. We always have, and we always will. And we want to be with you for the rest of our lives—together."

My breath hitches, and I reach up to wipe away the silent tears of joy that start to fall from my eyes as I gaze down at him.

"Will you marry me?" he asks, and I nod.

"I love you, Hailey Bennett. So fucking much," Sebastian says, brushing his messy dark hair back as he grins at me. "You're the best woman I know, and it would be an honor to be one of your husbands. Will you marry me?"

I nod again, and Reid clears his throat, dragging in a deep breath.

"Marry me, Hailey," he says quietly. "Make my heart complete. I love you to the moon and back, and I never want to let you go."

Their combined proposal is so beautiful, so heartfelt and filled with love, that I feel as if everything inside me is absolutely melting. My heart is full.

I nod again when Reid finishes speaking, but it's not enough. Finally, the words that have been building inside me break free, more tears spilling out with them.

"Yes. Yes! Of course I'll marry you!"

I have no idea how any of this will work since it's all uncharted territory, but the one thing I'm positively certain of is that it *will* work. I've learned by now that with Reid, Nick, and Sebastian at my side, anything is possible.

They surge to their feet in response, pulling me into their arms as I'm once again showered with kisses.

Nick reaches for my hand and slides his ring on my finger. It's brilliantly sparkling and lovely, with an exquisite diamond and a thin band that makes room for all three rings to fit together. Reid and Sebastian slip their rings onto my finger as well, and I vow to never take them off.

The piece of paper with their single bucket list item flutters to the floor as my soon-to-be husbands pass me between them, hands and mouths and tongues exploring me as if I'm their favorite work of art. My legs wobble and my breath comes faster as my head tips back, a plaintive whimper falling from my lips.

I close my eyes as Nick kisses his way down my neck and onto my collarbone. Reid slips a hand between my legs, and I hear Sebastian whisper something in my ear.

"Time to get our new naughty list started... *wife*."

BOOKS BY CALLIE ROSE

Boys of Oak Park Prep
Savage Royals
Defiant Princess
Broken Empire

Kings of Linwood Academy
The Help
The Lie
The Risk

Ruthless Games
Sweet Obsession
Sweet Retribution
Sweet Salvation

Ruthless Hearts
Pretty Dark Vows
Pretty Wicked Secrets
Pretty Vengeful Queen

Fallen University

Year One
Year Two
Year Three

Claimed by Wolves
Fated Magic
Broken Bond
Dark Wolf
Alpha Queen

Feral Shifters
Rejected Mate
Untamed Mate
Cursed Mate
Claimed Mate

Kingdom of Blood
Blood Debt
Dark Legacy
Vampire Wars

Standalones
The Very Naughty List

Printed in Great Britain
by Amazon